EMILY

Anne Redmon was born in the United States in 1943 and educated at the University of Pennsylvania. She has since then lived for long periods in London. At present she divides her time between England and America, where she teaches creative writing at the University of Michigan. She is a Fellow of the Royal Society of Literature.

Emily Stone won for her the Yorkshire Post Prize for the Best First Work, and her two other novels *Second Sight* and *Music and Silence* were published to widespread critical acclaim. Whilst being a highly intelligent and serious novelist, Anne Redmon also knows how to entertain.

ALSO IN ARENA BY ANNE REDMON

Music and Silence
Second Sight

Anne Redmon

EMILY STONE

ARENA

TO BENEDICT

An Arena Book
Published by Arrow Books Limited
62–65 Chandos Place, London WC2N 4NW

An imprint of Century Hutchinson Limited

London Melbourne Sydney Auckland
Johannesburg and agencies throughout
the world

First published in England by
Secker & Warburg Ltd 1974
Magnum Books Edition 1981
Arena edition 1989

© Anne Redmon 1974

This book is sold subject to the condition that it shall not, by way of trade or otherwise, be lent, resold, hired out, or otherwise circulated without the publisher's prior consent in any form of binding or cover other than that in which it is published and without a similar condition including this condition being imposed on the subsequent purchaser.

Printed and bound in Great Britain by
The Guernsey Press Co. Limited
Guernsey, C.I.

ISBN 0 09 9611007

ONE

Alexandra Courtney was my great friend and now she is dead. With a disregard for good taste characteristic of her, she called herself 'Sasha' because she liked Russian novels and because she thought Alexandra was a boring name. 'It's feminine for Alexander, after Alexander the Great, and I can't think of anything more tedious than to be named after a conqueror,' she said.

Everyone called her Sasha, but her family had 'Alexandra' carved on her tombstone. She died ten years ago, but I visited her grave for the first time only last week. I took no flowers; indeed I took no sentiment either. I felt fully the absurdity of trying to scry truths about my life from a polished square of rock; yet if I am to be honest with myself, that is why I did go. It is a nice irony that this is exactly the sort of action Sasha herself instinctively would have performed. Oh, she was a great one for sentiment and ceremony.

It is a sign of my present desperation that my life has driven me to do something so alien to my nature.

I took David with me for protection against whatever emotions I might be made to show on seeing her grave. David is my four-year-old son. Of course, with my 'psychoanalytically oriented background' (a phrase my mother often uses, flicking the letters off her tongue like beads across an abacus), I felt uneasy about exposing the child to a place where death is an unavoidable fact of life. A different kind of mother might have similar qualms about a bookshop crammed with pornography.

I found what I might have known all along: that the flattened mound of grass, the tasteful headstone, produced in me no immediate emotion whatever. David needn't have come, although he himself liked the cemetery. He found it a novel idea that people died.

I must have expected memories to rush out and rage about me – one would expect that from Sasha's tomb – but all my memories were extinguished by their contact with this municipal order, this stone chit which announced with no more passion than a form in Somerset House that she had lived and died.

Someone had put flowers in a rusty metal holder at the base of the grave. This surprised me. I thought her mother and father had reunited after her death and had gone to live in America perhaps taking Nanny with them as well. The family worshipped Sasha, and I daresay it was insupportable for them to be in any contact at all with the country where she had died.

It occurred to me that Gregory might have stayed in London, but somehow I didn't think Gregory would rise to dahlias for his sister's grave. Although his childhood feeling for Sasha was almost exaggerated, he had a flat, selfish nature – the sort which quickly recovers from mourning. He may have changed, but I haven't the slightest inclination to look him up and find out.

I wondered if it could have been Boris. David tugged at my skirt and demanded the ice-cream I'd bribed him with. This gave me the opportunity to dismiss the ugly thought of Boris from my mind. Boris wouldn't have remembered her so long anyway.

Then I knew. No one else besides Peter could have or would have travelled all this way with dahlias under his arm. I could see him getting off the bus, swinging his body in an arc, jumping lightly to the ground holding aloft his tribute to the dead with a shade of exultancy. I know so well how he must have looked. He brought me flowers often enough in the past. He would have spent all afternoon gorging his feelings beside her grave.

This certain intuition struck my stomach cold. I had gone on this depressing pilgrimage to find Sasha there over and above Peter, without Peter, for myself. All I found in breaking ten years' abstinence from conscious thought about Sasha was Peter . . . more and still more Peter.

David had found an open grave and with four-year-old crudeness and persistence wanted to see the dead person who would go into it. I left the cemetery with him struggling and whining. After only a quarter of an hour, I had had enough.

It has been a feat of will for me to steal up and contain my memories of Sasha against Peter's continual wash of talk about her. It has been necessary for me to conceal from him all I felt and all my doings of the past in regard to her. Neither he nor she ever really thought I had any feelings – not in their innermost hearts – and this I have turned to my advantage, bitter as I am about their opinion of me. Now it seems I must unearth her from my hidden mind where she has fitfully reposed for so long. Peter found my box.

I really ought to start a club (although I cannot abide clubs) for the husbands and wives of lunatics. I'd call it the Mrs Rochester Club, and our emblem would be a tray of pills on gules. As I walk through the streets, I sometimes wonder how many I see hold in their pockets latchkeys that they dread to use for fear that he or she has really done it this time. I wonder how many make a frantic mental check for aspirin bottles or razor blades, how many hide the money or the drink.

Peter has never really been insane, but he has dabbled with insanity for most of our married life. He has made a few half-hearted attempts to go crazy and then I have had him locked up, which is what he is after. He comes out shaken and grimly determined to march on until my seductive rival insanity reappears with her boots and black nightie to give his head another flick with her whip. He goes off again with the prayer that God will let him be mad instead of bad.

Each time this happens, Peter communicates to me (at or near the crisis of his passion) the intelligence that I cheated him out of Sasha. 'You promised me peace and you gave me a stone!' That is his favourite and most melodramatic jibe. My maiden name was Stone. He goes on to say that I killed Sasha . . . I never know whether he means her directly or her in his heart or whether he means Sasha at all. I haven't the time to interpret his ravings. Anyway, I pay the doctors to do it.

My policy has always been to let Peter *say* anything; but this time he has *done* something which embodies all the diatribes I have ever heard. This is what has rocked my endurance; what drove me to look at Sasha's grave.

For the last few months he has seemed better in himself. He always scorns me, but he has been less lethargic. He has done some work and he has paid some attention to David. There has been a subtle change in him . . . in his movements: the lighting of a cigarette, the quality of his walk have had more firmness in them.

A fortnight ago I returned home from work (David was with my mother), and in the dusky hall I heard his laughter . . . peals of ironical, explosive laughter . . . not mad and automatic at all. It was the sort of laugh a man might give when he has lost all his money and suddenly sees the humour in the situation.

'Peter?' I asked, my voice soft and cautious. For some reason I was frightened by the sound of his laughter even though it wasn't an eerie laugh. That one has no effect on me any more.

'Ha, ha!' he cried triumphantly. 'The very one I wanted. Emily, Emily!'

He was sitting on the living-room floor amid the strewn contents of my box, his whole body rocking with glee. My letters, my pictures, everything I have which is private and precious to me . . . everything was scrambled and trampled on. He had burgled my cache, the record of my secret self that no one, no one knew I had. He mocked me with it.

For a moment, I stood appalled at the door. I could not believe that Peter whose own secrecy is so holy to himself could have committed such a sacrilege against me.

'I have entertained myself this whole afternoon with your hypocrisy,' he said with some of his old dryness. 'I think it's time we talked.'

I said nothing, so he continued, 'You had it well enough hidden. I was looking for something else, never mind what, and I found it.' He looked at me slyly.

I knew better than anything else I know where it was hidden. It was hidden in the loft with the suitcases. I curse myself for panicking. Before I could stop it, I blurted out, 'Were you going, then?'

'I had begun to ask myself,' he said, 'why you wanted me to stay.'

'Is it another woman?' I asked idiotically.

'Oh, Emily, after you I would never ever go near another woman.' He smiled and shook his head. The curious thing is that I utterly believed him. 'This box,' he said, tapping it lightly, 'has given you and me a short reprieve. It makes some difference that you loved her too, but what kind of difference I will not know until you have given me some account of yourself.'

With muscles aged and aching, I moved across the room and slowly I began to tidy up: the letters written in her florid hand; the Bible and the doll she had given me because I had never had such things as a child; that accursed locket; the garish scarf she bought me – I never wore it, but I kept it – a snail's shell and a bit of lace. There was the key to Peter's old flat and all the photographs we'd taken of each other.

He watched me coolly as I smoothed and tucked each item into place. 'I wish you'd cry,' he said.

Sasha and I were at school together. Lennox was run by a Mrs Cameron, the haughty widow of a Scottish don. She thought clearly and measured words precisely. Although Lennox was a private school, Mrs Cameron was far from being ordinarily snobbish. She saw her girls as future teachers and parliamentarians. For her, the highest virtue was Achievement; Utopia was Girton College, Cambridge. Mrs Cameron's perfect woman was tidy and effective, self-contained and mistrustful of men.

I was sent to Lennox because my mother and Mrs Cameron were friends. My mother is a socialist, but then, oddly enough, so was Mrs Cameron. My mother thought that anyway she had done enough for her convictions by putting Jane and Anthony through the state system; also, I do not think she could resist Mrs Cameron's calling of me (in the manner of one calling a disciple) from the playroom floor, where I so well fitted together the bricks, shapes and beads which were the essential toys of my childhood.

I went to Lennox when I was fourteen. I disliked it, but I expected to dislike it, or rather, I don't think I expected to enjoy anything very much.

I have no idea how Sasha got there. Mrs Cameron, for all her convictions, was not exclusively interested in the children of meritocrats – there was a sprinkling of bland but clever debutantes – but Sasha had a quality that no one could categorise; and Mrs Cameron had no esteem for what she could not categorise.

Sasha must have been beautifully serious at her interview, and Mrs Cameron would have missed the mockery in her solemnity: that is certainly how she was accepted into the ranks of the elect. It puzzles me more that Mrs Courtney should have sent her there. Mrs Courtney sensed auras, so that the aura of Lennox, which was as strong and practical at Dettol, must have put her off.

Sasha's father, who had deserted them shortly after the war, had a seemingly mysterious control over the Courtney affairs. I say mysterious, because no one ever mentioned him. I think he paid the bills and saw to it that he was getting his money's worth.

Putting Sasha into Lennox would have been his little revenge on them all. I don't know that Sasha sensed this at all, but she hated Lennox with a high, articulate loathing. She wanted to be an actress, and to her mind, actresses had no business with Latin and PE.

My unhappiness at Lennox, before Sasha and I were friends, came from loneliness. I bore this cross with patience, because I had no idea that my life could be otherwise. The other girls despised me, but then I saw nothing surprising in their opinion. I was pale, thin and awkwardly dressed. I had no idea how to speak to another human being with anything like the ease that is socially required. I had been a bookish child, and I blurted out big words which expressed precocious thoughts. That I did my lessons well only made me the object of more scorn.

Sasha burst on to the scene late in my school career. One September morning, in my penultimate year, she was there, sitting dramatically hunched over her desk, sighing passionately. She seemed annoyed rather than unhappy, and yet, she seemed unhappy too. She spoke to no one, consequently, everyone peered at her, trying to ascertain why this interesting person was so fed up, and, indeed, who she was at all. She was almost uglier than I was, but she did not seem the least bit worried by her rather odd appearance: she disposed herself, rather, as attractive girls do, in a vigorous, self-confident manner. I eyed her cautiously, but my heart gave a yelp of hope. I knew at once that we were kin under it all, and that she had made an important discovery which I had altogether failed to recognise. She knew how to use her awkwardness to her advantage.

Wanting someone particular to be your friend must be very much like being in love. During the first few weeks of the term, I watched her continually. In everything she did she radiated solutions to me of my own problems. She used bigger words than I did; she had more elaborate ideas. No one laughed at her. Her uniform was untidy, but it was rakishly untidy (I am a well-ordered person when it comes to my things, but I could never apply this to my school uniform). She was very quick at her lessons, yet everyone listened with respect to her recitations. She remained somewhat aloof from the others, but she walked through any bad opinion they might have had about her as unmolested as Moses parting the Red Sea. Indeed, she was taken up as the school eccentric. People made jokes about her at which she graciously smiled.

I hardly dared to look at her; she would sometimes smile at me, a little knowing, quizzical smile, as if we had a secret to share only when the right moment came. I suspected, despairingly, that she smiled that way at everyone.

We came together because I was badly teased in front of her. I went to cry, a great girl like me, in the lavatory. I hardly ever cry, but when I do, I surprise even myself with the awful piteousness of the sound.

I had been standing near a group of girls who were lustily describing the habits of boys in the back row of the cinema. They were coyly surprised that so much passion could be generated in so public a place. Although it was my private, adolescent shame that no boy had looked at me with anything approaching interest, I wanted to say something that would draw Sasha's attention to me. I have a poor ear for the right cadences of any conversation.

I think I said, 'The thing is, you see, that men approach a sexual peak at the age of nineteen, whereas with women it comes later.' Even now, I can hardly bear to recall my saying that with no idea in my head that it was funny. They all burst into shrieks of laughter; even Sasha laughed. I stood quite still for a moment, playing with my fingers like worry beads. I clamped my self-control down on my rising sobs, until they burst and overrode all sense. I ran into the lavatory with the sensation that I had been sick. I turned on the taps, sat in one of the cubicles and wept like mourning.

A few minutes later, I heard a knock on the door. I swallowed hard, thinking that some teacher had come to view my shame; but, being obedient, I opened the door, hanging my head, and slightly averting my eyes.

Sasha stood there, her face trembling with pity and indignation. 'I'm sorry,' she said. 'Don't think I was laughing at you the way *they* were. I thought you were making a sarcastic joke at their vulgarity. They're so bestial, and you, I think, are very fine.'

I couldn't really believe my ears . . . that she thought I was fine. I looked down on my hands, wet with tears and blubber, and saw that I was still seated on the lavatory. Sasha saw my shame, and released me from it with her own, peculiar form of tact.

'Come!' she cried, her eyes burning. 'You come home with me for tea, and we will talk. I am sure that you are the only one here worth talking to!'

I thanked her timidly, hoping I was saying the right thing, and asked her if she was sure her mother wouldn't mind.

'Our house,' she said grandly, 'is always open to those who are persecuted for righteousness' sake!' I had some vague idea that this was biblical, and I liked people who could quote things. There she was, brandishing the cubicle door like the shield of God's armour, talking like Joan of Arc . . . I thought she was magnificent.

'I really don't do this often,' I said, as we walked home, 'if at all.'

'I know,' she said happily, giving a thrilled little skip through the leaves. 'I know, that is what is marvellous about you. I have watched you. I'm glad you cried. It gave me a chance to know you.' Then, as quickly as she was happy, she became sad. 'I know you don't cry, don't worry. That's why I admire you. You have the courage to be yourself, and I haven't. You should see how I cry! Rivers at the cinema, oceans when I'm cross. I haven't the slightest notion what I am, so my courage to be it fails me. Never mind.' She cheered up with this unburdening, and with a gusty sigh, she started off again, walking so rapidly that I found it difficult to keep pace with her.

At last we arrived, a bit breathless, at a house at the end of a large, redbrick row near Sloane Square.

If I had not had any religious instruction in my childhood, I had had a view of ethical materialism impressed very firmly upon me. They had got me before I was seven, and I knew then – I feel now – that money should not be possessed in such large quantities as to maintain large flats in Chelsea. I was instinctively mistrustful of this house as someone else, with a very different training, would be on the threshold of a house in Stepney. Still, the more something is frowned upon by one's elders, the more exciting that thing becomes. As Sasha turned the key in the heavy oaken door, I had the vague sensation of being at the mouth of Ali Baba's cave where all the glimmering goods had been robbed from the workers.

Sasha took her good address completely for granted; she was neutral to it. I mean by this that she never felt superior to anyone else because of it. She was delighted by the aristocracy; indeed, whatever political sympathies she had were royalist. She had a picture of the Queen, and stood up rigidly in the theatre for the national anthem (Sasha quite often embarrassed me), but she was never aware that these things have connotations, implications for the poor. She would have kissed the feet of a Habsburg, but she would have washed the feet of a beggar with equal enthusiasm. It would have offended me to do either.

My memory of that house is more important to me than any considerations about whether it should have been standing at all. I can almost run thoughts of it through my fingers.

The Courtneys had a first-floor flat. As far as I could see, they had no social dealings with any of their neighbours.

The hall was purposefully rich and sombre. The stairwell was vast. A ponderous newel post marshalled a column of oak balusters down from the dark space above. Everything gleamed with wealthy ugliness. After the front door was shut, the only light in the dark, wax-smelling column of air came from a stained-glass window. This depicted Tristan and Isolde, clasping each other with milky lack of feeling. But the light was soft and played upon the floor, purple and red and blue and green. It transformed the hall into a dreamy, quiet place.

Sasha used to sit and think on the stairs under the window. Her looks were appropriate to that place and in that light. There, she was transformed into someone almost beautiful. A Pre-Raphaelite would have loved her mass of kinky yellow hair, her pallid skin that bruised so easily. She had a wide mouth, and when she laughed, she showed big, splayed teeth. When she was daydreaming, as she did on the stairs, she would purse up her mouth to cover her teeth. This made her look as if she were mocking her own thoughts in a good-natured way. She looked a bit unearthly, like an amused angel, or so a painter would have seen her.

On that day, however, she burst the peace of the place with her excitement. She made an amazing amount of disturbance as she thumped up the thickly carpeted stairs, towing me behind in her eagerness to show me off . . . her new prize. She threw open the drawing-room doors, erupting the hush of her mother's afternoon.

'Sasha, darling, please! Such noise!' said Mrs Courtney, passing a hand over her ear. She sat at a green baize table with another woman, whose appearance was so astonishing that I stopped and stared at her, forgetting both my manners and my shyness. She was a massive woman, whose face had the colour and weight of carved sandstone. Her nose was fine and beaked; her straight, grizzled hair was arranged securely in a knot at the nape of her neck. Her mouth was somewhat grim in its lack of expression. Everything about her was monumentally still – everything but her active, black eyes, which pierced my stare and made me look at my scuffed shoes. She had a primitive grandeur: it looked a bit absurd in a London drawing-room, yet, it was awe-inspiring. I remembered that I'd seen faces like her's in the *National Geographic*. I decided that she must be a gypsy.

The two women had been playing what appeared to be an elaborate game of patience. When the heavy woman saw me, she scooped up the cards, and laid them face down with a decided thump. I saw that they had a very unusual design.

Sasha's mother had been studying the cards intently, rubbing the back of her neck with the quick, girlish movement that Sasha had when she translated Virgil in class. She jumped a little when Nanny hid the cards, and turned quickly round.

'Look, Mummy, Nanny! I've brought Emily Stone back for tea!' Sasha announced me as if I were a celebrity.

Mrs Courtney turned round to greet me, her face bathed in a vague, but beautiful smile. 'How lovely!' she said. 'I thought Sasha would never find a friend at that bleak school.' Mrs Courtney had a great talent for putting people at ease.

Her eyes were large and brown and sympathy-seeking. She used these eyes a lot, when shopping, at taxi-drivers, and, quite gratuitously (because I can never imagine her doing anything illegal) at policemen. When she was distracted by her own thoughts, which was quite often, she had the look of many divorced women of the older generation . . . a look of continual, deep surprise at having been left to cope.

Sasha had an irritating habit of calling her mother 'Mamasha', yet this title, affected as it was, suggested well her quaint prettiness, her quiet, maternal air.

The drawing-room seemed vast. It took me a moment to get my bearings in such a space. It had a high ceiling and tall, cold-looking windows; but the impression of expanse came more from the way the room was arranged. Pieces of furniture seemed to stand about with nothing to do: they were solid heirlooms, which had abandoned all hope of ever being used again. Empty vases stood on dusty tables, a horsehair sofa sulked in a corner, four bulbless standard lamps were placed at intervals around the room like landmarks (I could see no other use for them). This forsaken paraphernalia was arranged in an orderly fashion around the walls, leaving the wide floor to a somewhat dingy Oriental carpet, which looked as if it had died there.

But around the fire, there was a vividness which made the room seem larger still, as if the Courtneys camped out in front of it, like dukes in stately homes. A brass fender glowed warmly in the light and heat of the fire. The pretty French clock on the mantelpiece was almost obscured by old postcards from museums, and by pictures of Sasha and Gregory.

Sasha seated me in a bright chintz chair next to the hearth, not listening to my protestations that I was quite warm enough, thank you.

Nanny rose slowly and lumbered out to make the tea. She eyed me mistrustfully as she went. I had always thought of nannies as people, not women – fiercely chatty and conventional by way of an unspoken creed – who saved small boys, with flaxen hair and Fair Isle jerseys, from the damp on the banks of the Round Pond. I eyed Nanny too.

'Emily,' Sasha said to her mother, 'was quite stupidly teased today at school. I think they envy her. She is very clever.'

I was acutely embarrassed by this remark, but Mrs Courtney's kindness was excited by it. She swiftly seated herself in the armchair facing me, leaned forward, and carefully studied my features.

'I can tell, she said. 'She has a clever mouth.'

I was quite surprised by her behaviour, but Sasha seemed unperturbed by it, as if it was quite natural for her mother to say such a thing.

'Some people', Mrs Courtney continued, picking up her knitting, 'read character from the eyes. I think the mouth is more important, don't you?' she asked me mildly.

'What do you think of Mrs Cameron?' Sasha asked abruptly, making the question important by her tone of voice. 'I hate her.'

'Darling, that is very unkind,' her mother said, furrowing her brow over a difficult stitch she was trying to execute rather than over Sasha's remark.

'I can't help it,' she cried, leaping up. 'She's cold, and cold people are stupid, no matter how well they can do sums or translate Latin prose.'

'But, darling, you must always have compassion on the stupid; she can't help being stupid.' Mrs Courtney abhorred criticism, even though she did not understand what the criticism was about.

'My gels,' Sasha said in a confidential hiss to me; 'my gels are not heah to be trened as nursery maids . . . nor to marry the first man who comes along. My gels are to be educated, firrst and foremost, as women of purpose!' She got it perfectly, that faint trace of Edinburgh refinement, which passed almost unnoticed in Mrs Cameron's speech.

I must have been unusually solemn child, because that is my first memory of ever having laughed uncontrollably. Great guffaws rose from my stomach like a school of whales rising from the bottom of the sea to rejoice on the surface; tears of mirth ran down my cheeks, and I shook my head back and forth in delight at my own abandonment. Mrs Courtney tried for a while to look disapproving, but the more I laughed, the more she inwardly shook, until, at last, she submitted to her giggles, which burst forth pure and bubbly, like a child's. Sasha stood between us, clapping her hands, and fairly shouting with pleasure at the pleasure she had caused in us.

We laughed until Nanny returned with the tea things. We composed ourselves in Nanny's presence.

'Doesn't Emily have the most wonderful laugh!' Sasha cried, and, thinking of it, she laughed again.

I wiped my eyes, feeling more relaxed than I had ever felt in my life, I said, by way of making conversation, 'Mrs Cameron is a great friend of my mother's.'

I looked up, and saw that Sasha and her mother were no longer smiling. At once, my shyness came back. I was convinced I had offended them.

'Oh, Sasha,' Mrs Courtney said, 'Oh, Sasha, how could you!'

'I'm so very sorry,' Sasha said gravely. 'I had no intention of . . . I didn't mean to hurt your feelings.'

I looked from one to the other of them with amazement. 'But, you haven't offended *me* . . . I only meant to say that you had got her right!'

Sasha looked surprised, but I could not tell why. Now, I know that she was astonished at my lack of loyalty, my lack of family feeling. I saw her submerge her judgements often for the sake of loyalty, for the sake of family feeling.

'Oh, dear,' she sighed. 'I try to stop myself, but I find myself mimicking almost everyone I meet!'

A sudden fever of emotion possessed me, an emotion quite rare to me – one I do not understand. Tears started at my eyes, and my face was suffused with blushes. 'Don't mimic me ever. Please, never do that,' I said. I was sorry as soon as I'd said it.

She grasped my hand in both of hers. Her face was all compassion at my extremity. 'Oh, never, never, Emily,' she said softly. '*You* are to be my friend!'

I remember having a feeling of wild dislocation. I looked at Mrs Courtney in my embarrassment, then looked to her almost for help, but she was knitting abstractedly.

'You will, won't you, Emmy?' she asked, pressing my hand again.

At last, not knowing what to do really, I nodded, blushed, and consented to her offer. We smiled at one another with awkward happiness.

'Do you see, Nan?' Mrs Courtney said, 'the cards were right. Sasha has a friend. Extraordinary!' She spoke as if the extraordinary occurred to her so many times a day that the exclamation had become a merely formal thing to mark it.

'That's Nanny's Tarot . . . you must get her to do you some day,' Sasha explained, whispering to me, as if in confidence.

We were allowed to have tea in the nursery to celebrate, what we all appeared to think was our vow.

There are so many rooms which have great significance for me. I often wish the National Trust would branch out and preserve these private sanctuaries: Peter's for one – but that's another matter – and Sasha's nursery, for sure.

Her room was small, and had a cold north light, but this made it all the more snug. She did not sleep in it at the time I first knew her, because it was officially Gregory's room as well, but she had taken it over by right of conquest. Her possessions filled the room completely.

There was always a fire in the grate, and in the corner of the room, there was a smoky, silver icon of the Virgin holding with impossible stiffness an equally stiff baby Jesus. A small candle burnt in a red glass in front of the icon. Upon entering the nursery, Sasha always addressed herself towards that corner, crossing herself somewhat floridly. This practice made me uncomfortable at first. I got used to it after a while.

There was a large round table in the centre of the room. It was covered with a rich, slightly soiled Chinese silk shawl. Everything seemed to be covered with something. The curtains were made of green velvet.

She had papered the walls with pictures so close together that one could hardly tell the colour of the paint. Whatever she liked that could be stuck on the wall, she stuck on the wall. There was an old, dead bunch of flowers, a signed photograph of Clark Gable; there was a road sign, saying 'Disconnected Workmen'. She had Italian Renaissance Madonnas crammed up against travel posters and snapshots of her late lamented cat. There were a few sentimental Victorian lithographs, which I believe she took quite seriously, and there was a picture of Gielgud, brooding over Yorick's skull, which I believe she did not take seriously.

Piles of battered dolls lay on a chaise-longue, and piles of books lay upon the floor. Sasha never seemed to dislike a book. She was a glutton for literature, not a gourmet.

But Sasha's room, described like this, sounds scattered and sloppy. In fact, it was a deep, private place, full of yellow light. There was nothing in it of taste. It was more of a place of indulged imagination.

The room had a curious smell about it – something not entirely clean, and she had the same smell, of mustiness more than of sweat. I think she used some obscure preparation to keep her hair from rising straight out of her head like a bush. I had visions of Nanny brewing this up in a cauldron, but I think Sasha actually bought it from an old-fashioned chemist.

On that particular day, we settled ourselves in front of the fire with our China tea, and crumpets which oozed butter on to the plate. My mother was moralistic about butter: she almost disapproved of it. I was therefore shocked to see it used so liberally.

Sasha curled up like Alice in a large wing-chair. I sat, as decorously as I could, on a footstool, waiting for something to happen. I felt that there was a lot of good will between us, but I could not think of anything to say. Sasha said nothing either for a time. She sipped her tea and watched me unnervingly. She would often stare at me, nodding to herself as if to express agreement with herself at something she was thinking. I looked fixedly at the fire.

'I came in here,' she said, at last, 'so that we could be quiet and wouldn't have to talk. I don't think good friends should have to talk, do you? They should feel things together and not have to say.'

My parents always talked with their friends. In fact, their social life was entirely based on topical discussion . . . politics, social welfare, education. I had always thought that people went to each other's houses to put forward opinions and to argue them out with an armoury of facts. I sometimes wish I had been born mute, because that would have let me off having to converse with people. I was romantically struck by Sasha's notion. For the first time in my life, I felt that silence could be articulate.

For all the value Sasha appeared to give to silence, she was unable to be quiet for long herself. She whooped and chattered through life. Perhaps she appreciated silence in others. Perhaps she could not think of anything to say to me, having vowed to be my friend for life.

'I think you have been sent to me,' she said suddenly. 'You see, I have prayed for a friend, and here you are, sitting before me, so serious and so good!'

If there was something portentous in the way she spoke, I did not notice it then. I could only watch her.

'Let me see your hand,' she whispered.

I was puzzled by this, but I gave her my hand, palm downwards. She took it and turned it over, as if it were a precious piece of china. Her hair stuck out from her head, a cloud around a sibyl, and in the close, darkening little room, I felt an alien fear, which I liked and didn't like.

She stretched my fingers, bent my thumb, and pushed the pads of flesh on my palm. She traced the lines on my hand as if they were important rivers on a map. At last, she spoke with great solemnity. Her eyes shone with tears.

'I thought as much,' she said, 'you will suffer, like me. We will suffer together. I knew it. I sensed it. I'm psychic, you see.'

I did not like the notion of suffering at all, so I must have looked very uncomfortable. I wished for a moment I hadn't met her.

'Only great people suffer.' Her tone was lugubriously encouraging. 'The rest are just unhappy. Suffering is beautiful.'

She leant back in her chair, putting her long fingers together. She had pale slips of hands; her fingernails had an odd, spatulate shape. She receded into the shadow of the chair. I shuddered and was moved.

TWO

As far as my mother is concerned, suffering, if it in fact exists, is there for her to eliminate. My mother was good at mathematics in school not, I think, from an innate talent for the subject, but because she accepted without question that one was one. Her whole life has been unperturbed by questions, but disorder troubles her extremely. She could not have borne to leave an equation unfulfilled. If suffering looks ugly, then it is ugly. She sees no charm in ugliness and has no taste for the bizarre. She is made uncomfortable by things baroque or twisted out of shape; and she despises a sentimental view of unhappiness. Where she sees unhappiness, she tidies it up, unruffled by self-doubt.

She is too clever a woman to care about a short-term alleviation of pain. I think she prefers the word 'problem' to the word 'pain'. She never was a Lady Bountiful full of goodies for the homeless; instead, she sat for years on committees to house them. She taught biology in a secondary modern school until her doctor forced her to quit last year. She sends cheques to Oxfam still earmarked for the drilling of oil-wells. She says Mother Teresa gives her the creeps. She still tutors a great number of children. She teaches the illiterate to read and the innumerate to count. She bore and raised four children of whom I was the third and the second girl.

Now I reflect upon it, I see that my family was comfortably well-off, but this happy state of affairs was a source of guilt to my mother, so we all acted as if we weren't well-off at all. We had few things as children and what we had was simple; yet if one closely inspected the simplicity of these things, one could see that this sparse quality had been bought at a high price. Nothing, for instance, could have been more stark than my own bedroom: the flawless, the functional pieces of furniture suggested at first sight that a Quaker virgin of great austerity lived there – a girl who despised everything material. In fact, my mother had achieved this effect by a considerable expense of money on the latest modern designs.

Although we could have afforded them, we did not have servants, not even a daily help. We did occasionally have people living with us – people in some sort of jam – who lent a hand (and of course there was the au pair), but our household was essentially a cooperative unit. There was a list of chores nailed to the bulletin board every morning – chores for everybody including my father and even my mother herself. Somehow it was very jolly, like a kibbutz is supposed to be, and I think we all got a feeling from this system of the virtue of efficiency and hard work.

When I was at Lennox, my sister Jane had been married for several years. She and her husband taught English to immigrant children in Birmingham. She is the eldest child in the family so I was never very close to her. No, in fact I wouldn't be close to Jane even if we were twins. My brother Anthony had taken a respectable degree in history at Cambridge, and at the time I met Sasha he was living at home in a state of indecision about his career. Indecision in my family never meant, except in my father's case, the wringing of hands or a scratching of the head. Indecision meant a rigorous shaking of the problem by its shoulders until the problem pulled itself together in resolution and committed itself to a course of action. At the time I met Sasha, my mother was fully engaged in Anthony's struggle. They would sit up late at night challenging each other's political motives. No one noticed whether I had a friend or not, and I was quite happy to skulk in the shadows with my secret. I was in the habit of hiding things from my mother. Her consciousness is a swivelling beacon which rakes the horizon. I have never liked to be caught in the glare of her appraising eye.

I have always had a soft spot for my younger brother George. He was a strong-minded and independent child and he kept his thoughts to himself. When he was very young, he would sit dreamily alone softly singing to himself. For some time my mother thought he was mad. As a result of her fear, George was put through a battery of psychological tests which showed that his unconventional behaviour stemmed from an unusual talent for music. Thus justified, George was given a miniature violin and was left alone. George was one of my chores when I was a child. I am seven years his senior and I looked after him when he was a baby. I suppose I could go to him now I am in my present difficulties, but his life is replete with happiness, and I do not wish to beg from his store of it. He loves his work, his house, his wife, his baby . . . when I see him thus perched on life as if he were about to burst into song, I taste all the more strongly the gall in my own mouth.

My parents lived in Fulham long before that place had become fashionable. We had lived in a working-class area because of our politics, yet as we hadn't working-class friends or working-class habits, we were isolated from our neighbours. Our house was large and well-appointed. My school-mates lived in dingy flats and thought I was posh . . . that is my Fulham school-mates thought I was; at Lennox, they thought the opposite.

My father endorsed my mother's views partly because he agreed with them, and partly because he genuinely thought she knew best. Who can blame him? She had and still has an awful clarity that shines through his hazy nature like the sun through clouds. He was, before he sank into retirement, a sociology don at LSE, of all places. He is a gentle scholarly man, who likes to read more than he likes to eat. I used to watch him as he slowly read his heavy books on demes and groups. He would sit in the big leather swivel armchair in the sitting-room, swaying it from side to side with his foot, sucking at his pipe. Then he would lean back and close his eyes, letting the meaning of what he had read seep down into his mind and soak the fibres there. No one has ever cracked his privacy; perhaps my mother once tried to get through to him, but it must have been a futile effort, because from the time I was aware of them both, she no longer cared to find the key to his secrecy.

Sasha beleaguered me with questions about my family. She was hungrily fascinated by every detail I could give her. She listened with parted lips and shining eyes to my account of the mundane life we led. She wanted to know what chores I did, the colour of my father's hair, the kind of food we ate. She was awed by my mother's energy. She could hardly believe that a woman could have four children, a job and a large house to look after and not die from exhaustion.

I think I was never conscious of how much she needed information – how much she sensed her own family's separateness from the world. And so, she drank in this tedious brew of stories and transformed it into nectar in her mind. We lived, she was sure, heroically for ideas.

In the end, I had to invite her to tea, and she lived for the appointed day, referring to it constantly. I hid my dread, because I could not bear to disappoint her. My family's style of life did not embarrass me – Sasha, after all, already admired that – I was ashamed of something much less definable than Indian tea and packaged bread.

Sasha arrived very prettily dressed. She had little heels on her shoes, and at the door, she pinched her cheeks and bit her lips to get up a little colour. She obviously thought it was a bit of an occasion, because she stood expectantly in the hall, looking brightly about her. I suppose she thought that someone would come out to greet her. At last, my mother emerged from the kitchen, drying her hands on a tea-cloth. She turned towards the stairs, then noticed Sasha as a bit of an after-thought. She did not stop drying her hands, but slowed the action down, giving Sasha a summing-up look. She thought Sasha was overdressed. I read it by telepathy. 'Oh, hullo. This must be your friend, Sasha. Tea, George,' she hollered up the stairs. 'I hope you don't mind if we have tea in the kitchen, Sasha.'

Sasha looked involuntarily at her dress, then at my mother, as she retreated into the kitchen.

My mother's social attitude puzzled me when I was a child. Subtle resentments seemed fairly to boil up through the cracks in her clear, commanding personality. Although she was fond of pinpointing what might have been the flaws in the upbringing of others, she was reticent about her own childhood. I believe my grandfather was a Presbyterian minister, and I know my mother lived in a small Yorkshire town until she escaped to Oxford. It must have been there that she obliterated all trace of Northern accent and country ways. She had planed down, by sheer mental effort, the chip on her shoulder – but the shavings remained.

What bewildered me then in her nature is clear to me now. The whole thrust of her personality is social. Her mind is a social mind, her work, social work; her feelings – even they are social feelings. She has no private friends; she has comrades. As she interprets all life through the medium of society, her emotions throb to its workings alone. She has never been angry except in a cause, and in her mind, people personify causes. In her battleground psyche, Sasha became Sasha's genteel clothes and manners; the kitchen (of which my mother was enormously proud) became a kind of headquarters of working-class resistance where ladies could by justly humbled.

We sat in silence at the scrubbed refectory table. Sasha, now subdued, looked furtively around the pine-panelled room. She seemed, at first, bewildered, like an émigrée with only a textbook knowledge of the place she was in and the language which was spoken there. Suddenly, it became strange to me too. I had the curious sensation of being dazzled by the most familiar things: the smart Formica counter, the Spanish tiles and Finnish rug, the shining utensils, which hung in rows on the wall to suggest my mother was a better cook that she was (I think she liked the shape of cooking things, and so do I). Sitting there with Sasha, I became agonised by the spotless informality of it all.

My mother, with her crisp curls and black-rimmed spectacles, bustled about the cooking area. She spread honey, lifted with a swift movement the macaroni cheese on to a woven mat, and tidied as she went, so that no trace of preparations could be observed. I mentally saw the Courtney's kitchen . . . that dark place full of cooking smells. The walls were scarred and greasy from the gas stove, and Nanny had a disreputable old chair where she would doze or knit or read the *Daily Mirror*, mouthing the words as she went along.

We ate. My mother, suspicious that we weren't talking, shot us a glance: under that scrutiny, I became more incapable of speech.

George slouched into the kitchen. When he saw Sasha, he

stopped and gawped at her. 'Who are you?' he asked. My mother did not correct his manners, not because she believed manners were inhibiting, but because she couldn't be bothered with them.

'Sasha Courtney. Who are you?'

George did not answer; instead, he arranged some toy cars he was clutching in a line on the table. He pushed them along, making soft, growling noises in his throat.

'Eeeeeeeeow! Urk!' Sasha cried suddenly, in an ear-splitting, precise imitation of a racing car. She sat straight as duchess, with her hands folded in her lap. George burst into rollicking giggles. 'Do it again! Oh, please!' he cried. She shook her head, casting a glance of mock chagrin at my slightly frowning mother. George at once suppressed his pleas. He looked at Sasha with covert admiration.

My mother sat down and poured herself a cup of black, teabag tea from a pottery pot.

'Sasha,' she said. 'Are you Russian, then?' She spoke in a condescending voice, a tone emphasising the contrast between Sasha's extreme youth and her own maturity. The question, innocuous in itself, sounded very rude.

Sasha appeared to incline her head modestly for a moment's thought, but from under her brow, she shot at me a look of purest devilment. I was quite startled. 'Yes,' she said solemnly. 'My maternal grandmother fled the Bolsheviks in 1917.'

'Oh?' said my mother, coldly. 'Have another bun.' She knew Sasha was making fun of her, but she couldn't figure out how. I was thrilled by Sasha's daring.

Peter is standing in the shadows of the hall, listening to me think. I know he is there, because he stifled a cough. Listening to me think . . . I must be as mad as he is. Madness is contagious, not from the first sneeze of the infected, but from prolonged contact, like leprosy. My mind has started to wrinkle and buckle under the steady torrent of his paranoia. I have started to lose my nerve – that is the worst of it – and where will they be without my strong nerve, Peter and his family and David?

Since he found my box, he has stayed at home and I know why:

to goad my memories into language. Because I am, if anything, conscientious, I lay them out and catalogue their number. If I really thought this would revive our feelings for each other, I wouldn't mind his intrusion; but, I suspect his motives.

He is using me as a medium to contact her afresh. His memory, the only part of himself he counts as human, fades. Peter needs reasons to support his unreasonable feelings; he simply wants new reason to grieve.

It is almost true to say that I left home when I was sixteen. I had my meals at home, I slept at home, but the larger part of me detached itself from my mere surroundings and went to live at the Courtneys. Sasha overcame my mother's antagonism to her with one easy stride. She simply pretended that my mother wasn't there, a game I liked to play. She ignored her dip into cold normality by ignoring the existence of the swimming bath. She treated me, indirectly, as if I had been orphaned by black circumstances, which she knew but hushed up for the sake of my feelings. Shortly after the uncomfortable tea-party at my mother's house, she sent me a letter addressed to 'Countess Emilia Fyodorevna Stone', thanking me for a beautiful party, which she described with such lavish invention, that I nearly believed I did have an elegant little mama, who languidly attended a samovar while her lovers attended her.

She took to reading mysteries into my character. She bought a book on astrology and read up on Virgoans. She told me, with great awe in her voice, that I was 'aloof, analytical and pure'. I remember thinking about that a lot, hugging to myself that I was something, that I had characteristics.

It is only fair to say about Sasha that she replaced from her own store what she took away from mine. If to her mind I had no mother, then she must supply me with her own mother. I had tea with them nearly every day. Mrs Courtney made me clothes. I never wore them at home, because I sensed there would be a lot of inquiries into the precise nature of my friendship with Sasha and her mother; besides, Mrs Courtney had very bad taste. I kept the dresses and hats at their house, and Sasha built this into her game.

I used to love watching Mrs Courtney sew: the way she crossed her needle through the cotton, weaving delicately the strands under and over; the way she bit the thread, replaced the needle carefully in her pin-cushion; the way she lovingly folded the ugly, expensive material she used. If only she had an eye, if only she had taste, I used to think.

Nothing ever happened in the Courtney household. Mrs Courtney rested every day, but she rested from life, not from labours. The flat was always clean and tidy as if by magic. Nanny did the housework so slowly, so methodically that no one ever noticed she was working at all. The two women lived, almost above time, in a perpetual stasis of routine. Sasha accepted this, she even derived rest from it, but she was too active to like it. She plunged into time at school and splashed almost hectically about.

She took me by the hand, and like the Red Queen, she led me galloping across the chessboard. I doubt if she was as conscious of my grasp as I was of hers. I clung to her, knowing that at such a pace I would fall if I let go. I am not sure that Sasha took account of our very different natural rates of speed.

We became solid sisters against a hostile world, or rather, because of our sisterhood, we interpreted the hithertofore indifferent world as hostile. On my own, I would have shrugged and endured Lennox. On her own, Sasha would have got by on charm, but that would have been a feat fraught with danger for her. Instead, she made the place a symbol for us of all that was abhorrent in life. She took to smoking black cigarettes with gold tips and called herself a revolutionary. We smoked them in the lavatory and planned subversion.

She set the tasks; I carried them out, most of them; some, we did together. We let frogs loose in the biology lab – no, I did that, she was too squeamish. We spiked the milk with vodka, hoping the entire student body would reel about all afternoon. Actually, everyone complained the milk was sour, and we saw our combined week's allowance going down the drain. We rearranged clocks so that classes were missed. No one suspected me. This gave me a profound sense of satisfaction. The more I did, the more satisfied I became, and the more I realised how much I really did hate every brick in the walls. I savoured this hatred in my mouth. It was the first feeling I had that I could identify with absolute precision.

Sasha fed my flame. 'These grim Puritans with all their cant about usefulness! Bah! They think of us as machines, not people at all. Have you ever seen Mrs Cameron laugh?' She flushed her Balkan Sobranie down the drain and fanned the smoke out of the window with the *Times Literary Supplement*. She stamped and shook her fist. 'If only I could pull it down like Samson. I wouldn't mind being crushed in the rubble!'

'Sasha, listen,' I said. 'We have done only minor things up till now. There must be a coup. We must get them to close the school.'

We could not think of how to do this, but Sasha insisted it must happen on the Ides of March. We printed signs on a purloined typewriter. They said 'Beware the Ides of March', and we put them everywhere. Our previous actions had annoyed Mrs Cameron, but when the signs went up, she mentioned it in assembly. I was very proud.

We started our campaign on the fifteenth of February, but by the fifteenth of March, the dramatic society had called upon Sasha to be Beatrice in *Much Ado about Nothing*. She contented herself with displaying a large banner saying simply, 'The Ides of March has come.' I was not contented, not in the least. Some aura about my home made me feel such things should be taken seriously. When the students rebelled in Paris, I thought about Sasha and me. I would have enjoyed the blockades, and so, I suppose, would Sasha, had she been presented with an actual blockade. If Sasha, all those years ago, had really embraced the role of Marianne, I might have turned into a Robespierre with a dedication that frightens me. But as I have turned out, I have become completely frigid to politics. During a recent demonstration – a very large one – I experienced actual pleasure in going by tube to a concert. I looked up at the roof of the swaying train, as if to envision their feet far above my head, their inflamed attitudes far apart from mine.

Sasha really was better at Beatrice. This part she played made her a very good companion, and I soon forgot my barricades. With Beatrice as her guide, she became wickedly witty. Everyone admired her acting, even Mrs Cameron. With her praise, which she doled out with the fruit-punch after the performance, Mrs

Cameron expressed in a severe tone the hope that Sasha would have a distinguished career on the stage. The emphasis she put on the word 'distinguished' carried with it all the weight of disapproval she felt for undistinguished careers on the stage . . . Had she been asked to elaborate on the subject, I feel sure she would have said that an actor's life is 'essentially uncommitted', but I think another kind of revulsion stirred her as she looked at Sasha's happy, painted face. I felt woefully separated from my gaudy, excited friend as I stood beside her in my drab clothes.

She tried to teach me to act. She said if she was going to starve in a garret for art, she wanted someone to starve with. She could never see herself alone, but she could never have borne my life.

We chose Ophelia for me to read because I liked *Hamlet*. I remember I wanted very much to do the part well; I learnt it by heart. There was something in the notion of being an actress that slaked some kind of yearning in me. It had occurred to me that in taking on disguises, my own personality could enjoy a freedom, a secrecy which I had so far achieved only by silence: and silence, I knew even then, was not a sufficient cover.

Lennox had a small stage and a few modest klieg lights. The stage was mainly used for the propagation of Mrs Cameron's wisdom. The klieg lights were a bequest from an alumna who had been an enthusiastic achiever in the field of drama therapy. Those lights held great fascination for Sasha. She was always tinkering around with them. On this occasion, when I played Ophelia, she toyed around with them until she achieved a ghastly blue effect: she did this with an ostentatious expertise which I envied.

I stood inflexible on the tiny stage, trying to wrap the cloak of Ophelia's madness around myself. I spoke: the words sounded foreign to me, so that I enunciated very clearly to make them intelligible to myself, but no meaning came to me from them. I felt strangely that I was doing something forbidden. I tried hard to imagine Elsinore and found myself imagining a painted set of Elsinore. The more I tried to be Ophelia, the stiffer I became, until my head ached.

When I had finished, I looked down and said, 'I can't do it.'

Sasha cocked her head and gave a little smile. 'No, you can't. I wonder why. I can do it without any effort at all.' She had a way with her of never looking down on one's failure, so that with her, one never minded failing at anything. 'Isn't nature odd?' she said. 'I can't do maths, but I can act. You can do no end of algebra, but act, you cannot. Look . . . I'll show you how it's done. Would you be interested?'

Without waiting for my reply (Sasha always assumed that I would be interested in anything she did), she sprang in a balletic leap to the stage, where she stood very straight, with the elastic poise of a Degas dancer. She became very still. Her eyes bulged trance-like with concentration. My selfconsciousness began to slip away as I watched her, even though she had not begun to move or speak. Somehow, her expression and her stance had altered so that I forgot her maroon uniform and uncombed hair. She started to move across the stage: it was a gliding walk, interrupted by half-stumbles. She moved her hands uncertainly, as if she were fumbling for something, then gave it up with a jerky shrug. With a voice flat, sad and a little harsh, she sang the bawdy song to a tuneless air of her own invention. I saw at once that I had been wrong in thinking Ophelia a pretty, crack-brained thing. Sasha contrived to make the song obscene; in all of her subtle actions, she suggested a real woman whose mind had been nastily interfered with. I could barely interrupt her with her cues; I have never seen a better performance of the role.

'What you didn't do,' she said afterwards, 'was to find whatever there is of Ophelia in yourself. But then I think sometimes I have too much of everybody. You are lucky to be yourself alone.'

I relish the thought of Peter's reading that last sentence: in it is the explanation of his death in her. Her character was large enough, that is for sure, but not in the way he thinks it was. She was large in her capacity for borrowing others for her own art – a peripatetic magpie was Sasha – and I, not he, I lived with her rapacious imagination.

The worst of it was her flattery. Out of the few wisps of information she had about my personality – those she had extracted by questions and observation – she erected a whole glowing self for me which she handed me as a gift. Out of my good bone structure, she created beauty; out of my cleverness, she created brilliance; out of my very reticence, she created a mind too subtle in its power of reflection for speech. I couldn't act. Very well then, she put me in her imagination in a realm beyond acting. She decided I was a scholar, and once she had done that, she referred all questions to me, nodding sagely at my most idiotic opinions.

It was not until we were about to leave Lennox that I became aware that there were a few anomalies in her story about me. One day, Mrs Cameron checked my progress down the polished lino hall. She fixed me with her firm gaze. 'Emily,' she said, 'I want you to do something for me.'

'Oh?' I said, clearing my throat grittily.

'It's about Sasha. You're a sensible girl, Emily, and you've been a good influence on Sasha.' I felt at once that I was wearing orthopaedic shoes. 'I speak to you in confidence because of my friendship with your mother.' She paused here to transfix me with her own sensible eyes. Under such a cold beam, I was willing to promise anything. 'Sasha has a first-rate brain.' This information struck me somewhere deeper than Mrs Cameron's glance. 'I appeal to you,' she continued, 'because her mother seems quite incapable of grasping the situation. As far as I can see [and here she looked very severe], Mrs Courtney's secret wish is that Sasha should finish her education at a Swiss boarding school.' She looked at my mother's child, not me, knowing that as my mother's child I would appreciate the extent of such frivolity; but I could see only Mrs Courtney, looking with vague interest at the garden beyond Mrs Cameron's study, refusing to comprehend a word of what Mrs Cameron inevitably had said.

'That girl would have a place at Cambridge just like that,' she said, snapping her fingers.

I left Mrs Cameron with the shadowy knowledge that she had taken something away from me. Sasha and I never spoke of Sasha's intellect; we spoke of my intellect. We had tacitly agreed that she didn't have one, although the evidence of her work should have warned me. What truly bothered me, although I see it only now, was that Sasha was indifferent to her mental ability. She was no more proud of her intelligence than she was of knowing how to do an Irish jig (she knew how to do an Irish jig). She dismissed airily in herself what she seemed to admire so in me.

I had my little revenge. I told Sasha the whole, unexpurgated story of my interview with Mrs Cameron and at the end I asked, 'How are you going to act, how are you going to get any coaching at any Swiss boarding school, or even at Cambridge? They're just amateurs you know.' She had listened to the story with some alarm, but when I put on my finishing touch, she went wild with rage, first at her mother, then at Mrs Cameron. 'I see no future in life if I can't act,' she cried. 'I would sweep the stage and dust the props just to be near the theatre!' This was the crescendo of her tirade. In the end she had convinced herself that suicide would be more honourable for her than to stifle her natural inclinations.

I don't know what she said to her mother, but the next time I went to tea with the Courtneys, they were all aflutter with excitement about Sasha's career on the stage. 'My little Bernhardt!' Mrs Courtney called her, squeezing and kissing her every so often as if Sasha had announced her intention to marry someone particularly suitable. I never liked to see Mrs Courtney demonstrate so much affection.

It was decided that Sasha should have a place at RADA. I wish I had had her genius in getting around mothers. My mother had determined that I should go to London University, and it had never occurred to me to challenge her. I did hold out for reading English, which my mother thought a waste of time; but in order to secure my will firmly to London University, she acquiesced. She even invited a spare, eager don to supper. He, who was later to become my unbeloved tutor, spent the whole evening flattering me by asking my opinion of *Othello*. He treated my views as adult and valuable so that my wish to do anything other than attend the London University drained slowly from me. I was later to learn that Dodd had few opinions of his own.

I can see now why my parents wanted me so much to be at Bedford; at the time, I simply assumed that they wanted me to live at home. My brother and sister had been at Cambridge; it was clear that George would study music. They felt that at least one of us should go to the university where my father taught. My whole education was a function of their academic diplomacy.

Even though my place was assured, my mother gave me no hint that I would be accepted. If she was not wholly honest in her disdain for privilege, she at least never gave any of us the hint that we were beneficiaries of privilege. All four of us worked with survival in mind. As a child, I had the impression that I was competing with a whole country full of gifted academic wizards. To this day, I cannot bear to be bested in anything, not even in a game of chess. I laboured long and hard all my childhood for a place I had already won.

Sasha, on the other hand, treated her acceptance at RADA as a foregone conclusion. No one ever said that Nanny had seen success in Sasha's cards, but I am sure that her divinations came into it somehow. I always had a faint suspicion that Nanny peered into the offal of the Sunday chicken. I could see her in my mind's eye, murmuring over a flopping liver while the brussel sprouts grew cold.

Our afternoons were given up to rehearsals. I missed the times we giggled over buns in the nursery. Instead, we took to the drawing-room where, when the cups were pushed aside, we all fell silent for Sasha's Phèdres, her St Joans, her Rosalinds. Mrs Courtney would give the cues in a quiet, uninflected voice, while Sasha, dressed up in this or that faded evening dress, would speak, her voice as flexible as an organ. Mrs Courtney and I listened reverently to the voice of culture, while Nanny would sit farther off, silent and immobile except for her eyes, which watched Sasha with the pride of a mother cat.

Sasha often asked for my criticism. It seems a pity that I hadn't my present judgement. At the time, I simply marvelled with everyone else because it would have been nearly sacrilegious in that atmosphere to do anything else. I told her she was perfect, which she absolutely was not. Her voice was too sonorous, her gestures too mannered. Her pleasure at her own assured future was too great for her to bother about mere art.

They hung lucky charms around her neck for her audition; afterwards, she went into a gazing mood and our communication ceased. Of course, I saw her at school, but she silenced me with suppliant looks. She appeared to have gone into some internal wilderness to pray and fast until her fate was decided. Her arrogance had dropped like the wind, and she was becalmed. What hit me hard was that I was becalmed too. In her company, I had the illusion of a life full of activity and friends. When she removed the company, she removed all of those pleasures which I had come to think of as the products of my own fertile brain . . . as if it had been my idea to go to the cinema, buy a new dress and talk to people on tube trains.

It was during her period of abstinence from society that I received my fee for all that industry. I was accepted at Bedford College, London. 'We are very, very pleased,' my mother said when she learnt of it. No kissing, no hoots of triumph marked my passage into adult life; a Spartan nod, a stern smile – these were the marks of praise in my family. If I had not become so much an adopted child of the Courtneys, I would have been satisfied with my cold confirmation, this formal blow on the cheek which signified I was now a soldier of the intellect; but I was not satisfied, not satisfied at all. I longed to wallow in unction.

I took my triumph to Sasha. We sat under a plane tree in the school garden. I inhaled the spring air and mixed it with my new sense of freedom. I remember feeling that I was telling her a wonderful secret, even though it was no secret at all.

'I'm so happy for you, darling,' she said, her eyes brimming with tears. Those tears, in that moment, became the unction I had craved. She looked away and sighed, her tears really overflowing this time. 'I hope I am as lucky,' she added in a tremulous voice, and I was forced to comfort her. There was something in it all which left me feeling raw and short-changed.

She remained quiet and abstracted for a few weeks, until one day I received a letter from her asking me to meet her in 'the coffee house'. The note, for it wasn't a letter really, is in my box. It is pencilled in her excited handwriting. She wrote with quick little stabs.

'The coffee house' was a dim little café on the King's Road. Those were the days when the King's Road was dingy and arty – in fact, Sasha's garret was to be somewhere around Glebe Place (it seems funny now: she couldn't have a garret there now for under forty a week). For countless Saturdays we had cruised up and down the King's Road, poking into bookshops and covertly watching the men. 'He looked at you,' we would say to one another with wide-eyed surprise. We imagined 'lovers', as Sasha called them, from this extremely raw material. She was apt to fall in love at first sight, and would moon over some handsome boy for weeks, attributing to him qualities of hard intelligence and exacting ruthlessness. I grew my fantasies on more poetical-looking men. Who said that the gods torment us by granting our desires? I can't remember now.

That Saturday, the sun was shining, and cheerful beatniks (those were also the days of beatniks) straggled about the pavement, calling to each other and embracing each other in that casual but loud way people have when they want other people to envy them their ease.

The café was drab, with its dirty floor and old red lino tables. A smell of stomach-destroying coffee pervaded the place. I found Sasha crouched in a dark wooden booth, cradling an empty cup in her trembling hands.

We didn't speak for a moment. She looked at me with wounded, shining eyes.

'They turned you down,' I said at last.

She took several deep breaths, then smiled sadly. 'No, no, they didn't turn me down.'

'Then whatever's the matter?'

'My father won't let me go, and Mummy can't afford the fee.' She was on the edge of a sob, but she pulled herself back from it, just in time.

'But Sasha!' I was really pleased with myself here. 'You can get a grant! I have one.'

'Oh, no, no, they won't give me a grant,' she mumbled, brushing my solution aside. 'I shall simply have to find some place cheaper.' Suddenly, and I did not expect it at all, she careened right over the edge and plunged into the deepest, loudest sob imaginable. 'Ah, he's ruined my career! He's ruined everything for us, and now he's ruined my career!' She wept openly and loudly, throwing her head into her hands.

'Sasha, hush! Sasha, please hush! Not here, please!'

'No! It's all over, finished, and I shall die!' She wailed no less audibly, but in a higher key, like a small child. She pulled at her hair, and started to scratch her face. Everybody was watching. I became more and more embarrassed. 'Is she all right, dear?' the waitress asked. 'Yes! Yes!' I cried, and almost viciously pulled the limping Sasha out of the café. I don't know how I got her home, but it wasn't far, and I managed somehow. When we arrived at her front door, she motioned me away. 'I don't want to upset Mummy,' she said with a great air of one pulling herself together. 'Emmy, Emmy, you are so good to me.' She dashed into the house and closed the door in my face.

When I next saw Sasha, she was quite recovered, although a little sober. I had been very worried about her, but her improvement worried me still more. It was some time before I realised that if she had been given a place at RADA, she would have, almost certainly, been given a grant as well. It made me uneasy that she should have lied to me. I should have said something about it to her, but I could not, partly because she was unapproachable on the subject; partly because I couldn't have mentioned it even if she hadn't been.

THREE

There is a sense of invisible oppression, something which amounts to a haunting, in an unhappy household at three o'clock in the morning.

Four hours ago, I emptied the ashtrays and plumped the cushions. I look around this room and see that I have gone to a lot of trouble to make it attractive. God knows I have spent enough money on it. Nothing is frayed or out of place. David knows and respects the rules concerning the sitting-room. But, this place, this room, my whole house is scribbled over with our unhappiness as if some manic child, some poltergeist had been let loose with a black pen. Unhappiness lingers on the doorknobs, the coffee table, like fingerprints after the murder of the day.

The child does not suffer: children haven't the knowledge of suffering, even though they might experience it. He is wary of us. He sucks his thumb, and, eyes laden with mistrust, he looks from Peter to me and from me to Peter.

Peter, of course, is the Olympic sufferer . . . a professional, marathon sufferer. He refuses to recognise my suffering, as if the extent of it, like Red China, were too vast for him to comprehend. Instead, he calls on God to deliver him . . . from me. I do not believe in God.

Hatred fills my lungs like emphysema: it bulges in my chest. I can point to it *there*. My hatred sluices me to drowning.

I could reach for the telephone, sweatily grip the receiver and breathe down it to a stranger, a Samaritan. Sometimes, on the tube, I am tempted to spray urgent words at a total stranger, to expose myself dirtily to averted eyes.

Since I saw Sasha's grave, I have become possessed with the memory of her. In my mind I circle the plot above her bones, staring at ALEXANDRA COURTNEY, BELOVED DAUGHTER OF . . . until I am near hallucinating her ghost.

Sasha would have loved to haunt me. She died believing she would rise again. I have no time for such nonsense . . . no time. I am happily safe from any worry that I will see her again. Yet I think she died knowing why Peter and I would be unhappy, and I'd be willing to crack her bones open to find the answer.

I remember that trip to Italy distinctly. I want to remember it, not because it brings me closer to the truth, but because it takes me farther away from the truth. I remember enjoying myself just that once. I pick up the few photographs I have with the luxury of a rich woman with a box of exquisite sweets. I fall in love with places, like a cat. Florence was to me what a cushion is for a cat. The trip was arranged for Sasha as a consolation prize for having failed to get into RADA: not that anyone admitted that she had failed – that is merely my interpretation of what I saw. Sasha begged me to go with her. My parents at last consented to give me the fare in place of a birthday present, and they agreed to that only after I had promised to repay half of it when I was able. I never forgot that debt: Peter paid it with one of his grand Coutts cheques before we were married. My mother had to accept it because she had accepted our situation; she fumed for weeks in impotent rage.

We took the train because Nanny was frightened of aeroplanes. Sasha looked glum on the boat, partly because she was inclined to be seasick, and partly because she was not sure she wanted to be consoled; but the moment we reached Calais, she became unable to resist the excitement which had tempted her all the way from Victoria. Neither of us had been abroad before. She lifted up her head and sniffed the cool, tarry air of the port. 'Oh, Emily, Emily, we are in *France*!' her voice set me thrilling with being in France.

'Listen,' she whispered, 'they *think* in French!' She put on a pair of dark glasses as we went through customs, and looked at me over the brim. 'Do you think they'll suspect I'm smuggling diamonds? I do hope so!' As I was in an obscure way afraid that I was smuggling diamonds, I laughed with pleasure and envied her her dark glasses.

'Do you know we are going on the Simplon Orient Express?' she asked in an awed tone. 'It really does go all the way to Istanbul,' She did a little dance on the platform, chanting 'Istanbul, Istanbul . . .' the word became a cheer.

'Take me back to Constantinople, no it's Istanbul, not Constantinople . . .' I started to sing in an embarrassed little voice.

'No, you can't go back to Constantinople, oh, da, da, da, da, da, da!' She finished the song triumphantly. Several people on the platform smiled. The breeze blew, the train ground and shuddered with powerful purpose. 'Oh dear, oh dear, oh dear,' Mrs Courtney cried. 'I know we shall never get the right couchette. I know our baggage will be lost!'

'Nonsense, Mummy!' Sasha said pleasantly.

'I've got it all arranged, Mummy,' Gregory said from the shadow of a pillar, for Gregory had come as well.

Nanny looked mistrustfully at the train, but smiled and patted Gregory when he spoke. 'He's a good boy,' she said. Gregory shrank from her touch and looked annoyed.

With sedative noises, we got Nanny and Mrs Courtney settled in the corner of our second-class couchette. Once past Paris, the two women became pacific.

Sasha and I skittered like happy spiders through the clacking, rocketing train. We seemed to hurtle on our own, without the benefit of machinery, through the vast, airy space, and, godlike, we observed the poplars hazy as night began to fall, the women winding lazily towards home like so many dragonflies, their bicycles whirring like wings – a long loaf of bread for a tail. We became quite giddy with the foreign sounds and smells.

Sasha practised her French on anyone who was willing to listen. French didn't suit her full, somewhat throaty voice. She annoyed a high-toned bourgeoise, arrogant with gloves and chic, by quizzing her on her destination, her marital state. The lady evidently had exquisite linguistic sensibilities. She delivered a haughty insult:

'Vous êtes Americaines?' 'Yes,' said Sasha, 'we are from Omaha, Nebraska.' She marched me off to the dining-car, where we met an agreeable waiter who also thought we were Americans. He liked Americans. His sister had emigrated with a pleasant GI. The waiter showed us snapshots of his nephews in cowboy hats. Sasha listened with great interest to his life story, and he rewarded us with a free cup of coffee. 'Mains en travers la mer,' Sasha said brightly. The waiter winced and poured us out another cup.

Years later, Peter and I took the same train on a holiday taken for the purpose of patching things up between us. We had David for more or less the same reason; to patch things up. We sat in separate silences, refusing the comfort of the scenery. We were together only in that we both contemplated revenge on one another.

Sasha and I shrugged and grinned in rhythm with the French; we gawped at the Alps and flattered beaming Swiss on 'la beauté de votre pays'.

In Italy it became very hot. Mrs Courtney fanned herself intermittently with a restless petulant gesture. Sweat poured off Nanny, but like an Alp with torrents she paid no heed to it. She was knitting a hideous sock for Gregory. The sock grew in ugliness as we travelled; it bristled with needles, which would frequently clank to the floor or get lost under the seat. We would all shift to find them. This made me itch with nerves, but Sasha thought it was funny.

'I don't see how you can touch the wool, darling,' Mrs Courtney said.

'Uhnuhn.'

'Oh, for heaven's sake, Nanny, I don't need the sock until autumn. Put it away. You're driving us all mad with it!' Gregory spoke rarely, perhaps because his voice had only just finished breaking. He had, however, a querulous, dictatorial tone which made Nanny put the sock away. She beamed affection at him, but he flounced and groaned and went back to reading *The Unquiet Grave*.

I have never been able to get the measure of Gregory. He was seldom in London because he attended an obscure public school in Yorkshire where there was strong emphasis on outdoor activity. When he was at home, he spent most of the time in his room, where he painted somewhat septic pictures of naked women. I am sure his mother disapproved of his paintings, but she pandered nervously to his many whims. He was not spoiled like Sasha; he was anxiously served. My mother would have called him a 'problem child'. Under her tutelage, I am sure he would have painted very cheerful nudes in no time at all.

I found it difficult to keep my eyes from wandering towards Gregory as we sat in the fuggy, swaying compartment. He exerted upon me an unpleasant fascination. he was short and frail like Sasha, and like her too, he was pale; but, where her complexion was charged and changed by mood, his was always sallow. Even in the Italian sun, his skin refused to take on colour, so that when he stood, his face fixed and unsmiling, in a piazza crowded with happy, brown Italians, he assumed a look of almost allegorical significance. Gregory looked on life through lizard's eyes – eyes cold, and almost independent of his face. Like a changeling or fairy's child, he seemed old and full of lore.

It was to be understood that in some way Gregory had been wronged. His mother showed this in little ways. She allowed him to be insolent to her, although it was clear that his insolence hurt her. When he was about, she lost the natural, comfortable manner she had with Sasha and me. Gregory perturbed and bewildered her; she made placating motions towards him. He in turn, seemed to accuse her of something . . . stupidity, perhaps, or lack of proper feeling for him.

He appeared to have a strange influence on Nanny; he activated Nanny past her usual silent watchfulness. She would touch him, speak to him of her own accord, but he shrugged off her attentiveness as if by reflex.

He was not alive to the presence of anyone but Sasha. When Sasha and I talked with each other, Gregory would lift his eyes from his book and covertly watch us. When he did this, I would instinctively turn my head towards him and he would burrow again into his book as if to deny my glance. Sasha hardly spoke to him, yet I felt she was aware of him. She spoke to me more loudly in his presence.

Sasha and her brother had a rapport, but it was almost entirely telepathic. Either they did not have to speak, or speaking would have spoiled something between them. They had the quality of two vines, watered and nourished together, whose tanglement was intricate but somewhat fragile.

Sasha rarely spoke of him when he was at school, but one dark November day when she was bored, she showed me the stories they had written together as children.

They had invented a country called Loofay. The king of Loofay was called Bumblefarb, and his queen was Runcebella. As far as I could make out, Bumblefarb and Runcebella had no qualities of leadership at all. Bumblefarb liked to play with toy trains, which he ran around the parapets of his castle. Queen Runcebella was so fat from eating chocolate éclairs that she could not leave her bower. She lived on a gun-carriage especially constructed by her king; it ran on rails and was powered by steam. If the king wished to see Runcebella, he would pull a lever and she would chug up the ramparts to his favourite turret. There, they would survey their pleasant country, which rolled in plenty from the mountains to the sea.

Gregory had made an illustration of the king and queen on their parapet. I remember those paintings to this day; they were like illuminated manuscripts, accurate to the smallest detail and fired with colour. There was no doubt about it; Gregory was an accomplished painter.

There were volumes of these adventures. Mrs Courtney had stitched the pages together. I remember all of the stories. Sasha let me take them home, I pored over each intricately drawn page, reading as I had never read before. I had never had any fairy stories or romances. I hid them in my desk as if they had been pornography.

Gregory had a minor exhibition a few years ago. I kept away from the West End until it was over. I was afraid I might be tempted to do something unwise.

But there . . . I was remembering Italy. The photograph Peter dug out of my box, my reliquary of dead good times, depicts Sasha and me standing against the house like victims of a firing squad.

I have suddenly seen that Peter can get nothing from that. He can only guess the colour of the place; he cannot see Mrs Courtney backing dangerously towards the garden wall, her eye fixed on the viewfinder of her old box camera. 'Try not to squint, my darlings,' she said, and Sasha squinted violently for fun.

The villa was a few miles from Florence. It belonged to an expatriate cousin. This lady, whom Sasha described as a bit impractical, had been convinced at last by her solicitors that she must return to London to sort out her labyrinth state of affairs. She had taken the Courtney's flat, and we had her villa and its staff in exchange. There was an exuberant chauffeur-cum-gardener called Luigi. He had a bad-tempered wife, Annunciata, who cooked and kept house. 'She is quite literally a demon housekeeper,' said Sasha. 'I caught her wringing the neck of a cockerel. I'm sure she drinks its blood and casts spells on Luigi.'

Annunciata and Luigi had terrible quarrels which embarrassed Mrs Courtney and fascinated Sasha. 'Diavolo! Diavolo!' she would scream. There would be a bang, another scream, then silence. Annunciata would emerge with breakfast on a tray, humming a brisk little tune. Sasha said she thought the quarrels got her adrenalin pumping.

We had bitter coffee and hard rolls on the terrace every morning Gregory read the *Daily Mail*, which was, for some reason, obtainable every day in Florence. he read slowly, without much pleasure. Sasha and I would sit near each other in graceful wicker chairs. Sometimes we didn't speak, sometimes we spoke lazily of what we had done, or what we planned to do. Whatever we said seemed unimportant but pleasant, as if our murmurs added peace, adornment to the cool and restful, shuttered house.

Mrs Courtney took her breakfast in bed every day. Nanny kept her company except for the unimaginable occasions when she must have confronted Annunciata in the kitchen.

Nanny refused to recognise Italy. She did not complain about the heat or the food. She did not deplore the standards of hygiene. She simply ignored the fact that we were there. She sat nearly all day in the most capacious drawing-room chair, and continued her covert, anxious watch on this family.

Sasha had a comradely air with her mother, but in her behaviour, there was a quality of gentleness which seemed to imply that Mrs Courtney was very slightly handicapped. Sasha would now and then quietly bully her mother who seemed from time to time to go astray when it came to buying stamps or attending to train schedules.

Sasha had a very different mode of behaviour towards Nanny. She moved around Nanny friskily, shyly like a foal around an old brood mare. Nanny had for her an animal pull. She would touch Nanny a lot, kiss her on the cheek, whisper in her ear, then skitter away as if she dared a cuff. Sasha was in awe of Nanny; but then, so were they all, even Gregory in the slightly frantic way he would beat off her touch. I was the only one who felt no respect for her, partly because she didn't like me, partly because I never had the physical contact with her that she seemed so heavily to rely on as a method of communication. If she by chance brushed me in passing, we would both involuntarily recoil from one another. There was something indefinably at cross purposes between us.

Because I didn't like Nanny, I treated her with a too precise courtesy; I think she mistrusted me for that reason. Sasha was distressed that Nanny wasn't enjoying her holiday. 'Don't you want to see the holy pictures, Nan?' she asked. 'There's nothing holy about them pictures. I have my own pictures,' Nanny replied with a gesture towards her bag which held the Tarot cards . . . those arcane things, they made me shudder. She sat in the villa the entire holiday.

Mrs Courtney made brief forays to the 'holy pictures'. She liked Fra Angelico, and her face would assume a mild loveliness when she had been to see his frescoes. Otherwise she found the heat exhausting. She preferred to read thrillers on the terrace or talk to Luigi about bedding plants. He liked her, and they developed a tenuous little friendship over the flowers.

Gregory prowled off by himself; so in the main, Sasha and I saw Italy together.

My father had given me a history of art as I left from Victoria Station. He had once, he said, enjoyed painting, but he had no time for it now. He sometimes slipped into the National Gallery if he had a moment. He recommended to me Duccio and Piero della Francesca. He presented me with a book and a grave warning to go with it: 'You must guard against frivolity in an approach to art. Here you will get the basic grounding in the principles which will give you a lifelong enjoyment of the subject.' Then, in his hunted, gingerly way, he gave me a kiss. 'Try to have a good time,' he added with some embarrassment.

There was something in the manner of his giving that made me love the gift. I read every word of the book. I even tried to make Sasha understand the importance of line and mass and colour. She listened with only half an ear; with the other half she seemed almost to be listening to the paintings we saw, as if they transmitted tone as well as form.

She was fascinated by angels and archangels, by Madonnas, by crucifixes. Secular painting left her cold, but for the sacred, she had a greedy eye. She would disappear into duomo, baptistry or parish church, and regardless of the value of the altar screen, she stood with rapt attention. I would find her hovering over a bank of votive candles . . . there was something mothlike about her, as if she felt she had been starved of light. We said nothing about this obvious interest, this apparent hunger she had. She moved wistfully away when I appeared, but we did not talk about it.

Otherwise, we revelled in the place. Every morning, Sasha would pace the garden wall, pointing across the piney hills to the day's area of action. Luigi drove us everywhere, and she gave him instructions like a general from the battlements: today, we will overcome the Museo San Marco, today we will take Arezzo by storm! Sasha digested languages the way she ate ice-cream. She smacked her lips and rolled her tongue around a word. Luigi liked very much to teach her all he could.

We had a brilliantly good time. Sasha wore jokey clothes and never minded the coach tours or careening Fiats. We drank illicit Campari; she bought me a silly hat; we giggled at the lechers' 'Bella, bella!' and one wonderful time, we had to take sanctuary in a church to escape a pack of gods on Vespas. Even then, Sasha was a dangerous flirt.

But, she is dead now. When I think of her alive, I can hardly believe this *fact*. Life then seemed voluptuous with possibilities. We wriggled our toes in sandals and let ourselves be overpowered by sunlight. The sun in Italy is a rigged-up paint-pot, slapping at the buildings with unreal colours.

I must think about it as clearly as I can. It was the possibility of what the future held which enchanted us so much. We lay awake in the scented dark and talked.

'Do you think the cards are right? They say I shall be an actress

. . . or at any rate that I shall fulfil myself . . . yes, I know I shall be an actress, possibly a great actress. Does that sound conceited? No. I've decided it isn't. To say that is merely to be small and pettifogging. I loathe pettifogging.' When we talked in the dark, Sasha would pause a lot, as if she were feeling along a wall so as not to mis-step.

'You can see I can *feel* it sometimes . . . a sort of destiny. Do you know what I mean?' Sasha's romances seemed realised to me as she spoke in the lush night. Our days, after all, were filled full of Michelangelo and Botticelli and their quaint notions about the indomitable spirit of man.

We talked too, of course, about what I wanted to do; but even then, there was nothing I wanted to do so much that I could taste it, like she could. It worried Sasha that I could not summon up a vocation . . . that I was flat in the area of desires.

'You are inscrutable, Emily,' she would say now and again; she would look into my face as if she were scrying a crystal ball. She picked up the subject of my character quite often, as if it teased her mind, like a difficult Chinese puzzle.

'Perhaps it is enough for you to *be*,' she said once, apropos of nothing as we sat one evening on the terrace. I had taken up smoking during my last year at school on account of Sasha's Balkan Sobranies. It had quickly become a compelling habit; she gave it up because it made her cough. I have never wanted to finish a cigarette. Halfway through, I light another on the butt, but that is only in private or with people who know me. It seems eccentric to do such a thing in public. Sasha watched me smoking that evening and scratched her woolly head violently as if irritated, not by the extravagance of my habit (she didn't know the meaning of the word 'economy'), but by her inability to grasp something about me.

'I wished I looked like you,' she said. 'You look like a heroine, a bit like Greta Garbo, you know, cool and noble. And the way you smoke . . . as if you had a secret or a very important worry. You *look* profound . . . people only laugh at me, even when I'm serious. I think it's my mouth.'

I hunched over further in my chair and stared into the dark, too flattered for speech. She got up and did a few random dancing exercises. She often did these, in a swift, unapplied way. She said grace was important to her art, but I think she just enjoyed being graceful.

'There you are, Emily! Whenever I say anything like that, you have a little smile, so remote, as if your secrets were more important than I could ever guess.' She made an adept plié. 'I have to practice to be what you are.' She was a bit out of breath, for she had completed several pirouettes. 'Perhaps you're a witch and could change me into a mushroom if you liked. I think Nanny's a bit afraid of you, though she won't say why.'

'Gregory doesn't like me,' I said suddenly. She stopped in mid-stretch and looked distressed.

'Oh, God, what has he said this time?'

'Nothing, nothing at all. He just looks at me as if I were some kind of poison, that's all.'

'Oh, that's all right then,' she said, looking relieved. 'He just oozes a bit sometimes, if you know what I mean. I shouldn't think it was you, exactly.'

'Ooozes! Oh, Sasha you are funny!'

She listened to me laugh, her head cocked to one side. 'I do love your laugh. You don't laugh often, do you? You're such a serious person . . . you are in all ways compact . . . a little Puritan.'

'I thought you didn't like Puritans.' I felt my face contract.

'No. I don't like unnatural Puritans. I think I like anything that is natural. You haven't imposed that rule on yourself; the rule is your being. That is different. Anyway, you know I like you, so why look so stricken?' She touched her toes, then sat down. 'Poor Gregory. I wasn't really being unkind about him. He's unhappy. I don't know exactly why he is unhappy, but I feel his unhappiness in me because we were children together. I love him, but I find it hard to like him now. Is that a dreadful thing to say?'

The question was rhetorical. She breathed in sharply and changed the subject, even though I wanted to go on talking about him. He followed me around with his Nemesis eyes. Sasha never really liked to talk about her family with anything approaching honesty. Honesty in Sasha was as rare as my laugh is in me. My condemnation of Sasha is that she did not have any time for the truth.

We took the train to Assisi, Sasha and I. Nobody else had the energy to go as it had become very hot. I had a case of aesthetic indigestion after two weeks of earnest gallery-going, and I, too, felt hot and lethargic. Sasha, however, was absolutely determined that I should accompany her. She seemed to have a hidden wish that I particularly should see the place.

She was unusually silent at the Church of St Francis. We milled somewhat aimlessly through the crowds from coach tours. A businesslike and not very friendly friar sold us some postcards. An Italian wedding was in progress at the saint's tomb – all flashing cameras and flowers wrapped in cellophane, as if for a funeral. The bride and groom posed in an attitude of exaggerated affection for each other. I fidgeted, while Sasha, as still as a hunter in the bush, looked sharply around her, as if for tracks and clues. Her attention to the church was so great that it created a privacy around her that I did not dare to break. She appeared to be absorbed in every small detail of the place, the way a lover finds deep fascination in the household of his beloved. It was the first interest she had I couldn't share.

She ate her lunch woodenly; she stared unseeing at the Umbrian hills. She had a remarkable power of concentration, but I had never seen her in quite this trance-like attitude. I became annoyed with her. I went over every detail of the church in my own mind, yet I could not think what held her so; I had been indifferent to the place; not even the Giottos were particularly fine. My father's book said that the frescoes had been done by a pupil. I myself had wanted to get to Padua to see the real thing. But then, I considered, Sasha's taste had never been remarkable, or even good, for that matter.

After lunch, we climbed the high hill to the church of St Clare. The air shimmered in the sunlight. Weeds and dusty wild-flowers grew between the mellow paving-stones. The sensible Italians were at rest behind their shuttered windows. I panted in the heat; she climbed without a break in the quiet rhythm of her breath.

Upon entering the church, she smiled with satisfaction. I looked around the bare and simple place without much enthusiasm. It was, at any rate, cool. Perhaps, I thought, she smiled at that. A nun, a lay sister I suppose, was sweeping the stone floor with a besom. She swept with even strokes. On every other stroke, she took a step so that the action amounted to a dance.

Sasha led me into a room off the main church. 'Here,' she said, 'is what I have longed to see. The crucifix which spoke to St Francis is here. God called him from this painting.' She stood very still for a moment, then suddenly letting something go inside of her, she sank to her knees before the image.

It is odd . . . because of her reverence, I felt myself a sudden urge to kneel beside her in front of the stern, convincing Christ, whose outstretched arms for a single moment seemed to encompass me as well. My legs trembled and I turned away, unable to sustain my feelings of helplessness; and as I turned, I saw with a heavy shock, a woman veiled in black, veiled so that even her eyes were covered. She stood behind a massive golden grille. She seemed to be watching us intently. She stood very still. It took me a time to realise that she had been showing a party of tourists the relics behind her grille, and had probably wanted to know if we wanted to see them too.

Sasha continued to pray for quite a while. The nun continued to wait without any sign of impatience; my body stirred convulsively as I looked from one to the other, my vivid friend, the inexorable nun. At last, Sasha's limbs trembled slightly and she turned. When she saw the nun, she displayed no evidence of her surprise, but with respect, she approached the shrouded figure and asked her if she could see the relics. They spoke in Italian and I was unable to understand them. The nun glided from one glass and gold jar to another, explaining in a sibilant whisper what they contained . . . teeth, hair . . . she lifted each with the greatest reverence. My mother had a human foetus pickled in formaldehyde which she kept for her advanced biology students. She held it in no reverence at all. I sometimes wonder what she felt about me, swimming fishlike in her womb.

Sasha's face was intent upon these ruins. She spoke to the nun with childlike docility. I longed to escape – suddenly, I longed for England with something like a pain. That was the only time I can recall when I wanted more than anything to see my parents' Swedish furniture.

'We must see the crypt,' Sasha whispered. 'I wish I could have *really* talked with her.'

We descended into the cool vaults beneath the church. A pillar hid for a moment, what Sasha had come to see; the body of the saint laid out behind glass. The face was ravaged, brown, appalling with its beak of a nose and sunken eyes; but they had decked the corpse in a fresh, white habit, and around its head, they had placed a garland of flowers. Sasha looked at it with solemn eyes. When I think of her now, ten years dead herself, a sick feeling rises in me. I thought I had rid myself of that.

I was dizzy with relief to be going out in the sun again. A few doves whirred and strutted in the courtyard, and every being but myself seemed tranquil.

Quite suddenly, she turned on me. 'You thought it horrible, didn't you? I wanted to know what you'd think.'

'Horrible!' I cried, giving voice at last to my fear. 'Are you disappointed?'

She looked shrewdly at me. I was a little surprised at the acuity of her glance. I had half expected her to have been wilted by the place. 'Yes. A little,' she said.

'I don't see much in it . . . to me, it is like a lot of vultures gathered round a dead body. It's morbid.'

'But Emily, we are all going to die,' she said, as if explaining something to a child. 'They have simply accepted the fact. It is we who run away.'

We had progressed to the steps descending to the town. She sat down and fiddled with a flowery weed. At last, she spoke. 'I don't think we can really love life until we accept death, unless we see it as a simple metamorphosis. All this (and she waved her hand at the town which now droned in post-siesta activity) is more pure, more concentrated after death.' Her voice dropped to a low, faltering tone. 'I have about come to the end of Nanny's and Mummy's glass – whizzing. You know, they think I'm a medium. I've never let you see a séance . . . they hold them about once a week, and I have to be there or it doesn't work. Do you want to know a secret?' she asked suddenly. I nodded. 'I push the glass. I always have done.' She stood up. 'I didn't ask you because I was ashamed of myself, but now I'm not anymore. I'd like to tell Mummy, but it would kill Nanny, you know. She believes in the power of the dead and she's afraid of corpses like the one we just saw. Now those nuns . . .

they're not afraid of corpses or the dead. They must believe in life almost fanatically to keep that mummy there. They've decked her out for the Last Day when God will make her live. Don't you *see* the life in there?'

'No. A fear of death was all I got from that place.'

'Why didn't you kneel? I felt you were going to.'

'What? Kneel in the presence of death?'

'I thought I was kneeling in the presence of love,' she said 'which overcomes death. There, I've been pompous, but isn't that what they believe? I don't know; we never go to church because of Nan. All I have is that icon, which isn't much use as a theologian. It is what they believe, isn't it?' There was an edge of desperation on her voice.

'I don't know. I just don't know. I never thought about it,' I replied. That was the first time I ever saw Sasha in need of anything. I still do not understand what it was she wanted. I do know, however, that because I did not understand there was a slight shift of emphasis in our friendship. Our manners to each other became very faintly tinged with formality.

As for me, the churches soon bored me; as soon as I had catalogued the architecture for myself, I could think of little else to do in them.

After a week or so in Florence, I became restless and easily distracted. Sasha seemed no less interested in me, in fact, she was anxious to talk about this new, recondite passion of hers; but in thrall as I still was to her then, I gradually became aware of a lack in her as far as I was concerned. She did not supply and her God did not supply, what I wanted. Perhaps I never asked them, but I have a constitutional horror of begging.

I am still not very clear in my own mind about the precise nature of what it was that made me impatient with Sasha or why I emotionally mistrusted her faith (if you can call her sentimental longing faith); all I do know is that being at a new distance from her, I cast around in myself for something else to do. As the sound of her voice diminished in my mind, the sound of her brother's increased.

Once I had switched her off, Gregory emerged and became more and more insistent; it was as if his image had been all along an undertone, which asserted itself with pulsating and tuneless regularity in the absence of the main theme.

When we sat at dinner, I was conscious of his presence at my elbow. His manners began to annoy me to a fine sore point. He sucked, and shoved spaghetti into his mouth, biting it off and letting the excess slop onto his plate. He pushed peaches into his mouth with a casual greed: the juice ran down his chin and he made no effort to mask the sensual enjoyment he derived from this. He did it to taunt me, I could see that, because he must have sensed my disapproval. I would turn the crystal water goblet round and round on the linen cloth to keep from shrieking at him to stop. He would from time to time look at me with veiled insolence; otherwise, although he was never overtly rude to me, he would ignore me.

I found myself, without meaning to, proffering my naked legs in his direction as we sat in the sun on the terrace; I would start towards the bathroom in my dressing-gown, leaving it slightly open, when I heard his footsteps in the passage. At night, I dreamed obscenely of him; I say obscenely because the desire in my dreams was not ordinary. Peter does not know what he would have to do to satisfy me; let him work it out; I have disdained to tell him.

The heat that summer may have melted Sasha's English resistance to God and minted her an image which she never lost. The heat planted quite a different seal on me; it made my body slouch with languor and sensual desire.

I have always found the subject of sex distasteful. I detest lewd conversation with a fervour which in anyone else might be called Puritanical. I have always been fastidious about my body. I do not like being casually touched. In my early adolescence I was tempted to masturbate, but I bit my hands in bed at night so cruelly that I occasionally drew blood. The thought of defiling myself filed me with nausea. Apart from the temptation, there was little else which interested me in the matter except that I now and again was quite powerfully and unemotionally drawn to workmen in the street . . . people like that. Men like Peter left me cold until I was a bit older.

It is because of this fastidiousness in me that I am still mildly surprised, in a clinical sort of way, at what I did that last week we were in Florence, or rather, more at what I felt than what I did. I began to long for physical satisfaction as an alcoholic might long for a drink. It was a very sharp sensation – the sort men are supposed to have – and because of the heat and the opulent language, I relinquished any barrier I might have held against my acting upon this desire.

I found what I was looking for. One day (as I say, shortly before we left for home), Sasha went with her mother into Florence to buy some gloves. Gregory, who paid no mind to us anyway, had taken the bus to Siena for a few days. He resisted all questions as to what he wanted to do there. Sasha said he liked Duccio but was ashamed to confess it, although I cannot think why.

I stayed at the house. For a while, I wasted my time in trying to read a chapter in my father's book on the history of art, but I became restless. My restlessness that summer was terrible. The house was still and the heat hung on it, making every chance noise from the kitchen an irritation. I had the sensation that there was going to be a thunderstorm. I wandered into the garden, stricken by a heavy lethargy which seemed to eclipse my mind, making my senses so keenly aware that even the hum of insects seemed sharp and loud. I looked at the sky, but there was no suggestion of rain. Luigi was planting out some sort of heavy, green plant. I never bothered with learning the names of plants. I sat on a stone bench and watched him. His body was mature and muscular, if a little fat.

He looked politely in my direction and said something which I took to be conversational. I took off my sandals and crossed my legs up so high that a lot of my thigh showed. I enjoyed the sensation of myself doing what I was doing. I smiled at him, half thinking of Gregory. He looked confused and poured some water into the ground. I was irritated that he did not take my suggestion. If I could have spoken Italian. I would have invited him into my bedroom. He looked at me again, this time more sharply. I knew he wasn't happy with his wife; he treated Sasha with respect because he genuinely liked her, but anyone could tell how wistfully he looked at her legs when she didn't know it.

I inclined my head towards the house. Luigi shook his head, rather as a bird might do at a snake. I shrugged slightly, got up, and, leaving a trail of invitation behind me, I went into my bedroom, undressed to my slip and waited.

He appeared about half an hour later at the door. His eyes were hesitant, greedy, guilty and ironical all at once. I experienced a not altogether pleasant sensation of power, as if I were driving very fast on a road I did not know.

The thing itself took little time and I found it disappointing. My curiosity was, at any rate, satisfied if nothing else. It became apparent to Luigi, once he had awoken from his physical trance, that he had deflowered me. He was covered with shame and begged my pardon. I understood enough of what he said to ascertain that he felt I was too young to have known what I was doing. I dismissed him somewhat irritably from the bedroom.

After he had gone, I felt an unspeakable disgust at him and at myself, for although he had left my privacy intact, he knew, I felt, in what area it lay. I had a dreadful urge to kill him to keep him quiet, but I saw, in the few following days of our stay, that his shame ensured his silence. I was extremely glad it hadn't been Gregory.

In the end, I paid Luigi ten pounds. My mother had given me money for a present for myself, and he, in a sense, had fulfilled this requirement. I gave him the money in an envelope as we left the station. I saw him open it as the train pulled out. 'Whore!' he shouted in English after us. I think he kept the money though; they were poor. 'Oh dear!' Mrs Courtney cried, 'You don't suppose we left something behind? I could have sworn I heard Luigi shouting something. Did you hear anything, darling?' I said nothing, but smiled, curiously gratified by his reaction.

We returned to England, our pleasure expended. The Courtneys looked like a family on a long drive home from the seaside with sand and rotting picnic everywhere.

I sat apart with my self-loathing and for it I felt completely alien in their midst. Nanny's thighs swung heavily in the motion of the train. Mrs Courtney stared out the window, her face blank with preoccupations. Sasha chattered on with her observations which now seemed a bit pointless to me. I felt ashamed to look at her, for some reason – I suppose because of Luigi of whom she was fond – yet, in a curious way, my shame diminished her in my eyes. She suddenly seemed somewhat arch and frivolous.

As for Gregory, I did not look at him. Every time he hove into my sight, I closed my eyes and tried not to think of something he made me half think and half see on my inner lids.

FOUR

University life had transformed my brother Anthony and my sister Jane from mere adolescents into solid citizens, in both cases, the change being dramatic. I remember Anthony particularly, because he was closer to me in age than Jane. When he went up to Cambridge, he was a shapeless, undefined boy; when he came home for his first vacation, he had jelled, set into what he is today, a public man, a man of policies and thoroughfares. He gave the impression that he had only waited for the magic touch of matriculation to be born again. At the sound of the union division bell, his leadership qualities stirred, arose and coagulated into character.

Jane was much the same. The only difference between Anthony and Jane is their sex, and even that is not very marked, for Jane is very mannish.

As much as I disliked my brother and sister, I cannot avoid this about them; they had friends. Within their narrow terms, they had a good time; and the precedent they set produced in me expectations of a new life filled with parties and intellectual stimulation.

The latter expectation was fulfilled. I did well. The smell of new books is still perfume to me; the crack of the spine, the peace of the library produce in me a sense of purpose and well-being. But as for the former expectation – that of easy camaraderie – in that I was disappointed. With the sight of new faces, I allowed myself some hope. I peered at the other students, half wanting to find some indefinable quality that would draw me to them. I sifted through the arches of eyebrows, the bridges of noses and the quality of laughs; yet nowhere could I find a friend male or female, who would suit the cut of my needs.

Others, however, seemed to be drawn to me. I took this surprise with a measure of irony. I had, after all, been rejected at school by all but Sasha, and even more than that, I discovered that the reason for my pull on people lay merely and mundanely in my physical appearance. I had transformed in one respect alone, and it had taken Sasha's flattery and Luigi's lust to point it out to me; I had become extremely good-looking.

There was one man in particular who paid court to me. I have led a sparsely populated life, so I can easily remember him; his name was William, a thin, scholarly boy with too little beard and a pale face. In the space of a fortnight, William fell in love with me and proposed marriage to me – not that I particularly encouraged him. I let him take me to a film once, where he urgently tried to kiss me. We had lunch now and then. He said I looked as if I had some sorrow, but I had no sorrow then; I was only bewildered at his importunity.

William had a friend called Simon, who lived in digs. Simon had wiry forearms and rolled his own cigarettes. He gave bottle parties and I went with William to one of them. I had never been to a party before.

I do not actually disapprove of parties, as Peter says, I simply cannot think why anyone gives them. I remember that party particularly well, because I experienced there the only metamorphosis of character I was to have at university.

I stood in a corner of the room, drinking bad wine and smoking heavily while I watched the others. William stood at my side. Every now and then he buzzed at me like a May bug, but I paid no attention to him, partly because he annoyed me, and partly because I had a curious feeling which grew and grew upon me as the evening wore on. All my sensations appeared to recede from my outer self, to withdraw like the tide into me, leaving my body, even the facial expressions which animated my body, insensate, free of me . . . only tinged with me the way the shore is tinged with water after the sea has gathered itself to itself. I became numb to William's presence and unaware of the taste of wine; yet in proportion to my loss of bodily consciousness, my inner eye became acute. I became as detached an observer of the people who crashed around me as a scientist who watches struggling germs through a microscope.

They were drenched with sweat and sensuality. Girls half closed their eyes: eyeshadow soaks up the oil on the eyelids. Man's hand goes first to the waist of a girl, then down to feel the weight of her buttocks. Men and girls at parties, like that couple, like railway cars, forcefully lodging their tongues in each other's mouths; they stagger slightly to the sound of music. Excited girls laugh like frantic horses while their partners lunge at them and fumble for their breasts . . .

This sense of utter objectivity heightened in me until it became so nearly pure that I shuddered a little with the thrill of it. I saw with brilliant clarity that this state of consciousness was the answer, the key attitude to strike in relation to every disturbing enigma that life had so far offered me. From every question, every doubt, from every person, from everything that might root and shovel at my mind, I could withdraw. If the memory of Luigi disturbed me, then I could leave the disturbance high and dry; if parties made me shy, then I could abandon parties on the shores of my outward self; if William puzzled and annoyed me, I could retreat from him as flotsam. I saw that I could contract the sea of myself, and in that ebbing, distil myself into greater concentration.

William tugged at my sleeve. 'Are you all right? Have you had too much to drink?'

'William,' I said, 'I never want to see you again. I haven't a vestige of feeling for you.' I walked away, down the stairs and into the street, exulting in the magnitude of my discovery. He didn't dare to follow me. We met at tutorials; this embarrassed him, but not me.

In the same autumn, Sasha went to the Steadman School of Drama. We saw each other less and less, partly because of time and distance, and partly because of a slackening need for each other. We found ourselves both engaged upon growing up; we knew but did not say that we grew on separate trees.

'The Steadman', she called it in the tone a person might use in reference to a club famous to the cognoscenti alone (it was hardly on a par with White's). I am not suggesting that it was a tap-dancing school above a shop: it taught the Method and was patronised by a few known but not well-known actors of the avante-garde. Her enthusiasm for the place was defensive, not genuine. She spoke of it in the way a man speaks of an inferior restaurant he's taken a party to. The more things went wrong, the more she talked of 'teething troubles'.

'I've learned a lot of exciting things about movement,' she would say too often, or 'the value of certain tricks is enormous. One has to free the body, you know . . .', and Sasha, whose body had always been a miracle of quickness and grace, would make tight little gestures betokening freedom of movement.

The school was in Bayswater. It was housed in an early Victorian mansion of no character set in a long row of other, featureless, heavy-columned houses. Next door to it was an hotel advertised by a neon sign with half the light carelessly missing from it. She asked me to meet her there several weeks after her term had started.

The interior was no more inspiring to art than the interior of Lennox had been. There were the same lino floors, the same smell of disinfectant lingered in the corridors; but, whereas Mrs Cameron had ordained the dreariness of Lennox out of moral conviction, the proprietors of the Steadman had simply not the funds to make their school any more cheerful.

The upstairs drawing-room had been converted into an auditorium. A small stage had been erected at the end; it was hung about with hessian curtains.

A few students drifted about the place. For the most part, they were dressed in the drab of the times, all leather thongs, black jerseys and sandals. They wore furrowed expressions to suggest, one felt, that they were seriously artistic.

Sasha stood out amongst them like a brave flame amid a heap of dead coals. She wore a fuzzy woollen, electric orange pinafore thing over a black jersey, and black stockings of a weird, cross-gartered kind considered to be daring then. Her shoes were red and murderously pointed. In her way, she looked smart, especially in that dreary place with the autumn chill on the air; but I couldn't help thinking that she looked like a little girl on her first day of school, inappropriately decked out by a bizarre mother.

She was chatting with a great show of nonchalance to a milky-faced girl who had mournful, protuberant eyes. The girl hunched her shoulders apologetically and didn't know what to do with her hands. She seemed quite in awe of Sasha, who greeted me with noisy enthusiasm. The enthusiasm was overdone, and I got the impression that she was not altogether happy to see me. She seemed nervous and worried.

She introduced the other girl as Celia Russell.

'I'm interested in music, actually,' Celia said, as if this excused her for being there, 'but early church music got me interested in the drama as ritual.' She appeared to hope that I would approve of her remark.

'Oh, yes,' I said.

'Do you know the *Play of Daniel*, Sasha?' she asked. She had dressed with great care to look like the others, but a strong smell of soap and hand-cream and her accent betrayed her county origin. Sasha declared that she adored the *Play of Daniel*, then took me to meet her 'coach'.

'I think he will have great influence on me,' she said as if she hoped he would. His name was Jack, and his mouth moved as if on hinges, like a toy nutcracker. He thrust his poor man's hips into a woman's curve.

'Ah, you're the girl from the groves of Academe,' he said, smiling and hissing. I was childishly pleased that she had so obviously puffed up my coming.

Our conversation with Jack was brief, and we were left standing together in the draughty hall with very little to say to each other.

'What do you think of it all?' she asked. Her eyes, quickly moving and vulnerable, sought mine for reassurance.

I don't know why she suddenly repelled me so; I think it was the seeking in her eyes. Whatever it was, I had a strong desire to push her sharply like a small child pushes a greedy playmate. Instead, I averted my glance. 'I don't know enough about it to say,' I replied. I left early, making an excuse. I felt depressed.

I didn't see her for about six weeks after my visit to the drama school. We made and broke several engagements. Perhaps I had hurt her feelings, although I can't think how I could have done so seriously; she was always so self-assured. I think it was Boris more than anything else that kept her occupied away from me.

Anyway, I was quite absorbed in my work; but during that time, I would now and then glance over my shoulder and find her not there. I experienced vague twinges of loneliness without her. I have always done well on my own, and am very rarely conscious of a need for companionship. I think it is true to say that I feel actual relief when I am left to myself; but Sasha made me feel at ease, and I missed the sense of ease that she brought me.

It wasn't until November that I heard from her. My mother distributed the post before breakfast at everybody's place so that no commotion would disrupt the sacred hour when she and my father read the papers. My parents took *The Times*, the *Guardian*, the *Daily Worker* (as it then was), the *New Statesman*, *The Economist*, and several professional journals of the highest quality. These periodicals were circulated around the table in the most intricate order which had been devised to suit the relative interests of every member of the household. George, who had not come of age, was allowed to read a book.

As I opened Sasha's letter, I felt a curious twist of feeling. With hindsight, I suppose I could call it a premonition, if I believed in such things.

Darling Emmy [it said],

I cannot bear to keep it a secret any longer. I have found the most wonderful man!! Boris is his name. BORIS, BORIS, BORIS!! How I love to write or say the word. I am in love. I don't know if he is, but I have seen a lot of him. To confess to my stern judge, I have *been* with him.

I met him quite ridiculously, madly at Foyle's, of all places, where we peeped at each other most gloriously through the stacks.

His father is a Russian emigré, a prince, whom I haven't met, but I gather they're frightfully brave and tattered and have a Fabergé Easter egg in a glass case in a flat in Earls Court. He is brilliant and has just come down from Cambridge.

I long for you to meet him. I want you to love each other. He says he has a friend who would be most suitable, and could they take us to a v. *grand* dinner on Sat. night. Do please, *please* say yes. The friend is called Peter and is even more brilliant than B. if that's possible, and has just got a first in something or other, and goes to where you are going for graduate work in that too, whatever it is.

Your absurdly happy, Sasha.

I have quoted the letter verbatim. I have it before me now, as smooth and uncreased as it was on the day I received it. The joke is that I kept it mainly to be reminded of the first time I met Peter; the date was 15 November 1960, a month before his twenty-third birthday. Even though it serves no purpose, I like to keep such things on file. That is how I feel about Peter's discovery of my box . . . as if someone had raided a secret file.

'Heard from your little friend, Sasha?' my mother asked, peering over her spectacles at me.

'Mmnn,' I replied. I ate my egg with great concentration, and wondered at how quickly Sasha had allowed herself to fall in love. Although I did not realise it at the time, I was shocked that she should have gone to bed with a man after such a short acquaintance with him. I was annoyed that she had stressed so heavily this man's princely connections. It occurred to me that his origins were probably as far away from the Winter Palace as hers or mine.

I must try to remember that whole evening as objectively as possible. It is no use to me to recall my first meeting with Peter in the light of my present objections to him. I will go step by step through the growth of our early attraction to each other, but I have little hope that anything will emerge to enlighten me.

The Silver Samovar was the restaurant chosen for our 'very grand dinner'. The place has been pulled down; it used to stand in a sheltered corner of Kensington. I remember, coming into it as I did from the cold of the subdued little street, being confused by the light and the bustle. It was a bright place, not harsh in the way of cheap restaurant; an aura of expensive brilliance hung about the diners there. Waiters hurried to and fro with steaming trolleys, and in one corner a haughty looking maître d'hôtel set light to some meat stuck on a sword. He did this with wry finesse, so as to indicate that having a shashlik was rather vulgar, but nevertheless fun. I felt nervous and over-excited. I had never been to a restaurant before.

My party sat at a round table at the very centre of the room; they stood out from the others, the prosperous middle-aged men and their quiet wives, like lights against the foliage of a Christmas tree. They shone with youth and relaxed elegance. My first impression of Boris and Peter was that they were sleek, long-legged and sure, like the mannequin blades who accompany debutantes. With irritation, I felt my palms sweat with fear.

Sasha, gilded with light, sat between the two men: her face was in a glory. She had had social inhibitions like me; I knew she had . . . the lump in the throat at the sight of a handsome man, the hard, self-conscious laugh she gave when in a group of other girls. Like most adolescents, she too had worn that heavy shell of affectation.

I watched her for perhaps a minute while I gave up my coat, and knew that she had changed. She wore a scarlet, low-cut dress; her painted lids and lashes fluttered up and down as she flung quick, enticing glances at the men. She had gathered her woolly hair into a knot at the back of her neck, and she had artfully allowed some ringlets to escape along her forehead and behind her ears. She had broken through the invisible barrier of childish circumspection; in every gesture, she proclaimed some new idea about herself.

As I came in, and before she saw me, she was laughing. The sound of the laugh was low and gurgling; she threw her head back, and the movement revealed white, powdered, slightly sweating flesh from her chin to the cleavage of her breasts; I was surprised to see that they were large and enviable. She turned to the dark man and said something to him in an animated way that made him laugh. He too threw back his head, and I saw that this was Boris and that she had copied his laugh.

Peter sat at Sasha's left; he fiddled with his napkin. A cigarette wobbled idly and dangerously between his knuckles. He looked up every few seconds at Boris and Sasha with an expression of impatience mingled with a faint distaste. I sometimes think that if I had invented Peter's face, it could not have been more perfectly suited to my predilections. It was as if he had been expressly invented to click into the slot of my mind's eye. His face gave me and gives me still a profound intellectual satisfaction. I had looked unconsciously for him everywhere . . . and there he was. I was so afraid I would stare at him that I averted my eyes as I approached the table.

In my confusion, I looked at Boris, who rose to greet me with exaggerated courtesy. He was the sort of man who wears his manners like a boutonnière. He bowed to me with an air of flippant mockery at himself and me. Underneath the gesture which he merely wore, he was a man arrogant in the knowledge of his own virility.

He had a virile smile and virile shoulders, and when he sat down I could see his virile thighs straining at his trousers. The chair creaked beneath his weight. He was the most explicit man I ever saw. He had heavy brows and heavy-lidded eyes. Black hair grew all over his hands in wiry little curls. I was tempted to put out my hand and pull the curls and watch them spring back, or gingerly to touch his shoulder to see what he felt like. I was curious about him as if he had been a highly textured piece of statuary.

It was clear from the way he dressed that he wished people to think him foreign and extraordinary. He wore a red silk shirt and a velvet jacket slightly too small for him and much too elaborate for the occasion. Sasha smiled proudly as she saw me take him in.

'We are in the right place tonight. It is as cold as Siberia out there,' I heard myself talking as if from out of a phrase-book. I heard the sentence fall from my mouth as if I had not said it: my words were artificial and contrived. Boris looked at me with repressed distaste, as if I had handed him a bunch of plastic flowers. I blushed and sat down stiffly, making a frantic effort to find in myself again that door through which I could withdraw; but I was so conscious of Peter's scrutiny upon my furious cheek, that I was unable to enter into myself.

Sasha leaned somewhat recklessly towards me across the table. 'Have some champagne, Em, that'll warm you up!' For some reason, I was shocked that they were drinking champagne – it seemed wasteful and gluttonous to drink champagne unless there was a very good reason for it.

Boris peered down the neck of the bottle. 'Empty,' he said. 'Waiter, more champagne,' he called, snapping his short, thick fingers.

'Yes, more champagne,' Sasha cried delightedly. I was horrified that Sasha, who ordinarily had such good manners, could actually enjoy such a display of bad manners from Boris. In an effort to hide my disapproval, I turned to Peter.

'He's rude, isn't he?' he said, *sotto voce*. Boris and Sasha were so absorbed in conversation that they did not hear.

'Am I obvious or are you observant?'

'You didn't bridle, if that's what you mean.'

'Then you are observant,' I replied warming to the conversation.

'I am a mere dilettante,' he said, 'a dabbler in watching people. I hope to improve with age.' He toyed with his fork again for a moment, then abruptly turned to look at Sasha.

She was telling Boris about a performance she had seen of *Così fan tutte*. She loved opera more, I think, for the crush at Covent Garden than for the music. She had a habit of humming little snatches from arias, but she never hummed in tune.

She talked in a high, soft voice to Boris alone. I felt I heard her from a great distance. Boris leaned towards her and listened with idle amusement. His gaze shifted over her as she talked. He only half listened to what she said. I would have been annoyed if he had not listened fully to what I said, but Sasha didn't seem to mind his lack of attention. Indeed, she talked as if she did not expect to be taken seriously. Her voice was only a pleasant musical accompaniment to the real business and gist of the conversation. She punctuated her words with movement; she would lightly touch his hand as a kind of exclamation mark. She had not liked the Despina. She lifted her head and trilled a little, showing off her bosom to advantage. 'She looked just like a robin on one of those awful Christmas cards,' she said.

I had seen the opera too. I have always been zealous about Mozart. 'Well, Sasha,' I said, 'perhaps she wasn't much of an actress, but her musical sense is perfect. "Una donna a quindici anni" was exquisite.'

Boris, whose back was nearly turned to me, jerked his head slightly as if he had been interrupted in an important train of thought. I blushed yet again. Sasha, looking heavy-eyed, as if nudged in sleep, said, 'Oh, Emmy, were you there too? I went with Celia Russell. If I'd gone with you, I'd have had much more fun. Celia took the score.'

Boris laughed.

'I went alone,' I said. 'I enjoy going to hear music alone.'

'Let's order,' said Boris. 'I'm hungry.'

Peter turned again towards me. He first caught my eye, then shot up a single eyebrow as a flag in my defence. He made a face of such ironical amusement at the busy couple that I nearly laughed aloud.

He laughed too. It has been a long time since I've seen him laugh like that. He had a way of pursing his full mouth, pulling the corners down, then snorting delicately through his nose like a thoroughbred horse.

'You like going to the opera alone?' he asked.

'Yes.'

'That sort of thing becomes a habit. I started going by myself to the cinema, then to concerts, then for long walks. Now I find I am addicted to being alone. If you aren't careful, you'll turn into a recluse like me. Actually, you would make a pretty nun.'

'She would, wouldn't she?' Sasha interrupted with a bit too much spirit. Her ear had been somewhat numbed by alcohol and she spoke too loudly. 'That is if she had any religion, which she hasn't.'

'Haven't you?' Peter asked with interest. 'I would have thought you had. Wrong again. Do you, Sasha, have any religion?' He stressed each word to make the question weigh against her.

She faltered slightly in her gaiety. 'I'd rather not talk about it,' she said.

Peter gave her a diagnostic look. She flushed, and there was an uncomfortable, delicate moment between us three. Boris, however, charged straight through this English barrier.

'Did I ever tell you, Petya,' he said, his accent becoming thicker, 'that I used to be an acolyte for the Patriarch in Paris? I carried the icon when I was a little boy.' Peter knocked his spoon against his teeth. Boris continued with killing nostalgia. 'Ah, Sasha you should see the Russian Easter! I will take you on Easter to the Orthodox church and you will see the true Russian. They can never stamp religion from the Russian soul!'

With this remarkable statement, Boris grabbed the sleeve of the waiter, who now served us with borscht. 'Mitya, is that not right? They will never destroy the true religion?'

Mitya muttered something in Russian. Boris threw back his head and laughed.

'Mitya, tu es méchant!' he said, but he did not interpret Mitya's remark. Mitya, a sour fellow, was looking down Sasha's dress.

'I wish he wouldn't call me Petya,' Peter said to me in a low tone. 'It grates on my nerves.'

For a moment, Sasha looked at Peter with an odd admixture of anger and respect. She took a large swig of champagne, then put the glass down in a decided manner, as if it were a piece in a serious game. 'I have an icon,' she said quietly. 'It is very beautiful. So many people have prayed in front of it that it seems to have taken on some of their faith. If I had to part with all of my possessions, that is that last one I would give up.'

'So many of us felt that way, yet we were forced to part with them, even the icons. I am glad you have one. You understand it. They have life, you know.' Boris uttered this belief in a child-like, round-eyed way. Peter's lip twitched.

Suddenly, a tipsy rapture suffused Sasha's face. 'My icon is magic,' she said in a hushed voice. We all watched her.

Peter spoke first. 'Image, magic, magic, image, imagine. Do they all have the same root, I wonder. I don't think so, but it would be nice if they did. I shall have to look it up.' His tone, too acid, broke her wonderment. She looked bewildered that he could have hurt her feelings. I had a sudden wish to laugh aloud at his remark, but I suppressed it.

'You must forgive my friend,' Boris said. 'He has philosophy, and this makes him ironical.' He gave Peter a heavy look.

Although Peter appeared to despise Boris, he looked swiftly and directly into his scolding eyes. 'Sorry,' he mumbled, then, turning to Sasha, he said in a clear and courtly fashion, 'You must forgive me, I was merely being frivolous.' Boris gave a curt nod of satisfaction. I was at a loss to discover what connection these two men had between them.

'Oh, that's all right,' she said a bit too heartily. 'Don't let's spoil the evening. I want us all to be very gay.' She reached over and patted Peter's hand. He shrank instinctively from her touch.

The dour, libidinous Mitya provided distraction by bringing a plate stacked high with what appeared to be chicken legs.

'Sasha! You mean to be gay, you shall be gay,' cried Boris. 'Mitya, the tzigani . . . are they here tonight?' Mitya nodded, looking more searchingly than ever down Sasha's swelling front. This time, she smiled archly in response to his admiration. She was becoming quite drunk.

Peter, who seemed continually to talk in parentheses, said, 'My God, gypsies! Boris cannot be serious.' He looked at me with something like surprise, as if he had quite suddenly discovered that he found me attractive.

'Are you a philosopher?' I asked, emboldened by his interest. 'Sasha said you were brilliant at something.'

'Ha, ha!' he cried in his soft little way. 'Oh, mercy, no. I'm an archaeologist. That's even more useless than philosophy, you know. Did Sasha lure you here with my brilliance? I assure you, I have none. She spoke a good deal of yours before you came in. Do you think she is matchmaking?'

We prodded one another's minds with glances and half-smiles; yet neither of us gave a thing away. 'Probably,' I said, shrugging a little. He laughed.

Sasha stabbed her chicken-leg; instead of a bone, the thing contained hot butter which gushed on to her plate. She gave a Christmas parcel cry. 'Oh, look! What a delicious surprise!'

Her face was flushed; her eyes sparkled; she ate a mouthful, inhaling through her nostrils with sensuous delight.

Boris picked up her hand and bit it in imitation of her gluttony. 'My delicious little Sasha,' he murmured. She gasped a little with pleasure; a bit of food escaped from the corner of her mouth.

My ears buzzed with the heat and the drink. I ate primly, feeling that without effort, my muscles might weaken and behave as wantonly as hers.

Peter looked wiltingly at the sporting Boris. 'I only wish he had more imagination,' he hissed at me. He really did hiss, quietly, like an angry kitten.

They became more and more ridiculous. Sasha began feeding Boris bits of chicken from her plate. She was at once languorous and giggly. Boris snapped up the chicken. He looked like a great spoiled baby, commanding his adoring mother from an imperial high-chair. Peter sawed irritably at his food. I became more and more uneasy. The bustle of the place jarred my nerves. I felt suffocated by the crowd of bodies, crammed together, stuffing themselves like so many Strasbourg geese. The bodily function which I loathe the most is the process of eating. I would have left, but Peter held me there. Not that I expected anything from him in the way of a romance: his face, to me, was romance enough; his form held all about him that I needed. I liked his finely weird movements, the way he seemed to balance always on the edge of recoil. He touched his face, the table, his box of cigarettes with some regard in his fingers for the texture of each thing. He had the deftness in his eye and hand of a practised surgeon.

The gypsies came with the pudding. The lights dimmed and a small spotlight drew our attention to a small dais. The noise in the room lulled; a few diners stopped talking altogether and became expectant. Several sad-looking men in sateen Russian blouses began to organise balalaikas; their leader struggled with a microphone, muttering curses at its intractability. There was considerable bumping and scraping and high-pitched whining until he eventually tamed it. When they had finally arranged themselves, they sat in silence for a moment, as if the achievement of organising the stage had been enough effort for one evening. At last, they began to play in a weary, half-occupied way.

The first song was very sad. Boris interpreted the words for us. He leaned heavily on the table and told us the story of a maiden who betrayed her lover and jumped into the Volga, and so on and so on. He spoke loudly enough to get the attention of the people nearby. The man at the next table was particularly pleased. 'You can tell it's a good place if *real* Russians eat here,' he said to his wife in a self-justifying tone of voice. They were from the provinces, and he was trying to give her a good time. From her expression, it was clear that he was having a bit of a struggle.

But Boris, with each progressive stanza, became more and more of a stage Russian. With the encouragement of the nice man from Scarborough, he clenched his fists, and began to sing to himself in apparent anguish. He had a wonderful bass voice. Sasha looked half-drowned with love and admiration. When the song was over, Boris drained his glass with an affected flick of the wrist, and made to hurl it into an imaginary fireplace. He checked himself with a sigh, and put the glass down. There was a little polite applause for the gypsies and, no doubt, for Boris as well. Quite a few people were looking at him by this time. He looked well content with himself.

The gypsies (solemn, perhaps, because of their exile) tuned up again. With more bumping and scraping, they launched into another dirge.

Peter looked like a waxwork. I drummed my fingers counter to the rhythm on my knee. I cannot abide popular music of any kind: it encourages disordered sentiment.

The beat became more heavy with each stanza; each pulse throbbed the dirge with feeling. Sasha swayed from side to side and stressed the rhythm with small jerks.

Peter's back stiffened as she moved. Her eyes were closed; his trained upon her with an icy will to quench her crude abandonment. She fluttered up her lids; she did not see how we exhorted her to stop.

The music quickened. Boris snapped his strong fingers to her strong stressed movements. Her body had become a round submissive thing, a cushion on the rhythm, which erupted from her as if it were her own.

Her rapture frightened me, and yet, I could have stopped her with a word. She held me fascinated, my breath taken away at her ability to be transported.

Peter's blandness dropped; he changed his posture and became alert to her. The music strode with thicker beats. Boris arched his back and hit his heavy thigh with the heel of his palm. He grinned with his enjoyment of her.

The players pounded now and poured with sweat. With vacant stares, they held their eyes on Sasha as she swayed. They focused on her as they would upon a lathering drummer. In their heat, with otherwordly eyes, they brought their song to a climax.

And when she gasped with release, the audience whose eyes had fixed on her greedily throughout the song, turned from her. They buzzed their disapproval through the haze of smoke.

In a moment, she realised where she was and how she had enjoyed herself. 'Oh, Emmy,' she cried. 'Oh, Emmy, I'm going to be sick!'

With a hurried scraping of chairs, I bundled her to the ladies' room. There was a silhouette of a woman in a peasant costume on the door. It was an expensive ladies' room, lush with foam stools and shiny chintz. One expected to hear in it only the snap of alligator bags, the plop of lipstick tubes, the gentle hiss of taps. A vestal room it was, away from men.

Sasha retched over and over again into the basin. She made a wounded, personal noise. The lavatory attendant huffed, sour with judgement and distaste.

'You kids nowadays,' she said, as if this summed up her whole philosophy. 'Tarted up to the eyebrows and sick drunk. I never!'

The worst of it was that I endorsed the woman's opinion in my own mind. I was disgusted with Sasha's blundering. The sound of her retching froze my bones. My own image wavered before me for a moment in the mirror, and for a moment, it pleased me with its good taste. My face is in good taste. Then suddenly, stuck by a splinter of self-hatred, I saw the carefulness, the remoteness of my expression. With a drunken, addled anger, I wanted to smash the glass, but I braced myself, looked down, and the anger was gone.

Sasha, having finished vomiting, looked up at the woman. She adjusted her dress with tipsy care, and with tipsy articulation, she said, 'You, madam, are addressing the Princess Semenova to be, and it is her pleasure to enjoy herself as she will!' She gave a haughty snort and reeled out of the door.

'Well, I dunno,' the attendant said. In my Judas way, I gave her a tip.

'Do you have a pound?' Peter asked me when we got back to the table. He looked forsaken, stranded on an island of propriety and settling bills. 'Boris left his wallet at home,' he said a little dryly. 'But,' he continued, 'I suppose it was my treat anyway.' When I knew Peter better, I saw that he had suggested the place himself for his own reasons.

Sasha huddled in her chair, wizened by her debauch. Boris lolled next to her, bumping into her occasionally. They took no notice of each other. They looked like two tramps waiting for an all-night bus, no clear destination in their minds. The other diners looked at them with plain distaste.

'I'm terribly sorry,' Peter said. 'I'll pay you back. We'd better get them home safely.' He seemed so very responsible and serious then.

With the help of Mitya, who muttered Mosca-like into Boris's ear, we spooned him into Peter's car, an old Morris. His bulk made our task difficult, particularly because he didn't want to be taken home. I shoved an enormous tip into Mitya's hand; 'Spaseebo,' he said, refusing English on principle.

Boris insisted on kissing Sasha in the back seat. She looked truly miserable and kept saying she felt ill. She scuffled weakly, but succumbed at last to the ardent Boris. The car was over-heated and smelt faintly of vomit. Boris, single-minded, made it lurch with his exertion. Peter listened as he drove, with some amusement tinged faintly with fastidious dislike for his friend's ruttishness.

We stopped in front of a house in Holland Park. The hedge in front was smartly clipped. Someone was evidently waiting up for Boris. The drawing-room curtains moved; I saw black cloth, an anxious face, but I could not tell whether it was male or female. When the car drew up, the light went out.

'I thought you lived in Earls Court,' I said to Boris.

'I'm staying the night with a friend,' he said, giving me a bland, high-table look . . . the look of nobody's fool. I saw at once the connection between him and Peter which I had been unable to make before. Boris was suddenly as recognisable as one of Anthony's friends. He had had truck with sherry parties and higher education. He had done away so quickly in one glance with Boris of the steppes, that he fairly took my breath away.

That Sasha did not know of his duplicity, I was sure. She had so very little of the equipment of experience to judge how sharp and how distinct were the two sides of her lover's character.

I turned to look at her as Boris heaved himself out of the car. The prettiness she had set out with was now bruised. She had the same appearance as a piece of fruit at the end of market day, a thing thumbed and cast around. She smiled at me a little sheepishly then reached for his departing back too late to touch it. 'Boris,' she called shyly, masking the tremor in her voice which showed to me, at any rate, her yearning for him.

He tapped the window-pane. 'Good night, my little Sasha.' Thick horse that he was, his breath steamed in the winter air. He stamped his feet, then jogged up to the house. He fitted the key easily, as one does at home, then disappeared without a trace of waving or blown kiss.

I did not know at that time how far he had deceived her, but it took me very little time to calculate how far she had deceived herself. She shook my faith in her that night; it was the first crack before the crumble. I did not doubt her because of her behaviour; what horrified me was how blindly she had opened herself to pain. Any fool could have told her that Boris didn't take her seriously, and as she was no fool, she could have told herself. But she didn't. She *didn't* . . . or if she did – and perhaps she did – she didn't care. She had allowed herself to be completely vulnerable to him, and I condemn that in her more than I would have if she had been simply following her appetite.

Peter and I had to help her up the stairs. She was capable of walking, but incapable of thought, her eyes dazed. She said 'Boris' under her breath, wincing at some memory of him.

The fire in the nursery was low. The room had been lovingly made to receive her, the soft white bed turned down. The heavy curtains had been drawn, and the red glass glowed under the icon she had so advertised. That room! If there was anything I envied Sasha for it was her room which was so cared for, in which the cushions seemed to be perpetually plumped for her by magic hands.

Nanny sat in the winged chair so still that we did not notice her at first. I started when I saw her. Peter stifled a stare.

'Oh, Nan, Nan,' Sasha said. 'You won't tell Mummy, will you?'

Nanny regarded Peter and me hostilely for a moment, then turned to Sasha. 'You're tired,' she said firmly. From the emphasis in her voice, she meant to say that this was the dogmatic explanation for Sasha's condition. Most of Sasha's hair had escaped her bun and the mascara was smudged underneath her eyes. Her face always suffered if she was out of sorts; her skin looked soiled and pallid.

'You're tired and you look peaky,' Nanny said. She made a sign for us to go, interposing herself between Sasha and us like a grim angel. A stony fury petrified her face; her power loomed above us and diminished us. I suppose she had some notion that we were responsible for Sasha's clearly drunken state. Behind her strong, protecting body, Sasha seemed to fade; even the dazed look in her eyes went out: she closed them peacefully and let her body drop in perfect rest upon the bed.

'Good Lord! Who *is* that woman?' Peter cried when we reached the street. 'She looks like the Willendorf Venus, or at least how the Willendorf Venus would look if she had a face.'

'Who is the Willendorf Venus?'

'Oh, a stone fertility goddess, very ancient . . . doesn't matter. Who is that cavewoman?'

'Nanny?'

'You meant *she* is a *nanny*? You should meet my nanny! That whole place, that room. It's positively out of this century or any other century I can think of, except possibly the third millennium BC . . . No, no, they have an icon, and they appear to have fire pretty well under control.' His eyes flashed and he grinned wolfishly. 'Are you an *old* friend of Sasha's?' We started to drive in no particular direction.

'Yes. We were at school together.' He looked at me out of the corner of his eye. He drove the Morris as if it were a sports car with ease and daring and many gear shifts. I felt the probe of his attention: it made me feel uncomfortable.

'I find it hard to believe that you and she went to the same school. In fact I find it hard to believe and even a little disappointing that *she* can even read. But *you*, I would say you read the manufacturer's name on your cot.' He laughed not altogether pleasantly and sent the car erratically round a corner. I became aware of something dangerous in him. I squared myself to face his mockery.

'Where did you go to school?' he asked.

'Lennox.' We were driving into Sloane Square. He drove round it a little too fast, but not alarmingly. All the same, there was a tension in his movements that worried me. I narrowed my eyes and set myself against him.

'Lennox! Oh my upper-middle left eye-brow!' he cried, 'And where do *you* live?'

'With my mother and father in Fulham.'

'The elegance of socialists' children will never cease to amaze me' he murmured.

'The point is,' he continued after a pause, 'that you were *all* in disguise. I knew Boris was because I've known him for years and he is inclined, now and then, to shove reality to one side for a week or so. I, for one, always welcome his return to commonsense. But that your primeval friend Sasha should have attended a school for the education of lady parliamentarians is ludicrous. Is she always like that, or was it a pose?'

'She's always been like that as far as I can remember.' I disliked the conversation, so I answered him shortly.

'And you,' he went on, 'straight as a duchess, probably come from a long line of Roundheads. I don't know why I keep guessing. I'm nearly always wrong.'

His whinnied laugh maddened me. 'And whose child are you?' I asked with level cold. 'The son of a general? And was Eton or Winchester the nursery of your woes?'

He put on the brakes without regard for who might be behind him. 'That is remarkable. You got it in one. I am humbled. My father is a brigadier and I was at Winchester.' He appeared to be genuinely surprised. I felt and savoured my advantage.

'I'm going home now,' I said, opening the door.

'I'll take you,' he replied with automatic courtesy. His nastiness had dropped.

'Oh, no. I will find my own way. I assure you I will not be molested.'

He looked at me fully, this time. I could never withstand his stare; even now, I must avoid looking at him, in case he trains it on me. For a moment, I thought he might strike me, not that he seemed angry. He seemed, rather, to be possessed by a free-floating intensity as nameless and unreliable to himself as it was to me.

He spoke at last, haltingly. 'You are so rigid.' He leaned across and kissed me, then quickly pulled away, apparently greatly astonished at himself.

My anger was such that I was on top of it. I felt as if I stood on the crest of an ice-bound moor. He seemed small and far away from me. I left him sitting there, fingering the steering wheel.

When I got home, the house was dark. For quite a while, I walked from room to room. I lit no lights, I made no noise. I paced about until, worn out by my exhilaration, I went to bed.

FIVE

I try to remember what Peter must have looked like, what he must have been on the other end of the telephone when he first called me; but each time I replay to myself his cool, controlled voice, each time I see him with that air of poised detachment he had ten years ago, the sound and vision shatter under the images of him I have more recently acquired. My head buzzes with the scene of his attempted suicide last year. The memory of it appears to be out of control. Pictures of him in that hospital charge my brain against its will: like static, they interfere with the proper tuning of my thoughts.

It was I who found him; I who rode beside his helpless body in the ambulance. I, in fact, recalled him from the dead. I might have left him on the bathroom floor – the thought did tease my mind for a minute or two before I called the ambulance, but then I saw a vision of *her* like a monstrous spider looping towards herself his paralysed mind. He lay there like the parcel a spider makes . . . white and bound and curiously folded into himself. I am astonished at how grateful he is that I did call. I thought merely to counter his move. He talked the other day of 'the sin of despair' . . . it was not Peter talking, oh no, but someone talking through Peter. I found a little wooden crucifix in his pocket the other day. I think he's sneaking off to see some priest.

What a night that was and what a place, that casualty ward! A woman clutched a wounded child who shrieked and shrieked with pain. The child burrowed its nails into the mother's shoulders, gripped its legs with superhuman tenacity around its mother's waist, refusing morphine, refusing everything. The mother sat benumbed while nurses as ineffectual as birds flocked around her.

I had to fill out a form for Peter. They asked his birthday; that seemed idiotic to me to ask his birthday. The receptionist wore a little gold cross on a chain around her neck, but she wasn't sympathetic. She was impersonal and very busy.

Two orderlies wheeled Peter along a corridor. I walked along beside them, clutching the bottle which had contained the sleeping pills he swallowed. Everyone kept talking about the 'evidence', asking me about 'the evidence' as if I had been involved in some crime. In a vague way, I felt pleased that I had remembered 'the evidence'. It's such a joke that he took my sleeping pills. They are the only pills I have – I suffer from insomnia – but he, he has enough pills at hand to poison half of London.

I had to wait outside in the corridor while they pumped his stomach out. Every now and then the door would open and some white-coated person would rush in or out; I'd see a flash of white, the glint of torture-chamber objects, and Peter's feet twitching convulsively underneath a sterilised green sheet. He retched and gagged and gagged: it was a curious, bellowing noise that didn't sound like Peter at all. Any animal, human or otherwise, could have made that noise, provided, of course, the animal was big enough to produce the volume.

One of the doctors muttered something under his breath as he brushed past me . . . it sounded like 'bloody neurotics'. I noticed with interest that he was younger than I was.

An older doctor asked me a number of personal questions; he had a hard, flat manner, so I referred him to Peter's psychiatrist. He said Peter would probably have to go away for a time. I replied that I had become accustomed to this kind of separation in my years of married life. He evidently liked my dryness; we smiled a bit frostily at each other. He asked if this was Peter's first attempted suicide; I said yes – but I had forgotten something he had told me about the past. It seems so odd to me that such an important event in Peter's life could have slipped from my mind.

What I had meant to say, I suppose, was that it was the first attempt I had witnessed.

I kept watch over Peter that night until the psychiatrist arrived. A young nurse came in every so often to check his pulse. She looked at me with reverence as if I exhibited some singular devotion to my husband by hovering near his prostrate body. Indeed, there was an element of truth in her assumption.

I looked long and hard at my husband who had that night tried to leave me. Pink spittle bubbled at the corner of his perfect mouth; in better times, his mouth enchanted me like nothing else on earth. I used to like to bruise his lower lip with my teeth, I'd watch him smoke, talk, eat, for my pleasure at his lips' stretch, pout or quirk. They had taped a yellow tube along the arch of his fine nose. I ran my fingers gently down it and he stirred. I hastily withdrew my hand. He sank back into sleep. He seemed to be carved in stone like an effigy upon a bier in a cathedral. I tiptoed round him, savouring the first feeling of love I'd had for him in years. Then suddenly I saw that I, the doctors and their instruments had blocked his escape; I felt curiously gratified.

There! I've said it. I've parcelled up my memory in words. Words stop a thing from sliding round the head. That done, I can measure out the past.

He took me out to lunch ten years ago because I had excited his curiosity. He can never leave well enough alone: he is a male Pandora.

We met again on a day of high wind and sunny cold. He gave me a meal at an Indian restaurant near the university. The food was good, and the waiters clearly respected Peter's expert reading of the menu. His father had been stationed in the Punjab; in fact, Peter had been born in India and had spent several years there. 'It was all a bit Somerset Maugham,' he said grimacing. We both laughed, although I hadn't the slightest notion what he was talking about. He was referring, of course, to his mother.

Peter could be a fascinating conversationalist. He had many interests, and he spoke about them with a muted but contagious excitement. In every field, I felt, he might be a little gifted.

At first, we were shy with each other. I had met him a bit unwillingly . . . I don't know why I met him at all. I hadn't liked him, he had made me angry, but he was the first person I'd met since Sasha who had made me feel I wasn't encased in glass. But I did like him too. He made me feel jumpy and funny. The reason I gave to myself for going was that I could find out something about Boris . . . that too was true.

In the end, my fear of him dissolved in his good-natured laugh and in his apparent pleasure at seeing me. At midday, there was no mockery in him. I liked the precise way he pared an orange and dissected thoughts. It shocks me to remember what a clever man Peter was.

After lunch, he insisted that I should go with him to the British Museum. He said he had something to show me. He walked jauntily along, his tie flapping in the wind. I saw, with a little surprise that he was happy to be with me, not just happy to be out walking in the wind with a girl. I was pleased, in a guarded way, that he was pleased.

Peter derived such pleasure from the British Museum. He climbed the long flight of steps like an eager mountaineer.

To my family, the reading room of the British Museum was one of the major shrines of the civilised world. My mother, with what poetry she had, had written a little piece about it for the woman's page of the *Guardian*. The piece was about the emotional satisfaction she experienced when she entered the hushed halls and saw the scribes and wits of so many nations gathered there. The collective spirit, she said, of serious thought moved and encouraged her to higher ideals. My brother Anthony was almost fanciful about the place. He often reflected that Karl Marx once worked there; he felt, I think, that the spirit of the departed unbeliever might hover smilingly above his labouring pen.

My family had no truck, however, with the museum proper . . . the racks of urns, the cases of illuminated manuscripts. My mother once suggested that these mere objects, the relics of immoral civilisations, should be removed to less exalted premises. There was not, she said, room enough for the periodicals.

Peter's piety was all for stone. We slipped past shuffling tourists as if there was a secret to be kept. For the sake of the reverence I saw he had, I walked on the balls of my feet (stiletto heels were worn then; it seems funny to recall it).

'You know,' he whispered in a shocked tone of voice, 'two-thirds of all they have is in the cellar! Some of the finest things have to be stored away. To have a find exhibited here . . . why I should have to dredge up Atlantis!'

He looked around him, fingering each treasure with his eyes. 'Look at this, will you.' He pointed to a gigantic Pharaoh's head carved from a block of black basalt. Part of the face had been bashed away; only a cataclysmic accident could have damaged something so huge and hard. I pictured its topple, its thud upon the sand, which must have shaken the earth, then looked away. The arrogant passivity of the broken face lingered behind my averted eyes.

' "My name is Ozyamandias, king of kings . . ." ' I said half to myself. I never liked Shelley, but I felt I ought to say something.

' "Look on my works, ye mighty, and despair!" ' He capped the quotation, laughing softly to himself as if the poem were some private joke to him. He always loved to finish my sentences for me or for me to finish his, no matter how banal was the thought expressed. He likes to think of himself as having a special rapport with someone.

'But I didn't,' he continued, 'come here for the Egyptians.' He smiled a little and we wandered on. 'They used to frighten me so! An aunt of mine took me to see *The Mummy's Curse* or something when I was only eight or so. Silly bloody thing to take a child to see! My addled family! . . . But I suppose the film gave me an interest in archaeology, a *morbid* interest.' Here, he looked down his nose with solemn self-mockery. 'I was so frightened by the idea that people, quite ordinary people like us, could die . . . no, that's not what bothered me . . . it was that when one died, one might be turned into a *thing* . . . that one might become an object of horror to other people. Well, that is taken for granted, isn't it, that one's corpse will be an object of horror to other people. But what struck me then, although I wasn't aware of it at the time, was that I might become an object of horror to myself.

'I used to come here and stare for hours at those bandaged mummies trying to convince myself of the harmlessness of being a thing.' He made a helpless little gesture with his hands. I watched him with great curiosity as he spoke. I had to shake my head a little in order to comprehend his real concern over these objects which were so remote in my own mind from meaning anything at all.

'I did classics at school absolutely because of the mummies.' He poked his thumb up in the general direction of what I took to be the mummy room. 'Well, I couldn't do hieroglyphics, could I? And that finally released me from all this heavy junk.' He waved his hand as if to dismiss from the room the great granite sarcophagus in our path. You could have put his corpse ten times over into the massive thing; it seemed to have been fashioned to exalt the fact of death. I looked at Peter out of the corner of my eye. He had once again assumed his air of brisk arrogance. 'Do you have any Greek?' he asked suddenly.

'No, no Greek. I did a little Latin, which I enjoyed.'

'Ah, well, you *would* enjoy Latin, wouldn't you?' He stood back and looked at me admiringly. 'I can see you now as a Roman matron. *Dignitas, gravitas* . . . they're in your line, or will be.'

'Weren't there three things? *Dignitas, gravitas* . . . and what?'

'*Pietas*, but nobody has that nowadays.' He stood thinking for a moment. 'On second thought, or rather to get back to my first thought about you, the one I expressed so badly the other night, when I called you rigid . . .' he interrupted himself and looked at me quizzically, 'I hurt your feelings, didn't I?'

Something in his regard was not altogether straightforward; I sensed that he wanted a particular answer from me before he went on. I paced out a few careful steps away from his orbit, and leant, considering, against a winged stone lion. The very fact that I hung fire on a reply seemed to excite his curiosity; his eyebrow shot up in appreciation of my independence.

'No, you didn't hurt my feelings,' I said at last. 'You made me angry. You intruded upon my privacy.'

He laughed shortly. I got the impression that what I had said meant more to him than I had intended it to mean.

'How and why should you call me "rigid"? You don't know what I am. How could you?'

'Ah . . .' he said, 'how good it is to find a girl whose feelings don't get hurt. Your reply was sage, to say the least.' He chuckled to himself. 'Why, how should I call you rigid? I meant it as a compliment. Do compliments intrude upon your privacy? Is one allowed to discuss you at all?' He had about him an air of high exhilaration.

I cocked my head and smiled slowly to him instead of speaking.

'Come, and I will show you what I meant by "rigid".' He offered his hand. I took it gingerly. He had a warm, dry clasp and cushioned mounts to his palm. He held mine in his with respect. Peter is the only person I know who has had any real respect for me.

'Here, you must look,' he said with muted agitation. 'These represent my apology to you for making you angry.'

He stood in the middle of the long, dour room, which was by now deserted except for one dozy guard. I walked slowly down the path he had described for me, looking at first perfunctorily at the broken frieze along the wall; but gradually, my eye engaged upon them, and my feelings ceased to chatter in their presence. Nothing moved there, least of all myself, as the still procession marched into my mind of perfect men and perfect horses petrified in mid-career. Each breathing thing had been preserved forever and forever.

'You must see the Nereids. The Nereids personify breeze.' His voice made me start. I had forgotten he was there. He spoke quietly and moved with conscious grace.

We stood together at the statues' base. They seemed to poise above us in the air, their limbs thrust forward through their rippled cloaks to sweep across some plain of the imagination.

'There, do you see what I meant!' he said, excited that I saw it.

'Peter, these aren't *rigid*.' It annoyed me that he saw them so.

'What? Do you imagine they're alive? Of course, they're rigid . . . rigid in their perfection. At any rate, you have for me a quality of what you see.'

We looked mistrustfully at each other for a moment; then he laughed. 'Thank you,' I said, and so we forced ourselves past the time when we could have blasted his fiction about me.

Sometimes I go to see the Elgin marbles, that is, if I have a moment or two during lunch. I stand behind the headless Nereids and savour my desire to push them from their pedestal. They'd make a satisfying crash. I watch the reverent faces of the tourists as they gaze at frozen breeze. Occasionally, I have the urge to leap up on the pedestal and poke my head, fairground-fashion, above the broken neck of one of the statues. I'd like to wink and grimace at the pious thousands. I think I am the only woman in the world married to a reversed Pygmalion.

At any rate, Peter and I on that day felt sobered and a bit uncomfortable on account of the speed at which our intimacy grew. For a while, we perambulated, in the stately way of nineteenth-century gentlefolk, other halls stacked and crammed with Buddhas, urns and broken pottery.

'What about Boris, then?' I asked suddenly. I was surprised at how easily I asked this question I had so carefully rehearsed. We sat on a bench in front of a sandstone Aztec: it stuck its tongue out, and this somehow reminded me of Boris whom I had utterly forgotten in the course of the afternoon.

'What about him, then?'

A bored guard looked in our direction, hoping for some interest in our conversation. I lowered my voice. 'He can't be as simple as he looks.'

'Look at that squat Aztec. I think feathers always make them look absurd, somehow.'

I was not to be distracted by the Aztec's feathers.

'Is he a great friend of yours?'

'Who, Boris? I don't think of Boris in exactly those terms . . . I am a great friend of his, but he is not a great friend of mine.' He spoke with peculiar emphasis. 'Good things have come my way through Boris . . . several good things.' I thought he meant me, and I was pleased. 'We knew each other at Cambridge, but I am not at all sure that we haven't outgrown our friendship. The way he behaved the other night!' He threw up his hands as if words could not express it.

'But what about him? I mean, is he intelligent and so on?'

He gave me another one of his diagnostic looks. 'I imagine that is the first question you ask about anyone. I don't know what you mean by the word "intelligent", but if you mean has he had academic success, the answer is yes. If you can get him on to Slavic history, he becomes quite lucid. In fact, he worked very hard.

'He has a very abstract sort of mind, and yet, he doesn't quite like himself to be like that. He is that curious thing, a stony cold romantic . . . no, no, there I am, wrong again . . . Boris has a heart, but it is simply too ordinary a heart to interest him for long. And, there's this element in him too . . . he is ashamed of tender feelings. Such things, he thinks, belie his masculinity. You'd have to be a man to understand that. He generally takes on a dashing pose when Vernon's been breathing down his neck too hard. The pose you saw the other night was the Anatole Kuragin pose. He has others, most of them equally Byronic, but that, unfortunately, is his favourite. It is very tiresome to all who know him well, and confusing to those who do not know him at all.'

'Who is Vernon?'

'Vernon,' he said, with a shrug.

'No, who is he?'

'*Vernon* is most emphatically a *she*! He lives with her . . . has done for years.'

'Then Sasha has well and truly swallowed the line, rod and reel.' I remembered with sharp distinctness the gape-mouthed adoration on her face.

'You mean she didn't know?' He seemed surprised. 'He usually makes no bones about Vernon. In fact, I have always thought that some of the satisfaction he derives from seducing other women comes from their very knowledge of his bound state. He appeals to their masochistic side, you know . . . "You'll get nothing from me but pleasure, baby, and you'd better put up with it, or you won't get even that." He fixes women with his basilisk eye. He likes to think he is irresistible. Would she care if she did know?'

'Care?! She thinks Boris is going to marry her, or at least, that is the strong impression she gave me.' I saw her lurching out of the ladies' room of The Silver Samovar, declaring herself the Princess Semenova elect; the memory made me shudder.

'Oh, dear,' he said. He stopped and sat in front of a dusty Maori boat. I joined him.

'Look at the space that thing takes up. Why don't they give it to New Zealand House or something,' he said absently. I wanted to prod him for inattention. 'No, that is naughty of Boris, fooling her like that. I wouldn't think he'd approve of that. In his way, he is quite a moral man. Mind you, I'm not opposed to promiscuity . . . except in a fastidious sort of way I have with me.' He laughed apologetically, but looked into my eyes as he spoke. I looked away, embarrassed that I was so drawn to his neat person. He himself, a little flustered, went on, 'One thing I always liked about Boris was his way of firmly setting down the rules before anything happened. It's important to know the rules before you get involved.'

We nodded together with youthful sententiousness . . . as if people could know the rules by simply telling each other what they were.

'What is Vernon like anyway?'

'Oh, you must meet her. I think she's appalling, but that is only a matter of taste. She's an American, not that that makes her appalling, it simply makes her appallingness foreign, and therefore more disagreeable to me. She's very clutching, clingy. She's also very rich. She keeps Boris.' He laughed. 'My God, I sound like my father, but it's true: he lives on her. She takes everything he dishes out and calls for more. I cannot bear that sort of woman!' He uttered this last sentence with such vehemence that I turned to look at him. He spread his fingers out as if before a fire, then grinned suddenly. 'I am, as I said, extremely fastidious.' I thought, for a moment, he was going to kiss me again; however, he decided against it and looked at his watch instead.

'My goodness; It's nearly three o'clock. I must do some work.' He left me quite abruptly; I liked that.

I wonder what kept me from going to Sasha with the story there and then. I felt the pressing importance of telling her, yet I tore up every letter I composed. I would start to lift the telephone off the hook, then leave it, refusing, as it were, the final fence.

I half expected her to call me, but I knew instinctively that she would not. There was no apparent reason why we should not have gone on as usual; we had not quarrelled, but somehow I knew that Boris had placed a moratorium on our friendship, not by anything he had said or done, but rather that she knew and I knew that the two of us, Boris and I, were mutually exclusive friends.

I was not tortured by jealousy, nor did I have my own designs on Boris. I was obsessed with their behaviour in that restaurant: how they sang together; that they had given themselves away to the tune of that bumping, grinding, obvious music . . . I could not bear that. I saw him again and again striking the heel of his palm on his thigh; his hand went down and down, catching at the rhythm as it went; how he sang so lustily without caring who was watching or what people thought. And she, I have already described how she let herself go.

It was their reckless, thoughtless, easy lewdness I abhorred. If they had conducted their affair with circumspection, that would have been a different matter. I never had any orthodox ethical bias. I did not mind what they did, I minded how they did it. I felt a deep moral repugnance at their abandonment. That sounds so pompous, 'deep moral repugnance', but I felt it and no other words describe it.

The danger of their abandonment, and more specifically her abandonment, pressed around my ears. It was as if she had threatened to plunge me to the bottom of the sea. By acting so, she threw me down.

I think I did not tell her about Boris then because I could not bear the sight of her.

Peter ran counterpoint to my preoccupation with Boris and Sasha. After our second meeting, we frequently ran into each other in this or that place around the university. He would see me to the library, buy me a coffee, and in these simple meetings, we filled the time with looks, not words. We made mute gestures to each other signifying anticipation of delights to come in our relationship. He developed a knowing smile; I would raise my fingers slightly in acknowledgement of the smile, the way a prospective buyer hails the auctioneer at Christie's. There was no overt enthusiasm from either of us in the early days of our courtship, none of the exaggerated behaviour I have noticed in others when they think something is about to happen between them. We did not revolve about each other like eager, sniffing dogs. We made time for slow, pleasant observation: a mutual summing up of hints given and received.

We were so cool, Peter and I, as cool as geometry. We were equidistant, and we tacitly agreed to saviour the harmony of this circle. I asked no questions about him; he asked none about me. We did not do the usual prodding with hooks, experimenting with each other's temperaments. We did not thrash around in cinemas or cars or in his flat – that appears to be the way people mate.

We based our friendship, rather, upon a sensibility we had in common. We walked together through the wintry city, our arms, not linked, tangential. We would halt in tandem before some sight, such as a sign scrawled on a wall, or a man we saw once on a park bench, carefully peeling the fat from the ham in his sandwich – anything like that – and smile. His smile became synonymous with mine. We talked very little; I was happy not to have to try to talk.

Once, I saw my father busily engaged in conversation with another don. We passed so near to him, but I said nothing. I did not hail my father or tell Peter that there was my father. We slipped away from him like wraiths. When I was a child, I often felt like a wraith: quite literally, I used to see myself as disembodied. My parents would look at me or talk to me . . . I would respond with my body . . . yet I enjoyed the secret sensation of really being somewhere else. I remember thinking, on that occasion when we saw my father, how nice it was to have a fellow wraith in Peter.

'How would you like to meet Vernon tonight?' he asked me this suddenly one afternoon as we dodged the traffic on the Tottenham Court Road. In the manner of a matador, he neatly avoided a bus. He is in the habit of making surprise announcements at inappropriate times. My hands started to sweat: I shoved them into my pockets and stared fixedly at the kerbstone in order to avoid my stirred feelings.

'I thought you wanted to find out about her. If I'd known you weren't interested, I wouldn't have accepted the invitation. She gives godawful parties.' Peter had a habit then of using Americanisms. He would talk out of the side of his mouth. He admired toughness.

I was itching to go, but I found myself saying instead, 'I think it might be disloyal to Sasha if I went.'

'Oh, you sound so prim! Disloyal to Sasha! I observed Sasha very closely the night we met . . . and you, of course you. She is a queen who counts on courtiers, and you, I discern, have grown stale in her court. You show all the symptoms of a restless baron. It would do you the world of good to be disloyal to Sasha for an evening; you might get some perspective on your thraldom.' He smiled with satisfaction at his own analysis of my situation. There was so much truth in what he had said that I marvelled at him. He registered my wonder. 'Amaze your friends with Peter Meadows, the mind reader,' he said. We laughed.

'Anyway,' he continued, 'you might consider for a moment that in not going to Vernon's party, you'd be disloyal to me. I certainly cannot face it alone.'

Peter's great talent lay in his power to suggest ambiguity. He could do anything with a simple sentence. He spoke then blandly and shrugged his shoulders as if to dismiss the remark altogether; yet, at the same time, he gazed at me as if he had said something of the greatest significance. He hooked me with his eyes, unhooked me with his shrug, so that I swam round and round him, trying to unpuzzle his intentions. And while I struggled with his meaning, I realised I had agreed to go, which was, of course, what I had wanted to do in the first place.

At first sight, it appeared that Vernon had many friends. The room was filled to an almost hazardous capacity with people. But as my eyes became accustomed to the smokey half-light, I saw the other guests more clearly: they were so incongruous with each other that it looked as if Vernon had chosen them at random, closing her eyes and putting a pin in the university directory.

A much televised don with glazed eyes stood amongst a gang of adoring first-year girls. A somnolent Chinese endured the political theory of an aggressive Indian woman in a pink sari. I had seen him before in the library; he had been deeply absorbed in a book on landscape gardening. Fresh-faced boys squirmed like puppies towards the drink, and an elderly cleric cast his eyes towards heaven. Indeed, I sympathised with him: he suffered the martyrdom of being nearly pressed to death by the jostling crowd.

In fact, the atmosphere was much more like rush-hour at Chancery Lane tube station than that of a party. No one seemed to be having a good time, yet everybody talked as loud as he possibly could. The guests chattered in a high-speed, reflexive way, all the while refuelling with the most expensive-looking fare. Instead of the pencilly red or vinegary white wine which is usual at such parties, there was whisky served in heavy, handsome glasses. Platters of rich canapés covered almost every table. No one seemed to appreciate the trouble Vernon clearly had taken in preparing such succulent treats. Someone had put out a cigarette in the avocado dip.

The appearance of the room conformed rigidly to the unspoken rules of student flat décor. The walls were a deep red, the paintwork, even a rather fine cornice over the door, was black; the bookcases were crammed with okay paperbacks. It took me a little time before I realised what was wrong with it all . . . that the inevitable Toulouse-Lautrec posters, which in most digs are clichés to cover the cracks, were here from the first impression: they were well framed, and there were no cracks in the plaster to be covered. Unless Vernon was a builder and decorator herself, which I thought unlikely, she had had this jaunty rebel's room professionally done.

I craned my neck to catch sight of Boris but he was nowhere to be seen. His presence as a permanent lodger there, however, was indicated by several shelves of books on Slavic history, and by an ostentatious dressing-gown which hung in the bedroom where I put my coat. Another sign of him was a pair of silver brushes, highly polished, which lay on a man's dressing table. They had been placed, improbably, on a lace doily.

I, saying nothing, clung to Peter for protection against the writhing bodies round us. He stood straighter for my clinging and smiled down at me, but I wasn't thinking of him. My hands were clammy and I had a headache. I felt as if I were in a dentist's waiting-room. I tried hard to drink my Scotch, but my stomach was so nervous that I could only manage maidenly sips. Sometimes I wish I had a magic wand so that I could effect with it my disappearing act. I cannot withdraw from situations by my will alone; my ability to do this seems to function from an area in me that I do not understand. The more I tried, that night, to find my inner sea, the more my nerves and feelings flooded me.

Peter talked for a while to a girl he knew who seemed to find him very attractive. She showed a passionate, if not altogether genuine, interest in the dolmens of Carnac. 'We took our hols in Brittany, and stumbled on these *fabulous* megaliths. It's fantastic, these ancient things practically in *cow* pastures!' She actually batted her eyes at him. He finally shook her off.

'Where is Vernon, then?' I asked, unable to contain myself any longer. I had to see her, I had to, in order to know . . . but to know what? I am still confused about what it was that I had to know. 'Is she among these?'

'You wave your hand about as if they were so much riffraff to you, and so they are, they are to me too.' (Peter is inclined to provide a running commentary on my remarks and actions: this habit maddens me now, but I used to like it.) 'It's a funny thing, but now I think about it, she is rarely to be seen at her own parties. I expect she's in the kitchen. You really want to meet her, don't you?'

I was annoyed that it showed. We elbowed our way through the crowd, jostling people's drinks, but no one cared.

We found Vernon by herself, as Peter had said, in the kitchen. She was struggling in a half-hearted way with a recalcitrant ice-tray. When she saw us, she put the ice-tray down and shook the water off her fingers with a mournful air.

'Fucking thing', she said. 'Peter, do my ice-tray for me, will you?' It seemed difficult for her to articulate this obscenity, but having managed it, she looked from one to the other of us to see how we had taken it. As no reaction came, she looked sadly again at the ice-tray, while Peter, who simply ran it under the tap, dropped cube upon shining cube into an ice-bucket.

I watched Vernon with intense curiosity. She seemed bound by chains of inertia. She moved her arms in an upward fashion as if to drag the chains behind her. She was tall and very bony; I guessed that she was somewhat older than Boris, for although her expression was petulant and childish, her skin was mature. She had evidently decided to make the best of her unhealthy appearance by emphasising it. She was not unclean, but everything about her was lank and dank and oily; her dark hair hung limply down her back, and she wore an utterly plain, long black dress. This, then, was Sasha's rival.

In contrast to her personal appearance, her kitchen was immaculate. I watched her as she laboured with a tea-towel at the glasses she had washed so carefully; she rubbed each glass to sparkling. She worked so slowly and so conscientiously that I longed to snatch the cloth from her and finish the job myself.

'Where is Boris tonight?' Peter asked conversationally. He appeared to be in good spirits.

'I don't keep track of Boris', she said loftily. 'Help yourselves to a drink.' She had a deep, oddly attractive voice. She drawled her vowels deliberately, as if the American intonation pleased her. 'I haven't seen you for a long time, Peter. Where have you been?'

'I've been working very hard.'

'Well, that's nothing new, but be careful you don't overdo it the way you did at Cambridge; I'll never forget that . . .'

His look was so cold and annihilating that she stopped short. 'Who's your friend or is it your sister? You look a lot alike.' She did not seem to be affected in the least by his apparent dislike of her.

'Emily Stone. No relation. I'm an only child,' he replied noncommittally.

She sighed deeply. 'So am I. Dr Hammond says an only child doesn't know how to relate to his peer group. Don't you think that's true?' She had intended the remark to be conversational. One might have sighed and spoken this way about a cold, rainy day.

I felt a stab of savagery towards this thin, fretting girl. 'On the other hand, you don't have to cope with sibling rivalry either, do you?' My voice had too sharp an edge. Peter looked covertly amused, but Vernon blinked as if I had lunged my fist at her face.

'Why do you have to be so hostile? I didn't say anything to hurt you,' she said. She took the ice-bucket in the crook of her arm, stared indignantly at me for a moment, then left the kitchen, as if vacating the field with a parting shot.

I was prepared to laugh at Vernon, but she had taken her stand so well that I could not. I had stumbled, almost accidentally, on some real flintiness in her character. With the ice-bucket under her arm, and her dead-pan, staring face, she gave the impression of one of those Byzantine mosaics . . . an empress in chips of stone.

'That is Vernon,' Peter said. He spoke of her as if she had been an exhibit.

'What is the matter with her? Is she ill?' I spoke coolly, but Vernon had unnerved me.

'You were very catty to her, but I appreciate meanness in a woman. It shows an ability to cope.' I looked down, not knowing how to take his remark. He gave me new ideas about myself.

'Oh, don't take it seriously. No one takes Vernon seriously, not even Boris. She makes a profession of taking herself seriously. There is no room in her to accept anyone else's love or sympathy or even criticism of her. Literally anything you say to Vernon is taken by her as having a direct relation to herself. I long ago gave up asking Vernon how she was. She *tells* you how she is. She gives you an analytical breakdown of her state of mind.'

'What is she doing here? I mean what does she do other than accommodate Boris?'

'I think she takes some course or other, mostly in herself. She has been psychoanalysed for three whole years. Her doctor lives here, her analyst.' He mouthed the word 'analyst' as if it tasted bad.

'What do you have against analysts? Some of my mother's best friends are analysts.'

He cocked his brow and looked at me briefly; but he went on, ignoring my question as if by a conscious decision. 'No, it works this way: Boris and the doctor live on Vernon; Vernon loathes but lives on Daddy because she has to support her two expensive dependents; her Daddy lives on a chain of right-wing newspapers. The American press unwittingly sponsors free love and foreigners. Boris once showed me a copy of one of those newspapers, all pints of milk and quarts of good, clean fun, and rabidly anti-Communist, Catholic, Jewish, Negro, sin. Only when I'd seen that did I begin to have any sympathy with Vernon. My sympathy, however, was short-lived, but that's a long and entirely different story.'

'Do she and Boris have one of these loose arrangements? I mean does she cheat on him with the same jaunty air as he cheats on her?' He missed the anger in my voice. Perhaps I hid it, though I felt it.

'Jaunty? The idea of Vernon's being jaunty ever!' He laughed sharply. 'No, I think Boris longs for her to do unto him as he does unto her. My suspicion is that Vernon has the morals of a Girl Scout tucked under all that Allen Ginsburg gear!'

We fell silent. I reflected upon the snippets of my building dossier. He became restless and pecked at his whisky in the quick, nervous way of a bird at a bird-bath.

'No, you said the right thing to Vernon . . . a piece of steel spot on . . . that's what you'll be in ten years time.' (I remember he said just that.) 'I should have said that to Vernon, that sort of thing, ages ago . . .' He spoke in this disconnected way, then suddenly pulled himself up short. 'I'm tired of talking about these silly people. I'd rather talk solely about you.' He leaned against the sink and played self-consciously with the tap – off, on, off, on, off. He mumbled, as if half to himself, 'I love you.'

I remember now, the words gave me the shock of bad news. 'What?'

'I love you,' he repeated, this time incisively, unemotionally.

I had to look at him quite hard because he seemed unreal and I am not imaginative, not given to fantasy. He stood quite straight and still, as if to give me the necessary moment to take him in . . . a man who has knocked on a particularly important door. The expression in his eyes, above all else, made him believable. He looked at me, not with love, but with a curious air of certainty about me, as if he, by intuition, had understood that this was the right moment to speak: that he had merely voiced a concrete truth which existed not for him alone, but also for me, if I but knew it.

I mistrusted his words, but I liked them. I would have liked it if he had written them down on a piece of paper so that I could have looked at them as an important memorandum. I would have liked to have made anagrams with the letters . . . to touch, feel, become familiar with the words the way a blind man knows a face with his fingers.

I looked up at him again. His expression had not altered, so I smiled and offered him, with a certain formality, my face to be kissed.

He kissed me, then trembling slightly, lit a cigarette for us both. He smiled and shook and smiled, as if some exquisite but arduous moment in his life had come and gone.

'That is why I love you, you see,' he said, standing back, viewing me. 'Anyone else would have asked me *why*. Anyone else would have had a list of questions . . . about myself, my intentions, what I mean by the word "love" . . . Do you remember the story of the princess and the pea? You are a true princess.' He stood across from me, as if not daring to touch me in case I might vanish.

'I'm not sure you've piled on enough mattresses,' I said, for want of another remark.

He laughed silently and turned a little circle in the neat kitchen.

'How well you understand everything! You have an instinct for me, for what must be said to me.'

I felt numb and bewildered and I started to speak.

'Don't!' he cried. He was high and exultant. 'Don't spoil it!'

Peter has to have everything just so.

Everyone who is unhappy must remember a time when he or she could have walked out of the room, shut the door, and thus disarmed the goad of life. I could have left Peter, then and absolved myself of him forever; but I did not. I stayed out of weakness. I accuse myself of the worst weakness. He had cracked my shell and gobbled my most vulnerable part. He said he loved me. The words worked on me like a magic incantation: they realised me, gave me proof of myself. Does it sound self-pitying? I suppose it does, to say that no one, not my father nor mother nor Sasha nor anyone else had ever *said*, so that I could hear it, that they loved me; and there he was, so right, so succulent, so utterly full of charm – a man who gave me perfect aesthetic satisfaction – saying that he loved me. I felt those words to be an affidavit I could wave at the world, not because I knew myself what was meant by them, but because I knew the world attached great importance to 'I love you'.

Even then, I saw and knew that all the gimcracks in life, from Christmas presents to deep confidences, hung from the branches of these words. I knew, because I had gone without it, that love was the basic premise from which real treats and pleasures sprang. To be lovable, to have it known that you are lovable, is to give the world a sign that you are in the running for the best.

I did not thank Peter, as it were, from the bottom of my heart; I did not love him back, at that moment, in any conventional sense. What I did see was his significance to me: here, at last, someone had given me something I could really use.

Peter and I stood, awash with Scotch in Vernon's little kitchen, safe against the surge of party chatter in the mutual wonder we had at our new acquisition.

Boris was standing at the door. He was leaning on the jamb so that the muscles of his chest and arm were well displayed. I think he had overheard quite a lot of our conversation. He smiled at me impertinently as if we shared some joke against Peter. I stood as still as a stalked animal.

'Hello, Peter. Do you mind if I squeeze by and get a drink?' Boris's shirt was undone in a cinematic décolletage. He passed between us. He was aware of his body; he made me aware of his body.

'Oh, hello, Boris.' Peter paid no attention to this intrusion. Boris might have been the family pet. Peter is the most self-contained man at times. If he has finally lit upon and pinned down an emotion in himself, he becomes entranced by it. He paddles about in himself. He could make love in public spotlessly, effortlessly; his feelings would exclude all other eyes.

Boris raised his elbow, gulped down a glass of water, and smacked his lips, as if he got pleasure from using his most ordinary muscles.

'Now I know who you are,' he said, after staring at me for a moment. 'You're the girl from that restaurant . . . My God, I was drunk! . . . What's your name again?' He hit his head with the heel of his palm, as if to demonstrate that his memory for names came from the lack of importance he attached to people . . . from the lack of importance he had attached to me.

A thick barrier of thuds in my ears kept me from thinking. 'I'm Emily Stone, Sasha Courtney's best friend.'

'Oh, yes,' he said, 'quite so.' He gave himself away in a nervous little glance. His mistake was to shift his gaze. I thought he'd soon enough remember my name.

Vernon appeared in the doorway. 'Oh, there you are!' she said to Boris. 'Your father called and asked you to have lunch with him on Friday. I think you'd better call him. He's got another scheme in mind . . . probably thinks he's found Anastasia selling newspapers in front of Earls Court tube station.' She clutched her brow in apparent imitation of Boris's father.

'Oh, God, has he? . . . Listen, have you got anything to eat besides all this nibbly stuff? I'm starved!'

She fussed around the refrigerator, jamming and unjamming packets of this or that. She flustered herself into a little storm over the food. 'Oh, I'm *so sorry*, Boris. Honestly, I had no *idea* you'd be in for dinner . . . and with that gang out there . . . I really just didn't think.' She seemed actually worried; she sought reassurance from his eyes. 'I'll tell you what. I'll go out and get a Chink meal. I'll go round now.'

'It's *all* right, I'll fry an egg.'

'But it's *not* all right!'

'Look, Vernon, if it will really make you feel any better to go out into the freezing bloody cold right in the middle of your own party, then go. I honestly don't mind a fried egg.' His voice was plump and paternal. He patted her shoulder and she looked grateful. She started frying eggs, a pleased expression on her face. He gave her a little kiss, then half turned and looked at me with a query in his eyes. I gave nothing away, because I had not then decided what to do. There was a palpable lump of hatred for them in my chest. I could have hurled it then, to smash and explode them: but the lump sat on my lungs and made me voiceless.

SIX

Although Peter was very reticent about his own family, his upbringing, his past, he came to regard, after he had made his declaration to me, my history, and all the principal agents who had carved it out, as a source of endless fascination. I had no inclination to spill out my grievances; he hectored me for a list of them, but I think I sensed even then that he was testing my reticence, seeing how long I could remain warily silent under the duress he imposed upon me. Knowing Peter as I do now, I see I would have lost him if I had shown him but the tip of my bitterness. I told him what I could of my family with deadpan reluctance.

He asked if he could meet them, saying that I was if anything too enigmatic, and that he must have at least some mental picture of me to be getting on with. He said this in a somewhat businesslike fashion which I liked.

I had an urge to keep Peter a secret – to cut him off as far as possible from my ordinary life – yet secrets have no real value unless others are aware there is a secret. I reckoned they would know better I was hiding Peter if I gave them a glimpse of him, then made him vanish. They would at least get some idea that I lived in depth away from them. I therefore asked my mother if she would have him to dinner.

'Bring him along, by all means,' she said. 'Any evening will do.' By this, she meant that she would take no pains to impress him with anything but our own life-style (of which she was very proud, to do her justice). She asked no questions about him; she resumed correcting papers without noticing the importance I attached to him.

Later that evening, I overheard her asking my father if I oughtn't to be taken round to the Family Planning. My mother had a few zealous friends in that organisation who felt the benefits of contraception should be liberally given to married and unmarried alike. 'She has a young man.' Her voice floated up the stairs, like a cold breeze: there was such deprecation in her tone. I could never quite understand why she didn't like me; I always took it for granted that she didn't.

I brought him home, a few days, a week (I can't remember), after Vernon's party. Since that time, he had not left me alone. When I travelled on the underground, I sifted through the crowds for the faces of Sasha or Boris or Vernon, as if I looked through pieces of a jigsaw puzzle for the corners; but Peter was always at the top of the stairs to meet me. He wedged himself, as it were, between me and the telephone, and sat on letter paper like a demanding cat. Out of good taste, he said nothing more to me about his love, but he was always there. He made himself central. His picture was ever-present in my mind's eye.

I told him he would get no special treatment from my family, no three-course dinners made by loving hands; but all the same, he appeared at the front door freshly laundered and dry-cleaned. He wore a neat knit tie and looked extremely well.

My father greeted the well-organised appearance of Peter with grateful surprise. He gave him whisky in the living-room, an unusual gesture, and talked to him with nervous pleasure. I think of my father as having no emotions, but it was more, I now believe, that he had no emotional force. I suppose he cared that I had found an amiable looking young man.

'An attractive boy,' my mother said as I helped her in the kitchen. She spoke as if this was the full definition of his character. She was quick at judgements because she saw no shades of grey. 'Is it serious?' She chopped a cucumber too thickly with an excellent French knife. As her question was perfunctory, I did not answer it.

We had stew for dinner – my mother called it a 'ragout' because she had put a little wine in it. She bridled in front of Peter, and was somewhat ham-fistedly skittish (she had flirted with my brother-in-law). We drank Spanish Burgundy out of coloured tumblers.

'What do you do?' she asked him.

'Archaeology.'

'Oh.' She wiped her spectacles with a paper napkin. She had once arranged for her friend Georgina's son to take me to a dance. He, poor boy, and I were dumbly miserable the whole evening. He was a student of political science. My mother had been annoyed when I told her I thought he was a bore. The word 'bore' was never used in our family in that sense. I had picked it up from Sasha. My mother guessed this and said so with considerable disdain.

'Does your father by any chance have anything to do with charities? A Brigadier Meadows?' my father asked this eagerly – since he liked to keep tabs on a small world – though somewhat suspiciously, because he didn't approve of charities.

'Yes. A cancer research fund, not a major one.'

'That's it! I met him at a meeting once. I noticed because you have a strong look of him. I've been cudgelling my brains all evening trying to remember.'

'High Tory, I'm afraid.' Peter gave my mother a winning smile saturated with irony. I was surprised and a little shocked to see that he liked her even less than I did, and on practically no evidence.

'You don't share his views, do you?' she asked brusquely. They both embarrassed me.

'I haven't any political views whatever.'

A silence ensued.

'Don't you think involvement is necessary in this day and age?' She was riding it hard and it occurred to me that she still found him attractive. She leaned too heavily towards him.

'Not really,' he said, munching a slimy dumpling. 'This is delicious.'

'My parents find politics very absorbing,' I said looking down at my plate.

'I see.' He nodded politely as if I had told him they were keen rose-growers; he classified politics as a hobby.

Dinner at our house was always over in half an hour. No one leaned back and dawdled over cigarettes.

'I admire your kitchen,' Peter said, looking about him. He actually did like it.

'It's the dining-room,' my mother said coldly. She shoved the plates on to the counter, but he said nothing more. Braver men than Peter have been known to chatter witlessly at this sort of moment with my mother, and I liked it that he didn't.

She gave us coffee in the living-room. 'You'll stay for the discussion?' she asked, but it was an order. Peter looked about himself, somewhat alarmed. It was socially impossible, for him particularly, to leave directly after a meal. He turned his attention to the scalding instant coffee in its pottery mug. 'What's the discussion about?' he asked.

'Sex,' she said as she went to the door. Peter has too eloquent an eyebrow. My father looked deeply uncomfortable. He shifted from side to side in his chair, pretending to drink his coffee.

A group of children in their early teens trooped awkwardly into the room. They looked for all the world like carol-singers who, unexpectedly asked indoors were now called upon to perform more for their sixpence than they had bargained for. One of the girls gulped and flushed when she saw Peter and me on the sofa. I wondered with manic inner laughter if she thought we were there to give a demonstration.

'We started on diagrams and a little biology,' my mother said to Peter, filling him in, 'and we are now at the stage of talking seriously about responsibility.'

'I am sure it will be very interesting,' said Peter with grave good manners.

'You don't really have to stay,' my father said to Peter. 'Don't you think you would rather see a film instead.'

'Most of them are on the same subject.' Peter has an impeccable social laugh. I could see that nothing could drag him away.

My mother had arranged the kitchen chairs in a semi-circle. There was some jockeying about for who would sit where, but they all settled quietly enough and looked up at my mother expectantly.

'Tonight, we have my daughter Emily and her friend Peter Meadows. They are both at the university. Perhaps Peter would give us an idea of how sex is generally handled there.'

Peter turned scarlet. I could not think how my mother could say such a thing.

'I don't think so,' he said with remarkable poise. 'I'm rather bad at speaking. I'd much rather listen.'

There was some nudging and giggling. I could see that my mother had not managed to quell the adolescent tendency to think sex funny.

She cleared her throat, bypassing Peter as a bit of a weakling. 'I think tonight we will talk, not about morals exactly, but about moral responsibility in personal relationships.' My mother's tendency to use big words with children often gave them the impression that she took them seriously. As she spoke, they all looked unnaturally solemn. 'Maybe you, William, would give us a jumping-off place.' Her pointed finger appeared to galvanise him.

'Well,' he said, in his unruly voice, 'I think you mean that people shouldn't go round having sex with each other unless they love each other . . .'

'Exactly! But something more . . . Joyce!' She shot a finger in the face of a keen girl on the left.

'Maybe that they should think first if it will hurt the other person.'

'That's the idea! That's fine, Joyce.' Joyce glowed at her own good performance.

'Before you get involved in heavy petting or sexual intercourse, you should be sure of what, Nigel?'

'This is like an absurd catechism – I must say they are well drilled,' said Peter, *sotto voce*.

'That they are ready for it,' said Nigel.

'That you are ready for it and that your partner is ready for it! It's not a one-sided affair, you know.' My father, who had been sucking his pipe, got up and stole from the room.

'How do you know when you are ready for it?' asked a thin girl in a puzzled tone. She seemed genuinely mystified. I could tell my mother didn't like her. She broke the flow.

'I think you're ready for it when you know that you have a valid relationship with your partner, and that you can take full responsibility for your actions.'

'You mean,' said Nigel, 'that you could take care of it if the girl

99

got . . . er . . . pregnant.' From Nigel's blush, it appeared that he wished he'd been found under a gooseberry bush after all. Nevertheless, he had managed the right word, and my mother gave him a thin smile as a reward.

'Well, nowadays, Nigel, there are contraceptives that take care of that little problem. Don't be afraid to use them. It's all part of being considerate. I mean more than that, though . . . about a mature regard for other people's feelings.'

A devil niggled at my brain. 'You mean, Mother, that people should get married, don't you?' She looked at me as if I had spoiled the subtlest of stories. She was far too conventional in her innermost heart to advocate free love; in theory, however, she liked the idea of free love. She found steering heavy around this point and I had made a wave.

'You cloud the issue,' she said, so haughtily cold that Peter noticed it with a twitch in his face. I was never any match for my mother, and she was quick to let me know this.

'I think,' she continued in full self-possession, 'that the relationship I was describing often leads to marriage in its fullest and deepest sense.'

'What is marriage in its fullest and deepest sense, Mrs Stone?' Peter asked in the fruity, pleasant voice of a good student.

'A real friendship based on a rich sexual life where one partner does not dominate the other, but where they live in close harmony.' My mother fought with words like a clumsy knight with a dragon, and when she made any conclusive statement, she stood triumphantly astride her prey.

'You are incontrovertibly right,' Peter said, with the slightest gesture of throwing up his hands.

My mother's smile buckled a bit, as if the dragon had given an unexpected moan. 'Do you think you could make the cocoa, dear?' she asked me. It was clear she thought it time we left the room. The children looked a bit bewildered.

'I'll help!' Peter jumped up like a Boy Scout.

My father was furtively scrabbling at a bit of cheese wrapped in cellophane. I put the milk on while Peter thumbed somewhat ostentatiously through *The Economist*.

'What did you think of it?' my father asked, his mouth full of cheese.

'Fine.'

'She does a marvellous job, don't you think?' he asked hopefully.

'Oh, wonderful. Everything she says is undoubtedly true,' Peter said. My father smiled sheepishly and bowed his way out of the kitchen, clutching the cheese to his chest.

Peter made himself at home in a high-backed chair. He leaned on the table and unpicked a raffia mat with his fingers. His attention, however, was turned on me as I measured powdered cocoa and poured hot milk.

'You do that well.'

'What?'

'Make cocoa well . . . competently. I like to watch you. You don't fumble anything.'

Immediately, I knocked a cup.

'Don't let me make you self-conscious,' he said. 'Your mother is an unhappy woman.'

'Oh no, she's not. She is completely at peace with herself.'

'There is no peace in your mother. She uses activity to blind herself to her very lack of it. Everything about her is too pat, too automatic. She holds a grudge against God that He did not make her a man. I know. I'm something of an expert on unhappy women.'

'Am I an unhappy woman then?'

'Yes . . .' he paused. 'Yes, you're unhappy, but you're not yet a woman. You're unhappy *because* you're not yet a woman. You seek completion outside of yourself. I would guess that your mother gave that search up a long time ago. In a way, I admire her. She has a steely grandeur.'

Perhaps what he said about me was true at the time he said it. I don't know. When I think of what I am now, how I am boxed in to suffocation by myself, and how this suffocation has atrophied the very muscles of my will to escape it makes me want to cry; but I can't even cry. Most women can cry. A few months ago, he said to me, 'Your upper lip is stiff to the point of *rigor mortis*.' He says that because he is determined to make me suffer. To do him justice, he believes there is positive value in suffering.

I must have lost the inner nubility I had when I, so many years ago, put the cocoa-box down, spilling a little, and turned to face him, overcome at what he had said. It must have been nearly Christmastime – in fact I know it was – I remember distinctly how he sat behind the little spiked metallic Christmas tree which stood on the stripped-pine dresser. The tree was my mother's only concession to the season; she said Christmas trees were pagan anyway. She liked to style herself a pagan, though God knows why; a pagan worships something. His shrewd eyes attended every nuance of my mood; he coolly watched and waited for my move. Some feeling I didn't recognise ravaged my stomach and my brain.

'I love you, Peter,' I said. I hadn't really meant to say it.

He sat very still. His fingers stilled and his face became as flat as a painting. As I watched him, this expression began to dissolve and crumple, as if a hand behind the frame had squeezed the picture. I realised with animal panic that I had made him helpless.

He got up suddenly and took my hand, holding it hard. His palm was moist, and his eyes filled with tears; the shrewdness in them was altogether gone. He seemed to be flailing around in a pool of gratitude and tenderness. I could not bear to watch him or to help him out of it.

'I'll call you. I'll call you,' he said. 'Let me take it in for a bit.'

He left me standing there with a tray of cups full of scalded milk and lumpy chocolate. It seems ridiculous that one is capable of irrevocable action at the age of nineteen.

I clamped myself into order and took the cocoa in. My mother had moved from love to hygiene.

If there hadn't been something official between Peter and me, I don't think I could have called Sasha. At first, it had unnerved me that I had laid myself so open to him, and that he had laid himself so open to me; but, once the initial shock had worn off, I found a greater confidence in myself than I had ever known. The whole incident became less and less to me like a mutual cutting of wrists and commingling of blood, and more and more like a trade agreement. I saw that there was something really solid in my pact with Peter. He left me quite alone for a while so that I had time to grasp this: that our exchange of loyalties described a charmed circle around us which made us invulnerable to the rest of the world. If I had allowed him to go on loving me without my cooperation, a mere, charmless semicircle would have existed; the circle and the charm depended on the trade. Now we both had something to fall back on. As long as I had Peter, I felt that nothing could prevail against me.

I felt little gaiety or surprise at my new situation. I went out and bought some new clothes; I worked with great efficiency; and I went to see Sasha. I was not sure I would tell her about Boris, but I thought I might.

First of all, I was surprised to find Celia Russell there. She was the whey-faced girl from Sasha's drama school. She was rubbing her hands before the drawing-room fire, not as nervous people do when they cannot think of what to do with their hands, but in order to get warm; it was a relaxed gesture which showed she felt at home there. Sasha seemed at ease with her, but not intimate with her.

Sasha seemed very pleased to see me; this also surprised me. She admired my new dress and, leaving Celia in the lurch, rushed to the nursery to show me a pair of shoes she had recently acquired.

She chattered merrily on while trying to unearth the shoes from the depths of her cupboard. The cupboard had once been a toychest, and there were still remnants of its former state. She flung an old doll with chewed-looking bits of hair on to the hearthrug. I picked it up and examined it; the doll's colour was repulsively unlike flesh and someone had knitted it a bright green cardigan. I picked irritably at the little pills of wool which had collected all over the garment. 'Don't you ever throw anything out, Sasha?' I asked lightly.

She turned and saw me holding the doll. She was flushed with crouching. 'Oh, not Balkis. I could never throw out Balkis; she's like a friend, and you can't dispose of friends. I just retired her for when I have a little girl.'

'Why did you call it Balkis?'

'I don't know. Why not? I think Nanny once told me I was "balky". I was too. I can remember having a temper tantrum in Hamleys when I was far too old for that sort of thing . . . so I called the doll Balkis because she was balky like me. I used to have great games about her never doing what I wanted; she spoiled the other dolls' tea parties and refused to get dressed or be bathed . . . here's my shoes, at last. Do you like them?'

I didn't, but I said I did. Like all of Sasha's clothes, they were a bit extreme.

'You never had a doll, did you? Except I gave you one one Christmas. Do you remember? A bit silly of me to give you something like that. I should have thought that you probably liked games better when you were a child . . . you know, backgammon and chess and things.'

'I liked the doll. I still have it.' I thought about the doll she had given me; it was artfully made and had an almost human expression. I'd wanted to cuddle it, but never had because I thought I was too old; besides, it embarrassed me that I wanted to cuddle it at all.

'Do you know?' she said, suddenly standing up, 'that Celia Russell is in love with Gregory?'

'No, really?' I could not think how anyone could be in love with Gregory. Evidently, she agreed with me, because she said, 'Yes. Isn't it extraordinary?'

'But he's only seventeen. He hasn't even left school. Is he in love with her?'

'He more than tolerates her. Let's put it that way. We're all delighted.' She cast her eyes towards heaven. Celia was, evidently, an answer to prayer.

'How is Boris?' I tested the ground with this prod.

'Well.' She shut down conversation on this point with a decided slam. 'Oh . . . I have your Christmas present. I shall forget to give it to you if I don't get it out now this minute.' She busied herself with rummaging under the little day-bed which supported a heavy weight of books and clothes and other odds and ends. She hummed a little tune, and smiled secretly to herself as she brought out ribboned parcels.

'Let's see . . . Mummy . . . no, Nan.' She read the labels. '*Those* are for Boris.' Her secret smile deepened as she put a pile of gifts to one side. It had never occurred to me to buy Peter a Christmas present. I wondered if I ought to. She had wrapped Boris's parcels in shining foil, sprinkled glitter on the top and done them up in gold ribbon. There was a book, a record and a little box which

104

looked as if it contained jewellery. She gave the pile a little stroke, then returned to her search for my box. My anger at Boris rose; still, I said nothing.

'Gregory . . . Celia . . . aha! Now I have it. I hope you'll like it.' She handed me a striped and tinselled parcel of interesting dimensions. She smiled eagerly, as if there was no question of my not liking it. I found myself combating a deep irritation with her. She had an easy charity.

'I haven't got you anything yet.'

'Oh, don't bother,' she said gaily. She shoved the other boxes back under her bed.

I had a vague feeling that something was altered in her room, but I could not make out what it was. I put my parcel with my gloves, and we went in to lunch. It was a Sunday and they had a joint of meat.

Celia Russell ducked her head as she ate her meat, as if grateful for being allowed to eat their meat, as if she were one of the worthy poor at the convent gate. She wore, without any confidence in it at all, a barbaric necklace dripping with gimcrack gods and goddesses. I heard Peter laugh at the thing in my mind's ear. Celia's face demanded a twinset and pearls.

I had not reckoned on Gregory's being home for the holidays, but he was there, festering at Celia's side. He looked much older, more in command of himself. We greeted each other stiffly. I experienced a sensation of intense loathing for him. I looked away from him, but he was always there in the corner of my eye.

Celia passed him titbits and condiments from the table without his bidding. She looked on him with humble love, and he seemed to accept this with gruff condescension. There was something painful about Celia which didn't bear thinking about: she looked woefully out of place and pathetically eager to be in place there; but she was the sort of person who would have been out of place in her own home. I could see she didn't fit in Surrey either (she came from Godalming).

She talked a lot during the meal; in fact, she almost dominated the conversation. She had written a 'concerto' for the lute, and she spoke of it in a lot of technical language which she appeared to assume the Courtneys fully understood, their being, as she thought, conversant with things artistic. Mrs Courtney smiled approvingly and called her 'dear Celia'. Celia flowered visibly in such gentle sunshine. I became more irritated as the meal wore on, particularly at Celia's glowing self-abasement.

'How is the Steadman?' I asked Sasha, making a cross-current in Celia's flow.

'Oh, Sasha's doing so terribly well!' Celia cried, interrupting herself. 'Jack is making her do Nina in *The Seagull*, and she is quite amazingly good. Jack confided in me that he has never had anyone as good as Sasha to coach. I think he's quite *astounded* at his good luck. They're a marvellous pair, Jack and Sasha; they work terribly well together. I can't understand your secret with him, Sasha. He's a terrible pansy . . . Ooops! I'm so sorry, Mrs Courtney.'

'Oh, that's all right, darling. One does know a thing or two about the world.' Mrs Courtney smiled her fragile, encouraging smile. Nanny nearly growled. She was very strict in some ways. Celia didn't notice Nanny, only Mrs Courtney.

Sasha was evidently very pleased at Celia's praise. She and Celia started to talk shop. My irritation reached a pitch; then, suddenly, it all began to drain away. I felt the whole scene to detach itself from me, and once more I had that sensation of oozing into myself and becoming very dense inside, like pressed rock from outer space.

I looked around the table at the Courtneys and Celia as they mildly ate their Sunday dinner. They had a bovine appearance as they chewed. Nanny particularly looked like a cow; she regarded me hostilely, and I inwardly laughed at her, cow in disguise as she was. They all suddenly looked artificial, as if they were pretending to be people, when they were not really people at all. I thought it quite funny that they could eat off dinner plates with all that chunky Edwardian silver without realising their true position. I felt curiously successful . . . above them, like an orphan made good revisiting his orphanage. I tilted my head slightly and thought of Peter and smiled. I noticed how Sasha's teeth stuck out and how extreme and undignified were some of her facial gestures. I thought, for a moment, that I did not like her and that I did not not like her: she appeared to me objectified. Somehow this thought broke my mood, my detachment. I teetered for a minute on the brink of this thought, then descended again, a bit abruptly to my normal mode of being. As I came down, the sound of Sasha's voice rushed loudly in my ears.

'I'm trying to learn Russian,' she said. Celia gave her a significant, conspiratorial look. 'In order to understand *The Seagull* better,' Sasha added firmly. 'I've ploughed my way through the Cyrillic alphabet, and I find vocabulary easy enough to learn, but the grammar is quite incomprehensible to me. I was so chuffed at my early success with the words, that I went and bought a copy of the play in Russian. I can't make head or tail of it. I am sure one loses a tremendous amount in translation. It is so frustrating having to say lines which you know miss the flavour of the author's intention. It's a bit like eating meat without salt.' She spoke thoughtfully; she was in control of her subject. Indeed, she appeared to be more in control of herself than I had ever known her to be. She ate and moved unhurriedly. She had had a way of gorging food and of talking excitedly with her mouth full. There was something new about her, independent of us all.

I ate my cheese with a good deal of concentration. Thoughts came to the surface of my mind like concrete blocks; one thought built inexorably on to the other. I reasoned that Sasha could not have achieved this independence without a base for it; that all the evidence I had gathered pointed to one prime cause of her new composure, and that this cause was Boris. I was convinced from her behaviour that she considered her alliance with Boris to be particular and monogamous (if not married and permanent). Therefore, as something essential was missing in her information about Boris, I could only conclude that she had constructed her happiness upon a delusion which must at sometime, sooner or later, be made manifest to her. I wondered what she would do. A sense of heaviness pressed itself upon me, but I was not clear about its origin.

After lunch, Celia and Gregory removed themselves to the window-seat in the drawing-room, where they entertained themselves with medieval pleasures. Celia had brought her lute. She played Gregory some sections from her concerto while he drew her picture in the sad, cold, afternoon light. Sasha seemed content to listen. She sipped her coffee slowly, stroking the edge of the cup with her upper lip. She dreamed away at the fire.

'Let's go back to the nursery. I have something to tell you.' I said. I had in my mind to talk about Peter. I felt oppressed by something.

She seemed happy enough to come with me. 'I haven't seen you for ages,' she said as she settled herself cosily in her own wing-backed chair. She gave the coals a poke from her seat, then let the poker clatter to the hearth. The fire spurted up.

'Now I know what's wrong with your room!' I cried. 'You've taken your icon down. Where is it?'

She abruptly ceased to smile. I had not thought she would flinch from that particular question, but she did: she flinched quite visibly. 'I've decided to retire it for a bit like Balkis. I'm sick of it.' She muttered this apologetically and without venom. She looked to the wall where it had been, then at her fingers.

'What was it you wanted to tell me?' She brightened a bit.

'Do you remember Peter?' My head ached terribly.

'Oh, yes! The cynical man who looked as if he was about to kiss your feet. He worships you.'

'How do you know?' I asked incredulously. 'You haven't seen me.' For a moment I was diverted from my purpose by surprise.

'Oh, anyone could have told you that he was going to be in love with you,' she said with her old, easy quickness. Something about this seemed to please her. She sat up and leaned towards me. 'Anyway, Boris told me that Peter told him that Peter was in love with you. There! Isn't that nice?' She acted as if I myself did not know that Peter was in love with me. She smiled as she had smiled when she gave me her idiotic Christmas present; as if everything I had came from her, Sasha's bounty. Good old Emmy's finally got a boyfriend! What a relief! I thought she'd never make it. Maybe if I pull enough strings for her she'll even get him to marry her . . . The pressure in my head gathered momentum, then broke.

'Boris found out about us but not because Peter told him.' I could see that Sasha's mental volubility was for a moment checked. She stared at me and became very still. Who can resist being a bad omen? I felt like one of Nanny's Tarot cards.

'Boris found out about us because he overheard Peter telling me he loved me at a party. His party. He listened on purpose.' I enunciated each word very clearly so that she would not miss any of it. I had to check the vitriol which spurted up and threatened to engulf my voice. I hadn't known I was capable of such a feeling.

'Oh,' she said faintly. 'What party was that that Boris gave? His father is too ill for anyone to go there.'

'Boris's father is hale enough to take him out to lunch. Boris doesn't live with his father anyway. He lives with a woman.'

She shook her head and laughed uncertainly. 'Boris does not live with a woman. He lives with his father in Earls Court. Boris and I are in love. He does not live with a woman.'

'Sasha, I have been there I tell you. His clothes are there; his books are there; his dressing-gown hangs on the bedroom door.'

She gave a sudden, sharp scream of amazing ferocity. She stood up and flailed her arms about. 'It's not true. It's not true!' She looked very undignified. I was bewildered by my own calm.

'The woman's name is Vernon. I thought you ought to know.'

'Where . . . who is she? How could she? We're lovers. Do you understand? I love him more than I could have thought humanly possible.' She probed desperately with a look the truth of what I had said, then suddenly a deep sob welled up and broke from her mouth, almost as if she had been sick. 'I have put myself utterly in his hands. I don't believe he could betray me . . . not that feeling, no. He is everything to me. I took the icon down because of him. I have done everything because of him . . .' her voice trailed off, then suddenly raised itself to an incredible pitch. She seemed first pierced, then goaded by her grief. She turned on me, but she did not seem to see me. 'Where is she? Take me to her! I will see her, then she will give him up. She will see that he cannot mean as much to her as he does to me. She must take pity on me!'

'Boris is a serpent,' I said, 'a basilisk.'

'Boris is a basilisk, a basilisk . . . but I LOVE BORIS!' she cried as if this altered things. Tears poured down her face. 'Oh, I am wretched.'

'I will take you. Come along,' I said, with the self-possession of Virgil in hell.

I escorted Sasha to Holland Park. We did not speak. She seemed to diminish in size; she pressed her body into the seat of the taxi as if she wished to disappear into it. Her face was deathly pale and her eyes bruised with tears. I felt curiously passive and unconcerned with her condition; I wondered, instead, about whether or not Boris and Vernon would be at home, and decided that they would still be in bed.

Vernon answered the door. She was wearing a frilly nylon nightdress. I had expected something in leather, somehow, and was a little disappointed. She yawned and motioned us in. She did not seem to think it odd that we had come, nor did she appear to expect us to apologise for getting her out of bed. I had the impression that Vernon's sitting-room was like the lobby of an hotel, and that Vernon thought of herself as being a kind of concièrge.

Sasha stood in the darkened room, clenching and unclenching her hands. Her lips were almost blue, and her body shook from time to time. Vernon paid no attention to Sasha. She drew the curtains to let in what meagre sunshine there was, and she picked up Boris's shoes from the floor. She plumped the cushions, calm and businesslike as a maid.

She looked comic in her unsophisticated nightdress. Her collar bones stuck out. Her arms were thin, and I could see her breastbone through the filmy blue cloth. She had gooseflesh, and looked as if she would like to get a dressing-gown and slippers, but she stood facing Sasha, and rubbed her arms.

'God, it's cold! Would you like a cup of coffee?' Vernon had a gawky amiability that seemed at odds with the image she tried to maintain.

'Where is Boris?' Sasha spoke through chattering teeth.

'Why, he's in bed, reading the papers . . .'

'Then it's true!'

'What's true? Who are you anyway?' She stared at Sasha for a moment, then an expression of great wistfulness came over her face. 'Oh, I get it,' she said. She lit a cigarette. 'Look, I can't talk about Boris until I've had a cup of coffee.' She turned towards the kitchen. 'Boris is a . . . Never mind.' She shrugged.

Sasha sat down mechanically. She looked stunned, almost epileptic, as if she had forgotten she was there. She worked at her lower lip with her teeth. I sat poised and erect on the edge of my seat. I could not take my eyes off her. My senses felt heightened and sharp.

Vernon returned, bearing a tray stacked neatly with pottery coffee cups; there was a glass ball, containing a generous amount of good-smelling black coffee; and, looking out of place amid the heavy cups, there was the most fragile bone-china jug, full of thick cream. She set the tray lovingly on a stark white table, and began to pour the coffee. There was a ceremoniousness about her movements in which her angularity became her. 'Black or with cream?' she asked Sasha. 'White,' Sasha replied automatically. She took the cup absently, without really looking at it.

'I'll bet,' Vernon said, clearing her throat a little self-consciously, 'he's done something awful to you; but it can't have been as bad as some of the things he's done to me.' She looked sympathetically at Sasha, then gave a resigned sigh, as if in the sigh, she were expressing the lot of women everywhere.

Sasha looked at her for a moment with keen scrutiny; then rocked back in her chair and closed her eyes, as if something quite important had occurred to her. She opened her eyes, gave Vernon a faint little smile, then withdrew again into herself with an expression of great puzzlement on her face. She shook her head, as if to roll some pieces into place. 'I had expected . . . I'm sorry,' she muttered. She leaned forward to take Vernon's hand, but Vernon jerked too quickly to receive her touch, and Sasha's eyes went blank again.

At that moment, Boris wandered into the room. He was wearing old flannel pyjamas and he needed a shave. He saw Sasha and me, and he blinked.

'Good God! What on earth did you bring her here for!' He sounded really outraged . . . righteously indignant.

Sasha looked at Boris uncomprehendingly for a moment; then she looked at the cup she held. Her eyes narrowed, her chin set, then she hurled the cup at Boris with a terrific force. It hit him on the chest; the hot coffee poured all over him.

'*Ouch, God!*' he roared. Everyone was paralysed. Sasha picked up the tray, and before anyone could stop her, she turned it over on the floor. There was a tremendous crash.

'Oh, my cups, oh, my precious pitcher!' Vernon held her face in her hands, then at once was on her knees amid the mess, moaning and taking up slivers of china.

As soon as she had done this, Sasha became at once very jumbled and confused. 'A hateful thing to do, a hateful, hateful thing, you lied,' she kept repeating, then suddenly she said. 'Oh, God, Vernon, I'm so sorry.' Then she rushed from the room, her feet crunching the spilt sugar. Boris stood amid the broken crockery with a look of uncalculated amazement on his face.

I sped down the stairs after Sasha. She was on the street, about to get into a taxi. She was shaking from head to foot as if she had a high fever.

'Sasha!' I called after her, 'Sasha!' I ran to catch her up. She stood with her hand on the taxi-cab door. For a moment, I thought she was going to faint. 'Are you all right?'

'You enjoyed every minute of that, didn't you, Emmy,' she said flatly, almost tiredly. She got into the cab and disappeared from my life for nearly a year.

In the end, I took a long walk, crying bitter, squeezed out tears at nothing I understood. That evening, I rang her house and was told that she was not at all well and had been put to bed. When I remembered that I had left my Christmas present there, I experienced something like a real sense of loss. I knew I could never go and get it back.

SEVEN

It was a curious winter; I find all winters curious now in relation to that one which was the happiest of my life.

I watch people a lot, especially in the winter, as they bumble about the city in the cold rain. A bit like moths, people come to life, become even a little frantic, in places where there is warmth and light. They come together in shops or theatres or in pubs; they smile too vivaciously at each other; but otherwise, outside, people walk around in the winter as if they were on the moon. They pad themselves in thick clothes, and their faces are hidden by a mask of cold. It seems odd to me that we are able to support life in the winter.

I often think of old people and how cold they must get, especially if they haven't enough money for coal. You see them in the park, stiffly throwing crumbs to the pigeons, or walking slowly round a cold pond, circling winter ducks.

Children never mind it though. I take a day off a week, and this day I religiously devote to David. I always take him out, because I can't bear to stay in the house. He has never been a happy child, never. Sometimes I scruple over the little signs of his unhappiness, his nightmares, his finger sucking, his unnatural goodness. He effaces himself for our sakes because he knows there isn't room for him in our minds. He gives up his pleasure in order that we may resolve our struggle better. He knows his self-assertion would tip the balance. I think of him as a little foreigner who has accidentally strayed into a civil war. There is nothing I can do for him while I man my guns.

But I think of how he gallops across the park, the deserted park in mid-January: like a pent-up animal, he is almost manic. With flushed ears and frozen breath, he plays as if winter were perpetual Christmas, or as if it didn't matter that the earth were dead.

All winters make me think of that one in which Peter and I hung so closely together. I require him to remember it as he has required all of these memories from me. He insists on reading my testament – very well, he shall read it through. He will see how and in what way I want him back. I call his bluff in this exercise; he does not see me as wanting anything, but I do: I want him.

I was horribly bothered by what had happened at Vernon's flat. The smallest things annoyed me, and I had bad, obscure dreams; of reading books and not understanding the words, of missing trains because I was digging for something: the dreams had a strange ochre quality.

Peter waited for a week or two, I can't remember how long, until he had settled something in his mind. I do seem to recall that Christmas came and went without our exchanging so much as a card. I did not think of him much; perhaps I was very sure of him. In any case, I sought my consolation in work, not in him.

I had a special place in the library where I liked to sit. I like to have half a table to spread out reference works, a notebook, a thick, creamy pad of foolscap for essays, my handbag. I work neatly. There was a fellow who used to share my table sometimes. He would crouch on the end of a chair, jamming his impossibly filthy mackintosh full of notes scribbled down on bus tickets and envelopes. He wrote in a tiny, indecipherable code. He had an amiable, eager face, and would go through the stacks like a hunter, finger pointed, and 'Aha!' when he found what he was looking for. He never seemed to lose the drift of what he was doing. I saw him on the television once: he has become a well-known literatus. I don't see how he succeeded, working like that. I could never work like that.

One day, Peter came in and sat down in front of me and my books. He has a thin face, and it can look pinched (his well-defined nose and brow have sharpened with age); but that day, it glowed with a resolution and love. With his Puritanical features alight, Peter looks a bit like John Knox in ecstasy, if one can imagine such a thing. He was carrying an enormous bunch of white freesias which he pushed across the table. 'There!' he whispered, 'those are for you!' They must have cost several pounds, being out of season. They were wrapped in stiff, green florists's paper, and they had the odour of paradise. People craned their necks and smiled, applauding silently this grand gesture. It was a beautiful gesture: no one could help but believe that.

To see him was suddenly a relief as sweet as the smell of the flowers.

All such romantic gestures lead to kisses and affirmations in flats or rooms. I had not seen Peter's flat before – not out of any sense of propriety (although I do, I think I really do, have a strong sense of propriety), but because of the distance we had imposed between ourselves before. I don't know why we can't have the rigour, the self-discipline we had then. We have lost our dignity.

At any rate, he asked me, with a mock Prussian bow, if I would mind continuing our conversation in his flat. I think we both felt very awkward. We were making heavy jokes at each other in the car. Our breath steamed up the windows, and the freesias kept well in the refrigerated air. I felt self-consciously bridal and pretended to look at the flowers. He drove ineptly, taking corners wide.

He lived in a low-down part of Notting Hill Gate. He had attic rooms. The rest of the house teemed with loud, beggarly children, whose mothers, with hung heads and resentful eyes watched our ascent up the steep, smelly stairs. These, I thought, were my mother's poor, and I wondered if she had seen them in their habitation, or if she had, how she felt about them. These women fascinated me with their sprung wombs and soiled skirts. They looked stunned by their own inability to cope. My mother, I think, felt at ease only with the people she could cope for. I see now that she is a complicated woman.

Peter seemed blind to the poverty about him. I mean to say that he ticked his way up the stairs as agile as a squirrel up a tree, giving no salutations to his neighbours. One of them stared at me holding the freesias, gave an ironic snort and closed the door.

He fumbled in excitement with the lock.

'I don't take anyone here, but I want you to see it. I think you'll like it.' He was over-casual, like someone who says, 'Here, look at this poem I just wrote. Of course, it's only the first draft.'

A poem is a proper metaphor for Peter's rooms. I mean to say that he had constructed the place with a strict regard for the rules of harmony, in order to distil some potent feeling he had about what he was. He had chosen each colour, each piece of furniture, not simply because he liked this or that, but with great deliberation, precision and economy of style.

He watched me closely as I stood in the middle of the room, casting my eyes over this perspective and that object . . . drawing impressions into me as if with a net.

I loved that room. I think I loved it almost more than I did Peter. Peter's place had the balance and repose of a Japanese garden. He had accomplished, above all that squalor, a secrecy which made my pleasure in the room a little perverted.

When he was quite sure I liked it, he said, 'It might have been designed for you.'

I did not know how to acknowledge this remark, so I walked about a bit with reverence, as if in a museum. He had put dead branches in a straight glass vase set on a low table. The branches cast a shadow on the wall. Everything was clear or white or black or grey. He had not compromised himself by having colours. I felt everything there to be in perfect proportion of myself, the way one feels on a moor, or on a deserted mile of shingle.

There was a bust of a Roman dignitary on his desk.

'Where did you get this?'

'My uncle gave it to me. He approved of my interest in archaeology. Don't you think it is a good reward for doing what the family likes? It's fifth century.' The face of the Roman had considerable nobility. 'He oversees my studies. When I get lazy, he disapproves.'

I must have given him a sharp glance. 'Don't you tolerate any whimsy? He's better than your friend's famous icon. At least I don't invest him with any supernatural powers.' He stopped talking abruptly, and shook his leg a little impatiently. 'You look beautiful holding those flowers, but they'll die if I don't put them in water.'

He ran a tap somewhere. I looked out of the window. Far, far below, there were lean-to sheds and outside lavatories; clotheslines with socks and nappies hanging stiffly in the freezing wind. I noticed his heating was efficient. He put the flowers on the table; they released their fragrance more freely in the growing warmth.

'I took Sasha to see Vernon and Boris a while ago,' I said, pushing and testing myself in this new dimension.

'Oh, yes?' He fussed with the flowers.

'It was awful, Peter. She was very upset. We've not been in touch since.' I found myself quite safe there and able to talk about it.

'I should think,' he said, looking up, his eyes fully sensible, 'that she enjoyed every minute of it. I assume there was a scene.'

'Oh, yes, there was a scene, all right. She ran away. She wouldn't speak to me. When I called, her mother said she was ill in bed.'

He paused. 'I hope you don't mind my saying that I didn't like your friend Sasha much.' He stopped, looked, then went on. 'She has no idea of reality . . . not the slightest notion of it.' He checked himself because he had sounded too vehement. I lit a cigarette; a feeling of poise came upon me, then I said I didn't mind. I waited hungrily for his next words.

'I don't think, mind you, that one can dismiss her as a fool. I think it takes a lot of brains to act all the time.'

He sat on the floor, one knee up, an arm flung over it. He never achieved this state of repose anywhere outside his flat. I used to love to watch him sitting that way: the sight drained me of tension.

'She threw the cups and saucers on the floor.' Somehow, being with Peter there, I felt how ridiculous it had been and how histrionic of her it had been to throw the cups and saucers on the floor. In front of Peter, in Peter's room, she wouldn't have dared do such a thing.

'You mean at Vernon's? Ha! I'll bet she did! Was Boris there?'

'Yes. She threw a cup of coffee at him.'

'Ho! Ho!' he cried, but his real laugh followed silently. 'That seems just to me at any rate. Don Juans do get themselves into undignified situations. Well, well. And what did *he* do?'

'He just stood there blinking.'

'*Exactly* as I would have predicted, silly peacock. It was bound to happen sooner or later. You see. Boris thinks he is amoral, but he is only really immoral, and that is so depressing.' Peter used words like 'depressing' and 'tiresome' with a languid air. This little mannerism belied the impression he tried to give of classlessness. He is never aware of giving himself away. 'And you set this whole thing up?'

I looked at him quickly, but his mind was easily running on some vision of Boris.

'I suppose I did. I wanted to see . . .'

He caught a signal, perhaps a fidget of my hand. 'Of course you did! Whyever not rub their noses in a little honesty! They were all crying out for a director. Why don't you chuck in Eng. Lit. and become a theatrical producer? Obviously, you have a gift.'

'I felt guilty.' This seemed to me at the time to be an arresting insight into the uncomfortable emotions I had felt since I barged Sasha headlong into the truth. Guilt, in my family, was a dirty word. My mother had a profound distaste for all of the feelings which fell under that heading; to feel guilty about something one had done wrong was, in our household, a greater sin than the crime itself.

I heard my mother once describe an event from her Yorkshire childhood. I remember the story because she so rarely talked about herself. She had been discovered, one Sunday afternoon in mid-January, with a pack of playing cards which she had got from a friend at school. The friend had taught her how to play patience – this game had been, apparently, all the rage. My grandfather, the Free Church minister, took the cards and slowly put them one by one into the fire. He told her she would burn like that in the fires of hell. He then took her into the garden and made her stand for a quarter of an hour in the freezing cold with her hands under the cold tap, which was there for the purpose of watering the flowers, I suppose. The punishment, he said, would teach her hands never to be idle . . . and they never were again; but from that day, she said, her whole being revolted from ever admitting a feeling of guilt into her heart.

'I felt guilty,' I said again, greatly relieved that this was all. With great clarity, I saw that I had been hobbling myself unnecessarily.

'Oh, stuff and nonsense,' Peter said. 'You don't think that anything really *matters* to that sort of person? No more than a play really matters to an actor. The more noise a person like Sasha makes, the more sure you can be that her suffering amounts to very little. A kind of inverse proportion operates.'

He was so sure. Peter was at that time so sure of his theories. He made me feel as aware as an angel of the machinations and foibles, not only of Sasha, but of humanity. When I was with him, I felt my mind to be omniscient, detached and perfectly at rest.

It is difficult, even painful for me to recall the high degree of intimacy which Peter and I achieved in that year. For a whole year, we cut ourselves off from everything and everyone else. We reduced our lives to the simplicity of a pen and ink drawing with no background. Our faces and our feelings were thrown into sharp relief against the grey peace of Peter's room.

We had no friends, no friends at all. I refused all invitations to parties; I refused even invitations for a cup of coffee, not only from men, but from girls. Something in my relationship to Peter would have been marred by outside contact. There was a kind of purity at stake.

We hardly left his flat except for a breath of air or for a film. I, of course, still nominally lived with my family. I came in late at night and left early in the morning; they gave me the freedom of a boy. I thought at first that they might object to my spending so much time away from home, but in fact they ignored me even more than they had before, and no one mourned my passing.

My mother did once suggest to me that if I had any sexual problems, I might feel free to bring them to her. She said this in a roundabout way over the washing-up. 'Of course, dear, in your relationship with Peter you may find there are some difficulties which only an experienced woman might resolve. If any questions do arise, you know I am always here, and, God knows, I've never been stuffy.' There was just the shadow of a glint in her eye; it was enough to make me want to run from the room. Instead, I made no reply.

'In that case, dear,' she said with a frosty smile, 'I leave you to your own devices. I think I can say with honesty that I have trained you to make your own decisions. I have no wish to interfere in my children's lives.' I could tell she was angry at me, but I could not make out why. I suppose it wouldn't do me any good to know my mother's reasons for feeling so constrained with me. She liked the other children.

Still, still, she needn't have worried about Peter and me. We had an exemplary freedom with each other's bodies. If there was something a little automatic in my response to him, at least the response was pleasant rather than otherwise. Sex seemed an enjoyable by-blow of our relationship, but it never achieved a central position in our life together. Perhaps it did for him. I don't know. At any rate, to me it seemed functional. It relieved physical tension and loneliness rather in the way that eating relieves hunger and irritability. It made me feel neither closer to nor farther away from Peter.

What did matter to me was seeing Peter. Whenever I saw Peter, his planed cheek, his long fingers, I felt a sensation of relief. I would climb the stairs and find him in . . . each time I felt a sweet relief. I hoarded Peter. He was my cache of peace.

When I was without him, I did not feel in any way robbed of his presence; I felt, instead, a bit lost and irrational. I felt as if a part of my mind would detach itself from me, not to wander off into madness . . . it was not that sort of feeling at all. No, I felt as if this part of my mind would leave the province of my inner gravity, much in the same way that a rock leaves the face of a mountain, gathers speed and matter, to flatten scrubby trees and houses below.

Why can't he now take this feeling of mine into account? I do not merely love Peter, nor is he, like smoking, an unbreakable habit; he is as necessary to me as insulin is to a diabetic. I think I have questioned every aspect of Peter, but I have never questioned what is basic to me about him, and that is my need for him.

The fool maunders on about love. Yet all along, from our early days to this time, he has had my need and he counts it as nothing. Instead, he plunders and exploits my character, rummaging through my feelings, casting my precious thoughts upon the floor like so much rubbish. Peter has emotions to spare for us both.

Well, well, that is now; in the past, we satisfied each other perfectly.

In those days, for a very brief period in my life, I was able to put from my mind Sasha and all of her works. The more entrenched I became in Peter's flat, the more I unloaded myself of the collected feelings of years. I woke up, found my need of her had gone, then cast her out. With her, went my mother, insofar as I was able to root her from me, and all the piled-up junk of hurts and wounds I had nourished against society.

Peter didn't like her – Sasha, I mean. Like the boy in the story, he simply pointed out that the Empress Sasha wore no clothes. It had never occurred to me before that the gorgeous fabrics of Sasha's imagination had never really hung on her back. I was, at first, a little stunned by my realisation; then I came to be amused by it.

Still, in her way, she managed to hold her clutch upon my roots. She attacked me in disturbing dreams. How like Sasha to attack me in dreams! One in particular, I had quite often. I dreamed I had been called to an unfamiliar house somewhere in a very poor area of London. A great number of people stood about the doorway: they looked miserable with grief. When they saw me, they parted a way for me, but I got the feeling as I passed through them that they regarded me with the deepest hostility. I entered the house, which was deserted and entirely devoid of furniture. It looked as if it had been empty for a long time. I brushed away the cobwebs at the door to the front-room, then went in.

A coffin lay on a long trestle table in the middle of the room. Seven great wax candles, the kind you see in cathedrals, stood around the coffin. They had been alight, but they had gone out. There was a subtle but powerful stench of corruption emanating from the coffin. I could not actually smell it, but a sense of the stench which was not a smell of it, nearly overwhelmed me.

I knew, in the dream, that I had a clear duty. I was to go and kiss the corpse and relight the candles. I knew that if I did this, the people outside would crowd happily into the room and that the stench would magically disappear.

I started towards the coffin, but although I longed to be rid of the terrible weight of dreary horror that oppressed me, I was quite unable to move. Indeed, I was incapable of moving because of the very horror I wished to end. I stood for a while, paralysed by anxiety. The question of who it was in the coffin hammered insistently upon my atrophied nerves. For a while, I thought dimly that it was my mother; then, suddenly it came upon me that it was Sasha in the coffin, and I awoke with such violent terror that I was unable to find my voice to scream.

This dream recurred at intervals during that time, that year, but I never managed to complete the action. I have never been able to sleep properly since then. Sometimes I spend the whole night sitting on the sofa, staring at the wall.

My life, otherwise, settled down into a pattern of wonderful simplicity. Some indefinable quality in me, my will perhaps, solidified and became pointed towards achieving ends. I learned to study with great concentration, and my hitherto woolly essays became compressed, concise and confident. My tutor praised me; my fellow students envied and disliked me; and part of the wonderful liberation of my mind lay in my not caring for the opinion of either.

I sat poised, in Peter's airy flat, over my books; he over his. We worked together, interrupted only now and then by the noise of some disaster in the family below us.

Every now and then, we would come to the surface and talk, eat or make love. We cooked chops and frozen peas over his gas ring; neither of us knew how to cook anything else. Peter, who had no notions about religion in those days still had a horror of gluttony. He sneered extremely at artistic cooks and gimmicky new restaurants. He was repelled by the thought of what food turned into after it was digested or what it would become if left to spoil on the table. 'Miss Havesham's wedding cake, Miss Havesham's wedding cake,' he would say whenever we walked past the big bakery near the Tottenham Court Road.

So, we satisfied our physical needs, our need for each other's company on the surface of our lives; then, we plunged back into the contemplative peace of underscoring phrases from books with light pencil, rooting through references and jotting down notes.

We made no demands on each other whatsoever. Why can't he see the exquisiteness of our former equidistance? I see his face so cool in the angled lamp-light; I re-sense my own measured footsteps on the pebbly grey carpet, our grace, our ease, our good fortune. The more I rescue this vision for myself, the more miserably certain I am that I shall never recapture it. He won't have it; he casts excretion upon it.

Occasionally, we would break the usual pattern, open a bottle of wine and listen to music. He had a gramophone, quite a good one. One thing I do accuse myself of . . . I never questioned the source of his income. It became clear to me that he quietly possessed a lot of money – money is so much at the root of Peter's character – yet I never asked him about it, or his family, or his religion or his politics. I think I had a horror of spoiling our equilibrium. And he, he regarded my silence as the height of feminine nobility.

He was extremely fastidious about music. Having such delicate sensibility, he would not allow us more than one record in an evening. At first, we listened to symphonies (Mozart and Haydn were the only two composers allowed); then, he felt that a symphony was too big a work to comprehend in a flat, so, for a while, we only heard concertos. In the end, we were narrowed down to piano sonatas and string quarters; after that, we hardly listened at all. My brother George and his wife Amanda have the gramophone going nearly all the time. If they are not listening to music, they are playing it. Peter used to accuse them of a frivolous approach: that is one of the few things he has said that has ever really annoyed me, even taking into account all of the hideous insults he has levelled at me.

It was a concert, in fact, which indirectly broke our magic circle, but I never really noticed the damage until later.

It was my birthday, my twentieth birthday. Peter has always been generous: he gave me a white silk dress which rippled out like fanned air when I walked. My parents gave me a new block of shelves for the unit-plan bookcase which stood in my bedroom at home. My mother was beginning to feel my nine months of near absence from home. She showed this by using an unduly strident voice when talking to me even on trivial matters; she also gave me the bookshelves. The gift in itself was insignificant – the significance lay in her remembering my birthday at all. She had forgotten the last two.

Peter made me walk up and down the room. He watched the dress flow and fold about me. 'Whirl around,' he said, 'and again,' he said as I whirled. 'It is perfect. You are perfect in it. Do you have any jewellery? It needs a rich, gold locket . . . none of these modern, tinny things.'

'Sasha gave me a locket, a Victorian locket which belonged to her grandmother. I believe it is gold. It has an amethyst in the centre. She gave it to me when I was seventeen.' I realised that she had neglected to send me a card. I shrugged a little to cast off my memory of her past attention. She had once baked me a cake. She always sent me a birthday card. She chose cards with sugary pictures and trite messages, but I kept each one of them and I have them to this day. She had presents sent through the post, because she said it was so much fun getting a parcel from the postman. I would rip off the string and brown paper, then delve through layers of brightly coloured tissue-paper for my prize.

'If you go home and get it, I will take you to a concert tonight. You must appear in that dress; you can't simply wear it here. Suddenly, for some reason, I want people to see you.'

That summer (the summer before my twentieth birthday), we had been forced out of his flat by the heat. Attic rooms are always the hottest place in a house in the summertime. Even the white paint, the crystalline objects Peter had collected for himself, seemed to reflect, intensify and refract the hot sun, bouncing heat off the cool walls and causing rainbows through the prism of a vase. We became sweaty with the heat and restless with no work to do during the holidays. We took to wandering the streets in the cool of the evening. We never went to pubs and rarely saw a film. No one hailed us in the streets; we knew no one. We walked in perfect unison, almost glided, like ghosts, observing life while unobserved by any living thing. Sometimes we'd go as far as the West End. We'd watch crowds debouch from theatres: the women, fanning their flushed faces with programmes, fluttered round the street like silky butterflies in their rich-patterned summer frocks. Indian children played subdued late-evening games outside their parents' restaurants. Bare limbs in easy movement flash through my memory as I recall that summer; yet nothing touched us, as though we had been incorporeal.

During the daytime, we went to Holland Park. As well as being close to Peter's flat, it is the only park I know which has a proper crop of trees. We found a covert there in a thicket of bushes near the avenue of limes. We'd smoke and talk and search each other's faces in the shade. He wanted to hide then as much as I did.

My mother occasionally asked me where I was going. I always made up lies, but I never had a twinge of conscience about my lies. I invented a hectic social life which I peopled with characters I had observed in classes, on the street. I even revived imaginatively Sasha and Boris as actors in my plot. Now I think about it, I almost always told my mother what she wanted to hear – it was easier that way.

I arrived early at the Festival Hall. Peter was not there. Somewhat dazzled by the light and crush of crowd, I found myself a relatively quiet space near the wall of windows overlooking the Thames. On a rare impulse, I had checked in my nondescript coat, in order to do justice to my appearance which had enchanted me in front of my own mirror.

I tried to look out at the Thames – the reflection of lights, the tugs and barges ploughing through the dim water – but I found myself unable to keep my mind on any interest outside the area of my own features, translucent in the glass. My eye replied to my reflected eye, I felt a dizzying incapacity to concentrate on any other image, either outside the glass or on it.

I shook my pale hair; it swung, then floated round my neck, I smiled a bit. My image seemed to return the smile enigmatically, as if it knew something about me of which I was only dimly aware.

The dress Peter had given me that morning was perfection. There wasn't a centimetre of cloth to spare around my waist and bust, yet no seam strained. My stockings were completely smooth; no blemish marred my face.

I fingered Sasha's locket. Peter had been right about the locket; its antique charm, its heavy gold, lay perfectly disposed upon my breast. I breathed to watch it heave and glitter.

I lit a cigarette to pass the time and thought how truly this was my birthday. I had smoothed out my adolescent gaucherie like wrinkles on a lap. The clumsy face and figure of my childhood had miraculously transformed. I was pale as the moon, a new moon sliver, so slender . . . no longer thin, but arched, symmetrical.

A man, fortyish and quite as impeccable as myself, passed behind me. Our reflected eyes met, and he admired me. I smiled again, but looked away until he had gone.

Peter hasn't left me because he can't get over my face.

He arrived to find me mesmerised by this new vision of myself.

'You are extraordinary,' he said with awe, 'quite extraordinary. Is that Sasha's locket? It's absolutely right. I wish I had chosen it for you myself. Did she buy it for you? It looks very valuable.'

'She gave it to me from her store of heirlooms. She has quite a number of them, I believe. She said she would never wear it, but it would look nice on me.'

Sasha gave me the locket the year before we went to Italy together. I had it valued a few years back for the insurance, along with the other jewellery – diamonds Peter's given me, a sapphire ring his father bribed me with. Sasha's trinket is worth £100. She had no notion of the value of anything. How they all love to see me looking beautiful.

He handed me up the stairs as if I were a queen. His eyes moved quickly from face to face in the crowd. A few eyes flattered him on his creation.

'As it's your birthday,' he said, as we settled in our seats, 'I feel I can indulge myself a little in one of my faults.

'What fault is that, Peter?' I hardly listened. I was so intent upon catching another glance to confirm my new feeling about myself.

'I like to be envied . . . no, I like to show the world how well I choose. I suppose it amounts to the same thing in the end.'

When he was in that mode of feeling about me, he would hardly touch me. Sometimes, he would put his finger a bit tentatively on my arm to see if it were real.

The lights dimmed and the concert began. I remember so well . . . they played Mozart's 24th piano concerto.

I hardly ever go to a concert now. I sometimes go if my brother George is playing. I have to place myself where I can see George. I am happy as long as I can watch him throughout, sweating with concentration on the score. I can hear the music only if I can see it through his diving bow, feel it through his complete absorption in what he is doing. Otherwise, I am tormented by a cough, or a boil on the neck of my neighbour.

Peter and I had a record of the Mozart. We had listened to it countless times in the dark. I'd close my eyes and let each note penetrate my brain. I envy George that he can enjoy his music in the light. Music is the only art which can, at times, distract me utterly. I can hear the slow movement of the Mozart in my head: I hear it now, ineffably elegiac and consoling.

I sat rigid in my seat, rigid both without and within. I could not distinguish one note from another. I tried to hear it, but I could not hear it: my ears altered the music into an incoherent buzz.

I shook my head, this time not thinking of my hair at all. I shook my head as someone going deaf might do. I moved my foot. Peter glanced at me instinctively to stop my fidgeting. I had an impulse to reach out to him, to hold his hand and ask his help. I felt panic rising in my stomach. I did not dare. I dared not move. I merely smiled.

The music trickled on. I closed my eyes, trying to imagine myself alone in a dark room. My own eyelids fought aginst my pleasure; I saw them on my face, the face in the glass downstairs, the ghost through which I had tried to see the river barges. I opened my eyes again, and again I was faced with the heads of thousands, all apparently intent, as I would be but could not be, upon the music – music I could not replay, music which happened in one performance.

I wanted to get up and run away, but I was afraid to do that. I could only sit next to Peter. I smiled and felt my smile to become me.

I felt I had to grip on to something, but I knew if I held the seat that Peter would notice. At last, with numbed fingers, I reached for my locket and grasped it in my cold palm. I only held it; I knew if I stroked it, I would give myself away. My hand was cold, but the locket seemed to warm it. I hung on to it; squeezed it tight; it grounded me. Everything seemed unreal to me but the locket.

The music, people, even my own face seemed estranged from me, not detached but estranged. The very atmosphere I breathed felt synthetic in my lungs; I felt as if it were opaque and falsely tinged with yellow.

I squeezed the locket tighter. I nearly crushed the thing. I closed my eyes again, and this time, Sasha's face appeared before my looming imagination. She intervened between my imagination and myself. There was something solid about her. I heard her throaty chuckle over the sad piano notes, and saw her, sitting in her wing-chair, shake her woolly head and laugh. I saw her leap at her own connivances and jokes down the street, pulling me with her in her wake. This vision of her comforted me and yet I tried to push it from me. I felt bound and trapped by the comfort she gave me. Peter does not know I felt this way about her too. He never bothered to ask me.

At last, the music ended. 'Are you all right?' he asked, a shade of crossness in his voice. 'I felt you were very tense.'

'I have a really dreadful headache,' I said. 'I'm sorry to spoil things, but could you take me home?'

He looked at me shrewdly for a moment, but what was in my eyes was lost on him.

In the car, he said, 'I love you, Emmy, really I do.' He hardly ever said that. I don't know why he said that; but anyhow, it was lost on me.

What is he up to now? I try to think about him – to get the measure of him. I thought if I unearthed the past, I might be able to see something of him – to understand what is going on now – but I can't, I can't.

I wish he'd left things as they were. I could cope with him – he was containable within my mind the way he was. These years and years of defensive silences and barren pauses – I could somehow live with this. I can endure. This is my one human asset. I am the most durable of women. I have dealt with bills and psychiatrists, scenes, the child, and although the duties have been onerous, they were ones I knew how to shoulder. What else has my life been from earliest infancy but an ordeal by others?

He has changed since he found my box. He has changed, and I have come to the cold realisation that I have no point of reference now by which to judge him. It is almost as if what had contained him for me had slipped from my grasp, shattered to the floor and let him out; like mercury, he runs away . . . he no longer courses up and down in a way I can measure.

His whole pattern of behaviour has altered. He is now out a lot. He told me he'd found a job, but he wouldn't tell me what job. I don't know what he's doing any more. I've always known what he was doing.

The other day, he returned home with a whole stack of records. We haven't played the gramophone in years. He bought Schubert of all things – he knows I hate Schubert. He played them through the other night while we ate dinner. It was all I could do to keep from holding my hands over my ears. I had to escape that arch mellowness, that gliding noise. I ran from the house, and in the end, I walked all the way to Piccadilly Circus. I sat down at the foot of Eros. Someone tried to sell me marijuana. The lights flickered on and off; people wan from drugs jostled me; the steps dirtied my clothes.

I must not allow myself to panic like this. I keep telling myself I must snap out of this. I keep getting sick; my stomach heaves over but nothing comes out. My hands are starting to shake. What is he up to?

He cannot know what it costs me to put all of this down. He can surely see what an intolerable position he has put me in. Either I tell him or I lose him altogether; he had made that very clear.

Why can't I see him with my own feelings? He is to me, after all this time, like someone I barely know. It's as if I hear him operating behind a thin wall. I can only guess at what he is really doing, and even when I attempt to describe him to myself, my mental picture of him elides with other strange forces and is eclipsed by them.

I have, I suppose, to give account to myself in some way – account for the reasons I had in following her – but when I try to do this, I am as dumb in regard to her now as I was to her then. It was impossible for me to articulate the anxiety I felt after that concert. I felt as if my own hand had gripped my feelings to the point of strangulation, and since it was my own hand, I was extremely frightened that I could not make it let go. I let myself know, in no uncertain terms, how silly I thought I was being. I tried to work off my peculiar cold fear in the library. I tried to immolate myself in my life with Peter. I found only that the harder I tried to lose myself, the more potent my fear became. I had a frantic sensation of loss. What I had lost and when I had lost it – these things were not clear. It had something to do, I knew then and feel now, with the cutting off of an essential source. It was as if, on going to turn on the water, I had obtained a gurgle and a splash of unwholesome effluent, perhaps because I had neglected to pay the bill, perhaps because there was something radically wrong with the pipes. I was not sure which . . . I only found that I was thirsty and that I was without the means to slake my need.

All I knew was that I had an intense need to see Sasha again. I had no desire to speak to her; in fact, I regarded renewing my old contact with her as an absurdly retrograde step. We had been children together; we were children no longer. Her image was important to me, what she represented was important to me; through this, I felt I could focus on the nature of my distress. That is why I followed her, and why should I have told Peter that? He, with his glassy walls, he had no interest in my feelings. Our love excluded everything extraneous to it; he made this amply clear from the very beginning in every action or thought he expressed to me. He had no wish to deal with me; he still has no wish to deal with me, on any level deeper than that we arrived at in our original agreement.

I set out to follow her on a sodden day in September, nine months after I had last seen her. I followed her efficiently, like a private detective. I organised my search well. From quite early in the morning, I watched the drama school. I had equipped myself rather as women did in their vigil before the coronation, except I had no flask of tea or camp-stool. I wore an anorak and trousers. I became anonymous, and no one approached me with so much as a glance. I started my watch from a launderette, where I pretended to be doing my washing. I carefully made use of someone else's dryer; I continued my watch, from a café across the road where I had a cup of tea. I watched the reflection of the place in a bookshop window; then from the porch of the Hotel Europa, whose sign had not yet been mended. The wind blew up and around, swirling leaves and old papers from the gutters. It rained, indecisively, off and on. Housewives trudged past me, intent on their errands. Only a few, the old, the unemployed, eyed the weather with any interest.

I saw Celia Russell climb the stairs, and with a tearing of nerves, I expected to see Sasha behind her; but she did not come. The coach, whose name was Jack, arrived in the company of a boy. By eleven, I knew that my search there was exhausted. I took the tube to Sloane Square, and made my way to her flat.

I waited on the stairs of a large house at an angle to where she lived. I wished I had brought a haversack with me so that I might have appeared to be a stranded hitchhiker. People in Chelsea stared at me. The housewives of Bayswater, preoccupied with meals and children and cleanliness had counted my loitering as beneath notice. In Sasha's corner of London, ladies pursue idleness professionally. They dress up in hats and gloves, they take idleness that seriously, for the purpose of loitering around Harrods and Peter Jones. A professional is always a good critic. They stared at me, badly dressed at noon, with no apparent place to go.

When she at last came out, I was surprised at how, like a hunter, I was glad to see her. I ducked automatically, and instead of feeling the emotions I had anticipated on seeing her, I found my mind working swiftly on the best course of pursuit.

I followed her at a distance of about seventy-five yards or so, diving into doorways, joining bus-queues, dropping money on the pavement to conceal myself whenever it seemed she might look around. What I became most aware of in following Sasha was her gait. Naturally enough, in shadowing a person, that is the first thing one would notice. If one does not attend to the rhythm of every footstep and the subtle changes in that rhythm, discovery is inevitable. I was so intent on observing this instinctive rule, that it was some time before I realised that she was walking like an old lady. She walked very carefully, halting now and then. Also, she sat down once on a bench, a thing that threw me into confusion, for I was forced to hide behind her in an undignified hurry. I was maddeningly unable to see her face, because whenever she turned, I had to turn also. She wore a heavy black coat and a scarf, tied very firmly around her head. Although it was not very cold, she seemed to feel cold, because she shrugged into her collar every now and then.

She went on for quite a long way slowly and uncertainly, as if aware of precariousness in herself. She seemed to be absorbed in the danger of just getting around. At last, she stopped in front of a church, a small, ungainly building in front of which there was a large crucifix carved in wood. The crucifix was sheltered by a little peaked roof; still, rain dripped off of the figure's face and body, like sweat and tears, it seemed, for the carver of the piece had twisted the form into anguished contortions. She looked up at the figure, and for the first time I saw her face. I made no attempt to hide this time, as she was completely absorbed in her regard for the figure. Her pallor was terrible, her expression even more so. I remembered how in Italy she had yearned over banks of candles in cathedrals . . . her expression was now utterly different. She regarded this image with a kind of ruthlessness, a deadly seriousness, as if she were asking from it, or whatever it meant to her, not reassurance or even inspiration, but for some kind of concrete solution to a problem of great importance. As I watched her, I was alive with fascination, and after she had pushed the door open and let it fall, I counted to a hundred, then went in after her, audacious as a cat.

The church, which had seemed small on the outside, was inside dark and capacious. A little red light, like the light Sasha lit before her icon, hung over the altar. The light swung and winked in the draught from the door I had closed so quietly behind me. I moved swiftly behind a plaster statuette of some saint or other: he held a plastic lily. I stood as still as I was able for my trembling, and even with the wind buffeting the windows, the church became intensely quiet.

Sasha stood for a moment in the aisle, then made a deep curtsey, gripping the pew for support. She entered the pew and knelt, holding her hands together, but not bowing her head. She appeared to stare fixedly at the altar. Whatever she was thinking was expressed in the rigid intensity with which she held her back. She seemed, without moving, almost to propel herself towards the object of her devotion. I became aware that I was hardly breathing as I watched her. After quite a long while – but I did not count it in time – there seemed to be no time in it, her muscles relaxed; I heard her, even from my far vantage point, breathe out, and she was still.

She rose rather quickly, making a sign of the cross, made another obeisance before the altar, then moved quite quickly to a small, heavy door at the end of the church. She knocked; a man, in his middle fifties I suppose, opened the door. He was wearing a black cassock, and although his voice had a carrying tone, I could not catch his words. It was obvious, however, that he and Sasha knew each other and that he had expected her. She slipped in and the door closed behind her with the final kind of echo of a bank vault.

When she was gone, my whole body seemed to sink under me. As if they had been stiffened by her presence, my joints gave way; I would have fallen had I not checked myself in time. I felt utterly drained and exhausted. I cast my weight of bones on to the pew next to me and looked around in the desultory way of a tramp on a park bench. I started to feel how wet I was from the rain, how tired I was – not from my search, but tired in a more important way, from a long time back. I rubbed my nose fiercely; it didn't seem to matter there. It occurred to me in a half-hearted way that I had not rubbed my nose that way since I had been a small child, but I was too tired to think that out. A gust of wind smacked the door; the red light wavered; the church was silent once again. The silence seemed to deepen and spread, almost as if it were a body of barely perceptible gas, fanned up and almost increased by the wind which had disturbed it.

I thought I had better go, but my body made no move to carry out my thought. I noticed some badly painted pictures of Jesus on the wall: they appeared to tell the story of the crucifixion. I thought them in bad taste. I decided that wouldn't matter to Sasha as she hadn't any taste to speak of . . . I wondered if it mattered to me, but I shrugged, too tired to care whether it mattered or not. The church was still, in spite of all the baroque sufferings depicted on the wall.

The door twitched open; then shut. I leapt from my seat and dashed behind a pillar. My nerves gave me something like a violent pain as they wrenched back into action. I heard muffled voices, words spoken urgently; there was no affectation on the inflexion of either voice. There was another silence, in which the gloom and peace of the church seemed to gather round me again for a moment; then the door opened suddenly, its weight being held back by the arm of the priest. His other arm rested lightly on Sasha's shoulder, which was bowed and rounded. He seemed tall beside her. Her face, her form, her reddened eyes expressed a wrung-out smallness. He had in his aspect an air of self-possession. His movements and gestures were controlled but very slightly exaggerated. He moved with a consciousness of himself, but without self-consciousness, as he walked with her into the body of the church.

'Until Monday then,' he said. There was something faintly business-like in his tone. She looked at him, imploringly. 'I'm sorry,' he added. 'I can't say anything else to you, my dear, than I have said. You will see it, though, in the end.'

With an effort at a smile, she said goodbye, then she hurried down the aisle and was out of the door before I would have thought it possible. I pressed myself against the pillar and shook with relief.

Suddenly, the priest with an energetic stride reached the place where I stood. He looked at me very gravely, but with a certain amount of kindness. He even reached out his hand in my direction.

'What the matter?' I asked him sharply.

'I was going to ask you the same question,' he said quietly. I did not like the look of his face – too kind, too quiet, too aware – St Francis with the wild, wild wolf, taming the beast with love and understanding.

'You've been standing there for a long time and you look very worried. I have no wish to interfere . . .' He paused and looked at me intelligently. There was something formidable in him. 'But I can listen. I have listened a lot, you know.'

For a moment, his seriousness unbent me. He seemed fixed before me, a solid, black column of calm. His face and hands were clean, so clean, his cleanliness might have sprung from his bones, a self-regenerating cleanliness. He did not smile, but his eyes were full of fresh vision of me, full of an uncondemning realisation of how miserable I was. I had the sensation of having been admitted *in extremis* to a hospital where all the walls were white, where all the sheets were so clean they squeaked between my fingers, where everything was very quiet.

I opened my mouth to tell him the wrong I'd done her . . . to tell him how frightened I'd been at the concert, how I couldn't hear the music. My failures ached in my throat, but I couldn't do it. I couldn't say a word.

Suddenly, fury shot up in me like lava: it was completely unexpected, the anger; it tumbled from my mouth without my consent. 'Your sympathy! My God, look what it's done for her!' I could hear my flat ugly vowels smashing against the walls of the church, and with a terrifying speed, they seemed to ricochet back to me, as if my hatred had misfired and blown up in my own face.

He started slightly; I turned and ran away, feeling as if I had scorched the ears of God, in whom I had never believed.

Shaken as I was, I entered softly. Peter was reading, his long legs stretched out and crossed at the ankles. He tapped a sharp pencil against his forehead which shone like an apple in the lamp-light. A fine, upstanding lamp, that lamp of his: it had impeccable proportions and always gave the correct shaft of light upon the page. He read a heavy book which he held easily in his large hands. It was a tiresomely written treatise on runes. He read steadily with good concentration.

He saluted me with his pencil and a quick smile, then turned the thick page. I sat down on the floor and watched him, grateful for his beauty in the lamp-light.

He pursed his mouth in pleasure and amusement at my gloating regard. He liked it that he could read and not have to speak to me as I watched him. He always said I was the next best thing to a cat. He loves cats. My watching him work pleased him as a cat would have pleased him . . . a cat who settles, stares and rapturously purrs.

He drew out this moment he enjoyed. I could not look at Peter without that greed I always had for him. It seemed to steady me.

'When do you want to eat?'

'Now. I'll cook.'

'But you're working.'

'Bored with it. No one can write as dismally as this man. I know what I'll do – I'll compose a runic book on English prose and send it to him!'

'I'll cook.'

'You're a rotten cook!' We laughed. For some reason he thought it was funny that I couldn't cook well. He became protective towards me when I wrestled with tin openers or came to blows with chicken joints.

'Emily! Why on earth are you wearing those appalling clothes.' He put down his book and shut it. 'For heaven's sake, go and change into something decent.'

I kept a secret cache of clothes at Peter's. We enjoyed the secret and often referred to it. Peter is the sort of man who flicks ash off of women or pulls away stray hairs. He had a habit of dusting me, then standing back and arranging me. Even now he flaunts me out of habit.

We took a lot of photographs of one another at that time. He found them in my box. I kept them all. There is one of me from that period sitting and working at his wide, low desk, a crystal jug beside me. I look younger and less absorbed than I posed to be. I have one of him stretched out on his bed. He is smoking a cigarette and gazing at the ceiling. I thought at the time the photograph embodied his poetic detached intelligence. I was a fool for not seeing the weakness in his face.

'Where have you been today? You looked like my Aunt Mathilda who used to prowl for mushrooms in the early morning dew. She claimed to talk to the fairies.' He slapped two chops under the grill and put some frozen peas into cold water without any salt. He was even worse at cooking than I was.

'I followed Sasha around London. That is how I spent my day.' I was quite surprised to find I had effortlessly told him the truth.

'You what!'

'I'll tidy the sitting-room, shall I?' I felt sharply criticised and so moved off. He followed me, indignant.

'Sasha! You mean that scatty friend of yours. What on earth did you take up with her again for?'

'I don't see why I shouldn't take up with her if I wanted to. You act as if it were disloyal of me to take up with her.'

'You have no need of her,' he said shortly. 'I always thought she was bad for you, Em. The night we met . . . how can I describe it . . . I felt you looked up to her in a way. You seemed terribly under her influence, and she, she just took you for an audience. If you'd gone on with her, you'd have found yourself clapping and smiling, forever abasing yourself, putting yourself in the shade so that the light could better shine on her. And the way you looked at Boris . . . it was as if you'd caught your mother in bed with the milkman . . . What did you go to see her for, anyway?'

We'd never quarrelled before. His irritability threw me off my guard.

'I didn't go to see her. I didn't even talk to her. I tell you, I followed her . . . just to see what she was doing, just to keep tabs on her. I wanted to settle something about her in my mind.'

'You mean you *tailed* her! In this weather? It's plain mad.' He looked at me with devastating coldness. I've seen him look like that at David when he has disturbed some of Peter's things. He cannot bear anything to be out of order. He would sacrifice anybody's feelings for the sake of order. He must see now how he has never let me talk, never listened to me. I stood there almost unable to bear his punishment.

'Stop it, Peter. Don't. I'm worried about her. She's ill. Why do I have to answer to you? Why can't I see my friend? I had to see her to find something out.'

'You're shaking. Stop shaking. Pull yourself together. Do you hear? I'll not have you dragged down like this. We can't afford to have you behaving like that.' He was upset all out of proportion to the incident. His face was red his eyes more panic-stricken than angry. If only he really had been shouting at me . . . but he wasn't. He was shouting at himself, his own feelings.

'The chops are burning.' I met his hysteria with a level I'd found in myself of almost total self-defence, a cold control . . . I tried it almost experimentally. I reversed the chops and turned the heat down under the peas. He stood in the doorway, blinking, his face flushed. He has a tendency to cry when he is upset. I saw that I had won; he looked confused.

'Emily, come away from that. Please, come and sit down. I must tell you something. I've meant to and meant to, but I didn't want to spoil anything.' He was flustered by emotion and he scrabbled at my arm.

I turned off the cooker and said, 'Very well.'

We sat rather formally across from each other. I could not imagine what he had to tell me. I remained externally calm, but I was frightened, very frightened that, whatever it was, it might make me lose him. He looked sick and very troubled about what he was going to say.

'I had, while I was still at Cambridge,' he said inhaling deeply, 'a rather loathsome nervous breakdown.' He looked down at his hands, then at me with a heavy force of feeling.

I waited for him to go on, but he did not. I felt extremely puzzled that this appeared to be his confession. It was as if a quite sane person had suddenly told me that the key to the universe lay in the ability of human beings to touch their toes. I could not see that Peter's revelation had any significance at all, yet his face was red with the effort of telling me.

'Why what's the disgrace in that?' I asked.

He sat back in his chair and closed his eyes, as if I had taken away some terrible burden by my question and by that alone. 'You see everything so perfectly,' he said after a time, 'how I feel it as a disgrace.'

I can see now that he thought my bewilderment was vision, but I could not grasp this at the time. I was only glad that he had stopped looking at me in that vulnerable way of his and relieved that he had told me nothing worse.

'I don't see how disgrace is involved, unless you actually murdered someone. Even then, you'd have an excuse.'

He gave me too sharp a look, then, reassured about something he said, 'No, I didn't murder anyone. I did no harm at all.'

'You're all right now, aren't you?'

'*Voyez!*' he said, holding out his hand to show steadiness. Still, his voice was nervous.

'Then why did you bring it up? It's in the past.' I couldn't see the point of the conversation. It gnawed at me that I couldn't see the point.

'These things always leave a mark on me . . . a terrific amount of suffering is involved, you see. Things set me off still, hurt the scar tissue. Your following Sasha, now that . . . the first sign of my illness was that I started doing things like that; but instead of following people, I sent them anonymous letters, telling them what I really thought of them.' His snappishness dissolved; he talked rather dreamily about himself. 'I took up curious diets. I'd eat nothing but carrots for a while. I actually turned yellow. They thought I had jaundice – that is how they discovered me.'

He lit a cigarette, smoking it fitfully without regard to the flame, and his voice became careless, almost urbane. 'At last, I half killed myself by putting my head in a gas oven. I made myself comfortable, as people are supposed to do in such situations . . .' Here he made a deeply ironical face.

'Actually, Boris fished me out. Boris saved my life, isn't that funny? As you may imagine, my feelings about Boris are "ambivalent", as your mother and my psychiatrist would say. In fact, I believe that Boris took me along to meet you and Sasha that night in order to cheer me up . . . not that I was depressed. He simply finds my way of life incomprehensibly unexciting and thereby concludes that I am always depressed. What is so amusing is that he doesn't really like me and I don't really like him. We are bound together by a mutual sense of duty.'

'What has this actually to do with my following Sasha? I mean, I followed her for perfectly natural reasons. She is my oldest friend, whether you like her or not. I don't see why you have to be so portentous about it. I don't dare to talk to her because I'm a coward.'

He laughed quite a lot, relieved, reflexive laughter. Oh, how I wish I'd really let him know, told him what I had been about to tell that priest. But no, I answered as I always answer Peter, in order to suit his requirements, his rigorous requirements.

'I do love you, your simplicity. You sit so straight and give the simplest explanation on earth. The trouble with psychiatry is that it makes nonsense out of anything straightforward. One takes the symbols from one's own life and imposes them on other people so that the world, in the end, is reduceable to oneself. One's own mind becomes the lowest common denominator for every action expressed by anyone else. Before I met you, that was shortly after my breakdown, I was seeing neuroses in trees, complexes in running brooks, psychoses in stones and madness in everything.

'Sasha is your oldest friend and you are a coward! Are you aware of how elegant, how simple that explanation is? You do not know how many questions would have to be begged in myself before I could arrive at such a moral statement. You can have no idea what peace you have brought me this year. And I thought it would be broken by my admission. As it is, by your very silence, your faint surprise at my taking it all so seriously, you have removed such a portion of my morbidity that the doctor could never take away.' He leaned back in his chair and closed his eyes, making a precise arch with his fingers. He looked almost perfectly relaxed and happy.

His praise of me dampened my bewilderment, but in its place there came to me a faint, slightly nauseating sense of unease. After a pause, I said vaguely, 'My mother's friends all have psychiatrists.' In fact, I took psychiatrists to be one of the services provided in a well-ordered left-wing household . . . a little like laundrymen. He looked at me sharply again, but I had retreated where I can feel cheated without danger.

EIGHT

Once Peter allowed himself that one luxury of telling me about his weakness, other luxuries followed . . . things we simply could not afford. We have lived beyond our means now for ten years. I cannot see how we can retrench; yet neither can I see, being in debt to each other as we are, how it is possible for one of us to desert the other.

The obvious solution to our problem is divorce. We have both privately, and in agonising scenes together, threatened each other with the final death of the business; but by slow degrees it has become apparent in our marriage that we are not capable of living apart. We have separated, but we come together again with excuses, like the child, like Peter's moral scruples against divorce, like my anguished appraisal of myself as a torturer who needs a victim. I know that none of these reasons is the real reason for our continued connection; but where the real reason lies, I do not know.

A clean end: I like to imagine it sometimes. There would be an awesome silence and I cannot make out whether it would be awful or not. I like to think I would set up a wholesome life in a flat somewhere where Peter and David would never find me; but what would I do that is more wholesome than what I already do? I am not fool enough to think I would fester any less for a change of address.

I keep thinking I need some further form of privacy. The need for privacy assails me daily . . . hiddenness, retreat, immolation. I don't really want a pleasant flat and friends: I want solitary confinement where no one can disturb my peace again.

We still sleep together intermittently; but both of us are ashamed of that. It seems we shouldn't, given the way we feel about each other.

I know that by this time our marriage should be ended; but I have a sense of its not having begun yet.

The other night we had dinner together. Quite often, I work late to avoid this situation. We ate in silence. During the meal, we looked at each other; our looks expressed a bruised wonderment at our predicament.

I can still hear myself stirring my coffee over and over again just to make a little noise in the silent dining-room. He is thinner, no doubt about that, and older; thinness and age do not become him. My face becomes sharper with time . . . Jack Spratt could eat no fat, his wife could eat no lean . . . Peter and I are both Jack Spratts, thin and sharp-faced. We are mirrored in each other's eyes. I see myself in his; he sees himself in mine.

I felt myself to be as he sees me: cold and grudging, a merciless woman. I saw in his eyes the other night that peculiar, flattened expression that I have in the presence of my mother. Peter feels about me the way I feel about my mother.

And what do I see in him that he is so, justly or unjustly, alienated from me? What repels me about Peter is his basic self-indulgence. When I see that in him, I cannot attempt to understand him, to help him or forgive him. It is as if, seated at a large dinner, I was incapable of taking the first bite through nausea. He is bound, not to me, but to himself for life. When he married me, he married himself. His character has no outlets. He is hermetically sealed, and he wonders why he gets sick on his own poisons.

The curious truth is this; Peter and I are capable of satisfying each other mentally and physically: we have fed deep on each other's emotions. I am not such a fool that I don't know we are both, both to blame. Our impotence lies deeper than these things which occur on the surface of the brain; neither one of us – and this is the point – is capable of generosity.

That came to me suddenly, just as I wrote it: it is the first original thought I have had in years. We are both stranded on separate points of honour, but I do not know how it is that either of us can get down. What can we do? Our feelings are so corrupted, our mistrust of them is so great . . . I do not know how one starts to be generous.

Peter was generous to Sasha once: it is in that, his own generosity, that he loves her still. He calls up her shade, engineers her revenance very carefully so that I will see that once he was able. It's like the brag of an old man of past conquests. His blow is doubly dealt. He accuses me in his veneration of her of being sufficient to myself where she was not. All of this time I have been pursuing the idea that he took something from her, but he didn't; he took nothing that she didn't give out to everyone else. I too received her favours.

And why is her memory livid in my own? Why have I sentimentalised her to the point of keeping souvenirs? She was the only person I could almost take something from . . . but that is another story and brings out the worst wound. I'll come to that another time.

I said that Peter allowed himself new luxuries once he had revealed his secret. The most important of these, of course, was his decision to introduce me to his family.

In the year that I had known him, Peter had not once seriously referred to his immediate family. When I write this I wonder if it can have been true; but he did not – I distinctly remember that he did not mention them. This seems odd, not only for the obvious reasons, but also because his family plays such an important part in our lives now.

He was so reticent about them that I assumed for a while that they lived out of the country. He had told me he was born in India, and I supposed that they were still there, I imagined Peter's father to be a rather down-at-heel sahib, rich enough but perhaps slightly raffish. When Peter treated my questions about his parents with cold distaste, I developed this idea of mine. I had half-decided that there was some disgrace attached to his name.

He occasionally referred to his aunt and uncle, and this supported my theory. I supposed he'd been to boarding school in this country and spent some holidays with them. His aunt and uncle are by far the most agreeable people in his family, and, in fact, when Peter was a child they did take pity on him, Hermione and the Brigadier being quite the most hopeless parents I can think of. Aunt Beatrice is a simple-minded but motherly woman, and Uncle Frederick, though he has little sensibility, had enough sense to see how disastrous was his sister's management of Peter.

It was, as I have suggested, shortly after he told me of his nervous breakdown that he suddenly announced that we were going to call on his mother and father.

'But I thought if they existed at all that they lived in India!'

'They live in Eaton Square and have done so for twenty years.' He spoke curtly, but then softened. 'We are vey badly estranged . . . I have not been home since I left Cambridge. I don't want to take you there, in one way, but in another I do. I'm afraid I have a streak of conventionality which makes it necessary to me that you should be introduced. I have put it off, but I know that I must do it now.'

He was white and grim-faced in the taxi, and I myself was very nervous as we stopped in Eaton Square.

My in-laws are rich, and their richness is primarily expressed in that tall, stiff, yellowing house where they have their flat. David, on a visit to his grandmother called it 'the ice-cream house'. I was puzzled by this image for a while, but at last I saw the sense in it . . . the rich, vanilla confectionery of Empire-builders frozen in an architectural mould. It is my bizarre fantasy to think that houses such as theirs would melt in a warmer climate.

'My father works for charity to avoid hell,' Peter said, as we waited in that person's drawing-room. This statement was one of Peter's inaccuracies. A man of action, my father-in-law, but a gentleman with it, he works for charity because leadership and service are inextricably mixed in his mind and bred into his bones. It is a call of the blood to use his privilege responsibly. It has never crossed his mind that he will go to hell, because old whatever-his-school's-name-was's never go there. Peter's hatred of the man, so seemingly inexhaustible, warps his judgement.

A butler called Parker, who wore a white jacket and looked rather like a hospital attendant, had shown us in. The man regarded Peter with great caution, as if Peter might explode. He was obviously very surprised to see us. I wondered that Peter had not telephoned first. Peter ignored the man's unhappy expression.

'Parker,' he said, 'how's your rheumatism?'

'Not so good, the weather being what it is, Master Peter. Still, we mustn't grumble, must we? How are you getting along with your studies?' The butler droned this speech quite automatically and completely at odds with his worried eyes.

'Well, thank you, well.'

This exchange between Peter and Parker is the same exchange, with a variation on the words, that takes place between Peter and waiters, Peter and taxi-drivers. The rhythm of a litany is constant. I always think that the same ritual intention of appeasement is there too.

'Madam will be down in a minute,' said Parker, leaving us on a plush settee.

Peter rose and walked around the room with the stylised air of one who wants to think he is recalling old, once dangerous things which he had subsequently defused by virtue of his own sophistication. He arched his brow. 'Every time I come here, I am impressed with the bad taste of it all . . . furniture to be afraid of . . .' Bland but brittle, he waved his hand at a perfect Queen Anne table as if to indicate the originality of the judgement; as if to despise a Queen Anne table one's taste had to be exalted far, far above the ordinary. He appeared to me as he had done on the night I had met him . . . a connoisseur of art in a gallery full of bad reproductions. He poured me a drink from a silver tray. He swaggered a bit and his face was the picture of delicate hauteur.

In a sense, he was right about the drawing-room. It was interior-decorated, that was clear, because the place was full of interesting but completely impersonal colour schemes in slub silk and deep-pile Wilton – contrasting textures in turquoise. Great hunks of silver stood about on little spindly tables – rose bowls, candelabra, cigarette boxes, all engraved like so many trophies handed out for the virtues of money and a good name.

I had never been in such a place before. There was something in the sheer, towering defendedness of all that money which impressed me. I didn't like it, but it impressed me. The decoration of the room made its owners completely impenetrable to an outsider; there was no suggestion of individuality about it, not even a work-basket or pipe or an ink-stain to give one clue about the identity of Peter's parents.

I imagined Peter's mother to be awesomely smooth, as untouchable, as unknowable as her own drawing-room. I was prepared for a former beauty, who would deftly extract a cigarette from one of the silver boxes, turn on a well-shod foot, sit smoothing her lap, and with a slight shake of her silver hair, would pose me hard questions, asked with impeccable style.

I therefore could hardly believe her when she slipped through the door, closing it ever so carefully behind her – so far was she from my expectations. A little woman in her fifties, she moved apologetically. Her hair was slightly lank and she had no style at all. What was remarkable about her was the expression in her eyes. When she saw Peter, she stood absolutely still by the door . . . she didn't stare at him – because staring is altogether an outward gesture, almost an aggressive thing, implying an opinion on the part of the beholder – no, she did what must be the opposite of staring; she yearned for him, longed for him, sucked him in with her eyes, feasting on his appearance as if he were an essential to her diet sorely, sorely missed. He looked away. At length, she spoke with a timidity which somehow did not coincide with her gaze. 'Well hello, darling, this is a nice surprise.' She kissed him directly on the cheek, not like Sasha's mother, who brushed past and kissed in the air. He flinched slightly from her kiss. She took note of his blink and moved confusedly to sit on the edge of a deep armchair.

'Mother, I have brought Emily Stone to meet you.' His manner was too distant, hollow. His face struggled with the effort to maintain this manner.

'Oh how do you *do*!' she said with inappropriate enthusiasm. She seemed to be trying hard to focus on me. For a while, she said nothing, only looked at Peter with tremulous self-deprecation, as if apologising for her former greed. I think if she had said anything at all, if she hadn't looked at him with such intolerable, self-abasing love, he would have been all right. Instead, his dignity, which he had possessed up to this point, heightened and hardened in his face to cruelty. He looked rather like a painting of a Spanish grandee.

'We're getting married,' he said, shortly. 'That is why I came.'

Why hadn't he mentioned it to me before? I still cannot get over that. Why did he have to say that? He hadn't asked me . . . I wanted to tell her, but I kept absolutely still for the danger there was about.

He had used the most brutal kind of shock tactic. The woman sat flailing in her wound, bewildered by the pain like a child. She turned to me, a stranger, rather than look at him. She had barely taken me in before; now she asked for my support as if I had nothing really to do with Peter's announcement . . . rather as if I had been an innocent bystander at the scene of an accident which had dealt her an almost insupportable blow. She begged me with her eyes that I would cushion the shock.

I had that heightened sense of control which comes in an emergency. 'Mrs Meadows,' I said kindly but firmly, 'I can well understand how you feel; but Peter and I have no immediate plans. I am sure he blurted out the news in natural excitement. He did so want you to know.'

She looked at me for a moment with dumb gratitude like an animal – her thanks all for the tone in my voice rather than the words I had spoken which she appeared not fully to understand. All the same, cagey and cowering slightly from Peter, she got to her feet. 'I think I must go and tell your father,' she faltered. Panic drives Hermione: it is her motivating force, and in her fright, she invariably flees to the source of it for protection against it.

Peter was tense with irritation. He seemed not to have heard at all how I had soothed her, how I had extricated him from a head-on collision with her.

I watched his working face for a moment then took a gamble. 'Don't you ever use me like that again!' I judged exactly the sharpness of my tone. He looked at me with astonishment.

'I hate my mother,' he said by way of explanation.

'Clearly,' I replied, 'but I have no wish to be involved with *your* hatred of *your* mother.' I was gratified to see him look with shame at his hands.

At this moment, Peter's father entered the room. He opened the door and closed it behind him with the swift precision of the managing director at a board meeting.

I had considered Peter's face, his demeanour to be sharp, a little angular; he is a soft model of his father who stood rigid with controlled anger in front of the fireplace. A little like the Duke of Edinburgh in his bearing (not that he takes on any other self to complete himself), he looks as if he is made out of permanent pleats.

He gave me one swift, calculating look which made me instantly wary of the man's intelligence. That look of his, which is also Peter's – if I hadn't my own interests to look after, I would tell them what a mistake it is. To give such a look to an Arab in a bazaar would save you money: no one would cheat a man with such an eye. But in dealing with transactions of an emotional nature, such a look is a bad mistake: it is a dangerous thing to show all of your weapons before you have judged the armoury of your opponent. A more sure way to dominate is to let your subject underestimate you on first acquaintance.

'I understand from Peter's mother that you are to be my daughter-in-law,' he said with a frigid smile. He ignored Peter entirely with his eyes; Peter's chest sank visibly in his father's presence. I saw this only with my peripheral vision. I knew instinctively not to let my eyes swerve from the Brigadier. I smiled a little and inclined my head.

'How do you do,' I said, holding out my hand. With great relish I saw I had him. He was forced to move five paces towards me and shake the hand I would not let drop. Having done this, he had no alternative but to sit down.

'In my wife's shock, she forgot your name,' he said. Although he did not look at Peter, he directed a withering shot at him from the corner of his eye. The indirectness of the look gave it peculiar force and point.

'Emily Stone.'

'Stone. . . ?' The question was automatic, not friendly nor enthusiastic, nor even hostile. The Brigadier keeps a mental file on all the landed gentry of England; he would refer to the file in a storm at sea, if the occasion arose for its use.

'The Stones of Fulham, father,' Peter said with cheap sarcasm.

'My prospective father-in-law lectures at LSE. They live by choice in an area of sociological interest.' He had tried to make his voice slick with disdain, but it wobbled in the middle of his speech; because of this, he produced the disagreeable effect of childish bravado.

The Brigadier paused for a full few moments, thus gathering to himself every advantage. I recognised the swell of his anger beneath his silence: it had a great deal in common with my own brand of anger.

'You will realise, Miss Stone,' he said at last, 'that my son's visit today is his first in two years. Had he announced himself before coming, it is unlikely that I would have allowed him in. Although it is altogether laudable that he should inform us of his plan to marry, I think he would have served your interests and our interests better had he written to me and let me know in that way. In the past he has shown himself to be acutely concerned with my wife's delicate nervous condition. Had he been sincere in his anxiety, he might have spared her the shock she has suffered because of this announcement. He must know that even his appearance has a detrimental effect on her health.

'In marrying my son, Miss Stone, you must know, and it is my duty to tell you this, that he has a history of mental instability.'

He turned his full face to Peter for the first time in the entire interview; it was composed in an expression of extraordinary malevolence.

'I am sure Miss Stone does not admire you for what you have done to your mother.'

Peter blinked from the pain his father had caused him; then with a lunge of earnestness, terrible for its being out of character, he said, 'She knows it *all*; she understands *everything*!' He trembled, close to tears.

The one power below the ultimate power Peter has over his father is the power to embarrass him. The man really blushed under his little moustache. In this state, he turned to me without thinking. 'We would be delighted, Miss Stone, if you and your family would come to dinner some evening. This meeting has been painful not because of you, I hope you realise that, but because of the shock it has given my wife and myself to see our only son after such a long and unhappy parting.' Decency to all others beside Peter is the Brigadier's extravagance in such situations – situations which have recurred with tiresome regularity during my married life.

'I am not sure, father, that I shall ever return with Emily or without her. She can hardly have enjoyed your humiliating me in such a manner,' he mumbled and looked down at his hands; he looked curiously boyish. He sat foolishly amid the ribbons of his dignity, making no attempt to gather them up when even the rags of it would have done. His speech, brave enough in words, sounded aimless and empty – a tired approach at mere face-saving.

Peter's father blenched. I was then at a loss to explain such a dramatic change in this aspect. Now, of course, I know that Peter's mumbled words constituted the most potent threat to his father that he could utter. How the Brigadier must have suffered those two years of Peter's self-exile! Their tormented involvement is meat and drink to the man. Ah. Peter! His weakness lies very much in not seeing his own strength, or, if seeing it, scrupling to use it.

'We've had our differences, Peter,' his father said almost gently. Peter looked up at him quickly from surprise at this *volte face*; his father's eyes held him even though he tried to look down again. 'But, look here, you were a boy two years ago. And now, here you are a man . . . about to get married . . .' he broke off; there had been the slightest catch of emotion in his voice. His eyes suggested for a moment a reserve of thwarted tenderness for Peter – how deep a reserve it was difficult to ascertain. Peter leaned involuntarily forward, but his face, still wary, showed a kind of tired bitterness. His father carefully removed his glance from Peter; he became at once impersonal and brisk, and Peter slightly relaxed. 'We'll see,' he said.

'I am sure that Mr and Mrs Stone will want to meet their daughter's future in-laws,' the Brigadier said quite calmly as if nothing had happened. 'Besides, I know it would please your mother to know Miss Stone better and, for that matter, to see you again. She has quite pined in your absence.' He added the last sentence, I remember, with great lightness, almost with humour, so that it would appear that Hermione had only been a little sad and you know how women are, always making a fuss about their children. He has this talent, the Brigadier, of making it seem, in the subtlest phrasing of the most ordinary remark, that he and Hermione have the most normal marriage on earth. His towering rages at Hermione fall from his deft lips to the pigmy height of flirtatious tiffs. When he chooses to present it in this way, Peter's breakdowns become growing pains. Even now, I have to shake myself slightly during such a conversation with his father to remember that Peter is thirty-four years old. But as I have said, I never underestimated Peter's father and have thus been spared the chagrin of making any serious error with him. Poor old Peter . . . to this day, he still believes his father is a bluff soldier. He talks enough about the man's machinations, but his approach to his father is always obligingly direct.

This is the way the Meadowses take one: they left me that day with the feeling that I had great mental agility which I had exercised well on my own and Peter's behalf. I felt, when I left that house with Peter, that I had won a particularly taxing game of chess. In fact, one essential point had escaped me. I had so well used my wits in the game that I had forgotten its purpose. It did not occur to me until much too late that Peter had won and that he was the sole victor. He had made me tacitly accept a final engagement to be married without having made me a proposal first. I had felt the necessity of being with Peter, but I had never projected this feeling into any desire to make it permanent. Had he proposed to me directly, I might have accepted him, but I would have done so with reserve. In an ordinary engagement, I might have felt trapped. Things would have emerged, feelings so far untouched, differences too big to be hurdled in marraige. As it was, he propelled me into a dramatic situation where I had to decide all at once whose side I was on. By doing this, he overrode all the caution I would have had in the normal way. From that day, I was engaged with him in the just war against his family, or at least I considered the war to be just at the time. The urgency of a just war was there, at any rate. What I did not see was that he had recruited me into a far more dangerous, a far less clear conflict where I never know whose side to take. He had joined me to the deepest of his multiple selves, and from that position I am never secure. He hates me for knowing what he is, but he hates me worse if I retreat. He is bewildered and lost if I become myself – and so am I, so am I.

Hermione takes tea with me now and then. Occasionally I allow her a shopping spree for David. I watch her hesitant over milk or lemon, fumbling at her purse for the correct change. I listen with half an ear to her interminable griefs. She accuses ghost people of committing terrible wrongs in the past. I stand aside as she rubs against David, beseeching him to love her. She will snatch him up, put him down, snatch him up again, interrupting the child's solemn games. She bewilders him and he has a sense of pity towards her. Perhaps it is his sense of pity which bewilders him. He cares for her very much, more than anyone else, but he is most at ease at my mother's house. My mother is not fond, but she is proud of his achievements. She makes sure he is always constructively occupied.

That is a digression. It is my mother-in-law I watch with an almost clinical interest. It was she who set the course of my life in motion, as if she had lurched into the key switch of a computer. But no, not the key switch, surely not the key switch. She threw a key switch, and Sasha threw another.

Peter's mood, when we reached his flat, was almost ecstatic. In retrospect, it seems very puzzling that this should have been so; he had, after all, just received a number of carefully judged body-blows from a father whose ability to reduce Peter to jelly at the slightest touch is truly phenomenal. I wasn't puzzled at the time; I was drawn in, carried along, not by ecstasy of my own, but by his. Sasha used to do that to me. I am the best companion in the world for the self-drunk. There is something in another person's inebriation for me . . . I can lose myself in someone else's mood: it's almost like being at the films.

'Emmy, Emmy!' he picked me up and put me down. 'You were magnificent!' He poured us a drink, whether to celebrate or to calm his nerves I could not tell. 'Was it awful for you? Aren't you glad I've spared you up till now? I had a dreadful feeling you thought I was ashamed of you, but you see how . . . I was ashamed of them. I turned it over and over in my mind. I couldn't bear you to see how they were; I thought how you might despise me . . . but I knew I had to do it, had to go back or I would have been escaping, and thank God you were with me, all cool and acid. He thought to divide us with his dire warnings, but he neglected to see how perfectly attuned we are. He has seen everything I've ever done in terms of a conventional kind of courage, in terms of backbone. It is "spinelessness" he hates me for . . . that is why I couldn't take you to see him before I told you about the breakdown. I knew he would mount such an attack and I couldn't be sure how you'd take it. I have a habit of half-thinking that everyone sees me through my father's eyes – a wriggling incompetent. But it never occurred to him when he tried to destroy us back there what a rock you were, how you might see my failings with the eyes of love.' He threw himself down into the leather armchair; he was full of gaiety and triumph.

'You said we were getting married . . .' His mood had got the better of me. Somehow I felt it was banal of me to mention it.

He shrugged and smiled a little mischievously. 'You and I, we understand each other so well. We have reached that level, have we not, where it becomes tiresome for you to go home every night. There is no point in going down on one's knees to someone with whom one kneels. Good heavens, Em, did you expect a proposal? I'm sorry.' He chuckled to himself, but somehow he included me in his laugh so that I felt whatever doubts I had were based on vulgar and conventional notions. I did not wish to let him know that such thoughts had crossed my mind. I looked vaguely at the branches in the vase, the Roman head; and supposed it would be all right.

My mind was stuffed with circumstances, gorged on enough events to feed my feelings for a year; in that time I might have digested what had happened to me. As it was, my responses lagged, my mind became dumb in regard to the forces which hollered round my brain. I seem to remember myself in that week before Sasha sent her letter in a state of near trance. I tried to grip on to the memory of Sasha in the church, of Peter at his parents' house, but each thought slipped from my grasp, as if all that had actually happened to me had been illusion. I did not mention to my parents that Peter and I planned to get married, partly because the news did not seem real to me. I was not disturbed; indeed, I was becalmed. None of it seemed to matter very much. I was vaguely anxious, the way one is in a dream. It seemed to me that I had got on the wrong train, but as I was unable to stop it, I did not tax my energy with hysteria. I started to take aimless walks by myself. I did not look at anything on my way, nor did I think about my life; what comforted me was the feeling of my footfalls on the pavement. That, at any rate, was solid.

It was after one of these walks that I received the letter from Sasha. Like the others, I have it here before me. I wonder what Peter felt when he saw it. I expect he had a double shock: one, that I had kept it; one, that the thing itself is so intrinsically hideous. It is an almost obscene relic, like something from the Police Museum.

It took my parents a little while, on my arrival, to remember that I had a letter from Sasha. They had some people in for a drink. These were Nigel and Frieda, a couple who taught at my mother's school. At any rate, Nigel did, and Frieda wished that she did and said she would as soon as little Dominic could be left at the day-nursery which everyone was so keen on getting started in the area. They all said what a scandal it was that the working mother was not adequately provided for by the state.

The conversation, however, was weak. It was clear that my mother and father found little very interesting in Nigel and Frieda. Nigel and Frieda were painfully conscious of Dominic, who was crashing his way through the kitchen cupboards, flinging pots and pans in all directions.

'Oh, Emily,' my mother said in an awkward pause. 'I just remembered . . . the most peculiar boy was here with a letter for you. He said he was a brother of that friend you used to have, the one with the Russian name. It all seemed very mysterious.'

'How fascinating!' Frieda cried, taking up in her tone my mother's implication that this was probably part of an absurd cloak-and-dagger game played by children.

It was always a pleasure to hold an envelope coming from Sasha. She wrote on thick, expensive stationery which made each letter as important as a parcel. You would hold one of her letters in your hand before you opened it, just to sense the weight. You would see how fine your name and address looked in that dashing hand. She wrote a name as if there were some pomp in it.

The handwriting on this envelope was very bad, shaky, as if she had had to make some conscious effort in every stroke; as if without conscious effort the hand would have slipped and run berserk across the page. Children don't write like that; they write unsteadily simply from lack of experience.

I knew at once that the letter contained something grievously odd. I took the letter into my mother's smart living-room, that place so full of swivel chairs and paper flowers, bottle-lamps and hessian textures that no news received in it could really be bad news. How can one suffer while seated on a Danish sofa – each clean line seems to cast doubt on any other human faculty but reason, to pour contempt upon any state but order, to disallow any purpose for oneself but a functional purpose.

I held the letter in my hands, not daring to open it. Had she seen me following her? Was she now denouncing me as the cause for her obvious unhappiness? It came clearly back to me, what I had witnessed in the church: the black coat, the tight scarf, her body clenched in prayer; and her formidable companion, I saw him too.

I put the unopened letter carefully on the coffee-table. The child in the kitchen was having a tantrum; his gargled howl came muffled through the door. Instinctively, I snatched the letter up again and held it to my chest until I could be sure my privacy was safe. It came to me suddenly that Sasha might be taking the veil – announcing to me her final withdrawal from the world, laying it at my door, her decision. I saw the Poor Clare at Assisi, rippling through her waterfall of black and how she commanded Sasha's esteem. How like Sasha it would be, how like her medieval mind where every commonplace was punctuated with some glory. I ripped open the envelope in a sudden spurt of irritation.

Dear Emily (in the past it had always been 'Darling Em'),

I must see you unless it's too hard for you. I'm afraid I'm very ill – they say I'm dying. I've had this thing for ages and didn't make much of it, but I knew they were so worried; then there was test after test, and I overheard them talking. I asked Mummy outright and she broke down. She blames and blames herself, but it's best I should know, isn't it? It's an unusual disease . . . I don't think I want to remember the name and so I never can, funny, isn't it? Something to do with the nervous system . . . I thought that sort of thing was all in the mind and I wish to God this was but it isn't and there's irony for you. It's so like me to have an obscure disease. They treat me like a broken egg, but I must get things straight, so please will you come, my oldest friend.

Love, Sasha

I remember I knocked over George's bike on the way to my room and didn't pick it up, quite deliberately leaving it there after I had made the motions of stooping and grasping the handlebars.

I sat down on my narrow child's bed in my narrow child's room. I sat there for quite a long time, feeling nerveless and formal, but quite real, quite solid. I noticed little things I took for granted with sharpened clarity – the typewriter with sticking keys, the bookshelf . . . my birthday present. I looked with interest at the spines of the books, thinking to myself that there was not one among them which I had not been required to read or asked to like. The Braque reproduction my mother had issued me with hung askew on the wall. I got up to straighten it, then suddenly, I took it down and put it on the floor face down. I never liked Braque; I didn't know anything about art anyway. I turned to the bookcase and started to unload it, placing the books in even piles on top of the picture, but then I suddenly stopped and returned to the bed where I sat and thought what was the use anyway. I looked around the room again, trying to lodge my eye with something I liked, something personal to me. Sasha was dying. I looked again, but there was nothing, nothing at all there to show I had any preferences, any character. I tried to think of something I liked, but when I did, I couldn't come up with anything. The effort made me feel confused. I flapped my hands a little, not knowing what to do.

I smoked half of five cigarettes, letting the dark grow around me. 'I like cigarettes,' I thought, but then I remembered that countless other people liked cigarettes too. I saw Sasha making a plié on her Florentine balcony. She had said something about the way I smoked, but I couldn't remember. I heard my mother's voice from the kitchen: she was lecturing George. I wrapped myself in the eiderdown and slept deeply until morning.

I awoke the next morning with a comforting sense of a disaster passed, the kind a nightmare sometimes brings in its wake; but when I sat up and saw the letter, I became aware that the wound was on-going.

It was Sunday and my family were reading the papers, calling out to each other snatches of opinion on the state of the world. George was doing exercises on the violin. His room had been partly soundproofed by polystyrene tiles. I would have spoken about it to George, only George was a child. Later I found out what a sentient child he was; he would have been able to sense, if not understand, what I felt. However, the time for that is past. George allows me only now and then to talk of inward things.

I tried to get out of the house unnoticed, but my mother, who had moved alone into the living-room with her coffee, saw me put on my coat.

'Emily, dear, I would like to speak to you if I may.' She smiled professionally. I went in to her, in a curious way glad of her. She sat upright in a round armchair.

'We see you so little now. You know, of course, you slept through supper last night. In fact, since the term began, you've hardly been home at all.' She paused. 'You haven't done your share of the chores.' I looked at her incredulously. Chores. I saw myself, in accelerated motion like Charlie Chaplin, washing dishes, making beds, chopping onions. Yes, work: joy through strength. The film flickered ridiculously through my mind, busy, busy, busy, push, pull . . . I heaved a mountain into place and planted the Red Flag at the top. Maybe she was right. I opened my mouth to speak, but she looked at me hard through the fortification of her black spectacles, thus interrupting me.

'I do not wish to pry into your private life.' She smiled understandingly. 'But it is my responsibility to see that some work is being done by you . . . academically, I mean.' I felt oddly disappointed. 'You must not abuse your privilege, forget the privilege of attending a fine university.

'I think it would be fair of me to ask if your relationship with Peter interferes seriously with your work.'

I said nothing for a while, looking closely at my mother's face in the silence, nearly peering into her face which did not alter in any way its expectation of a reasonable answer. I looked again, trying to make sure she didn't notice anything odd about me, but she didn't.

Then suddenly, I seemed to see my mother at a great distance, as if we spoke to each other across the length of a vacant room: as if some unexpected but mysteriously knowable force had removed the furniture of our life together, leaving the perspective and acoustics of the room completely changed.

As if taking up a suitcase and departing from a former habitation, I said, 'Peter and I are to be married this Christmas.'

I was only a little disappointed that she showed no emotion at my announcement. Indeed, I had hardly expected her to.

'Well, that's nice, dear. Something I think we all expected.' I think she was subtly relieved he was going to make an honest woman of me. For all her bravado, she was her father's child – a Puritan to the bones.

'Of course, we would be very disappointed if you failed to finish your education. You won't find yourself fulfilled in marriage unless you find some outlet for your mind.'

'We work well together,' I said simply. 'Perhaps I will even take a higher degree. You see, Peter has a lot of money.' I must have said this with a bit of a sneer, because she replied with a certain false jauntiness, 'Well, dear, it always comes in handy.'

'You give your permission?' I asked. My head was buzzing with other questions I wanted to ask her, not that any of them were formed. In a way, I wished she would keep me there, press me harder about Peter, the wisdom of our marriage.

Instead, she shrugged slightly. 'You've always been a self-sufficient child, Emily, even when you were a baby.' She had never mentioned my babyhood before; I always went on the assumption that I hadn't had one. She must have fed me and held me and changed me; I looked at her with new curiosity.

'Yes,' she said, responding to my glance, 'you never clung or cried like the others.' Her face, not ordinarily accustomed to sadness, now slacked into sad lines, not wistful, but defeated. She looked a little old. The expression, however, lasted only for a moment. 'I think you have the sense to run your own life; I have never stood in the way of what my children really wanted. I have brought you up to think for yourselves.'

So I took the letter to Peter because I couldn't live alone with it. I felt real urgency, for the first time in my life, to tell someone something. For all my reserve, I knew instinctively that if I did not communicate my news, it would explode internally and poison me. I took myself carefully to his flat, like one with a busting appendix.

I sat on the edge of his bed while he read it. The only shabby thing he allows himself is an old dressing-gown he had at school; in it, with his toes curling and uncurling on the cold floor, he gave my letter his full attention – direct, hard, deductive attention. He looked a little like my idea of Sherlock Holmes. He read the letter several times.

'You're upset, Emily,' he said at last. There was a flicker of accusation in his voice that warned me from elaborating on my emotion.

'I confess I am.' He approved of my answer. He smiled as if to say, 'that's a good girl, you're not giving way to it'. For this self-restraint, I got my reward . . . he actually turned his mind to the problem.

'I am not sure,' he said in a slow hesitating voice, 'but I *think* you may be prematurely anxious about this. I mean, by the law of averages, people very rarely die of diseases without a name; or at least, they generally know the name if they are dying of it.'

That sounded eminently sensible to me. As always in that flat, things had a way of becoming concrete and within my grasp. My life took on a structured quality which it never had before and has never had since. He thought deeply, then spoke again.

'People like Sasha, however, quite often create dramas for themselves, settings like deathbeds and greasepaint of an unhealthy colour in order to get attention. Your friend is not an actress for nothing, you know.'

'I want a cup of coffee.' I let his thought sink in while I almost tenderly made his bed and noted with pleasure that he had been reading a book I had recommended him, *Seven Types of Ambiguity*.

He came back with coffee for us both. He had a meditative look which became him. It is the one mode he has still in which I can remember the need I had for him then.

'If you ask me, which you have done, I would say that Sasha probably wants to attract your attention for a specific reason, and that is not difficult to fathom. She is getting revenge on you for what you did to her over Boris, which is really very stupid of her because she would have found out anyway and I daresay she richly enjoyed the scene, much more than she would have had she found out in the ordinary way.' He paced, smoked and expounded.

'But what should I *do*?' I felt suddenly very comforted in asking him what I should do. His mind, coiled around a question, worked quickly to digest it; his whole face expressed the energy of thinking. His rationality was forceful then; it was that I loved him for.

'The best way to deal with that sort of thing . . . that sort of threat . . . is simply to cooperate. In other words, don't go.' He smiled in the knowledge of my admiration.

'But I must go.' I slurred over his idea, hoping for further direction from him. 'I would never forgive myself.'

'Emily, Emily! that is the first time I have ever caught you out in a lie! You must go because you have to find out.'

We grinned at each other. We both felt moved by his perspicacity.

'Would it make you feel better if I went with you?'

I nodded, warming to the idea of being a little helpless. 'We will go together. Now. And we will get to the bottom of this.'

I watched him dress. He was quick and finicky as a cat. He rubbed a spot off his boot with a little spit.

Half-way there in the car he said, 'I have an idea that this will probably get you over her for good.'

'It's nice of you to help like this.'

'You lay my ghosts, I'll lay yours. I like the way you haven't panicked.'

I was glad of Peter then. He made everything seem so simple. Sitting next to him in his Morris as he skimmed the empty Sunday streets, I felt more for him than I ever had. I can still remember the way he looked, how well he drove, his body correlating perfectly with his eye. Everything about him was distinct – from his clean profile to his spotless cuffs. I wanted to touch him, yet I held him in too great esteem to touch him.

'I told my mother we were getting married,' I said. He watched the road carefully, but he lifted his chin and smiled with satisfaction.

'Fine,' he said. 'That's fine.'

There was no mistaking Sasha's illness. As soon as I saw her, I knew there was no getting round it. She sat in the drawing-room in front of the fire; her whole being was shrivelled and frail from the inside out. Her hands rested slack on her lap; her shoulders sank in indifference to the heat of the fire or to the cold of the draught. The room seemed bigger and chillier in proportion to her frailty.

Nanny had let us in, as unconcerned at who we were as a proprietress of a low boarding-house. She turned her back on us without a greeting and trudged up the stairs ahead of us, wheezing and gripping the heavy banisters as she went. She was wearing old, fluffy bedroom slippers which bulged under the weight of her fat feet. Something, which I presumed to be Sasha's illness, had robbed her of her own sense of presence and importance. Instead of seeming massive, she looked merely fat. She went off to the kitchen, as I'd seen her do many times before, but this time there was something cynical and sluttish in her walk, as if she thought whatever task she was about to do stupid and unimportant.

Mrs Courtney had gone to rest.

Sasha stared at the fire. Whether she was hypnotised by the flames so that she did not hear us come in, or whether she noticed but simply did not care, I could not tell. She looked like the old lady down the road who slowly dies. She looked out of her window, but does not see. Once, David waved to her from the street. She looked away with a kind of sarcasm. Sarcasm and irony go unremarked in the old, but they have it – they have it.

Sasha had become thin and pinched – a little yellow. There were small bruises here and there on her skin. The circles round her eyes had a thick, brownish quality. She wore a white scarf, tied tightly around her head.

'Sasha,' I said. She stirred, but still did not look round. Then she turned her head and looked at me. Her eyes had a frankness in them that I had never seen before; she looked directly into mine. I realise that in previous interchanges she had always looked a little to the side.

'You got my letter,' she said as a statement of fact.

I was too awed by her to speak. Although I am not an intuitive person, I did then have an overwhelming feeling that she was about to die . . . a case where emotional evidence is so strong as to be accepted as datum; and in the face of death, I had nothing to say, nothing at all.

'What's the matter with you, Sasha?' I had forgotten that Peter was there. His voice made me jump – it was phlegmy, as if after a long silence. She looked at him too with a little surprise.

His appearance was strangely, almost dramatically altered, so much so that with a thud of pulse and brain I saw in him another man. His face was flushed, his eyes iridescent, his body tensed. He was moved almost to tears with pity.

She scrutinised his face, and with an odd, puzzled frown, she said, 'I'm not quite sure, some nervous debility I believe. I told Emily in my letter.' It seemed to cost her some effort to be coherent, for she closed her eyes. 'I'm so tired,' she said. Then suddenly, her voice cracking and sliding into a terrible sob, she cried, 'All my hair is falling out.' She put her hands to her head, pulling a little at the scarf and mourned and mourned herself.

It was horrible to watch her. She became a horrible thing I wanted to shun like the pictures of disaster in the newspapers; like a woman losing her child amid the pop of flashbulbs, or the decimated bodies at Belsen.

I had the curious sensation of something happening to me at great speed – something speedy and noiseless like the moment before a terrible car crash, something that was happening to me without my having willed it, something I could observe without horror or despair – a perception into the eye of disaster where everything is perfectly still, void and without a pupil. I hung there in shock while she cried.

Suddenly, breaking the petrified scene with his quick movement, Peter crouched beside her. Eyes shining, trembling like a girl, he was at her feet. 'There . . . there . . . there . . . there . . . Don't cry, don't cry!' He patted her knee almost furiously. 'I'll tell you what. We'll take you to the seaside. Would you like to go to the seaside? Of course you would!

'It really doesn't matter about the stupid hair. You look very nice in that scarf. I shall buy you a new one. How would you like a scarf from Dior? Easily managed, nothing to it. I'm as rich as can be.' He was not quite conscious of what he was saying. He talked reflexively as people do to animals or infants who are dumb in their pain.

And he did comfort her. She did stop that awful noise. I would have shaken her or killed her in a moment to stop that noise. The sound of pain or mourning drives me nearly to a frenzy. But he knew what to do; it had never struck me to do that.

She wiped her eyes and blew her nose on his handkerchief. He was still crouched beside her, but he smiled gently at her now, and gently he took her hand. 'Will you come with us? We'd love to take you out. I imagine you get very bored and turned in on yourself here, don't you?'

She looked at him very solemn and grave. 'Yes,' she said. 'I'll come. I love the sea. They never let me go out now. They are all so unhappy about me, they don't know what to do with me.'

'Now,' he said, getting up; he didn't smooth his trousers as he usually does. 'You'd better get some rest. All that crying and fighting can only make you weaker. You won't get anywhere struggling like that.' He smiled again with an encouraging nod.

Sasha could not take her eyes off him. She rose with a little difficulty, watching him all the time, still very grave and unsmiling. It was a steady gaze that seemed as necessary to her as it would be necessary to fix one's eye on a man who was pulling one out of a heavy sea.

'Goodbye for now.' He stood very still so as not to alarm her. 'We will be back tomorrow morning. We'll make an early start, so be ready at nine. You mustn't let us down. Don't let them keep you in unless the doctor himself says so.'

She nodded and left the room obediently. At the door, she said, 'Thank you, Emily.' Her eyes were quiet. He had made her quiet.

Even at the time I knew we were altered. Of course, I had no way of knowing how much or for how long; but just as there is one, almost imperceptible moment, when I stop and smell the doom of winter in the air each year, so I knew then that the season of Peter and me had changed.

'I think it's time we got drunk,' he said. He put two glasses and a bottle of whisky on his table. He poured it out with a precise and careful movement, measuring it like medicine. He pursed his lips and brusquely handed me the glass. It was a melodramatic thing to do – to suggest we got drunk – but there was something cold and professional in his manner, systematic almost, that frightened me a little.

I was grateful for the warmth that sprang from the whisky. I felt very confused, and I found I could not look at Peter without a sense of embarrassment. He seemed cool enough an hour after the event, almost hard-boiled; but I was embarrassed for what he had done at Sasha's, at how easily his pity was tapped. He saw me look, then avert my eyes. There was a flicker or hostility in his eyes, then he too averted his gaze. 'I suppose I can take it that you are convinced she is ill,' I said at last. My flat voice sounded more emotional than I felt. I felt nothing.

He took another drink, then sank back in his chair. His face fell naturally into an expression of pain; in other words, the few lines that had formed on his face had been formed by that expression. People who have ulcers have a permanently sour, furrowed look which after a while becomes natural to them. At the time I was not aware of the significance of this look, but it was so marked and unselfconscious that I stored it away in my mind.

'I didn't want to get into this, Emily,' he said half to himself. He mused for a moment longer, then pulled himself together with a sharp jerk. He leaned on his elbows, poured some more whisky, then pulled a piece of thread off the carpet. With a little effort, he made his fingers spider-like on the glass-topped table. Abruptly, he changed his tack and lit a cigarette. 'I don't know whether she is ill or not,' he said on an exhalation. 'I think probably she is . . . but she is suffering. Surely that is all that matters.'

I had wanted him to say something else, something more concrete. 'Oh, come on Peter. You've certainly reversed the position you held this morning.'

'This morning I did not know she was suffering.' He stabbed out his cigarette, looking fiercely at the ashtray.

I could not see that it was relevant whether or not she was suffering. For that matter, I could not see what it was to Peter that she suffered. Her suffering was to me merely an ugly gloss on the fact of her imminent death.

Nothing ever mattered to me so much as Sasha's dying. To say I mourned her would be to lie about the truth of my feelings. From the moment I knew for certain that she was mortally ill (and I knew it at once from the stiffness in her bones and the frankness in her eyes), I began to give her up.

As Peter and I sat there, withdrawn from one another by our private visions of her sinking body, I felt a kind of *rigor* paralyse my heart. Perhaps if I could have had a fit of hysterics, I would have been better. Peter has now come to accuse me of not throwing myself about like he does, but I could never let myself do that. At least I can say that I have kept my dignity.

I had never thought about death before. I cannot abide to think of it now. Peter's morbidity sickens me, and in a way it puzzles me too. Death may be fundamental as he says, but unlike sex, it has no use. To me, there is a certain frivolity about death – but then, Peter thinks it leads to something else and I do not . . . or at least if it does, I have long since lost the energy to speculate upon it.

'She is lonely and afraid,' he said, at last breaking the silence. 'There is no alternative but to see her through.'

I saw an alternative, but I sensed that I might lose him if I mentioned it. I must never lose Peter.

NINE

Although it had rained in the night, the dawn of the day was fine. I met Peter at the corner of our road where there was a bus shelter and a small green. My parents were both at work, but I still had an urge for my journey to the country to be formally clandestine. Accidental secrecy was not enough.

For all that the sun was coming out, the weather still forbade a trip to the seaside with an invalid. The leaves were sodden underfoot and breath steamed the air.

I would not have recognised Peter had not the people in the bus-queue stared. He pulled up to the opposite kerb in a blue Mercedes Benz. He looked thin and slightly comic at the wheel of that large car: it made him seem a little small.

'My father didn't like the idea of my taking his car, but when I explained to him about Sasha, he was extremely pleased. He called it an "errand of mercy", really he did.' Peter laughed unpleasantly.

'You did go to see him again after all.'

'Well, we couldn't take her anywhere in that old Morris, could we?' He snapped at me irritably and fiddled incompetently with the switch to the heater. The car was already too hot; its suspension was too smooth; its seats too comfortable. I felt drowsy and began to have a headache.

'He treated me like the prodigal son, emphasising "prodigality" more than sonship. He thinks it's all due to you – I mean my request for the car – he thinks it means you have turned me back on the straight path. This hulk is the fatted calf, his most prized possession.' He hit the dashboard contemptuously.

Sasha and her family had been waiting for us in the drawing-room. Sasha reclined slightly in her mother's chair. She was wrapped up in a fur coat several sizes too large for her. It seemed to be her mother's coat, but I could not remember having seen it before. A pile of rugs had been placed on her lap. She wore gloves and a long knitted scarf, a badly made thing in bright pink – a colour which never suited her complexion at its best. She gave the impression of a huge doll, a guy perhaps, which had been dressed in a millionaire's nursery: she lay that still and expressionless.

Mrs Courtney sat in a hard-backed chair at right angles to Sasha. There were signs about her of earlier weeping. She looked slouched and tired, but her eyes moved perpetually, first to Sasha, then to herself, as if something could be done by her eyes to enliven Sasha.

Nanny sat opposite Sasha on the chintz sofa. She watched Sasha with the concentration of a snake. Her head swayed slightly as she stared, but the stare had no effect on Sasha.

Peter took Mrs Courtney's hand and introduced himself. She fidgeted with his hand, not shaking it but holding it as if he were a familar friend. 'You will take care of her, won't you?' she asked him confidentially. 'She's been quite insistent on going . . .' she broke off, but her look eloquently expressed how she had never been able to deny Sasha anything. 'Haynes said it would be all right,' she muttered. I assumed that Haynes was Sasha's doctor. I tried to catch Mrs Courtney's eye, but she was all for Peter.

He responded by fervently pressing her hand. 'Of course we will take good care of her. Of course we will. I have my father's car. It's very warm and comfortable, and as soon as she shows any signs of strain at all, we'll bung her in and come straight back home. You see, I think the sea air and a change will do her an enormous amount of good.' Peter was as familiar with Mrs Courtney as if she had been his aunt. I would have said he recognised her from somewhere.

She smiled up at him, grateful for a man, and nodded over and over to herself – a little gesture Sasha had inherited from her. 'Yes, yes, now you say it, I am sure it will be good for her.'

Still, she fluttered over Sasha until we were out of the house. 'You won't get cold, will you darling? You won't exhaust yourself?' She kissed Sasha and breathed on her unconsciously. 'You will take care driving?' Almost every remark that I ever heard Mrs Courtney make took the form of a question. Sasha looked at her mother as if to beg her to stop. She was very much bundled up and her face looked small amid the furs. I watched the sorrow which Peter had damped down flare up again, distorting Mrs Courtney's face, I left the room quickly, my modesty offended by such nakedness.

It took us some time to get out of London. Peter had some difficulty in manoeuvring the car. He tugged awkwardly at the steering-wheel, making arcs round corners too wide for safety. I could see why Peter's father had been reluctant to lend him the car. It was obvious from the traces he had left behind that he took the car seriously. There was a pair of handsome pigskin gloves folded neatly on the dashboard; a freshly laundered yellow dust-cloth lay next to them. Even though I was not familiar with such cars, I still noticed an irregular number of dials and appendages to the instrument panel.

I sat behind Peter and Sasha. I felt uncomfortable both outwardly and inwardly. I did not like the cushioned motion of the car and the smell of polish and new rubber. Luxury of that kind stiffens me so that all my movements feel forced in its presence. I refused to give way to the expanse of the foam seat. I sat tight and awkward watching the backs of Peter and Sasha.

Peter cuts his hair unusually short. I suppose he thinks the ascetic qualities in his face are enhanced by this, but from the back, his head looks shorn unnaturally, like a prisoner. Now and then our eyes met in the rear-view mirror; impersonal, they were, both his and mine from our intense awareness of Sasha's presence. She had not spoken since we left her house; her whole body radiated a deep dejection. She looked this way and that out of the windows, but briefly and without keen interest. She shrunk into the comfort of the seat; she seemed to be received by it.

Once out of London, Peter became less tensely preoccupied with the road. All of a sudden, she pulled herself up with an effort and spoke. Although her voice was small and broken, we were both startled to hear it.

'What are you studying?' she asked Peter. She gave the question a sound of importance as if she had been thinking for a while how to phrase it.

'Archaeology. It's a long process.' He spoke with deprecating modesty as if to excuse his studying at all. 'I suppose I shall have my doctorate in a year or two; then I shall be all set to dig things up.'

She paused for such a long time that I thought she had forgotten him. 'Do you have to have a doctorate to dig things up?' From her slow way of speaking, she appeared to be genuinely interested to know the answer.

'Oh, heavens, no! I've already dug up a great deal. I've tunnelled through cairns in Scotland and been through Brittany like a mole, but only in the capacity of a navvy. One is made to feel very lucky to be allowed to exhaust oneself with a pick and shovel. I've lived in the most appalling conditions, eaten the dreariest food and endured the harshest weather without the pay they'd give to a ditch-digger. No, when I get my degree, I shall be able to organise digs and oversee other sweating students. It's a bit like the fagging system. I shall richly enjoy sending them down into muddy pits.' He talked nervously, making his vowels brittle and flat, employing the clipped consonants of their common class.

'Ancient civilisations . . .' she said, pronouncing each syllable slowly and lovingly as if the very thought charmed her. 'I think I'd like to find out about ours, Celts and Druids . . . not so much about what they used as about what they thought.'

'Actually, that is my main interest – Celtic prehistory. But the Saxon tribes and the Scandinavians interest me as well. I would really like to find out how our ancestors stood before the Romans, before Christinaity . . . before all of these more familiar ideas took hold. The Church, for instance, was very clever in building on rather than destroying ancient beliefs. I mean they regarded converted peoples to a certain extent as valid organic societies. Some of the Breton saints are actually pagan gods translated into a Christian ideal . . . but I'm sure they adopted cultural ideas as well . . . or rather that the people never really threw out certain ideals. Here! I'm giving you a lecture. Am I tiring you?' His voice had an animated, happy sound.

'No, go on . . .' I caught something of her old energy in her tone.

'I have a strong, and perhaps romantic suspicion that in these highly superstitious cultures there was a thread of crude moral consciousness. Of course, there are so many threads – the Phoenecians brought influences from Mycenae . . . you can tell that in the design of the dolmens at Carnac – that it is difficult to untangle them and come out with any clear vision of an aboriginal idea. But still, it is my view that each thread survives in this braid-like structure. You can tell this from the way some ideas co-exist in one modern mind . . . ideas which are quite inconsistent with each other. Take, for instance, the Norse emphasis on an insane kind of courage in battle. A man who went berserk in a fight – a berserker, he was called – was the most respected member of the community. He was holy. Now that is quite inconsistent with turning the other cheek, with Christ's disapproval of St Peter's violence. Yet my father holds to a stern Norse view of courage in a way which is totally inconsistent with the religion he claims to believe in. I'm not saying that the two ideas are necessarily incompatible. I just think that our interpretation of Christianity is shot through with more ancient attitudes.'

He had spoken with considerable energy. What he had said was clearly of some personal importance to him. We had never spoken much of his work before. With a mild sense of confusion, I realised that I had not asked him about it.

'I try to keep myself clean from society, from any of its formulated ideas. Almost everything we feel we think has barbaric origins.' His voice was full of that fastidious pride which still feeds so deeply on his character. I knew how he had raised one eyebrow when he spoke.

'Barbaric?' Sasha asked with mild surprise. 'What do you mean by "barbaric"? Do you have contempt for what you study?'

Her tone was lighter, less muffled that it had been. He had excited her curiosity. All the same, he looked at her mistrustfully. She had this way of wounding feelings accidentally. Her interest in people was so prodigious, her ability to criticise so deficient that she would point out moral flaws in one without the faintest notion that she might have been offensive. She spoke of faults and virtues as one who, puzzled by an object, takes it to the window for closer inspection. It was the quality of satisfied curiosity in her voice which confounded anger in her friends. 'Oh, *that's* the way you are,' she seemed to say. In her own way, Sasha was a scientist. Peter evidently recognised this, for he replied without rancour.

'Contempt? Not in any particular way towards the ancients. For humanity in general, yes, I suppose I have contempt.' Peter is an ass. He does not, nor did he ever, have anything like a proper contempt for humanity.

'Really?' She sounded gently disappointed. I longed to see her face.

'I spent,' he said, forcefully changing gear, 'the better part of my life in public schools. If it isn't barbaric sending a small child away to be brought up by strangers I'd like to know what it is. It took me two years at Cambridge to realise exactly what had hit me.' He paused to steady his voice. 'And since the customs of our upper middle class have damaged the better part of my nature, it is my mission to discover their most profound roots.'

'I thought archaeologists were mainly concerned with opening tombs.' It was clear that she referred in her mind the subject of tombs to her own imminent death. Peter took her up very quickly to staunch her thoughts.

'Oh, they are, they are and so am I . . . tombs and analysing potsherds. A most absorbing task, putting together potsherds – great precision, great concentration is required. I also like solving mysteries. I confess to a great admiration of Sherlock Holmes.' The corner of his eye sought Sasha's face.

She looked at him for a moment with wan gratitude. I saw her profile clearly. 'That's who you remind me of,' she said after a pause. 'I knew it was someone. You remind me of Sherlock Holmes.'

Peter, flattered, spurted the car ahead at greater speed. I was annoyed by his susceptibility to such a very little bit of praise.

Neither of them spoke for a while. She sank back again into the seat and rested her head on her hand. The car slicked along the country road, silent as a glider in the air. The richly lined interior absorbed all incidental noise so that the silence became unnatural . . . deaf silence. I became impatient for one of them to speak again.

'When you talk of ancient peoples, ancient beliefs, it makes me think of Nanny,' she said at length, so softly that I could barely hear her. Peter's back stiffened with attention.

'I used to live by Nanny's omens, her own personal form of magic; I know Mummy did, though since I've been ill, neither of them has touched the cards . . . you know, they read Tarot cards once a week, every Thursday afternoon. It became quite impossible for me in the end to support such a weight of superstitions, even a flock of birds had some immanence. What was so intolerable was that I lived always for what might happen, never for what was happening. Now that I know what is going to happen – and that is the last thing on earth I wish to have happen – I feel freer somehow. I love Nanny terribly, you know: she has more strength than any of us. Whatever is truly primitive in her is good. After my father had left us and we were all so upset – frightened really I suppose – she would simply hold me for an hour at a time. She never had to be told that I was unhappy; she sensed it.'

'What do you mean by truly primitive?'

'Oh, unselfconscious,' she said quickly, 'like Adam and Eve.'

'You're a Rousseauist, then, believing in the noble baby and the noble savage.'

'I don't think I am. After all, I just said I thought poor Nan had done us wrong to ply us all with superstitions and that I had been wrong to believe them. I don't think anyone's very noble really. What I think is that we're all basically lovable – but that sounds a bit foolish.' She shrugged and smiled apologetically. Her strength had rallied a little as she talked.

'Not if you really mean it,' he said grimly. She ignored his remark and fell to gazing out of the window.

'When do we reach the sea?' she asked after a while. Peter had been driving badly. His back was hunched with brooding – an unusual posture for Peter who as a rule had a military bearing.

'In about half an hour,' he said. He looked at her (I saw him in the mirror) with curious force. His eyes were all alive with an unidentifiable feeling.

'Have you ever thought about what a tidal wave would be like?' She asked him the question as if she wanted to know what specifically he thought.

He hesitated. 'Yes, I have.'

'I tried to write a poem once about a tidal wave. It sounded so much like Shelley that I tore it up. I don't think I had much idea of what a tidal wave would be like then. The idea of being crushed seemed romantic to me then.'

' "A wave to pant beneath thy power" . . . I know.' He paused. 'I used to write poetry,' he added. I saw the back of his neck turn red.

'Did you?' She looked at him, and although I could not see her face, I knew she looked admiringly. 'What sort of poetry?'

'Quite honestly, I'd forgotten all about it until you mentioned it. It wasn't good poetry. I don't know if it was poetry at all. I wrote about preoccupations, obsessions . . . a lot about hermits and saints living at the top of towers.'

'Oh, I know, St Simon Stylites.'

'Yes. That's the one . . . and St Anthony in the desert. I wrote about him too.'

'You sound disillusioned, like a lapsed Catholic. Are you a lapsed Catholic?' Her voice was gentle and inviting of confidences.

'No. I was a madman.'

'Oh, come, Peter. It isn't mad to write about the saints.' There was a cajoling, almost flirtatious undertone to her remark.

'He means,' I said, 'that he was quite literally mad.'

She was still for a long moment. I saw his eyes in the mirror. They cast about to find mine.

'I knew you had suffered something,' she said quietly.

'Most people condemn it as a form of wickedness,' he murmured.

'Do they really? How extraordinary!' she said. For a while, they were both quite solemn.

It is hard to write such things; of such things it is hard to tell.

My life now, my adult life, the only span of time of which I will be aware . . . I let the thread of it fall each day unnoticed to the ground. I am no longer concerned with what tangles the yarn. I am either above this concern or beyond it – I think I am – as unconcerned as I am about the cat in my mother-in-law's knitting-basket. I do not care to knit, nor do I care to make aesthetic patterns of my life.

Peter and Sasha are my proof against such folly. He gives, she gave such tangles and twists the name of suffering. The word gave her and gives him meaning. After his attempted suicide, he raved on at me well into the night about his guilt, which consisted of a retreat from suffering . . . something about the wickedness of despair, something about an acceptance of pain because of the crucifixion of Christ. I didn't understand a word of it.

What maddens me is their lack of commonsense, their lack of practical animal commonsense. In the face of pain what animal would not retreat from it? Any rat flees pain, and if the pain is inevitable, the creature fights back, snarls from its corner. I can see the point of Peter's self-destruction far better than I can understand his present insistence on accepting misery. He's gone behind my back again and seen some priest. I know it . . . just as he went to see Sasha, just as he sought his psychiatrist. He will hurl himself against every possible door until one gives.

I, on the other hand, have my pain which is ceaseless and dull. She never knew about it. I've never told him. My pain started years ago, sometime after she was dead. My pain is that I think without respite day and night. I think in long sentences and paragraphs. I think in pages. There are appendices to my thought which is not philosophy but compulsive action of the brain.

I can no longer stare out of the window, listen to music or to someone else's conversation without articulated thought forming in my mind. Each feeling clots too quickly on my brain and dries in scabs of words.

That is how I look upon it sometimes. At other times, I see not the content of my thought but the form of it as being architectural – a wall of thought, elastic and contracting like a metal watch bracelet. I think, therefore I am not.

But no matter how great the pain of this contraction, I will not call for help; I will not give it the name of suffering. Suffering requires the audience of God. And how can I accept the existence of God when I am not really certain of the evidence of my own being, when I know that Sasha realised herself only through what hurt her?

On that October day, I was, however, younger and had not begun to think. So I drew my coat around me and pretended to sleep.

We reached our destination at about eleven. Peter had taken us to a place near Eastbourne. It is called 'The Seven Sisters' because of seven chalk cliffs which range around the shore. Peter remembered it from childhood. His aunt lived nearby and had taken him often to see the cliffs when he was a child. It was so like Peter to have ignored the unsuitability of the place for an invalid. The only descent to the shingle was a steep staircase gouged out in the cliff-face and reinforced by wood. Besides, a thick mist had settled beneath the brow of the cliff.

Sasha got painfully out of the car. Peter did not look at her, but he seemed tensely aware of her. Sasha stood in the car park. Shivering in her fur coat she moved unsteadily across the gravel like a new-born foal. After a moment or two, she stood with greater confidence. Her face was wretchedly pale, but her eyes were changed. Her vision, now alive and well, took excited flight and darted here and there to swoop and catch impressions of the place.

'It's a long way down,' he said. 'Are you sure you'll be all right? We could go someplace else.'

'No, no,' she replied with a touch of impatience.

The car park was large, built to accommodate a great number of summer trippers. There was a green shack at one end where a hand-painted sign said TEAS. We were the only people there except for an old man, who on seeing us came out of a little hut and, slinging a ticket-machine over his shoulder, advanced slowly towards us across the wide expanse of deserted ground. We waited, Peter and I, still and shivering for him to come; but Sasha struck out for the cliff's edge over which the mist puffed like steam over the edge of a cauldron. The old man made a great business of selling Peter a ticket, twirling the paper from the machine with exaggerated style. He was nervous and fumbled a bit. He seemed to care about what we thought of him. He did not seem to notice how monstrous the car looked all alone like that with its pompous bulk and sneering bonnet.

'Let's go down,' Sasha said when we reached her. She was excited. Peter drew a glance from me.

We descended carefully the long stairs into the mist which grew thicker around the bottom. The steep cliffs were hardly visible. They looked like ponderous shadows and seemed, through the mist, to have an oily texture. The water gurgled and lapped around the shingle.

'I'm afraid this is a terrible day,' Peter said apologetically. His voice sounded muffled in the fog.

'Oh, but the air is good. The moisture feels so good on the face!' she replied enthusiastically. When we reached the shingle, she stood for a moment looking about her, then she started to run. I could see her, her mother's fur coat flapping heavily behind her. She looked weighted down with it and she made very slow progress across the thick shingle.

'I don't think you ought to run,' Peter called after her.

'But I will!' she called back. 'This coat is too heavy. I'm going to take it off.' She threw it down on a rock.

I stood at the bottom of the cliff and looked up. I could see only to the middle of the staircase; I felt as if I were underneath the grey sea.

Peter started after Sasha, picking up her coat as he went. The coat swung out and made a rippling noise. He laughed, a delight concealed in his laugh. 'Put this on, you silly girl. You'll catch cold!'

She laughed and spurted ahead. There was a sound of abandonment and pure enjoyment in her laugh. Soon, she almost disappeared from sight, taking Peter with her.

I walked to the water and stared into it. The waves were grey as the mist; they came up in short agitated little curls. The mist smelt heavily of salt, and all natural sounds were thickly muffled by it. I heard deafly their boots plunging into the shingle; their voices had the quality of song. They called to one another like birds flinging wind from their wings above the ocean.

Peter hove into sight for a moment. His face was pink and pretty as a boy's. He skipped three stones across the water, taking pleasure in his skill; then suddenly, he flung himself back into the mist, taking no thought on his change of direction; like a boy, he turned on the ball of his foot with energy and speed. He crashed strongly up the shingle towards her voice which called his name.

I stood still and watched the water roll. After a while, my eye became bloated with the spectacle of waves.

At the moment I write, I wish with the might of a child that she were still alive. It is true that a large part of me hated her – still hates her – but there was something in my total feeling for her that focused my mind. I watched Sasha the way an aerialist watches his partner across the high wire. She balanced my mind and channelled it towards herself. Now she is gone I feel there is something about my being and my life I can't quite grasp.

Of course I realise now that I wanted her to die. I am intelligent enough in retrospect to admit what I was too dishonest to see then; but what I cannot understand fully is why I wanted her to die. While I watched the waves I was filled with high feelings I did not choose to describe to myself. I now recognise it as exaltation and relief . . . partly that, but there is something else I can't quite get to.

I made my mind busy with thoughts of death . . . made death posies in my head to throw upon the water for Ophelia. I watched the sea for signs of Charon's boat, thinking myself clever for matching the desolation of the place to the River Styx.

I remember now that I remembered then how Sasha and I had taken a long walk one summer morning. We had started out in Sloane Square and went, via the park, all the way to Kensington High Street. We meant to take the bus, but never really looked for one because we were enjoying the day.

We passed the Albert Memorial. Since childhood, that monument has given me dark qualms. Albert, sitting under his huge black canopy, was to me at nine the king of death overlooking the kingdom of death.

Peter and his Egyptians! All of Peter's fears are contained in the stomach of that old prince.

'In memory of Albert,' Sasha had said, looking up at it while I did my best to look at it without betraying my fear. 'The poor dear queen must have had a very bad memory if it had to be prodded with that. It's something a bit more than tying a knot in a handkerchief, isn't it!' She laughed at her own joke; and I remembered as I stood by the sea that she made a face at Albert. The memory of her puckered-up face made me shake my head at how she had tempted fate.

'I don't see how they could have called that style Gothic,' she went on, 'when the whole point of Gothic is different.' She looked up at it again and shook her head. 'Oh, ye of little faith,' she said.

I cannot say that Sasha was exactly insensitive, but she had a way of tripping involuntarily over the wires that held up other people's fates; of snarling people together; of stirring up their disguised feelings.

I remember we walked on to the shops. She bought a pair of electric green shoes and embarrassed me by swaggering past unsuitable men. After an Italian workman had breathed some appreciative remark down her neck, she seemed satisfied and we went home by bus.

Looking out to the sea, I wrung my hands and thought of irony. At last, my mind feeling stale and unsatisfied, I turned and strove up the bank of shingle. Sasha was sitting on a rock; she was flushed and sweaty and out of breath. Her actual presence made me uncomfortable again. Peter stood above her and looked sadly at the shingle. He did not acknowledge me as I came up; instead, he scuffed his toe on a rock. I concluded that they had finished their romp and had been waiting for me.

Sasha looked inquisitively at me as I approached; then she looked at Peter. She had the look of one attentive to important, distant sounds.

'I think we'd better have lunch,' Peter said. 'Do you think you could eat, Sasha?' He was polite but I got the impression that he had been disturbed by something.

'I've got an appetite for the first time in months,' she said, looking up and smiling. I felt that she too was uncomfortable.

We all looked up at the steep stairs we had to climb, then dejectedly at each other.

'Well,' said Peter, 'I suppose we'd better assail the Eiger face.' She smiled at his remark.

He stood over her, waiting for her to rise which she did slowly. He fiddled nervously with a stone. Suddenly he threw the stone to the ground with surprising force. She was so watchful of him that I wondered what had occurred between them while I had been staring at the sea. For all that she was tired, she concentrated intensely on Peter.

'What a stupid thing to do, to bring you all the way down here!' he cried vehemently.

'Never mind,' she said gently. 'Never mind, I've really enjoyed myself.' She put a few fingers on his arm but withdrew them as soon as she saw him stiffen at her touch.

She found the climb quite an effort. Peter had to support her the whole way. I waited until they had nearly reached the top, then slowly I started the ascent, leaving the shingle cuffed and spoiled behind me.

Peter would have done well as an impresario. His money is to him an extra limb with which he arranges scenes and actors around him. Even when he was quite young, as he was then, he used his money in this way. I, his constant prima ballerina, have danced about his sets to serve his mutilated emotions, wearing this frock, striking that attitude until the motion has exhausted me. But Sasha, ironically enough, never took the stage although he tried to make her – or, at least, she never took it on his terms. She transmuted what he gave her into her own interpretation of herself and never even bothered to show gratitude for things.

On this occasion, Peter had brought out of his hat a cosy restaurant in a wood near Tunbridge Wells. Smoke curled from the chimney through the trees; the window panes were leaded. It looked like the dwarves' cottage in *Snow White*.

The place inside was deep brown and lit by firelight. We were seated in a dark corner. A few chrysanthemums stood in a vase on the table.

Peter had been silent and agitated in the car on the way from the sea. He now rubbed his hands and smiled with satisfaction as we took our places. I think he had worried that the restaurant might be vulgar with horse brasses and artificial flowers. Such things are very important to his well-being.

He now inhaled deeply the smell of wood fire, the chrysanthemums, and looked at her and me. She too inhaled the scent of the room, more deeply than he had. The smell of a mixture of foods permeated the place. She smiled. Her eyes had gained a quality of depth from the surroundings. She had slept in the car and looked refreshed.

'How do you feel, Sasha?' I hastened to cover up the sound of strain in my voice with a smile. She looked from me to Peter and from Peter to me. Although she smiled, she appeared to be puzzled by something.

'Oh much better, darling. Much better for the fresh air and the sleep.'

Peter touched her arm, and although she did not draw back, her fingers flickered on the table-cloth. I realised that we had both been staring at her hard. I looked away.

'I've ordered you a very light meal. A cheese soufflé, then a little fish and a light white wine. I hope you can manage it.'

Peter played with a bread stick, one of the Italian kind, dry and crisp like thin bone. Peter drew round the table-cloth endlessly his own monogram, PM, PM, tracing it on to the linen.

His aunt gave us a monogrammed damask table-cloth for a wedding present. I never thanked her for it because it was stupid of her to think that we would ever use a monogrammed table-cloth.

Sasha had relapsed into stillness. every now and then she would do this: let her body fall like a sack, her eyes staring away reflectively. She had never been reflective in the past, despite her tendency to daydream. She had always been responsive in company. She hauled herself up, now and then, to attend to what was going on.

I think I'll use Aunt Winifred's table-cloth for Peter's shroud. I think I could just about carry it off.

Peter fidgeted until I thought I would scream. He snapped the bread stick into minute pieces and ate them one by one.

They brought Sasha her soufflé. The wine was subtly sweet, suggesting a whole breezy summer. Peter would bottle all experience if he could. I remember the day so well. Details spill over in my mind.

Sasha ate her soufflé wearily. Peter and I watched her as she ate. She glanced up at us with a mild but slightly mistrustful look of an animal interrupted by stares in the middle of its feed. I was embarrassed, and looked instead on what I was eating – although I cannot remember what it was I ate. Food is a nuisance to me and I have little sympathy with the appetites of others. At one time, however, I used to enjoy watching Sasha eat. In Italy, I enjoyed watching her eat. She devoured platters of pasta and zabaglione. She would hang over an ice-cream cone, rolling her tongue around it, having so much pleasure from the ice-cream that she seemed to enjoy the excess of it which splashed to the hot pavement, the glutinous stains on her skirt. She wore sunglasses too. They made her look enigmatic as she enjoyed her ice-cream.

She ate her soufflé with a look of stifled nausea on her face, as if she ate it to be polite to Peter whom she watched with great care and attention.

Peter has a curious attitude to food. It disgusts him and he eats very little, yet he knows all about it. He can order a perfect menu at a restaurant, but once faced with it, he can only nibble at the edges of each dish. I think he worries about the morality of eating at all.

It began to rain lightly outside and a little wind had got up; I could hear it in the chimney.

We were the only occupants of the dining-room. The restaurant seemed to be run by a family or a group of friends. There was the sound of talking from the kitchen, talking in a low, familiar key, and the clash of cutlery being washed or sorted. The silence we found ourselves in became uncomfortable. I wished I could think of something to say.

'What did you do before you fell ill?' Peter asked. His question sounded out of place. He spoke as if being ill were an occupation in itself.

'I was studying to be an actress,' she replied, a faint tinge of surprise in her voice. She looked at him alertly, aware that he knew this already. I telescoped myself the better to listen.

'I had to stop some time ago because of the exhaustion . . . no, that's not altogether true. I stopped partly because I no longer wanted to be an actress.' She made a broad, dismissive actress's gesture. She laughed into her glass with her new sarcasm.

'You look so surprised, Emily. Did I go on about it that much to you?' I said nothing, but felt puzzled by the way she spoke. There seemed to be in her mind a new connection between ideas. Her whole aspect was changed as if she had aged. She seemed in slower gestures and more careful speech – even in her sense of irony – to have gathered time into herself; to have sucked it up over a short period; digested it and become older.

Indeed, although I didn't recognise it then, she had discarded her old jauntiness, her manner of the precocious child. Having drastically altered time in herself, she confused me.

'What made you want to be an actress in the first place?' He spoke abruptly and made her start. As she had acquired age, so she had acquired a certain dignity which made Peter's question seem a little impertinent. However, as she seemed anxious about Peter in some way, she smiled encouragingly at him.

Peter casually tapped the tines of his fork on his plate, masking with the gesture his eagerness to hear her answer. He took a bite of food without much apparent pleasure or appetite.

The white scarf which she wore had fallen a bit over her brow. In this position, with its folds and amplitude, the scarf had the look of a nun's wimple. It set off her weary face, contained the weariness within its bounds so that her exhaustion seemed to come from too strenuous an inner life.

Sasha was a capitalist with time. She invested herself in every moment of her life so that everything with her seemed doubly real and doubly felt.

'I wanted to live more,' she said after a moment's thought. Peter's eyes, his grey eyes with their snapping, lashless lids, showed such an extraordinary interest in what she had said that they seemed almost independent of his face. His face was carefully in repose.

She met his stare with her own eyes, but she met it obliquely as if some idea of him were taking form in her mind. I could not tell what this idea was, but it seemed important as, having thought it, she sat back on the cushioned seat, placed her hands in her lap, and gave up time to see him.

Peter put down his fork and acknowledged her vision of him with a quick look of uneasy surprise.

I remember with what wonder I prized his elegant shoulders, his wary, intelligent face. I always liked particularly the fullness of his lower lip.

Sometimes, when I least expect it, even now, I am seized by the image of Peter swamped by a feeling of awe at his every aspect. I am tortured by greed for every detail of him, his hands, his forehead, his eyebrows so that I can hardly bear to look at him until the moment passes.

The food was particularly delicate and well-prepared, but each bite I took made my stomach bulge with nausea. We ate as a polite distraction from what was really going on. We made our jaws work by conscious effort, not in the normal automatic way.

'An actress,' she said at length, 'has life written for her . . . *lives*! At one time I thought I would like to be a thousand different women. I was overwhelmed by a kind of delirium at all that choice. Wouldn't it be wonderful, I thought, to pick and choose one's character luxuriously, like from an enormous box of chocolates! Now I am reduced to being one woman . . . a lady of reduced circumstances.' She laughed at her own joke with genuine amusement.

Peter laughed too. When he laughed, his face had a soft, happy look that it never achieved at any other time.

'But why did you change your mind?' I asked, unable to contain my curiosity any longer.

She looked at me queerly for a moment, her fork poised over her fish. 'Boris made me change my mind,' she said flatly. 'The circumstances of our break-up forced me to see what I was, and after that there seemed little point in trying to be anyone else.' There was a hard edge on her dispassionate voice which made me think she struggled not to wince when she spoke.

I battled with an obscure fear. The glistening sauce seemed a reproach; the goodness of the wine seemed a reproach. I looked down at my plate. She looked at me with sudden earnestness, as if to reach out, but Peter interrupted our first contact of eyes.

'But Boris is the biggest actor out,' he blurted. 'I know Boris well,' he added in a quieter tone seeing how intense her expression became at his words.

'I'll warrant you that I know Boris better!' said she, laughing aloud almost hysterically. 'Of course, he's an actor. He takes his fantasy life to fanatical extremes. He was far more audacious that I ever was!' She fumbled at her handbag, an ugly pouchy thing, her favourite (she had had it from our days at school). 'Do you know he gave me this?' She placed, as a card player reveals a crucial ace, a diamond stick pin upon the table. The gem sparkled wondrously in the muted light; pronouncing its true worth.

'It's real,' she said, her eyes narrowing. 'I had it valued.' She spoke incisively, drawing her lips back from her teeth. After a moment, she went on more quietly. 'It's from his family. I wish he had given me anything less valuable, anything at all, but I must return this before I . . .' She put the gem back in her handbag, and leaned with her eyes closed against the back of the seat. 'I can't eat any more,' she said.

'Surely you can't want to have anything to do with him after the way he treated you!' Peter spoke so loudly and sharply that we both stared at him. He withdrew slightly from us and straightened up his shoulders. She cast her eyes down for a moment, then swept them up, giving Peter a shrewd look. She pursed her mouth with the faintest touch of impatience.

'You seem to assume,' she said good-naturedly and at odds with the expression in her eyes, 'that he treated me badly. I was brought up on that assumption myself – that a man is always to blame. Poor Mummy has always been helpless because she thinks she is helpless, because she just naturally supposes that my father damaged her beyond repair when he went. I flung myself at Boris. I went to bed with him against my conscience in order to indulge my greedy feelings. I would have to sink to the depths of hypocrisy to blame him utterly for what happened.' Here her expression abruptly changed. 'Besides . . . in his own way, in his own way, he treated me well.' She paused, but neither of us spoke nor hardly dared to breathe for fear of disrupting the passionate flow of her narrative.

'You talk about acting a bit contemptuously, as if it were immoral the way the Puritans thought. Is there no ritual in your life? Have you no idea of yourself that you wish to urge on others? Have you never wanted to put yourself in someone else's shoes, feel their feelings and think their thoughts in order to identify the better with their lot?' She leaned forward falling on her elbows rather than putting them on the table. Her hands trembled and she spoke with great urgency.

'Everyone acts out his own belief about himself. Only some of us have more than one belief. Boris was serious with me; that you must believe. He was serious with Vernon too. Boris was inconsistent with me, that is all.' She finished the sentence triumphantly. Clearly, it had cost her something to arrive at this conclusion.

'I thought you said you decided that acting was a useless profession,' I said.

'I said I stopped wanting to be an actress because I took it much too far. Vernon wants Boris for what he is most importantly to himself; I took him, wanted him, loved him for what he pretended to be and because he took me for what I pretended to be . . . only, only I was unaware that I loved his supporting role and he was unaware that he loved my prima donna.' She tried to laugh, but her voice cracked with weariness. Suddenly, tears began to ooze from her closed eyes. Her eyelids were translucent. They shivered a little, shaking the tears out. The tears shone in the bruised circles around her eyes. The flush from the sea air had disappeared from her face like wiped-off rouge. Her cheeks were sallow. She did not move her head to hide the tears, and her body crumpled as if from an inward blow.

Peter looked down at the cold, half-eaten food upon his plate. His face flushed violently. Some emotion had flooded the capillaries in his skin so that his cheeks looked smitten by the inner force of blood. 'Don't cry! Stop crying! Stop crying this instant!' His voice shook with the sound below it of chaotic rage. He scraped his chair against the floor; he knocked his cutlery. I was terrified by his violence. I thought he might strike her. Then suddenly, in one of those instantaneous flashes of knowledge, I saw what to do with Peter. I turned my face to him and stared at him with a peculiar coldness and distaste, as if he were a drunken stranger. He saw, because he was watching for someone to give it, my stinging command; and in a moment, he dropped his gaze and threw away his anger. His body trembled slightly everywhere, as if his nerves had been unstrung from some central point of control. I turned half-way to Sasha, but when I saw her face, I looked away.

She had opened her eyes at Peter's command and meekly obeyed it; yet, when she had seen what had passed between us, her eyes widened in surprise. Her grey, tearful eyes were caught by the transaction between us the way a child's eyes are when he is interrupted in some petty sorrow by a greater emergency.

She never lost her childlike quality. She had in her, before her death, the elements of old age and of childhood.

I have no sentimentality about children. In fact, I dislike them. On the ordered social surface of my brain I have the ordered normal reaction to children. I give away the money Peter gives me to children's charities; but each year I live, the surface of my mind becomes more brittle. Like old paving-stones which crack, the surface gives way to life beneath.

A child is a greedy, suckling animal. If you look at children objectively, you will see that even their pretty wrapping of clear eyes and pure skin is only another tool for survival. Most people would kill their children if children were not beautiful. A child is the coldest creature on earth and the most parasitical. If you observe a child at play, you find the original scientist, the original intellectual. No movement is without purpose, the one purpose that is pitched to the intensity of lust, and that lust is for knowledge . . . of the geometry of bricks, of the properties of clay, of the use of its hands and eyes, of the power of the word.

'I'm sorry, Sasha,' Peter said when he had recovered himself.

'There's nothing to be sorry for,' she replied. Her voice, always musical, had a slight crack in it, so that when she spoke each word sounded new, as if it cracked with freshness. 'I cry very easily. Emmy can tell you; I cry at the cinema.'

'Sasha even cries at the opera.' There was eagerness in my tone that I had not meant to put there.

'You were right to stop me, really. Self-pity is an awful bore and will get me nowhere.' There was something graceful in her manner, yet not soft. She looked warily at Peter. Sasha had emotional agility the way a dancer has physical agility. She was capable of sustained balance on her toes, and able to leap to abnormal heights with great speed and seeming effortlessness.

All emotion was now gone from Peter's face. He now looked at her as if she were a difficult problem in chess. She, with the manner of someone playing something swifter and less intellectual sat slightly back and erect. She looked as if she had been playing an expensive poker game well into the night.

His move was to leave the table which he did abruptly. As he left, he smiled at me fully, a great flare of warmth. The smile still puzzles me. It disturbed me then because it made me feel that the conversation had been about something I did not understand.

Sasha and I were left alone. We sat facing each other across the table. The purple chrysanthemums had not been smartly arranged as they might have been in a city restaurant. The stems had been left on and not trimmed to a low height and made artificial and stylish. The flowers were tall, upright, and stiff so that their neat heads interrupted my line of vision. Whenever I looked at Sasha, I saw her through the branches of the chrysanthemums standing in the clear water which cast a moving white shadow upon the table-cloth. The sun now shone weakly, an afternoon sun which was amplified by the water in the vase.

The dining-room was completely quiet except for the crackling of the fire. The other tables, laid out, awaited other diners. Hotel cutlery has a particular weight and sheen; it evokes memories of journeys and provincial towns and the restlessness which comes from being itinerant.

When Peter left, I felt relieved from the obscure anxiety which had needled my mind all afternoon. I allowed myself to be calmed by the stillness of the dining-room. Sasha looked at me over the chrysanthemums and gave a strained smile.

'I like Peter,' she said. Her glance oscillated self-consciously between her hands and me.

I smiled at her nervously. I was suddenly grateful for what she had said – terribly pleased that she liked him, as I would have been at long awaited personal praise. That Sasha liked a thing I had, made that thing, whether material or immaterial, look important and official in my eyes. My appearance, my taste in music, my ability to study, even my old winter coat which she had liked: all these she had ratified with her delight in them; she assured me of their value by her smile and secured them to me forever.

No one else I knew liked Peter. In fact, no one seemed to care whether we loved or didn't love, whether we suited each other or not. My mother had no interest in our match: she had neglected to tell my father of our engagement. We lived unrecognised as ghosts in a society where no one believes in ghosts.

I smiled again at Sasha. 'We're getting married,' I said. I didn't tell you.'

Suddenly, I wanted to say everything: that I hadn't told her because I hadn't seen her; that I had wanted to see her and did not dare; that I had followed her to the church that afternoon; that I missed her; that I was sorry I'd hurt her with the news of Boris and Vernon; that I was frightened, sad and glad all at once that she was going to die.

This emotion of wanting to speak flooded my consciousness and drowned all other sounds as if someone had turned up the volume of a powerful radio. The words were so loud I could not hear them, so loud I could not speak over them. I frantically reached for the controls, and in a twist of the knob, I was again in silence.

'I know,' she said. 'Peter told me.' Her eyes were grave, almost sorrowful. Was it then that she knew how unhappy we would be? Did she sense in the slightly sybilline nature she never quite abjure the utter impossibility of either of us ever giving an inch? Sasha! the sybil from her cave of eyes! How well she gave impressions, how well she suggested depths in herself! I do not know how I can believe such things, and yet, I half do.

Sometimes I search my own eyes in the mirror; lately, I have taken to searching my face like a crystal ball, and like a crystal ball I get nothing out of it but an impatient wish for the revelation of a secret. Yet no revelations come and the truth is only hinted at between my formal hedge of lashes. The more I look at my face, the more my self eludes me: it becomes a face in the crowd without emotional content for me. The money I earn, I spend on clothes and pots of make-up. I feel more that I am somebody for myself if I describe a character on that image which never seems to be clearly mine.

'I feel as if we have quarrelled, although we haven't quarrelled . . . not in the open,' she said, after a short pause. She chose her words with a care unusual to her.

I wanted very badly to speak.

I have no real ability to communicate with other people. I know this and accept it as something of a blessing. I have never wished to be intimate with anyone else but Sasha. But why Sasha? Why Sasha, of all people, for whom I think I felt a little contempt? She had no taste, and although her mind was good, she was worse than stupid. She squandered her brain frivolously on other people; she hadn't the guts to be alone, to think alone.

A few years ago, I hit upon the comforting notion that I might be a Lesbian. The idea was so neat – it so elegantly explained my need for her, my wrath at Peter – that it brought me, for a time, considerable relief. The advantages of the theory were altogether too numerous. I could mourn Sasha frankly as a lost lover; desert Peter and David as bad mistakes; define myself according to the strangeness of my predilections; regard myself as a part of a persecuted minority; find a kind of warmth with another woman; and receive complete absolution from myself on the grounds of my unhappy childhood.

The only trouble with the theory was that I could not put it into practice. Try as I might, I could not mourn her; nor could I rouse the slightest memory of desire for her. And as for leaving Peter . . . the notion has become a running joke I have with myself.

If only I had been in love with Sasha . . . but the truth of the matter is that I never really even loved her, so that the idea of having been *in* love with her is a far-fetched one, full of false encouragement.

It was a close thing: I nearly loved her, but I did not.

I know that love exists; that it is possible because it is observable. I laugh at myself as I deftly analyse the images in the poetry of love. My brother George and my sister-in-law love each other. When I visit them, I feel awkward and out of place. Amanda and George have an exclusive luxury of warmth which they expect from each other in much the same spoiled way that the rich expect centrally-heated houses, giving no thought to the poor who have no hope of such things.

George plays the violin and Amanda plays the piano. They play together with an almost passionate rapport. Now and then, he'll stop to listen to her play alone; he'll close his eyes and smile as if he drank her music. When he does this, her fingers seem to take on suppleness and skill; her art increases as he needs it.

To be with George and Amanda is to be in agony at their ease with each other, their gratitude to each other. I cannot take Peter there any more; he cannot watch them unless he gets stinking drunk. Peter's stomach rises at his own inability to love. He's like a half-impotent man who fears the very sexuality of others, who murders a strange girl because she tortures him with the mere existence of her sexuality. Once, at dinner there, Peter turned his considerable cruelty on George and Amanda; but all he achieved was their pity and their further tolerance.

Peter does not know that I understand this secret of his.

But for Sasha, I would not have minded myself being untouched by human hands. She tampered with it – the end of a frozen finger – and rubbed to life in my wintry self a seemingly simple desire. Sasha made me wish I could talk. At times – and this is more important – she made me think I was talking.

I sit among my iron delights: my music, my books and my smart clothes. I derive pleasure from solitary walks; but no one intrudes upon my silence, not even the child.

I watched her face that afternoon when the sun slanted in between bouts of rain, and so sick was I with the desire to talk that I could not utter a word.

'Emily,' she said softly, witnessing my distress, 'I was angry at you, it's true, for showing me what Boris was . . . doing; but I have thought and prayed (she had prayed), and now I see that you were only showing me the truth; and nothing is possible without the truth, is it? It was my reaction that was wrong, and I hope you can forgive me.' She looked at me swiftly, then went on.

'Ironically enough, I always valued you particularly for your rigour, your refusal to compromise. I have always felt such a butterfly next to you.' She shrugged her shoulders and gave a foolish little smile. I was agonised by her directness, and in a sense, I thought the less of her for it.

Peter had been standing behind me. He jingled the change loudly in his pocket. 'I've paid the bill,' he said. 'Now I must take you home as I promised. You look exhausted, Sasha.'

She slept on the back seat of the car. She slept as if she had been deprived of sleep for two nights. Her mouth hung open and she dribbled slightly. I once saw a man in an oxygen tent – that was when Peter was in hospital – he lay like a corpse in a plastic bag, all yellow and still. She lay like that as if all but the minimal energy required for life had been spent in that day.

Peter and I did not speak for a long time although now and then he would turn and smile at me when we came to traffic lights. He seemed grateful for my silent company.

As we entered London, I said, 'What happened on the beach?'

'You don't miss anything, do you? Her scarf fell off. And she talked about her belief in God.' His face reddened. He clearly did not want to say any more, and I did not try to make him.

TEN

I have a clear recollection of Peter in the week or so that followed our trip to the seaside – a clear recollection which springs from the clarity of Peter himself.

The feelings, the imaginings he had had on that day seemed to have sharpened his wits and the outline of his personality. He smoked too many cigarettes and talked a lot, gesticulating with his cigarette, stabbing the glowing end of it in the air to make a point. We spent a lot of time together; but things had changed.

He seemed restless and appeared to want to avoid his flat. We went to a number of films; we did not talk about Sasha or about anything that had happened between us three, although this occupied both our thoughts.

We walked and walked. He took me to Mass at the Brompton Oratory – by accident, it seemed, as we walked that way, but, knowing him as I do now, I can see that it was one of Peter's plots. His face, hard with scepticism, softened wistfully as he blinked at the altar, then hardened again. I have a kind of disgust for anything Baroque. I felt uncomfortable under the twisted cherubim and was disconcerted that he did not seem to notice in what bad taste the place was done. He shook his head and we walked out in the middle of the Mass. He had developed a short, rapped way of speaking. He asked me in this tone of voice what I thought of it all. I said it was their business if they wanted to believe in such a thing, but it had never appealed to me. He looked at me critically for a moment, then asked me with faint sarcasm which registry office I preferred us to marry in. I did not reply. Regarding him warily, I walked on ahead, hunched in my coat.

The weather that autumn was extremely cold.

Soon after that, my parents-in-law asked me and my family to dinner, and even though I could see the idea made Peter uncomfortable, he acquiesced. I was surprised he had capitulated so easily. He appeared apathetic about the idea; his inner excitement was for something else.

I later learned that my father-in-law thought it extraordinary that no one had made any move to make our engagement official. Such is his family pride, he could not understand how my parents were not eager to cement the connection (he still thinks in terms of connections).

He did not see down to the true social depths to which we had sunk; how far from the ritual expression of births, marriages and deaths we lived. My mother had waved her hand and nodded her assent to our engagement between exam papers. As for Peter's talking to my father, requesting my hand in marriage . . . this had never crossed even Peter's mind, for Peter knew the score: Peter knew he might take me away without my being missed.

I remember when I was a child how I hated my mother's job. To have hated my mother would have been impossible; she was such an impersonal force. Hating her would have been like hating the moon: the emotion would have been an utter waste of time. But I could and did hate her job. I suddenly recall how I would stand at the window, the bay-window overlooking the street, waiting for her to return from school. We never went to the schools she taught in: she said it would have given us unfair advantages. Whenever I saw children uniformed in the blazers of the school where she spent her day, I felt such pangs. I would stand at the window waiting, but when she arrived, bustling and busy with thoughts of tea and many more articulate siblings, I would go upstairs to the 'Playroom', as it was called after the American fashion, and draw picture after picture of 'nice ladies', I called them, with beautiful, long hair. I remember mostly about my childhood a constant sense of yearning.

An indolent, hostile French girl gave George and me the necessary supervision during the hours our mother could not be with us. My mother was one of the pioneers of the *au pair* idea. Estelle spoke very little English and was a little inclined to teach George and me French. The only words I remember are '*bête*', '*méchante*' and '*stupide*'. These were the only words she spoke slowly enough, albeit through bared teeth, for me to understand. She harangued us in a torrent of angry French, yet oddly enough, I remember Estelle kindly. I think I sensed even then that her anger had little to do with me, and at least she was all there; she never seemed to be reading instead.

My high mother with her fierce spectacles and smart but sensible shoes! I remember her height and the look of her feet in the shoes. Although she was thin, her feet bulged slightly underneath her adult weight. To me the word 'adult' means my mother – a creature infinitely distant whose function in life is to read, to discuss, to expound, to have interests. An adult to me has 'Interests'; that I have none myself gives me a wry satisfaction.

The only things Peter's mother (and for that matter Sasha's mother too) and mine have in common are gender and humanity. Perhaps this explains why Peter admires my mother. I always felt that Sasha subtly admired her too. She looked at her rather as she might have looked at a particular sleek cat. Peter's admiration goes deeper: it arises partly from his feelings about my mother's behaviour at the dinner party.

My father, to do him justice, would not wear a dinner jacket for the queen. He had these small principles, these small, stubborn demonstrations of independence, and no matter how deep into Belgravia he trod, he would not compromise them. All the same, he did not go to the Meadows' dinner in a cloth-cap; he went attired rather like a Russian ambassador in an old-fashioned suit and a silk tie. He may have dressed in such a proper fashion for my sake; it is his usual custom to wear a black polo-necked shirt when he goes out to dine.

My mother, as we ascended in the lift, looked up nervously again and again as if she feared the cable might snap. Certainly there was this possibility (the lift was very old), but I prefer to think that deep in her self-confident soul there lurked a twinge of social vulnerability. I remember feeling uncomfortable – no, that's too strong a word for it – I felt vaguely uneasy that she looked better than I did. Although I have better features than my mother, she had and still had style – a well-shod, well-groomed neatness of character which she expresses in her clothes. She knows herself and her style. I remember she wore a crisp, almost sporty perfume which filled the lift with its odour of flowers wrapped in green tissue-paper.

The Brigadier greeted us with a precisely judged formality. *He* knew the form even if nobody else did. This, in an intelligent man, is his manner.

'Sing tow row row row row row for the British Brigadier', I found myself repeating idiotically in my head.

I must say for my father-in-law that he is as beautiful as Peter and that he has a better tailor. Was it my imagination, or did he look upon my mother with some pleasant surprise at her attractive appearance? I am certain, because I know my mother well, that she recognised with her eyes his potency.

There is a classless aristocracy of the attractive. A navvy with well-set eyes and an oval jaw can look, without causing offence, at a lady who knows the power of her legs.

I think that the Brigadier had not expected my family to be at all socially acceptable; for a moment, he looked confused.

Peter stood aloof, more than aloof, by a rosewood table; indeed, he seemed as remote as a man who might occupy a different time. I always found him most desirable in that attitude of remoteness. I took it then for detachment, for a sign of mental activity taken to the point of otherworldliness. Well, we believe what we want to believe. Any fool could have told by the autonomous movement of his hands, his fingers always flying over an invisible keyboard, that the look on his face was the only thing remote about him. His mind picks and unpicks his emotions with the same rapid compulsive motion as his hands.

My father and the Brigadier eyed each other coldly.

'I believe you and Mr Stone have met before,' Peter said, his voice thick with the parody of his father's manner. My father looked about himself uncomfortably and so did the Brigadier. It later emerged that my father, who was against charity in a welfare state, who regarded charity, indeed, as subversive, had aired these views at a meeting at which the Brigadier was present. Peter was quite aware, when he made this remark, that the two had quarrelled acrimoniously.

'Only briefly,' said the Brigadier with icy self-restraint. Everyone drank deeply in the profound silence that followed.

At this point, the door opened and Peter's mother slipped into the room with the apology on her face of a schoolgirl late for class. She stood at the door and smiled worriedly. As there was nothing else to look at, everyone looked at her. On seeing this, her smile solidified, her body solidified so that she seemed incapable of movement.

'Come along in, Hermione,' said her husband with a mixture of impatience and indulgence. 'Come along and meet Mr and Mrs Stone.

Hermione managed it by the back route: she walked along behind the chairs and close to the wall. When she reached her husband who stood by the fireplace, she seemed relieved.

A corner of my mother's mouth jumped up in a smile. She had, I think, genuine compassion for weakness in those of a social class lower than her own; but she despised it in her equals and superiors. Hermione waves her weakness at everyone she meets like a flag of truce, but 'surrender' is a word my mother doesn't know.

After my mother-in-law had said good evening to us, she backed towards the fire as if she needed to extract real warmth from that decorative thing which served to make the centrally-heated room more stuffy.

'I understand you are a teacher, Mrs Stone.' Now that his wife had come, Peter's father energetically turned his attention to my mother.

'I teach biology in a grammar school,' said my mother. She made a gesture with her glass as if to indicate how obscure she thought this career to be . . . obscure but essential to society.

There is a disquieting suddenness in Hermione's manner. Now she lunged her neck forward and said, 'How very interesting!' She spoke too loudly out of nervousness. 'How do you find the time, the servant problem being what it is?' she added feebly.

'We have no servants. We have well-organised children.' My mother replied briskly, the way people who have never had a day's illness in their lives speak to those who are chronically but not seriously ill.

'How I *do* admire you. Charles (she flashed a look of hostility mixed with trepidation in his direction) is always telling me I should get out and do something. I always mean to, but I never find the time.'

My mother gave her a brief smile, the kind one gives to a cracked woman on the street. Hermione's accent was precious and upper-class; in her fright, she fluted her pure vowels too loudly – it was that, I think, that my mother so disliked.

'Reads too many novels,' said the Brigadier, ignoring his wife. 'Ought to get out more. Do her the world of good.'

Everyone looked down at his drink.

'What about you, Miss Stone? Do you intend to follow in your mother's footsteps?'

'Follow?'

'Do you want to teach?' he added a bit testily.

They all looked at me, especially my mother, who smiled mysteriously.

'Emily is a scholar,' she said shortly. 'She has always preferred books to company.'

'Ha! First time we'll have had a clever woman in the family.'

Evidently, Mrs Meadows was used to such remarks. She blinked mildly. 'Get me a drink, will you darling?' she asked Peter.

Peter rose slowly to do her bidding. He walked towards the silver tray under the lamp where the bottles crowded. Everything was so clean – no, the table, the bottles, the tray were past the point of cleanliness – everything was so deeply polished that one thing reflected in another, giving the impression that a great wealth of hospitality and comfort lay on that table. They were polished above and beyond the call of cleanliness. This is the way of the rich: they have transcended cleanliness. Another thing about the rich is that they do it all with mirrors.

Peter and his father looked at one another. The Brigadier gave an almost imperceptible nod, and Peter poured out a large whisky.

'It is strange that you do not wish to teach, coming as you do from a family of teachers. You, sir, are a don. Or so Peter tells me.' The Brigadier continued bravely as one in the habit of courage does against all odds. My mother nibbled a cheese football and refused the comfort of her deep armchair.

'I am,' replied my father, who had settled himself squarely. He blinked mildly in the way a don is supposed to and smiled.

'Yes,' my mother said, 'my two elder children teach as well . . . or at least, Anthony teaches to broaden his experience. His final goal is politics. The younger ones, Emily and George, seem to have no interest in it. George is a highly artistic boy . . . a musician. But although Emily has never discussed it with us the plans for her career, I feel she has no vocation for teaching. She is an academic.' Everyone has always hung that label round my neck. Sometimes as I sit in the library I wonder if it is a true label. My mother smiled at me bitterly. On the Brigadier, she lavished a much more familiar smile.

Hermione leaned forward so as to be nearly doubled up. 'Oh, you have four children! How fortunate! I wanted four children when I was a little girl. I remember, I had four dolls. I called them my children, and when I grew up I'd have four children just as I had the dolls. But I could only have Peter, just Peter . . .' she trailed off, smiled at Peter wistfully, then sank back into her own middle-distance world.

The Brigadier and my mother exchanged looks of mild astonishment. I, in my turn, was faintly surprised that such a transaction of eyes should take place between two perfect strangers.

Peter leaned his elbows on his knees, his legs apart. He turned his glass round and round in his hands. His face looked unfamiliar to me in this atmosphere of high parental patronage.

'It is difficult to tell about children,' the Brigadier said affably, more affably than his expression told. 'We thought Peter would be a soldier like myself. When he was a boy, he played war games. We still have the lead soldiers. He and I'd spend hours getting up famous battles, eh, Peter?'

He smiled a little shyly at Peter, but perceiving that this reminiscence evoked no response from him, he turned again towards my mother, who had stiffened slightly in disapproval. My mother wished it to be known that she did not approve of war. George and Anthony had never been allowed toy soldiers *or* toy guns; Anthony had magically avoided National Service.

'I dug up the bones of old soldiers from old battlefields, father.' Peter laughed with a barking noise, not naturally, as he does, through his nose.

'Old soldiers never die,' said his father in the same dry, mordant tone that Peter often uses. He got from his father this habit of making obscure, faintly antagonistic remarks.

Peter and his father have more in common than either of them like to admit. At times, I have clung to the image of the Brigadier in my mind as a sort of symbol of hope for Peter's future. In his subtle, sardonic manner I see Peter as I first knew him. The upright bearing and the cold smile speak to me of what I thought was Peter's strength.

When Peter's last illness had put him in hospital, that time he attempted suicide, my father-in-law took me to lunch at the Savoy. I dressed with particular care in the furs Peter had given me one birthday; I inscribed on my face a haughty beauty with which to turn him to stone, partly to avenge Peter, but more importantly to avenge myself.

He neatly dissected a trout, removing the bones expertly placing them to one side of his plate. He patted his mouth deftly with the linen and observed that in his opinion, the temperature of the wine was not quite right. As the light struck his cheek, I saw the mould of Peter; as he placed his fingers together in an arch, I saw the manner of Peter; his nostrils flared, his eyebrows went up with Peter's delicacy. It was as if Peter's old animus had left his body drugged and unperceiving behind the iron lattice of the nursing home and had entered his father. I could hardly eat for nostalgia.

But he's as weak as Peter, weaker really. At least Peter knows he's weak: it is the knowledge of his weakness which persecutes him so. He feels he must always measure up to the standards of moral grandeur which his father affixed to his head in his childhood. I am half-inclined to tell Peter (indeed when he sees this account he shall read it) what I know of the Brigadier's weakness.

The immaculate Brigadier helped me to flattery in the Savoy. He felt, and would speak frankly, bad about my marrying into such a family (meaning his wife and son, but not himself) where one found oneself in the situation where people were likely to be carted off (here a euphemistic glance at his plate) at a moment's notice. How was one to plan one's life around it? And we had been so absolutely marvellous, even my mother and father, although God knows why they should have been so kind.

God alone knows, I agree with him, why my mother, who never took the slightest interest in me before my marriage should turn into a tower of strength after it.

The Brigadier informed me that he had the highest opinion of my character, while with his eyes he gave me a more personal compliment. I found myself agreeing with his estimation of me as I watched our common handsomeness in the glass. I felt I had come a long way from the macaroni cheese in Fulham. We indulged our secret rapport as Peter lay stunned on his narrow bed.

After the winey lunch, my father-in-law took me home in a taxi, and by subtle looks and the slightest pressure on the elbow, he let me know that all I had to do was to express – no, thrillingly half-express my assent – and he and I, well . . . two adults in such trying circumstances, such blasted hopes, such emotional frustration (this had been the tone of his conversation during lunch) . . . we could be forgiven for finding solace in each other at such a time. Of course he could not have known how little I want anything but revenge upon them all. I left him in a state of agitation which I never mean to satisfy. I almost forgot to visit Peter that night for the emotions which stirred in me. I visit him religiously when he is ill. In this last, most serious illnes he has had, I found I could talk to him quite fluently for hours while he stared unseeing and unhearing at the dusty, ice-green wall.

The dinner table, although large, was too small for the excessive number of pieces on it: crested silver with mint sheen; candelabra; salt cellars; forks, knives and spoons for every conceivable course. Tureens and serving-dishes lurked around the room as if to suggest an even greater wealth than was displayed. Bone china laced with gilt gleamed from a background of fine linen; the very candles looked as if they had been milled from the most expensive wax.

At one end of the table, Peter's mother sat peeping out from behind this armoury of grandeur as if she were at a loss to know what to do with it all. At her own shining table, she looked like an uninvited guest. The Brigadier, however, seemed pleased by the appearance of things, for he gave his wife a curt nod of approval.

My mother sat erect as a Calvinist in a brothel. She seemed nervously to suspect moral contamination from too long a sojourn in such an atmosphere.

A plain-faced maid in a crisp uniform served us with soup. As no one could think of anything to say, we all took elaborate interest in this bit of strange business.

'How is your friend, Miss Stone?' asked the Brigadier.

'My friend?' Words crept slowly in the paralysing ambiance.

'The girl who had some fatal illness. You and Peter took her to the country in my car.'

'Sasha,' I said. Saying her name, I wanted to repeat it.

'What on earth is the matter with Sasha?' asked my mother with a tinge of irritability. My mother was disturbed by the thought of illness and she had little sympathy with it. Somehow one was made to feel in our house that catching even the 'flu was a sign of having the wrong outlook.

It was because of this, perhaps, that I answered with some acerbity. 'She is dying with a nerve disease.' The word 'dying' and yet again 'dying' echoed in my brain.

'What a shame!' my father said. 'What a shame for you, Emmy. You were fond of her, weren't you? Emmy went to Italy with Sasha and her family.' My touching, ineffectual father. What a shame, what a shame.

'But that's an awful tragedy!' Mrs Meadows started up in her chair. 'How old is she? She was galvanised like the Dormouse.

'She's twenty . . . twenty,' Peter said defensively as if to say that twenty was a perfectly respectable age at which to die. His expression was stiff and tight, but he leaned slightly forward so that he would not miss a word of the conversation.

'Twenty and dying . . . how frightful! At twenty, my head was full of parties, nothing else' (and one could see from the peculiar wistfulness on her face that twenty for Hermione had been the golden age). 'Isn't that so, Mrs Stone?' Making an exaggerated effort to talk woman to woman with my mother, Hermione squeaked out the question in the accents of a duchess.

'I don't know about that,' my mother replied icily. Everything in her look suggested that at twenty her mind had been on higher things. Indeed, I'm sure it had been. I have never known my mother waste her time on mere enjoyment. She looked at Hermione like Mme Defarge.

As abruptly as she had entered the conversation, Hermione left it, sinking deep into her chair at the head of the table as if it were the corner next to the kitchen chimney. She blinked blearily at nothing at all. She shed my mother's sneer in a wash of vagueness. She seemed, from where I sat, to wander in a forest of silver trees. I saw her through the candelabra. Hair straggled loose from her bun, and the silk shawl she wore was in danger of falling off her shoulders now withered and crepey with age . . . the White Queen with thoughts of jam yesterday.

The soup we all drank now with a furious concentration was surprisingly wonderful, with its flavour of cream and herbs. Hermione, sipping at her spoon, seemed suddenly to recall something. She looked round the table in a state of barely concealed anxiety and her eyes lit at last and at length upon Peter, who, pushed beyond endurance by her wistful gaze, said, 'It's really delicious, mother, a delicious soup.' There was suppressed fury in his voice. Peter is above all a man trapped by his own pity.

For some reason, Peter's remark seemed to provoke an obscure, muffled anger in the Brigadier. He looked up from his plate, first to his wife, then to his son; his eyes expressed a frightening malevolence. The atmosphere this created was so strong that both my parents looked up. Peter flushed and his shoulders fell. My father shifted uncomfortably in his seat.

The Brigadier put his spoon in his plate and, almost imperceptibly, pushed it away from him. 'Food,' he said under his breath as if it were a curse.

Hermione's wound showed on her face. She, with wealth enough for two cooks (and it is her wealth they live on), had made the soup herself. Hermione's great talent – her only talent – is for cookery. The only times I have seen her happy is when she is in the kitchen measuring, sifting, tasting, stirring. On her face is a look of real pleasure. But the Brigadier cares for nothing but steak and potatoes; he thinks it is demeaning for his wife to cook.

I looked levelly at the Brigadier, hating him not so much for his rudeness to his wife but for his patronage of Peter and, by implication, me. The one thing I have loathed above all things in life is to be treated like a child. Even when I was a child I hated it.

I turned coolly to my hostess. 'You must give me the recipe,' I said. 'I do so want to cook things that Peter likes best.'

The Brigadier, although pale at my defiance, retained his self-control. Peter swayed slightly, and with more emotion than I thought the situation should have provoked, looked at me with piercing gratitude. But Hermione responded to my kindness most of all. Like a thirsty baby towards a bottle, she lunged her head in my direction, a greedy smile upon her lips. Had I not been so far away, she would have pawed me. She has that unattractive mannerism. When I go to visit her, I make certain that I sit where she cannot reach me.

'I have a collection of recipes from all the houses I used to visit when I was a girl . . . you must see them. You see,' she said, leaning forward and warming to her subject while the soup plates were removed, 'the servants were the only people kind to one when one was a child. We had a wonderful cook. She was really like a mother to me. I spent hours watching her. She baked the most delicious bread . . . I can still see her kneading it so skilfully. In the end, I came to her help . . . this was my great joy. My mother never knew . . . sometimes at a dinner party I would have done the pudding and I'd sit there and laugh to myself.' She giggled conspiratorially like a little girl. It was unusual for Hermione to connect sentences so coherently, but her emotion, which was clearly deep and from an embarrassingly private part of her, lent her eloquence.

Whether my mother suspected danger from the reckless tone of the conversation, or whether she did not like stories about cooks and great houses, I did not know. She gave a swift look at the maid who passed the plates when the subject of servants was introduced; but that inscrutable female Buddha seemed so entirely absorbed in her task, that she did not seem to hear. My mother changed the subject.

'Now we're all here, perhaps it would be a good idea to discuss the plans for the wedding.'

The way she said the word 'wedding' . . . No one from my family had attended my sister's wedding, not because there was anything shameful about the wedding, but precisely because a wedding was such a respectable thing. Jane asked that no one should make the trek to the Birmingham registry office. She said she didn't want any fuss, but I think it was rather that she felt she gave way in going through the ceremony to the force of collective superstition. She had proudly lived with Tom for years.

My mother had been in the closest confidence with them and she still is.

I can still see them now, Tom, Jane and my mother, sitting round the kitchen table after the tea things had been cleared away one early evening. Tom has always smoked cheroots. Jane never had any need to do anything with her hands; they were always folded in her lap, never twisting or turning or picking. Tom wears black-rimmed spectacles and a black leather jacket. His costume rarely or never varies. He comes from a working-class family in the Midlands and is inclined to talk about roots, although his accent has been very much refined in the course of his marriage to my sister. I don't know why this is because she talks a lot about roots too.

Tom has always loved my mother. He once told me what a 'fantastic woman' she was. This he said because he could never think of anything else to say to me, and he considered that in flattering my mother he flattered me. To her face, he pays her clumsy compliments which she accepts in the spirit of good fun.

I remember Tom once saying my mother 'accepted' him. Poor silly Thomas: Jane and my mother have twisted him round until he doesn't know one end of the social scale from the other.

On that particular evening, however, I remember they talked about free love. I, being nine, mouthed to myself the words 'free love' as I sat on the floor with my sketch pad. And what was free love? The words appealed to me. I had a vision of two lovers flying in the clouds.

I think the conversation must have taken place when they first started living together. My father being away at a lecture series, my mother put Tom and Jane in her double-bed for the night.

I had seen a magazine at school . . . *Vogue*, I think it was (I still have a secret love of fashion magazines). What really captured my imagination had been a wedding dress. A model with skin like thin paper and eyes like a fawn stood amid shimmering, glossy leaves. She wore a high-waisted dress made of the lightest white silk and a lace veil fell from a crown of flowers on her head. The lace was heavy, white and highly textured.

My mother and Tom and Jane buzzed on . . . the words wedding and love and marriage . . . my ears picked these out of the buzz. I sketched mightily, as quickly as I could in order to complete the drawing of the beautiful bride before they finished talking. At last, quite pleased with the results, I thrust the sketch into Jane's hands just as they wandered to the door, still talking, to prepare for the evening ahead.

'Look, Jane, I have designed a dress for your wedding. Why don't you wear a dress like this?'

Jane laughed silently and passed the drawing to Tom. He smiled and gave it to my mother. My mother, whipped up, I think, by the presence of the lovers and by the thought of the night of delight that lay in front of her elder daughter, burst out laughing. 'The things these children pick up at school!'

'Don't I know it! Jane said. 'With my girls I always have this to contend with.' She pointed at my drawing as an example of something I didn't understand.

'I for one,' said Peter, 'would like to be married in church.' His parents, apart on everything else, apparently had some anxieties, some views on Peter in common; for in the simultaneous, telepathic way of long-married people, they looked first at each other then at him, then at me with surprised relief.

For a moment, I looked at him to say, 'In church? Why in church? What do you mean in church?' but something made me hold my counsel.

My mother, who is a dedicated atheist, looked at me dead

straight, but my father interrupted her. 'Why not?' he asked indulgently.

'And what do you think about this, Emily? What are your feelings on the matter?' Her voice was even and calm, but I could tell from her expression that she had hopes of me yet. Not ordinarily a betting woman, she urged me on with her eyes. I poised indecisively, giving Mother a good run for her money.

'Are you religious my dear?' Mrs Meadows thrust her head at me. There have always been zealots in Belgravia, but they come as an unpleasant surprise. My father-in-law attends Matins every Sunday, and he is inclined to agree with me.

She had given me my moment with Peter.

'My friend is,' I answered. 'I daresay Peter with his usual kindness has considered her feelings in the matter.' I looked at him very sharply. I must say this for my mother, when she is around, I see things clearly – the lines of things are not blurred with charity.

I had struck beautifully home and I savoured my advantage. Peter reeled slightly with the shock of having been discovered. I knew then what I had begun to suspect: he had been visiting Sasha on the sly.

My mother's hopes had quickened.

'But,' I added, looking only briefly at her, 'I have no objection to being married in a church.' My mother is too sophisticated to make faces; on this occasion, however, she found self-control more difficult than usual. She looked sharply away, tightening her lips into a small round screw of irritation. Now she is older, one can tell how she has eroded her face: the lines round her mouth show great use of this expression of annoyance at being crossed. I grow older too; do the same fine lines emerge?

Hermione beamed at me with rich affection. Her colour had heightened and she seemed somewhat larger. Everyone looked at the Brigadier to avoid her eyes.

'My wife is a devout Roman . . . not that Peter and I have ever gone along with it, eh, Peter? Hermione is a convert, of course.' Peter had never told me that his mother was a Catholic. Why had he never told me? Somehow it is an area open for discussion between people who are about to marry – their parents' religion – or rather it is a thing which comes up naturally in the conversation.

My mother, lavishly anti-Catholic (because of the Spanish Civil War in which her second cousin had died fighting for truth and freedom), my mother, who found any form of faith repugnant, cast an eye in Hermione's direction – an eye satisfied with the confirmation of her first opinion: Hermione *would* be drugged by the opiate of the people.

It became increasingly apparent, however, that Hermione was drugged with something rather more than the opiate of the people. 'You don't understand, Charles . . . it's a great comfort,' she said slushily. Peter, with all of the usual critical look gone out of his face, regarded his mother quizzically.

'Well, married in a church you may be,' said my mother briskly, drawing attention to herself with the gesture of a teacher commanding silence, 'but a grand society wedding is out of the question if I may speak plainly (and when did she not), isn't that so?' She turned to my father for confirmation. Her businesslike tone somewhat allayed the bald vulgarity of this statement; but all the same, from the juddering noise my father made in his throat and from the way he looked wildly to the chandelier for guidance, it was clear that she had embarrassed him. She was slightly tipsy, a bit cock-eyed, flushed and over fierce.

I must add here that the Brigadier is quite allergic to vulgarity, so as a punishment, he withdrew at once his admiring glance from my mother, and, as if substituting another lantern slide, looked back again at her with pained hauteur.

My mother looked confused, then angry. hell hath no fury . . .

My father with a smoothing motion he quite often uses said, 'I think my wife meant merely that with so many commitments, we can't really afford . . .' here, despite his theories of economics, he blushed painfully.

The Brigadier, as well he might, given his wife's propensities, was inclined to show mercy. 'Who can nowadays?' he waved his hand, an unfortunate gesture for it included his whole starry, winking table.

Hermione, who had fixed me with her eye like the Ancient Mariner ever since I had defended her right to cook, now leaned more closely forward. 'I'll *give* you a dress! I've always longed for a daughter. I'll . . . we'll go to Dior and you can choose anything you like . . . such a beautiful face, such a beautiful figure! How clever of Peter to find such a lovely girl!' Her generosity, so long pent-up, spilled over, gushed out as wild as water from a dike. Her baggy face was florid with wine, her eyes, urgent and tearful, quested mine. I merely looked away as city people tend to do when they see an accident.

Peter's voice was so even, so almost conversational, that at first no one reacted at all to what he said. 'I don't see why you are letting this wedding achieve such proportions in your minds when none of you have been invited to it.'

Everyone was so transfixed by Hermione's flushed face that his remark took a while to sink in. He did not, however, have to repeat himself. My mother and the Brigadier turned as one man. It makes me laugh now when I think of the similarity of the expressions of their faces. The look of thunderstrook outrage at the insolence, the nerve, the daring of Peter to speak so in regard of his own wedding! My mother and his father, had they been able to resolve their political differences, would have been soul-mates.

Although she did not believe in striking children my mother had her own methods of keeping children in line. She had a stare which struck the malefactor cold – even my father could not stand up to it. In my dreams, I have sometimes met this image: an unseen figure locks and bolts silently a heavy door set in a high wall. It is a metaphor for my mother's look . . . no, I would have said that a year ago. The image expresses something of my own internal self-regard; for when my mother commanded me to override what Peter had said, staring me down through the silver candelabra, I lost, somehow, all desire to please her, all desire to knock and all desire to enter her good opinion of me. I saw in a single and revolutionary moment what I had, in all probability, avoided looking at all my life. That my mother disliked me, I already knew. That I disliked her with an active kind of desolation, this vacuum which extends and annihilates, was new to me. She saw me through her scruples and all I was to her as her child was a proof of them: for this, I hate her more than anything else. Yet the hatred with which I set out to destroy every vestige of her former reign on my heart has wasted me beyond all telling. This is the only thing I know.

'And what do you think about this, Emily?'

'We will marry exactly as Peter wishes.' They all looked at me except Peter who did not dare. His leg was tense against mine underneath the tablecloth. Once the words were out of my mouth, I saw the power in them with which I could confound not only my mother but anyone else I chose. I had the power to say no.

'Oh dear, and I thought, oh dear,' Hermione half rose, and from her mouth came an ominous eruptive sound. Then quite suddenly, she was sick, half on the tablecloth and half on the floor. She retched and retched again, spittle coming out of her mouth in between times. And she wept with shame and drunkenness.

'PETER, GET THAT WOMAN OUT OF HERE!' His father was rigid with fury.

Peter sat for a moment quite stunned, then he rose to take his mother by the elbow. 'Oh, and I wanted it to be so nice. Oh, I'm sorry, I'm sorry . . .' she cried brokenly.

It was then my mother came into her own and made Meadows family history. Up she bustled as brisk in contrast to the rest of us as Florence Nightingale would have been in contrast to her cholera patients. Compared with her, the rest of us, who sat numbed with amazement, seemed hopeless and dawdling. Exaggerating Hermione's drunkenness (for the woman could still walk), my mother hoisted her in the fireman's lift, leaving Peter not really knowing what to do with himself.

'Nonsense, dear,' she said to Hermione, 'there's nothing to get so upset about. This sort of thing happens to us all now and then. I should think you have a touch of gastric 'flu. There is a good deal of it about. U-u-u-up we go, steady now! There's a good girl.'

Hermione cast a pitiful backward glance at her husband. 'I'm sorry, Charles. I suppose I was nervous.' His regard for her was mere contempt; with this he shrugged her off.

My mother bundled her from the room. 'Come along, Peter, give me a hand.' (Peter's hand was the last thing needed.) 'We'll get you to bed and you can have a good rest!' She was in her element now, my mother, the meeter of emergencies. Her voice rang truest in a panicked crowd, and Peter, whose instincts yearn for order, followed her directions without questioning.

The Brigadier, my father and I were left in silence with the pool of vomit which glistened with the silver and the sheen of the linen in the candlelight.

ELEVEN

That was the end of Peter as I had known him. It was not that he then stopped loving me – in fact, the very opposite was true – it was I who stopped loving him. I was not aware of this at the time, but all that had seemed important about him to me, his parents had destroyed. From then on he took his mollusc heart around in his hands and offered it around to the mercy of the world. There was nothing (and he saw this quite clearly), simply nothing more they could do to him after that; and suddenly he saw (through Sasha, he said) that there was no point at all in defending himself any more against anything or anyone.

It was cold the winter Sasha died, but that wouldn't have mattered if it hadn't been for the walks. The walks started in earnest after that . . . Why do I say that? It isn't true. We had walked before – the whole summer long – we were always taking walks before; yet although we walked, we did not walk in earnest until then. We had merely ambled in comparison. We had been together; our union had been complete and it hadn't mattered whether we went abroad or stayed at home. We could have been in Peking or Andalusia that year we had together, and everything would have been the same. Neither Peking nor Andalusia would have impinged on our consciousness. Such places would have been like filmic background: nothing we had seen had been to either of us anything at all more serious or relevant than shadows shifting round us.

But these walks were different. Every step we took seemed solid, seemed to propel us to some destination. We did not walk as we had done in order merely to change the set around a fixed plot; we walked this time (and now I see it although I didn't then) to change the plot itself. At least, that is what *he* did. I had no part with it.

All the bottled up force of his personality seemed to surge from him like a pus – a never-ending well of it; even though I was there I kept my distance from contamination. My boots kept pace with his urgent restlessness, but in my mind I avoided him like the plague.

His mother, it appeared, was the source of his anguish . . . I'm not too sure, I didn't listen very carefully. There was something about an acute common tenderness they had when he was a little boy . . . how she took him to the zoo or circus, I can't remember, and how vividly she made him see the stretch of the panther's neck and the anachronism of elephants. And then there were her nerves which came like tidal crises. Had I seen how his father had shattered her with judgement? But he had judged her too, that was the awful thing. Her weakness appalled him; the extent of her frailty imposed on him an almost endless obligation to protect her not only from his father's irony but from his own callousness. His love for her was genuine. This he felt he knew now for sure. If the dreadful scene had taken place even a month before, he would have sneered at her with his father when she was sick and in doing so would have sneered at himself; but now he was filled with an almost unbearable compassion for her.

He tried to drag me into it; to drag me down with him. Each time he spoke of these things in his furrowed way, I felt a sense of being dragged down deeper. I was oppressed beyond words by his new, feverish longing for self-discovery. I still remember the feeling now – as if he had been sitting on my chest – I could hardly bear to look at him as he maundered on; yet now and then I would catch a glimpse of his handsomeness: its very elusiveness was tormenting.

He had displaced himself from where he was in me, and I discovered no place in my heart for him to lodge in. His words simply rolled off me as if I hadn't known him. He doesn't see how he disappointed me. He does not see why I became so flatly opposed to him from that time. He had presented himself to me almost wholly as one man and I had accepted him – as far as I was capable of accepting anyone – as that; and then he shifted ground.

What he doesn't manage to understand now is how little I knew then of any of this. He had caught me unawares. I was twenty, and all I knew of the situation was that he depressed me in that mode. It did not occur to me to make any detached summary on his character at the time. I more or less took it for granted that he would recover himself.

We walked. Round and round the Round Pond we walked. He grasped at straws of nature; made observations about little boys and galloping dogs. He seemed to want to get in touch with something . . . something other than me. He fed the pigeons and talked to them. He was childishly pleased when one took bread from his hand.

He made no secret about seeing Sasha. She was the touchstone for his memories and for his considerations on his feelings. I would stay in the flat and tidy up when he went to see her. He had become forgetful. He'd leave the gas fire on and he'd let clothes and dishes accumulate. The flat was my one consolation. I scrubbed it down; stripped it of every speck of dust. I guarded it against corruption with every inch of myself.

For she was there. She was there with me and her death leaked out on to me; it oozed from her to him to me. Death is catching.

I would not go to see her. I would not. Of that I was privately resolved. He wanted me to; he pressed me to, but he cannot conceive the horror I had of her. Her flesh fell from her in my dreams like slabs of rotted marrow. This vision was impacted in my brain, and more and more my mind withdrew from it so that quite often I saw Peter and every other living thing as being very small and mechanical . . . like clockwork toys.

That's what Peter wants to get out of me, I'm sure – he wants to know why her death frightened me so. But even if I would tell why, I could not. The thought of my own inevitable demise does not depress or excite me. I am not a physical coward. I found that out when David was born. The pain eddied round me, but I was not a part of it. The woman in the next bed screamed and called on the Mother of God. I had no respect for her screaming like that. You have to take what comes without screaming: I think that is my only moral law. Peter mumbled desperate prayers that night he nearly died; from what place they spurted, I do not know. I only know I value too highly my intact sphere of privacy to do such a thing.

No, Sasha's fading had a different significance to me. I don't know what it was, but I know how I felt – powerless and horribly fascinated.

And so I waited. In mid-November, I took leave of my family altogether and moved into Peter's flat. This departure caused no alarm in them: in fact, it was a departure which had already been made. I simply told my mother I was going, for what on earth was the reason for staying? She rather agreed with me, and said she approved of trial marriages. I packed what few things I had and went. I had no real desire to be near Peter, but I could not leave the flat unfortified. I became obsessed with the notion that he might burn it down in the night.

Peter's reaction to this move was extraordinarily emotional. I made no announcement of my intention, but simply appeared with my suitcase which I unloaded on his bed – our bed – while he was out. He returned, from Sasha's I suppose, to find me half installed.

'Oh, Em!' he cried. 'Oh, Em, how extraordinary you are. How little you need telling anything . . . how much I needed you.' His hands trembled over me; he kissed me, blotting his tears on my hair. He made love to me, me specifically, with violent emotion. I allowed this with my teeth set against it. I couldn't stand the sweat of it, and when it ended, I got up and bathed, scouring from my skin every trace of his feeling. I hung my clothes in his cupboard and neatened the shoes at the bottom, hoping, in the sight of my grim distaste for him, that this was just a passing phase.

And there I stayed. The holidays were nearly upon us. I pinched my face together and worked with tireless energy.

I did everything I could for him, doesn't he see? I slaved that balance might be brought back. I was there constantly, mending, darning, polishing, cooking. I even took him to Kew one wretchedly cold day thinking somehow the rhythm of our walk together might restore the past. Ice encased the trees and the grass was stiff with frost. Each twig, each pine-needle was made crystalline by its ice case. I caught my breath at the sight of such universal frost against the bleak sky. The sky that winter looked as if it would never change its colour.

He missed the beauty, the beauty of that walk which he would certainly, certainly have seen before, through lofty trees with strange names at Kew. I pushed a bough heavy with ice. The twigs clicked together and their sheen they had of ice refracted in the dismal sun.

'Listen, Peter,' I said, looking round. 'Listen to the ice.' But he turned away and wandered down the path with no thought of it. He wanted to talk. He was animated by the cold.

'Sasha's father is coming from America to see her,' he said that day.

'How is she taking it?' I had to muster strength to make my voice sound even.

'She means to see him. She feels she must. She wants to resolve everything with everybody. She has a great urge to do this.' I wondered about Boris.

'What has she resolved with you?'

He looked away. 'That remains to be seen. She says a great deal which is helpful to me.' We walked on a space in silence. 'You concern her in a funny way,' he said after a time.

'I?' How could she torment me so. She had no need of me.

'She'd like to see you again. She hasn't long,' he muttered. 'Why won't you come, Em?'

My attention oddly wandered to the trees. 'I think I would spoil things between you. It's obviously important to you both, your relationship.'

'What don't you see, Emmy?' he said softly. He kissed me and capered across the lawn like a child let out of school. He broke off a sprig of pine and gave it to me.

After that he became more garrulous about her, and this would have been intolerable to me if I had listened to all he said, but I made no reply to his remarks. Instead I'd busy myself with the kitchen or the bedroom floor. How he took my meaning, I do not know. His absorption in her was so complete that I think he hardly noticed how dire it was for me that everything in him had changed. And this I will never forgive her for. She made him raw – raw to every pigeon in the park, raw and vulnerable to my body, even to the children downstairs. One day, he came in and said, 'You know, Emmy, those children downstairs have been going around in this weather without any socks on. Their knees and feet are red! Do you think that woman would mind if I gave her some money for clothes?' And the next day, I saw them in the garden wearing woollen tights. The woman acknowledged me on the stairs, the first time since I'd been there. 'Thank you miss,' she said shyly, and vanished behind the door.

I watched and watched. Every minute I was watching, as if I stood breathless behind a door while noises of incredible destruction were going on inside. Adjust the Roman head, straighten the branches in the vase, scour Peter's room, clothes, sit, sit, as if in an eternal waiting-room. I smoked a thousand cigarettes, like an expectant father. I painted arcs around my eyes and paced.

I saw them continually in my imagination. They were always before my eyes, Peter and Sasha, and somehow she always pealed with laughter, real laughter, rising from her belly, as I'd seen her when we were children. She'd sit down for a laugh so that she could enjoy it the more. And he . . . I saw him swimming about in her merriment with a kind of joy, reckless and unable to contain himself any longer . . . both of them without inhibition of any kind.

Peter was splashed by her death all over. He came in splashed, covered in her smell of camphor and soap and oil. She burnt like acid where she fell and peeled his skin off.

Oh, Peter! Can't you see how she ripped you? He doesn't see, his only memory is of that involuntary smile she gave him, but I saw his face shining. She stripped him down to his pity so that he had nothing else left. It was *she* who broke what was intact in him, not I. I have done everything to mend.

I don't know when I conceived the idea of going to Boris and Vernon, but it had always been in the back of my mind that they might be of use some day. The idea came and went like a cramp in the stomach; there was a sense of mission in it, dangerous mission. I dared myself with the thought of confronting them with my news of Sasha, and the thought became a palpable lump, an object rather like a hand-grenade which my mind toyed with. I'd take it out every now and then, throw it in the air and catch it, musing on its capabilities as a weapon, its effectiveness; then put it away again for a time, never forgetting that it was there. 'So Sasha is intent on resolving all quarrels,' I'd think, then let the thought drop. I had a sort of mental picture of their indifference to her pain, how their sluttish lives had been untouched by her. My vengeance boiled at this and their hardness of heart attracted me like a magnet. Every now and then I'd see Boris revelling in his flesh. The picture was extreme and it made me close my eyes with headache. That they alone had escaped the touch of her disaster moved me most of all to hang round telephone-booths. I discovered that I never went out of the flat without the correct change for calling them. Sooner or later, I knew I was going to do it. I don't think I foresaw or even tried to foresee the consequences of my action; the action became enough, supreme in itself. The metaphor I made for myself appeared to me with increasing vividness: I would rip all the lies surrounding her away, I would explode a taste of reality into the midst of these posturing actors. I became intensely curious to see what would happen.

I had managed to keep these thoughts at arm's length before the holidays began. I have always been addicted to work. In work alone I can bury all self-consciousness. There is no sight in the world more comforting to me than a thick, blank pad of paper nested in a pile of books, provided for with sharp pencils. Unlike Peter and Sasha, I could never be seduced from work. I think often of how much both of them could have accomplished. Sometimes I believe it is the very inutility of their personalities which maddens me.

When the holidays started, however, I had to cope with idleness – idleness on a scale I had never known before. There are only a certain number of times one can polish a small floor before the action appears absurd. I began to see how brilliantly my mother had constructed the household of my childhood. At no time were we at a loss for guidance. Once out of this commune where achievement was paramount, I felt a sense of underlying panic that forced its way to the chambers of my mind which contained the substances of which I have spoken, and activated them.

The pressure of living with Peter day and night became almost more than I could bear. Day and night, day and night, he carried his love and gratitude for me around after me, a sacrifice I longed to snatch from his hands and smash to the ground. I had no words to beat off his torrent of love, his paeans to Sasha, his restless activity. I became paralysed with a sense of desperation.

I know I could have left them there and then, but such a course of action never occurred to me at the time. I was wedged hopelessly between them, I was grist for them, and all the words I might have fought them with forced themselves down to my interior self rather than out to object. For how could I have lost them, either one of them? They were essential to me, both of them, and I would have gambled heavily on my basic food for life had I uttered one word of the fear I had of them.

In the end, I called Vernon quite casually. I had had no plans to call her when I went round to the shops. I simply found myself surrounded by a phone-booth with the receiver in my hand.

Vernon spoke sleepily although it was ten o'clock in the morning. I half expected venom to pour from her when I revealed my identity, but I was extremely surprised to discover that she was positively pleased to hear my voice.

'Of course I remember you,' she said. 'In fact, I've been trying to get hold of you to tell you our news.'

I was too astonished to reply.

'I don't think you'll ever guess how important you've been to our lives,' she continued rather breathlessly as if to a very old friend. 'You really brought things to a head with us that day. We were married in July, and I'm going to have a baby!' Her whole tone was exclamatory, but the undertone was stale. It was as if she announced this news tirelessly to their every conceivable acquaintance in the same artless style. 'I think it's very important to get everything out in the open, don't you? So many English people flinch from a crisis. My analyst was really thrilled. He's been trying to get the same results from me for years. I can't tell you how much better I feel.'

I waited for a moment until she had quite run out of enthusiasm. 'I have my own news . . . of Sasha. Could I see you and Boris tonight? I really think you ought to know.'

'Well, that would be fine. Why don't you come over at about nine and have a drink.' Even on the telephone, I withdrew from her exaggerated friendliness.

The time I spent in waiting for nine o'clock was almost timeless in the anxiety I felt. I had to bathe twice, for the sweat, and when the moment came for me to go, my heart and stomach heaved with fear that I would somehow give myself away before I accomplished what I had set out to do.

They didn't seem to notice how I shook. In fact, they took very little notice of me at all. Vernon was making a pie, or at least she was stirring lukewarm water into a bowl full of ready mix pastry. I found it, for all my nerves, an effort not to tell her that pastry should be made with ice-water. Pastry was one of the few things my mother could make well, and it was one of the few things she didn't get out of a packet.

Vernon wore a white, frilly apron over a strained maternity smock. She was about five months pregnant, but she stuck her belly forward to make it look bigger.

The two other times I had been in their flat, it had been very well-ordered and clean, but now the furniture was dusty and the bookshelves looked unkempt. 'I'm sorry about this,' she said, licking a finger and waving the other hand over a pile of dirty dishes, 'I'm spoiling myself.' Her skin was very clear and she had a healthy look. However, she had not washed her hair for some time.

She plucked languidly at her apron. 'My mother gave me this when we were married. Typical of her. I've lived with Boris for five years, and she sends me a whole load of ruffled aprons and virginal nightgowns that won't even fit me in my condition for God's sake.' Indeed, she had found some difficulty in making the ends of the apron meet around her belly.

Boris was sitting in an armchair reading a book. 'He's reading Pushkin,' said Vernon in a stage whisper. He seemed to find the text very absorbing, for he had not glanced up at my arrival. I felt very conscious of him, and although I couldn't look at him for long, I felt curiously exhilarated by his presence, and by the fact of his not looking at me. He had altered and looked older. He wore a corduroy jacket and an unimaginative tie. I searched in vain out of the corner of my eye for his former mystery. He was eating peanuts abstractedly from a slightly tarnished silver bowl.

'He's trying to give up smoking,' she said, again in a stage whisper. 'I've finally convinced him it is bad for his health.'

I left Vernon with her pie-crust and moved stiffly around the living room picking up objects at random from the tables and peering at the bookshelves. A book on Natural Childbirth was spread open on the sofa at a line-drawing of a naked woman squatting. Her distended belly pushed through her knees; her face was utterly devoid of expression. The page was marked with fingerprints and a fleck of raspberry jam. Next to the book was another on child psychology, and underneath that lay a pile of knitting.

'Boris, why don't you make Emily a drink?' Vernon called. 'I'll be with you in a minute.'

Boris grunted, then put the volume of Pushkin on the floor. He looked briefly at me without acknowledging me, poured some Scotch into a filmy glass and handed it to me. He returned to his book.

I sat carefully, very carefully on the edge of the sofa, not daring to move much for what was inside me. Vernon came in and sat down next to me. There were still bits of pastry on her hands, but she started knitting clumsily, flour snowing on the blue wool.

'Are you going to have a boy then?' My voice sounded far away to me and completely artificial.

'Hope so,' she said, sticking out her tongue in order to concentrate on executing a buttonhole.

'Congratulations, Boris, I didn't know you and Vernon were married.' I dragged words heavily from me, but once out, they seemed to have come from someone else.

'Thank you,' he replied.

I sipped at the whisky without enjoyment. I do not like to drink. I do not approve of drinking. In my own way I am a Puritan.

'He's so tied up at the moment. He's on his Ph.D. and once we get *that* over with, we can begin to relax and enjoy ourselves.' She apologised for his indifference with this speech. I reckoned he wouldn't humiliate me for long in such a way.

'What is the subject of your dissertation?' I asked him so directly that he could not help but answer.

'The influence of the Orthodox Church on Pushkin.' He snapped the book shut with some irritation and stared gloomily at Vernon and me.

'Were you and Vernon married in an Orthodox Church?'

'It would have killed my father if we had done otherwise,' he said loftily.

'Peter and I will be married soon.'

'Peter Meadows? No kidding.' Vernon spoke without much interest, but then she was in the middle of a complicated stitch.

But my announcement galvanised Boris, who suddenly fidgeted his hands together between his knees and then leapt up and strode around the room. 'Peter . . .' he said in his bass voice. The tone expressed a sigh, a misgiving, a concern for Peter. His eyes became meditative. 'How is he? Is he well?' The question was more than polite.

'He's fine, just fine,' I said defensively.

'Peter was Boris's best friend at Cambridge,' Vernon said. 'In fact he tried to get Peter to come to our wedding, but there was no reply to the invitation. We figured he was having one of his turns.'

'It is sad to lose one's friends,' Boris said suddenly. He paced across to the fire and kicked at a coal. He looked over his shoulder at me with faint accusation in his eyes. I could not help but notice the power in his movements.

Without warning, my head became tight with pain and I knew the time was ripe for the fulfilment of my mission. 'I am losing a friend at the moment,' I said. 'I am losing Sasha.'

Boris humped slightly as if he shouldn't be surprised.

'You said you had some news of her. What is it?' Vernon spoke about her as if I were just anybody friendly.

My forces gathered to my throat and then expelled themselves too hard: 'Sasha's dying. Dying. I thought you'd like to know.' I stopped, but I wanted to go on saying it.

The effect I had striven for really occurred. Vernon dropped her knitting and Boriz froze in mid-pace.

'What!' they cried.

'She's dying of an incurable disease.' There was unction in repeating it.

'Sasha's dying. Oh, how sad,' Boris said softly. I didn't know he was capable of such softness. 'And I behaved abominably to her . . . Ah well . . .' He shook his head, almost shrugged and that was his demonstration of guilt, that and nothing else. Ah well. Ah well, indeed . . . he, a hit-and-run motorist a hundred miles from the corpse. Ah well.

Big, handsome Boris stood there in his physical glory, his wife pregnant by him, and shook his broad head and scratched it with his hairy hand. His trousers groaned with his thighs as he sat down shaking his head some more. I saw him on frail Sasha, a thick thumb squashing a moth.

It was a little time before I realised that Vernon was crying. She had put her knitting down on her lap and her hands flopped uselessly by her side. Her mouth and eyes were open. She cried shamelessly like a child, not attempting to hide her emotion. She looked peculiar crying, and I studied her with interest. 'What is she to you?' I found I had asked.

'You mean you don't know?' Her voice was faintly incredulous, but still she wept. 'I just assumed you knew.'

'I do not know what she could possibly mean to you, unless she has some sentimental value.' I had said more than I had meant to say. I had tried to be careful not to leave myself unguarded by a sneer.

'You mean you don't understand what she did here?'

I could barely combat my hatred of her which wriggled round my brain like a nest of snakes. 'I do not,' was all I could manage to say.

'In all my life,' Vernon continued miserably, 'no one has ever given me anything I didn't have to pay for except Sasha. She came here with every reason, with every intention of getting revenge . . . I have thought about it and thought about it . . . but this was it . . . she saw how I felt, and she couldn't manage it – revenge I mean. She gave me back Boris as much as if she had handed him to me on a silver platter, not because she didn't want him; she saw I wanted him more.'

I looked at Boris sharply, but he appeared not to be listening. He only shook his head as before, slowly from side to side.

'She hit Boris: that's revenge.'

'Well, I,' said Boris, slowly rising, 'deflowered her.'

'Do you think she'd mind if we went to see her?' Vernon asked timidly. 'I wouldn't want to upset her.'

'Somehow I don't think that Emily knows the answer to that question, Vern,' Boris said quietly. He stood quite still beside me. She looked at him somewhat uncomprehendingly, but he motioned her to silence. I saw I had to go.

'Give my love to Peter,' he said at the door. There was command not request in his voice.

How much more self-hatred is necessary, I wonder, before I expiate her death? It isn't conscience I feel – I have no nice ability to distinguish between right and wrong as Peter seems to have – there never were any rules for me to break. What I do have is a black hole in my inner universe, a vacuum in myself which her death left: it sucks my will, my sap into itself and I am left without a thing to call my own. Peter has no idea of his good fortune; he has the luxury of self to scribble on, to foster or destroy as he sees fit. He mourns her, he has the temerity to mourn her when her death was nothing to him compared to what it was to me. I sometimes think I have swallowed myself whole.

After I saw Boris and Vernon, things took a turn for the worse. I don't think I had realised how I was playing my last card with them, the very last will I could muster. I still have no clear idea of what I wanted from them. I had had some vague picture of a general holocaust where all four of them would meet and sing a final, grand and tasteless quartet – Boris, Vernon, Sasha and Peter, each demonstrating before my public eye his own essential poverty of depth and true invention. Thus, I was not only stung and bewildered by their reception of my news; I was robbed finally and at last of any personal immanence for any of them. Sometimes I see myself in this way: as a beautiful costume without an actor in it.

Do I have to remember the suffocation? I have no wish to remember that. My mind contracts with fear at the thought of it . . . but he must know; I must justify myself to him. It started in the night . . . something sitting on my chest pressing harder and harder until I woke . . . he was there beside me but I couldn't move, I was paralysed for eternal minutes, and when I got my movement back, I shook so hard I was afraid to wake him. For he *shouldn't know*. I was more frightened of discovery than of the thing itself. At first the days were clear of it, and then it came without my knowledge or consent and I was utterly helpless against it – the muscles round my lungs would petrify and I'd claw at the window catch, claw at the air – it was like being buried alive.

It would happen while I was at the sink or while I was making the bed. Once, I was overcome at the greengrocer's . . . I started to ask for a cabbage, and in the middle of the sentence, my breath solidified in my lungs, my lungs felt cold and heavy, like two bags of ice. I had to flee into the street and people stared at me as I gasped for air.

The worst of it by far was my own inability to struggle. I, the victim of an unspeakably enormous avalanche, was unable to move one inch to the right or to the left of its path.

Peter came and went; I hardly noticed him. I no longer found him an irritant; beside my strangler, he was nothing at all. He was important to me only in that I had to conceal from him that half the time I was stifling. I became very meticulous in observing the former rhythm of my personality. I studied each gesture I made and each word I spoke before I allowed them to become action. My mind constricted tighter and tighter around each effort at communication; I scrupled to say 'hello', and anguished in the night over the sum of the day's words.

He did not notice; he never noticed.

We walked around St James's Park and he fed the huddling ducks with scraps of bread. His person was a white-hot fever; he had come down with her; he was ill with her.

I measured my breath by its steam in the cold air. I was careful not to waste it. Evil seemed to peep at me from the trees. The eyes of the ducks pierced me with their malevolence. Ducks have wicked little eyes. Every Christmas I have to steel myself at the sight of their bloody heads, their battered bills hanging limp along the butcher's slab.

'Do you know what Sasha did?'

I couldn't speak, so I nodded very carefully.

'She wrote to Boris. She sent him back his diamond and she asked him to come and see her before she went.'

'When?'

'The other day. She asked me if I thought he'd mind or if he'd think she was getting at him in some way.' He was wound to the highest notch. His long fingers trembled like wires across his forehead. His hands sought everything . . . a pebble, a feather or my hair for its texture. He cast himself around.

'Oh, Emmy, I can't bear to sit and watch her die. She is so cheerful and she is wasting away to nothing! I could pick her up with one arm. She suffers horribly sometimes. I know she does; but she never complains.

'Do you know? I never understood what you saw in her. That shames me terribly now. And yet I feel . . . Oh, Emmy . . . that I have to convince *you* of her extraordinary goodness. She worries for her family . . . there's been all this business about Nanny . . .'

'What about her?' My voice was so stiff I could hardly get it out. I felt I had used up too much breath in asking the question.

'It was Mrs Courtney, she lashed out at Nanny . . . there was a terrible scene in front of Sasha. Mrs Courtney threw the Tarot cards on the fire. It was a bitter gesture, as if she were burning heretics. The cards seemed to writhe . . . the hanged man and all those frightful figures. She told Nanny she must go; that she had perverted their minds and told horrible lies. Nanny sat there with this terribly frightened look on her face. She looked utterly lost and completely uncomprehending. "Where can I go? There's no place for me to go." She kept repeating that. "How can I leave the girl?"

'Mrs Courtney's face – how can I describe it – it was tired and implacable. You know, she *did* have a grievance against Nanny. It's always the way with earth mothers; they imprison their children in a cushion of superstitions and the merely physical.

'Sasha . . . Sasha was amazing. She confronted the two women with the extraordinary fact of *herself*, with a kind of instinctual wisdom:

'"Oh, Mummy, we can't do without Nanny now, no more than we've ever been able to do without her. Nanny, don't go, you mustn't do that. You're like a sister to Mummy, you mustn't desert her . . ." She flung herself at them with a kind of passionate intercession. It wasn't so much what she said; her presence produced its own kind of authority. She revealed herself to them rather as the baby in the judgement of Solomon. Their love for her was somehow called into question by their wrangling. It was as if they tore her apart with it, and seeing that, they could not carry on. She rendered them incapable of doing each other harm because they neither of them could do *her* harm.'

He drew a nervous breath. I clenched my handbag and said nothing. He continued; his words pounded like nails in my head.

'She worries for me . . . she is so gentle and so genuinely horrified by everyone's misery. She sees me in a way that no other person has ever seen me. She is unruffled by every accusation I make against myself. I am a fool next to her, but the amazing thing is that I feel quite glad to be a fool. Whenever I go to her, I am in such a state . . . I could spring on her and give her artificial respiration; but when I actually see her, I feel reproached for the worst kind of insensitivity. She is more alive than I am.

'I wish I could believe with her. I never thought to see true religious faith. My only essays in that direction were so filled with hypocrisy – a wish to see myself justified in my own eyes – that I let the whole thing drop in disgust . . . but *she* sees mercy under the bed and in the knotholes of trees. *She* sees mercy even in justice. Nobody disgusts her, nothing threatens her . . . and all the while, she calls herself a sinner, which is something I read about and used to laugh at; but she has no idea of its being an affectation, and with her it isn't. Do you know what she said to me? She said she'd given up all pretensions to moral rectitude when she realised what she'd done with Boris and Vernon . . . particularly what she'd done to Vernon.'

He stood there waving his bag of bread around. His voice was pitched near hysteria.

'Sasha never had any pretensions to moral rectitude,' I said stiffly. Her whole life swaggered before my eyes – the luxury of her life, how she rifled it for pleasure. She was a whore, a greedy whore with her imagination. She sucked luxury from the simplest things . . . a pair of shoes or a laugh. What virtuous conviction did she have? When did she ever muddy her hands for the working class? Even my mother had more moral rectitude than Sasha.

He looked at me curiously, not quite sure, for the first time, of what I meant in regard to her. I ventured to reply, to smooth the cynicism out of my remark, when suddenly I knew my rib cage wouldn't move and panic expanded and exploded in my brain. The last thing I remembered as I fainted was the expression in his eyes – a deep suspicion of me.

I was not ill for long. Nobody in our family ever is. I refused to see a doctor, although Peter tried to make me. His questions were most dreadful. Why had I fainted? Had he said something to upset me? Was it the strain of worrying about Sasha? Had he been insensitive? He was all around me. He seemed to be everywhere. His sympathy and his anxiety abounded while above all else I wanted to sleep.

At last, I moved back to my mother's house, telling Peter that I had seen our family doctor and that he had ordered for me a complete rest. I told Peter I had kidney trouble.

My mother greeted me with surprise. She was doing the washing-up when I returned. 'Oh, it's you,' she said as I came into the kitchen carrying my bag, but my presence did not interrupt the flow of her scrubbing and sluicing. 'Have you and Peter quarrelled?'

'No, I'm not very well, that's all. The doctor told me to come home because he thought you were better equipped than Peter to look after me.'

'Nothing serious, I hope,' she said impersonally.

'He says I have a bit of kidney trouble. I fainted in St James's Park.'

'Ah, honeymoon cystitis,' she said nodding sagely. 'Well, I'm afraid you'll have to use the spare room. I've let yours to an unmarried mother.'

'Well, I shan't be here for long. Do you think I could have a cup of tea?'

'You know where everything is,' she said. A look of tired impatience crossed her face. She turned around and dried her hands on her apron. She looked towards me but not at me. 'I hope you've eaten. There's nothing left.'

Her indifference spread about my self like a dentist's injection . . . a prick of hurt to what was sore and then the numbing, a state both feared and longed for. I left her sluggishly and went to bed.

Days and nights drifted by me in the spare room. The place was always cold, and the unused sheets never seemed warm to my body. Somehow I thought my mother might stay home and look after me – it was, after all, a holiday – but apparently, she had other things to do. I dressed during the day and wandered round the house from room to room. I'd pick up childhood objects and scrutinise them in a puzzled way: they seemed oddly unfamiliar. I rummaged through drawers looking for something, I can't remember what, I think it was an old sketch pad.

I could not think of anything to say at meals. My father asked politely about my health and I think he muttered something incomprehensible about Peter and was it wise? But I found it difficult to get the gist of what he was saying. My brother Anthony came home one evening, and my parents were occupied mainly with his news, but I have no clear recollection of what his news was.

Most of all I slept deeply and dreamlessly, but when I woke, I felt tired, nervously tired. I tried to think of Peter, but his image eluded me. I could not picture his face.

I do not know how long I was in this comatose state; it can't have been very long, maybe only a few days. I had ceased to feel suffocated; indeed, I had ceased to feel anything at all. I do know, however, when I came out of it. I was sitting slumped on the edge of my bed; it was dark in the room; I remember. Suddenly, I heard a dreadful shriek pitched far beyond hysteria, then another and another – screams of someone made almost inhuman by agony. There were a lot of footsteps and then a babble of voices. I rose; I felt my hands touching me all over; my fingers went compulsively over my face and body, and in one tremendous surge, I found myself running down the stairs towards the noise.

My family had crowded into the kitchen. I broke through them and shoved past. A small girl of about two years' old lay on the floor in a pool of steaming water. The electric kettle hung drunkenly by its cord over the worktop, and on her knees beside the child was its mother, the woman who had taken my room. The child lay absolutely quiet, its eyes wide-open with shock. Its skin was scalded purple. The woman made no noise, but silently and with a kind of dignity, she gathered the child to her.

'Don't!' my mother cried.

The woman looked at her queerly for a second. 'Get an ambulance,' she said, lifting the child with infinite tenderness to the sink, and talking to it in a low, crooning voice. She bathed its skin in cold water.

'My little girl, my honey. My little lamb, don't cry,' she repeated. Her voice though soft was clear and strong; it fought through the panic in her eyes. She cupped the splashing water in her hand. The child jerked a bit and saw her with bewildered trust; then the pain deepened in its eyes and it started to scream again.

All at once, I knew I had to see Sasha. I did not want to see her; I had no reason to see her, but I needed to see her, because no matter how foul with disease she was, I was parched for her. I snatched my coat and bag and ran breathlessly to the King's Road. I strode up and down the pavement, up and down, waving my arms about me to flag down anything that would take me to the Courtney's flat. At last a taxi stopped. The traffic was heavy and we moved unbearably slowly.

Gregory did not want to let me in. He stood for a moment blinking through the links in the door-chain with his brown watchdog eyes.

'Let me come in,' I repeated with great urgency. 'Please, let me come in.'

He unchained the door and admitted me. He had not turned out the hall light. Even in the shadows, I saw he had grown up; only the expression in his eyes remained the same. As we walked up the stairs, I noticed a new firmness in his thigh – the slouch of his hip had become agreeable. The sodium lamp outside shone through the window which depicted Tristan and Isolde in stained glass. Gregory's body moved through the shadowy pink and gold. I could see his muscles stiffened against me in this light. He did not speak to me when we reached the landing, but shrugged in the deeper gloom of that place and left me there alone. I opened the big double-doors to the drawing-room and stepped unannounced into the light.

Mrs Courtney sat alone in the chintz armchair beside the fire; her hands lay idle in her lap. The green baize table had been put into a corner of the room. I noticed its absence because of the part it had played in evenings of the past. The table was now covered in a slovenly way with old papers and bits of dress material. There was the sound of a needle popping round and round the inner circle of a gramophone record. The gramophone, which had always occupied the nursery, had been messily rigged up on the floor beside the secretaire, on which it might very well have stood instead.

'Oh, Emily, it's you,' she said completely unsurprised. 'We

haven't seen you in such a long time. How nice of you to call. Could you turn over the record? Or turn it off if you like.' She printed out the sentences automatically, sentences of good-breeding made in early childhood to last a lifetime, sentences which conveyed the necessary pattern of hospitality without having any of its substance. The tone of the voice lacked warmth; it lacked coldness; in fact, it lacked any temperature at all: the whole flexibility of it was gone.

I was hard-pressed to do what she asked of me. I kept my eyes on the doors and would have pierced the walls between the drawing-room and the nursery if I could have done it.

She had been listening to Schubert. I have always found him mawkish. I looked at her warily over the top of the record sleeve, but I observed that she was quite composed. She sat straight in the padded chair with what would have been called dignity in a taller, finer-looking woman.

To avoid trembling, I replaced the record very carefully.

'I wish I could get Sasha to put records away like that,' said her mother in a conversational tone. 'She has scratched that one a lot from playing it too often and leaving it carelessly about. She's always had *nice* things, but she's never taken care of them.'

I turned to go, but she started up again. I was sure that she had noticed my desire, but she ignored it.

'When Sasha was a little girl,' she smiled slightly and cocked her head in saying 'when Sasha was a little girl', 'she used to be fond of materials and stuffs. Even when she was very tiny, she would deck herself out in my scarves, you know, and come in to me looking so terribly funny . . . but she never cared much for toys. Perhaps I spoiled her by giving her too many.' Her conversation flowed sweetly and quietly like a broad river; her eyes shifted slowly from place to place in the room, studying each object they met with the curiosity of a stranger. I became slowly mesmerised by her.

'*I* always like the toys – traditional ones like fluffy animals and baby dolls, pretty ones, you know – but she never liked a doll until it had become really scruffy. Do you remember Balkis? But Sasha is so independent, isn't she? There was no sense in forcing her to like things just because I did. More often than not she'd give Gregory her toys, which was a good thing as he is more possessive.'

She drew in her breath quite sharply. 'I expect she'll want you to have some of her things once she's gone.'

'It's as certain as that?' I made a strict effort to curb my feeling of wildness and yelling.

'Oh, yes, my dear. I'm afraid there's no hope of recovery. We've put the poor child through agony – test after test – and she's so brave.' She sighed wearily. 'I've accepted it now. It hasn't been easy. She's been my favourite, you know, although perhaps I'm wrong to say so; but,' here she leaned forward slightly, as if to make a point, 'we've had so much together, you see; we've been so happy, Sasha and I with each other. One mustn't be greedy.'

She leaned back to her former position and let her eyelids close. 'In her way she's lived a full life. It has been fuller than mine.'

Suddenly the doors opened and a small, neat man entered the room. He checked his energetic step at the threshold and walked with reined-in power to the centre of the room where he stopped and looked intelligently from Mrs Courtney to me, then back again to her. He had the quickest eyes I ever saw. His whole manner seemed to suggest that he had compressed himself from really a much larger size into something more compact for the purpose of greater speed and mobility. His features were so like Sasha's that I recognised him at once as her father.

Mrs Courtney didn't move, but when she opened her eyes and saw him, she revealed in them a new kind of pain: everything about her face showed a deep and perplexed feeling about him.

'This is Sasha's father,' she said quietly. 'Geoffrey, Emily Stone is one of Sasha's oldest friends. She's come to see me. Isn't that nice?'

He nodded shortly but did not speak.

'Geoffrey's come back,' she said simply. They exchanged a brief but powerful glance. She looked down at her hands, somewhat embarrassed, not by any love they had shown between them, but by the strength there still obviously was in their connection.

'I came in to see if you were all right. I heard the music stop. What were you listening to?' He was clearly embarrassed by nothing. He spoke with a certain toughness – a conscious American accent. He reacted to her mood like a dog sniffing the wind; he smelt something in it.

231

'Schubert.'

'Let me see.' He took the album from me. '"Tot und . . .", Death and the Maiden! Martha.' He looked at her, clearly disturbed by her. 'She isn't a maiden anyway. I thought she might be, but she's more grown-up now than most people ever are.'

There was something in what he said which, curiously enough, lightened her expression.

'Well, we'll put that away for a start.' He lightly chucked the record on to the sofa. 'I'll make you a drink.'

'Where is she!' I cried suddenly. I had held the breath of my feeling until it had burst out. 'I've come to see *her*.'

Mr Courtney poised himself on the ball of his foot as if expecting danger; Sasha's mother shrank from my suddenness. After a moment, she said, 'She's gone to a concert with Peter. They've gone to the Albert Hall. There's no point in her not going, you see. There isn't a scrap of hope. He's so gentle with her. It's very touching.'

I was drained of all energy — I sat down heavily on the straight-backed chair — so much had I counted on her being there.

'You look ill, my dear,' she said. 'Are you all right?'

Her voice came to me through the thick blanket of my tired flesh. 'I had hoped . . .'

'Why don't you come round and see her tomorrow, Emily? She's been wanting to see you.'

I shook my head.

'Do you think?' I asked. 'Do you think I might go and sit quietly in the nursery for a moment?'

She looked at me worriedly. 'Of course,' she said, 'of course.'

As I stumbled down the hall, the old scent of the place bore down through my nerves and touched my senses with a peculiar force . . . the faint smell of varnish, the faint smell of lavender. Lavender was the stronger scent and it came from the linen cupboard, and through the scent came the essence of every object which inhabited their lives: things especially removed from the ordinary, objects lucky to belong to them. Even what was common to most households was exalted in my eyes to a numinous, sweet-smelling place above its station.

I had no need to look in the linen cupboard to remember utterly what it contained. I once went there to get Sasha a towel. She had been trying to dye her hair black (it had turned a peculiar shade of green, which we had both thought very funny). On opening the cupboard, my senses had caught fire with the scent of lavender, the sight of the secreted, folded linen, the touch of it, cool and fresh. Sasha was laughing in the bathroom; water guzzled in the sink far off; I could almost taste my happiness at knowing these people who regularly conversed with happiness.

The nursery door was slightly ajar; it was dark inside. I swung the door open and waited for a moment, in case I might see some threat inside, and then entered, switching on the light quickly and closing the door after me. The room was completely transformed. She had stripped every surface of its treasures and had done away with the booty of her life. She had taken down her pictures; the dingy wallpaper was marked with where they had been. She had removed the heavy, tablecloth from the round table in the centre of the room; the thing stood there now without apology – old and battered and stained with ink. The piles of books and records had gone from the floor, and the postcards and gimcracks had disappeared from the mantelpiece.

The old daybed, which had once supported countless dog-eared loved possessions had been replaced by her own bed which was made up hospital fashion, with the sheets coolly smoothed over its breast.

The place was clean. I realised it had never been clean before. The cleanlines rose out of the bareness of the room; there was no sign of meticulousness for its own sake.

The only thing of hers which remained was the icon: it stood out now vividly, a gash of red and gold, on the barren wall. Its opulence curiously added to the simplicity she had achieved. The deep black eyes of the Madonna held mine for a moment, but I looked away, I walked carefully to the bed and sat down, feeling that to make a sudden motion might disturb the atmosphere.

She had bought a cheap plastic crucifix and had stood it on her bedside table. Next to this was a little card with a motto on it. I picked it up; it was a quotation from some saint or other. I can't remember all of it, but she had underscored the words 'either He will shield you from suffering or He will give you the unfailing strength to bear it'. I have remembered that all these years precisely because I find it so inscrutable. Just as I was about to put the card down, I saw through it in the light that she had written something on the back. It was a list written in a very shaky hand. It said: 'Boris, Emily, Daddy, Vernon, Nanny, Gregory, Mummy, Peter.' I couldn't think what she had written my name down for. I shook my head and replaced the card where I found it. I felt dazed and a little sick. I moved restlessly and shook my head, trying to remember why I was there; and then it occurred to me in a flash that there was nothing to stop me going to the Albert Hall. At this realisation, my body humped in involuntary movement as if convulsed by an electric shock.

I stood; I moved. In a dreamlike sequence of motions, I found myself sitting in another taxi-cab. I heard myself directing the driver; my voice seemed to proceed from somebody else. My own thoughts seemed to have little to do with me. My thoughts, I say . . . there was one thought, which was that if I reached her and spoke to her, she would not die.

I ran from where the taxi left me. The stretch of pavement between me and the door of the Albert Hall appeared to me as loaded with danger as the firing-line of a battle ground. From behind me, I knew that Prince Albert was watching me from the seat of his memorial. His eyes shot rays into my back.

I reached the foyer breathless with relief. The place was empty, huge and silent. A dozy ticket-taker in uniform blinked as he saw me.

'You're too late, miss,' he said. 'We can't let you in. They've started the second half already.'

'I don't want to go in!' I gasped. 'I don't want to go in. I've come to see a friend who's in the audience. I must see her. It's very important. It's a matter of life and death.'

'I'm sorry, miss . . .'

'I must see her. Please. All I want to do is to stand by the door to wait until she comes out. I have to get by. You must let me by.'

'I'm sorry, miss . . .'

'I don't care about your bloody rules! I told you. It is a matter of life or death.' I fumbled at my bag. 'Here. Take everything I have.' I tried to lift the notes from my purse. I had five pounds. The money wouldn't come out for my impatience. I wrenched the money out; it floated to the floor. I up-ended the coin purse letting a shower of coppers and silver clink on the stone floor.

'For God's sake, take everything I have, I must find her!' I pushed past him and ran. He started after me, but then the money swayed his eye and he stayed, picking up the pieces after me as I sped up and up the staircase not knowing where or how I was going to find her and Peter . . . Peter.

I went from level A to level B to level C to level D, marking the gates as if they had some profound significance. A door swung open and there was a shout of Bach, then closed and muffled trumpets I heard, and then a mass of voices coming as if from far away singing music which swung my mind off its heels and reeled me around with its triumph.

Their names ached in my throat. Sasha, Peter, Sasha, Peter. I thought the dam to my voice would burst and I would flood the hall with sound to drown the music.

A woman stared at me. She held a tray of ice-cream. I ran on and cowered, trembling and panting, behind a pillar. I must see her. I must. Where is she? Where could she be?

Another door opened and an acute soprano voice shuddered out voluble love. Then the door closed. I clung to the wall with my back, pressing my back into it, willing with all my mind to disappear through it to the warm dark of the other side where they were among the thousands of breathing bodies who calmly received and possessed the music. And while the warmth of this thought bathed my mind, it maddened by body. I could not reach them. The little windows in the doors winked with secrets and held me back from sound. The place was a spherical shell against me, and I, helpless to crack it, stood weeping little baby-sobs and gnawed at my hands.

Just as the guard approached me, the doors swung open and streams of people debouched from the hall amid the crash of applause, and he, with a shrug allowed himself to be deflected from his purpose by their numbers. I pulled myself away from my place against the wall and started frantically to search the crowd.

Everything moved so slowly. They all moved so slowly. They packed themselves together and smiled lazily at nothing and at no one. A few gabbled; I could not understand what they were saying;

they spoke English but I heard it as some other language. The warmth of their bodies, their jostling movements became sickening and disgusting to me. I wished I could mow them down with the glare from my eyes. I started to push. 'I beg your pardon,' someone said. 'I'm in a desperate hurry. I must get through. I shall be ill if I don't get into the fresh air.'

I shoved them all aside. People are nothing but a pack of cards. I shoved my way down, and there I saw them, Sasha and Peter, standing on the pavement between the steps and the street.

A fine, cold rain silted down in the area of light. The mash of people pushed for taxis against the rain. Peter stood patiently with her, shielding her from the crowd with his arm, and over her head he held a black umbrella.

She sank into his chest as he supported her. She appealed to him with her wasted body to give her the strength to stand. She neither looked up at him nor pressed against him; she peeped calmly out of his protection like a child nested in an eiderdown. And he did not look at her or increase the pressure of his arm around her: he was rooted and solid for her, he held his own for her, and he was increased in relation to her clinging weakness.

They stood utterly still . . . he with his umbrella and she sheltering under it. The rain came down all about them but did not touch them. Their figures seemed to the eye inseparable for the complete repose in which they stood.

I have never before or since seen Peter in such an attitude. Even from where I was, I could sense the rise and fall of his breathing, a soft, contented swell and drop that comes in a good sleep. His nervous hands were firm; he stood naturally erect as if this were his common posture. I could see his profile in the sharp light: his cheek looked soft and young, and the hair on the back of his neck seemed somehow touching to me.

I was shocked a little by her legs; they had hardly any substance now, and her ungloved hand dangled like a disconnected wire from her shoulder.

They stood apart from the crowd; yet in a way, the simplicity of the form they made together, unified under the umbrella, seemed to interpret the milling others to me as being sheltered and enhanced by them.

But none of this would have had any meaning at all if it hadn't been for her eyes, and but for them and for the expression of her they nearly proclaimed, every thought I have thought of her since would have been a complete waste of time.

As I stood on the step, immobile from my vision of her and Peter, she slowly turned her withered head towards me and met me with her gaze. She evinced no surprise at seeing me, nor did she raise the alarm to Peter; she merely looked, and in that look was contained and concentrated everything about her I had ever sensed. It was as if she had always had an inscrutable name which I had half-known and which she now fully told me. She had become the sum of her parts and she now stood before me with the result – no more impassioned by it than she would have been by a simple mathematical fact.

She was as vulnerable in this look as if she existed there without skin. Everything she ever was offered itself forward, even though everything she had ever tried to be had fallen into complete disuse. Between what she inly was and what she outwardly expressed, there was no longer any barrier. Peter's arm and Peter's umbrella were the only protections she now had against all the villainy in the world.

She looked at me, and looked at me, and from the mere presentation of herself, her expression deepened and held itself open to me as if she understood me with an indescribable gentleness and delicacy.

Suddenly, I felt more intensely tired than I ever had in my life; I felt tired and bleakly ill as if I had suffered for a long time from a kind of internal bleeding which even I had not so far discerned.

And this is what I have never been able to admit even to myself: I felt starved and gross in my starvation, like a repulsive bony animal which sucks the fur off its paws for nourishment.

I looked at her again: her eyes were wounded with my wounds. She offered me compassion.

Involuntarily, I started down the steps towards her, and was nearly at the bottom before I realised what I had done; I had told her without words my most shameful secret, but more than that, much more than that . . . she had always known it and had pitied me in one way or another from the very source of our friendship. At this realisation, my hand froze on the rope she offered me, and with a kind of contempt, I let it drop. She sought me again with her eyes and again, but her glances were now wads of wool, ineffectual against my armour. I gave her a little ironical smile and turned away.

When she was gone, I walked home past the Albert Memorial. I laughed a little at it. Its domination of the sky had ceased to matter.

TWELVE

Peter called me the week before Christmas to say she had died. They had thought she was improved; they had had some hopes. She had, however, taken a sudden turn for the worse, and when Peter went over there on the morning of the 18th, he had found them aghast at their fresh discovery of her corpse. He had seen her; he had thought he would be horrified, but 'such peace, such peace' on her face, he said. In a flash, I saw a smile carved in *rigor mortis*. He was surprisingly calm, and so I left him to it, telling him I would return to him when I felt better.

The truth was, however, that ever since I had seen her and taken leave of her in the week before her death, I had felt unusually fit and brisk. And when I learned that she was actually dead, the news came to me as a distant misfortune to somebody else. I had almost, but not quite, said 'What a pity' to Peter in that tone people take when they formally commiserate with another. Now she was gone, I felt as if some obscure accusation against me had been lifted. I was relieved that she, who knew too much, had been bumped off without my having had to lift a finger.

I remember the day of the funeral I didn't go to. She was buried on a cloudless, brilliant Saturday. I got up early that cold, blue day, washed carefully, dressed neatly and went down to breakfast.

My brother was up already. He plucked in an irritating manner the strings of the violin which he was about to practise playing.

My mother was reading the *Guardian* while eating cornflakes abstractedly.

'Peter called at an ungodly hour,' she said, 'and asked if you were going to some funeral. He didn't want to disturb you, he said. He seemed very strange to me. Whose funeral, may I ask, is being held today?'

'They'll have a hard time breaking the ground,' I thought to myself. I could see them out there in the cold, clean air; from early morning they would have been trying to break the ground. Or perhaps they had done it already. Now I think back on it, I am sure they had done the digging the day before. Someone with murderous sorrow in the mind would have had to make all the arrangements. Sasha once told me when we were children that she would like to have a joyful funeral, like that of a black musician.

I capped my egg and dug into its goodness. The egg tasted as fresh and delicious as it was yellow. I wondered what kind of coffin Sasha had worn to her funeral.

'I asked you whose funeral?' my mother demanded somewhat sharply.

'Sasha's funeral. Sasha is dead.'

'Good heavens! How perfectly terrible!' my father cried. 'That young girl you went to Italy with? I remember your saying she was ill. What did she die of?'

I was tempted to say she died of old age, but that sounded mad to me even as I thought it; so I suppressed the thought.

'No one quite knows. No one ever mentioned the name of the disease – a nervous illness I think, but I'm not too sure.'

'She was very neurotic,' my mother said with some self-satisfaction. She had met her only a few times.

'Neurotic? Yes. I suppose she was neurotic.'

'Aren't you going to the funeral? Peter said it was to be held at three o'clock at some Roman Catholic church. I took the name down.' My mother had stopped eyeing the paper while she spoke; she now turned her appraising glance at me, her chin not quite resting on her hands, but balanced there on the interlocking fingers.

'No. I'm not going to the funeral. Sasha has been dead to me for some time. We are no longer friends.' My words came so clearly out of my mouth that they astonished me.

'I didn't know they were Catholics,' my mother said as if she had half suspected it all along. She made a face at her cool coffee and rose to get some more from the pot.

'They're not. It must have been a last ditch affair.'

'She was afraid of dying, then?' My mother isn't afraid of anything, and she regards other people's fears with contempt.

'No. She and Peter worked themselves into a fervour.'

'I didn't know Peter was religious; although he spoke of marrying in church, his sexual morality is hardly orthodox.'

'I am not certain. I believe he has become so during his acquaintance with Sasha.'

'How are you going to cope with that?'

'I'll manage. May I see the paper?'

Everything was so easy, so clear. I read a story about an excavation in Mesopotamia. I cut it neatly with a razor (which was provided at the table for this purpose) to give to Peter. I also read a story about dangerous substances in cleaning fluids. I never read the front page of a paper because I dislike topical subjects.

I went shopping. The day was uncompromisingly bright – so blue, so cold – not a cloud anywhere I could see. The snow had solidified on the ground.

My mother asked me what I was going to do. I stifled the temptation to tell her to mind her own business. Instead, I told her that I was going to buy a Christmas present for Peter.

There were a great many people about. Crowds ransacked and looted the shops which invited their own destruction by seductive windows flaunting manikins with glistening hair. I walked up and down Oxford Street – up and down. People bumped me and stepped on me, people with vacant expressions who didn't say sorry.

Nobody looked at me; nobody saw me. I wasn't in anybody's eyes nor was I in anybody's mind.

A giant plastic Father Christmas nodded idiotically from a giant plastic sleigh above Selfridge's. Eight giant reindeer also nodded electrically; their eyes were lit up by light bulbs. The whole street was festooned with lights and medallions depicting toys of one kind or another.

'*Adeste Fideles*' blared hoarsely from some loudspeaker above some shop or other. No one looked cheerful. I felt like one of the figures on top of a gigantic musical-box.

I remembered something from my childhood. I had had a friend in nursery school; she believed in Father Christmas. She told me, and I can dimly recall it, in the Wendy house, that we must play that we were asleep and pretend that Father Christmas would come down the chimney. I remember now being thrilled at the thought of Father Christmas. I had a distinct picture of him quite different from his commercial portraits. I think I went so far as to talk to him at night.

I imagined that my mother didn't know about Father Christmas, and that if I told my family about him that he might come to our house too. I assumed he hadn't come because he hadn't been invited.

I can still see how they laughed, Jane, Anthony and my mother. Their derision is still painful to me. I locked myself in the bathroom and cried for an hour.

I nearly bought a shirt for Peter, but I rejected it because it was too expensive. I leafed through several books, but everywhere, the people crawled like flies about me. I thought it would be nice to swat them.

Somehow I made my way to Conduit Street. Things were better there, but then I thought of Sasha's cold body, so I went into Christian Dior and bought myself a scarf and a bottle of perfume. I decided I needed a present more than Peter did.

I was pleased that the assistant called me 'Madam'. She was tough, well-dressed and shrewd. The heels on her shoes were perfect. I could see she admired my taste.

There were silver balls and silver branches decorating the window of Christian Dior. Perfume bottles and brooches nested so cosily there in the grey silk that I felt a little shiver of happiness as I left with my parcels. The sky seemed less glaring over Conduit Street.

I hugged my parcels to myself. I looked with some gratitude at my image in the transparent window. There seemed to me to be a pleasant, glossy finish over the integrity of my features, almost as if someone had given them a final coat of shellac to protect them from the corruption of time.

In the background of the reflection, there was a waiting taxi. All at once, I decided that it was about time I went back to Peter's flat. I turned, hailed the man, and directed him to take me there.

I took my scarf from the tissue paper (I had had them wrap it up especially in silver paper) while the taxi ticked and lurched down the Bayswater Road. Such a swish it made around the silk – the scarf was blue and gold and purple. I caressed it with my hands and then my cheek, then fastened it around my neck. I wanted to see myself in the driver's mirror, but I did not look for fear of giving something of myself away to him.

Suddenly it occurred to me that I would like to see if Boris and Vernon had gone to the funeral. I knocked on the window and told the driver to take me to Holland Park instead.

When I arrived at the expensive-looking house, I paid the driver something extra for his compliment of eyes. I could see he saw me as a part of the houses's smart façade . . . something unreachable and faintly tinged with glamour.

Boris and Vernon were not at home. Vernon's mother answered the door.

'Are you a friend of Vernon's?' she asked chattily. She was neatly but unimaginatively well-dressed in the style of a certain kind of wealthy American matron. She didn't look like a monster to me.

'I'm over here for the baby, you know,' she said conspiratorally. 'Giving them a hand, you see.'

'I see. Do you know where they have gone?'

'Tsk! Aw!' She threw up a hand. 'It's so sad. They've gone to a funeral. One of Boris's old girl-friends died . . . very young . . . only twenty or something. They're both very upset. I said to Vernon, "You'll only upset the baby," but she said it didn't matter . . . it would upset the baby even more if she didn't go because she was sure she'd be in hysterics just thinking about it if you see what I mean. Boris says this girl was a very saintly person. I suppose you didn't know her?'

'No. I didn't know her. I'm sorry. I must go now.'

Instead of going to the flat, I walked into Holland Park itself. Up and down the avenue of trees I trod, round and round the tree-lined paths until my feet were tired. I liked to be in the shelter of the trees. The trees were a shield against the animate sky.

Why did I say 'animate sky?' How ridiculous to suppose it is anything but dead to the very socket of infinity.

I sometimes like to think of this poetry of pure deadness. I was exquisitely moved by the men walking on the moon . . . the moon so beautiful from below, the symbol of lovers . . . so utterly useless above. I consider the dreadful stars burning unseen in the blackest depth of space.

This I can barely admit to myself: that Peter rattles me silly with his inhabited universe. He is crushed by love, bound to the inexorable gravity of this love he feels sure exists but which he cannot find: while I, I am free to walk in the void, but solitary, solitary, solitary. I have no human race to run.

I sat on a bench bequeathed to the park by Lady Something-or-Other who was also in her grave. I looked at the trees. I can see myself sitting there in my good-looking clothes – a well-tailored coat and round my neck this blue scarf from Christian Dior. I sat with my legs together, my hands folded round the parcel on my lap. I can see myself as decorating the park.

Suddenly, I got the impression that Sasha was watching me. I got the distinct sensation that Sasha was actually watching me from the lime trees boughed above me, as if she were the Cheshire cat smiling equivocally through the twigs.

I wish I had had the courage to look, but I did not. Instead, I looked trembling at the parcel on my lap.

'Do you want it, Sasha?' I asked softly. I felt she wanted it. 'Do you want the perfume? Will you go away if I give it to you?' I asked her very softly. There was no wind . . . not even a sigh of wind.

I knelt on the ground, not in an attitude of prayer, but for a purpose. I unwrapped the elegant grey parcel and took the bottle from its elegant grey box. It was quite an effort to remove the glass stopper. In fact, I had to saw away at it with a nail file.

When I had opened it, I held it up towards the trees where I thought Sasha's face was watching me, then I poured the perfume into the ground. I had to shake it out mostly. The scent was overpowering. I wanted to be sick.

With that libation accomplished, I hoped she had gone away, but I couldn't be certain; so I got up and walked away as quickly as I could, my teeth chattering with the cold.

I went to Peter's flat and waited without moving until he returned some hours later.

He didn't bother to turn on the light when he came in. He didn't see me sitting rigid in his black armchair. He seemed to crash about – he knocked something over as he went into the bedroom – but he made no sound to himself.

For a while, everything was quiet; then I heard him start to sob. He made big, ugly, sniffing noises in between the sobs which rose from his lungs and forced themselves out as if his vocal cords were too small for the immensity of breath he wanted to expel.

After a while, I got up from my chair and went to him. My body felt stiff and old. I sat down on the bed next to him. I wondered that we had wallowed there together only a few weeks ago.

He started violently. 'Sasha?' he asked weakly. He sat up and looked. When he saw me, the hope went from his face and he lay back on the pillow. 'Oh, Emily, where were you?' His voice was laden with tears and mucus. I did my best not to despise him.

'I'm here now.' I switched on the light. His face was streaked with dirt. He had abdicated everything I had ever liked about him: his poise, his balance was gone and buried with her. His suit was crumpled; the loftiness of his expression had quite dissolved. I wondered rather what to do with him; his sorrow had to be disposed of. I felt a kind of fastidious distaste for the job, but suddenly, with great clarity I saw it as a job – something no more and no less than clearing out a long neglected attic. I knew that if I didn't sort him out, then and there, he would thereafter continually encroach upon that part of me which I was now determined to keep hidden and very tidy.

He blinked at the strong light and ran his fingers through his hair.

'It's all over,' I said quite firmly. 'The whole thing is completely and finally over. She'll never come back, and nothing you can do will ever bring her back. She cannot listen to you anymore. Do you think she's listening? I'll tell you something . . . you're talking to the thin air.' I wanted to laugh at this. For some reason I thought it was funny.

I braced myself for his hostility; instead, he looked at me with an air of puzzled innocence. 'I wasn't talking to Sasha,' he said. 'I was mourning her. I thought you would be too.'

I compressed my lips together and avoided his remark. 'I'll make you a strong cup of coffee,' I said. 'There's no point in your lying about in a pool of tears.'

I went to the kitchen; the place was sordid with half-eaten shop-bought buns and filthy coffee cups. I put on the kettle and immediately set about restoring order.

He appeared at the door. He rubbed his bleary eyes with his clenched hands. He leaned against the wall; tears oozed from under his closed lids. He had sponged up wretchedness; he was sodden with grief. I wanted to tear him into little bits.

'Leave that, Em. I want to talk. I must tell someone how I feel.'

'"Let's sit upon the ground and talk about the death of kings?" Oh, no. I won't do that. Here.' I handed him a cup of coffee. He took it from me, but let the coffee slosh into the saucer.

'We've got to tidy up, you and I.' I handed him the towel. 'Why don't you help?' I couldn't look at his pulped face. He was to me like the unknown victim of a terrible accident.

'You don't seem to have taken it in that our best friend was buried today. My God, I was there all day . . .' he shook his head . . . 'I don't think I've seen such sorrow as Mrs Courtney had . . . and the funeral . . . Sasha in a little pine coffin . . . she was so little. I could follow her, support her right up to her death, but after that whatever she knew about it failed me. The awfulness of it simply overwhelmed me . . . and all the time, I thought, "It's worse for poor Emily."

'I came and told your mother this morning where the funeral was being held. I didn't dare ask for you. I thought I would only make you more ill . . . but here you are, looking as if you just returned from a shopping spree. Why didn't you come with me, Emily? I had no one. Boris and Vernon were no use.'

I vigorously polished a spoon sticky with instant coffee stains. 'I thought you and she had God.'

'*She* had. I had only what she had. I stood next to her and inhaled what she had, but now I am without the slightest notion. She drew me out of myself and now she is gone I am snapped back into myself like an elastic band. The feeling of loss I have is very nearly intolerable.' He said this without much emotion; he almost droned the words.

I thought that I had better do what I had to do quickly and efficiently.

'Ah, Peter,' I sighed, 'how very little you really knew of Sasha. Ever since I first knew you, I always sensed that you were braving it out on the edge of your naïveté, and now it seems that you have fallen in.' I spoke in an almost light tone. I continued to wash the dishes. I knew it would be fatal to look at him.

'What do you mean?' he asked after a long pause.

'You said you wanted to talk. I wonder if you really want to hear what I have to say . . . what in all honesty I must say about Sasha. I had hoped to avoid such a confrontation, but here you are, taking it all to heart – the death of the best actress there ever was. I was willing to play along with your illusions about her because I have a horror of interfering with your privacy. I would have negated our whole relationship if I had nagged you or niggled you . . . or even said what I thought. I think I have been fair. But now you bully me: Why wasn't I there? Why didn't I sustain you? Sustain you in what! Reneging on yourself; bathing yourself in false comfort; returning to that infantile state you told me you were in before you met me? No. I shall never sustain you in that.' I firmly turned off the taps, took off my apron, and walked past him into the sitting-room. My feet felt good in my shoes; I enjoyed the sense of controlled progress. I switched on the steel lamp and sat back in the leather chair. I lit a cigarette and enjoyed the sense of danger. I knew I'd lose him if I wasn't careful: somehow that heightened my calm.

After a while, he blundered in after me. He was pale and pinched; he had withdrawn behind his eyes. 'What do you mean . . . false comfort? Surely there is no such thing as false comfort.' He was talking mostly to himself. I cannot describe exactly how he looked; he looked afraid.

'I mean to say I've watched you carefully all this time you've been with Sasha, and I have come to the conclusion that you are doing nothing more than trying to retreat through her to your mother. You've always granted that I see everything. I'm being hard now because I have to.

'You've always had this weakness – this weakness of trying to trust others. You're like a child. You throw yourself on other people's mercy. You have always been eager to destroy the perfect circle of you and me – that elegant balance – for a tangle of limbs and promises. I've never allowed it because I know what's good for you, and that is why you sought me out in the first place.

'You trusted your mother, and your mother deserted you because she was unable to support you. I consider it very dangerous that you have lately tried to whitewash her.

'You trusted Sasha . . . and see: she has died. And now, now, I can see you are ready to throw yourself on the mercy of God, which in essence means opening yourself up so that every dog in town can have a little bit of you. When are you going to learn that you can trust no one but yourself?'

I had never talked so well. One word walked easily out after the other: my words stepped as shiny as my patent leather shoes. I could almost see them as they slowly encircled him. He recoiled from me, but not enough; he couldn't take his eyes off me.

'I don't think you've ever loved anybody,' he said with a kind of amazement.

'I can give you something better than love. I can give you order.'

He stood silent for a moment. He shook his head with confusion. 'You talk as if Sasha were disordered . . . Sasha had the purest form of order . . .' He was agape with memory, he could not finish his sentence.

I had the sudden strong desire to murder him. His blood flowed from his head in my imagination.

'BUT SASHA IS DEAD!'

'Are you sure?' he muttered idiotically.

'If you don't believe it, you'd better go away until you do,' I said. 'Because when you do then you can come back and we will carry on as before.'

I returned to my mother's house quite confident of my success. I had taken no real reading of Peter's face when I left him, but I knew, without the aid of eyes or intellect that the ground was essentially mine. Over and over again, it occurred to me in my imagination that I had possessed the flat and he had left. I would wake up in the morning, expecting to find myself in his bed. I was not disturbed on the discovery that this was a dream. I merely collected my thoughts, as if they were a pack of cards scattered in a game of patience, and dealt again. I was aware that I had planted in his mind the seed which would grow, given enough time, to overshadow Sasha.

I became positively glad she was dead.

After the funeral, I found myself surprisingly at ease with my mother. A slow disclosure of our common bond took place. I became rather interested in her as she trotted faultlessly through the strenuous pace of her day. I helped her silently in the kitchen, and in exchange for that, she gave me back my room. The unmarried mother had gone back to her family. The little girl had been badly damaged: the grandparents, therefore, took pity on them.

My mother made no move towards me, but little by little she appeared to become aware of me, as if I had released a scent that she recognised.

One day, whilst I was chopping mushrooms, she asked me if Peter and I had broken off.

'To tell you the truth, mother, we have had our difficulties. The religious differences you mentioned seem to have come up awkwardly.'

'I *did* wonder,' she said with something akin to relief.

'There is nothing that cannot be finally resolved. I am merely waiting for Peter to come to his senses. I expect he will.'

'I must say, you show remarkable self-restraint.' There was grudging admiration in her tone.

'I have always been self-restrained,' I said. 'Self-restraint marks my character . . . rather, it is the mark of my character. Shall I finish these, or do you want then for tomorrow? They look as if they're going off.'

'You'd better finish them then . . . Peter is a very unstable boy.'

'I'm aware of that. I have stability for us both.'

'I believe you do, Emily.' She pierced me with her beacon glance. It bounced off me as if I had been a rock. 'Of all my children, I have worried about you the least. You never seemed to have need of me or anybody else. You were always a very private child.'

'Oh yes. Fine and private. I am that.' I finished the mushrooms and made everything neat and workmanlike. My mother and I exchanged a brittle smile. I think we understood each other.

With some relief, I got working again. I found scholarship as refreshing as some people find the crossword puzzle; first this fact, then that – each fact uncontroversial, a series of ideas given which I could neatly arrange upon the page. The facts made little patterns; I have never had much interest in what the patterns stood for. Indeed, although I have spent my life studying, I have never had any illusion that my work was important in the slightest degree. Actually, the very uselessness of what I do charms me.

I made a kind of game out of waiting for Peter. My mind played with his image rather as if he had been a doll. I dressed him up in my imagination in this attitude or that. Mostly, I saw him braving it out in poverty with me, rather as if I'd cut him off without a penny; I saw him unnerved by his own inability to cope. For some reason, I had visions of him struggling in quicksand. Now and then, just for fun, I'd press the nerve which used to activate my feelings for him; with some pleasure, I found it thoroughly anaesthetised. I'd look over all the old photographs we'd taken of each other. There was one of Peter I'd particularly liked – I'd taken it in the summertime while we sat one day in Holland Park. His face was mottled with the shadow of leaves; his shirt was voluminous in the wind. The camera had caught the cords of his neck and the swelling of his throat as he blew out smoke from a cigarette which he held tensely between two fingers.

That Peter had told me some central lie about himself, I had no doubt. The trouble was, I didn't really care. I was only interested in how long it would take him to come back, rather as if our relationship demonstrated something new about the law of gravity.

In the end, my patience was rewarded. The Brigadier called me in mid-February to tell me that Peter was once again in hospital. It appeared that he couldn't stop crying; the wall of faith she had built had given way under the pressure of his tears. The Brigadier spoke of this flood as if it were the greatest inconvenience to him; his voice had a fractious note in it. For a long time, I interpreted the Brigadier's attitude towards Peter as merely callous; I have come to sympathise with him more. He is a man with an hysterical sense of order . . . a superstitious sense of order. Peter in his disintegrated state is a threatening bearer of omens to him. My marriage to Peter has been an overwhelming relief to his father. I like him because it is he alone who admires my talents as a wardress.

Peter had a private room; I can remember that well. It was at the end of a long corridor of closed doors. An Irish nurse with kindly eyes walked with me down to the end. She had hopes of me, I could tell.

He was sitting in the dark; his legs were intertwined around each other, and his fingers made knots with a handkerchief. He seemed not to recognise me when I came in. As soon as the nurse was gone, I went to the switch and turned on the overhead light. The room was painted an icy green; there was a feeling of great barrenness and emptiness about it, almost as if he weren't there. It was devoid of human occupation. I sat down on the bed and looked at him for a long time, saying nothing. After a while, he uncoiled his hands and put his head in one of them.

'Do you hate this place?' I asked him. He didn't seem to hear me, then he slowly nodded.

'Then I'll get you out of here,' I said.

He looked at me in the oddest way. 'I didn't call you because I know you can't stand crying, Em. How are you going to live with me if you can't stand crying?'

'Because you can't stand crying either. You and I together never could. It was Sasha who made you cry. She ate away at your stoicism, your cynicism, like a cancer. You'll just have to take the knife to her, that's all. I rejected her for the same reasons; that is why I can help you.' He quickly withdrew to guard the treasure in his heart.

'Peter!' I hissed at him violently. 'Which is better, then, a life made intolerable by love or a life which is tolerable without it? If you had any sense you'd take me at my word that half a loaf is better than none!'

I left him with his complicated fragments.

The story of his cure is long and tedious.

How can he forget that it was I who hauled him back up the rocks of his consciousness; that it was I who unflinchingly took his abuse; that it was I who allowed him to be sick all over me with his yearning for Sasha? But he has forgotten it. He cringes like a dog before my good sense. He unpicks my explanations for his behaviour with his quick, destructive brain and throws the ravellings in my teeth. He forgets his need of me, that need which in the end made him beg me to marry him. My ordered coldness is as necessary to his life as Sasha ever was. Our characters deeply interlock on the point of his survival.

Then, he found me an efficient enough queller of storms. Since Sasha's death, I have been riveted together with steel bolts; he clung to me hard enough then to keep his conscience and his tenderness from breaking him to pieces. I found us a house. I furnished it with impeccable good taste. I built a solid wall around him of uncontroversial delights. I gave him the best food (I made him like good food); I made his cellar run like Lethe with excellent wine. I spent his money for him; but I spent it on him. I decked myself out like a goddess and seduced him to the entrance of my shrine with every subtlety my brain could manage. I even bore him a child I didn't want. And he agreed to the point of collusion with my dispatching of his fate.

Yet underneath it all – I know because I have the wit to know – he agreed mechanically. Never once in our married life have I been able to restore the tension and balance of our courtship. Just after he attempted suicide, he said to me, 'Where did you put the nourishment when you took it out of the food you gave me? Did you sterilise it then?'

Sometimes I dream I am in Belsen, sorting through a pile of bodies rather like a postal clerk until I reach one uncannily familiar – a starved woman at the bottom of the pile – it is myself. I somehow feel I ought to have some pity on her, but I won't. She'd only ask for food I hadn't got.